America the Beautiful

America the Beautiful

Love & Justice in Black & White

Bruce Angus

Bruce Angus

To the life and memory of

Daniel "Danny" Hambrick

June 1, 1993
July 26, 2018

Nashville, Tennessee

The author would like to thank a cadre of persons from his Air Force years and beyond who peppered his life with their humanity...and who represented the promise of possibilities:

Captain **Chris Mineau**, Vietnam F-4 Phantom Pilot, ejection/crash survivor.
Captain **Gary Baxter**, Vietnam O-2 Forward Air Controller.
Captain **George Crow**, Vietnam UH-1N Huey Pilot.
Two Vietnam **Huey Door-gunners,** fellow students in Jungle Survival Training, Panama, after their Vietnam combat tours.
Lt. Colonel **John Morrow**, Vietnam B-52 Navigator.
Captain **Dan Harmon**, KC-135 Pilot, Global Refueling Missions including Southeast Asia.
USAFA Cadet **Scott Chavez**, too short to be included, too good to be excluded.
Captain **J.J. Rankin**, Mathematician.
Captain **Poppo**, Geo-political and Humanity Master.
Lt. Colonel **Arnold Church**, Korean War F-86 Sabre Fighter Pilot.
Lt. Colonel **John Deming**, Chaplain and Counselor to the Damaged
FBI Agent **Chris Whitcomb**, Hostage Rescue Team.

"Six degrees of separation?
Try more like two or three."
Dr. William "Bill" Dutton

Legal disclaimer: All persons named in this story are fictional creations of the author and do not correlate to any real person, living or dead.

PART 1 - **CRIME**

1.1 THROUGH THE LOOKING GLASS (pg **1**)
1.2 THE MOUSE TRAP (pg **2**)
1.3 CALL OF DUTY (pg **5**)
1.4 LAST DOLLAR LOTTERY TICKET (pg **10**)
1.5 THE PUNISHMENT (pg **13**)
1.6 MY WAY OR THE HIGHWAY (pg **18**)
1.7 I JUST NEED SOMEONE TO LOVE (pg **23**)
1.8 THE SECRET OF NIMH (pg **28**)
1.9 GANG VIOLENCE (pg **37**)
1.10 TIL DEATH SO US PART (pg **40**)
1.11 THE CANVASS CAN DO MIRACLES (pg **51**)
1.12 WILMA !!! (pg **57**)
1.13 MY MONA LISA (pg **58**)
1.14 CAN A BROTHER GET A FAVOR? (pg **60**)
1.15 BORN AGAIN: LABOR (pg **62**)
1.16 VISITORS OUT OF THE BLUE (pg **69**)
1.17 SIGNS THAT MIGHT BE OMENS (pg **82**)
1.18 A FRIEND IN NEED (pg **84**)
1.19 BELOW THE RADAR (pg **85**)
1.20 THE CRIME (pg **97**)
1.21 NO JUSTICE NO PIECE (pg **100**)
1.22 CHANGE YOUR TUNE (pg **101**)
1.23 TECH SOLUTIONS (pg **108**)
1.24 GANG-BANGING IN NORTH NASHVILLE (pg **110**)
1.25 DISCIPLINE TAKES DISCIPLINE (pg **115**)
1.26 BENCHED (pg **117**)
1.27 BLACK IS THE NEW WHITE (pg **118**)
1.28 THE HYPOCRITIC OATH (pg **123**)
1.29 SAY CAN I HAVE SOME OF YOUR PURPLE BERRIES (pg **126**)
1.30 SENT DOWN TO THE MINORS (pg **128**)

PART 2 - ...AND PUNISHMENT

2.1   TEACH YOUR CHILDREN WELL (pg **131**)
2.2   HOMEWARD BOUND (pg **135**)
2.3   MINING FOR GOLD (pg **144**)
2.4   FATHER KNOWS BEST (pg **147**)
2.5   CHASING RABBITS (pg **152**)
2.6   ON THE ROAD AGAIN (pg **159**)
2.7   PRIDE AND PREJUDICE (pg **163**)
2.8   PEEPING TOMS (pg **169**)
2.9   SYMPATHY FOR THE DEVIL (pg **172**)
2.10 TIME FOR A LOOKEY-LOOK (pg **192**)
2.11 CHANGE IS GONNA COME (pg **199**)
2.12 DRESSED IN A LAW SUIT (pg **203**)
2.13 MICROSCOPIC PEP TALK (pg **205**)
2.14 DAMAGE ASSESMENT (pg **206**)
2.15 YOU'RE SO VAIN (pg **209**)
2.16 THE THUNDER ROLLS (pg **211**)
2.17 DO YOU SEE WHAT I SEE (pg **216**)
2.18 ALL IN A DREAM (pg **220**)
2.19 MAKING FRIENDS (pg **226**)
2.20 NEGOTIATED SETTLEMENT (pg **232**)
2.21 DENNIS RODMAN GROWTH SPURT (pg **233**)
2.22 I DON'T WANT TO BE LONELY TONIGHT (pg **234**)
2.23 A CODE THAT YOU CAN LIVE BY (pg **236**)
2.24 KUM BA YAH (pg **245**)

PART 3 - **PYGMALIA IN BLOOM**

3.1   WILL YOU REMEMBER ME (pg 249)
3.2   LOVES BABIES AND SURPRISES (pg 252)
3.3   ANGEL FROM MONTGOMERY (pg 254)
3.4   NEEDLE IN A HAYSTACK (pg 255)
3.5   ROOM WITH A VIEW (pg 260)
3.6   THE MILE HIGH CLUB (pg 265)
3.7   SEE THE USA IN YOUR CHEVROLET (pg 267)
3.8   I DID IT MY WAY (pg 275)
3.9   CH CH CH CHANGES (pg 277)
3.10 THE BEAT GOES ON (pg 278)
3.11 HELP! I NEED SOMEBODY (pg 280)
3.12 DO YOU HEAR WHAT I HEAR (pg 281)
3.13 LET THE SUNSHINE IN (pg 282)
3.14 IS IT TOO LATE TO SAY I'M SORRY (pg 283)
3.15 BOOTSTRAPS (pg 285)
3.16 STILL WATERS RUN DEEP (pg 287)
3.17 TELL ME SOMETHING GOOD (pg 292)
3.18 MOVIN' ON UP (pg 295)
3.19 THERE'S SOMETHING HAPPENING HERE (pg 297)
3.20 NO-KNOCK WARRANT (pg 300)
3.21 FRIEND ZONE (pg 306)
3.22 GUESS WHO'S COMING TO DINNER (pg 312)
3.23 MINI ME (pg 316)
3.24 WHY CAN'T WE BE FRIENDS (pg 317)
3.25 I GET BY WITH A LITTLE HELP FROM MY FRIENDS (pg 324)
3.26 LOVE THE WAY YOU LIE (pg 338)
3.27 THE IDES OF MARCH (pg 341)
3.28 BLACK HAWK DOWN (pg 346)
3.29 GOT TO BE GOOD LOOKING CUZ HE'S SO HARD TO SEE (pg 351)

3.30	ARE YOU SAD BECAUSE YOU'RE ON YOUR OWN (pg **361**)	
3.31	THE PARENT TRAP (pg **362**)	
3.32	WHAT'S THE BUZZ, TELL ME WHAT'S A HAPPENIN' (pg **364**)	
3.33	IT'S AN ILL WIND THAT DON'T BLOW SOMEBODY SOME GOOD (pg **365**)	
3.34	WHAT IT IS AIN'T EXACTLY CLEAR (pg **366**)	
3.35	FIND THE COST OF FREEDOM (pg **370**)	
3.36	MIEN KAMPF (pg **380**)	
3.37	EVIDENCE (pg **390**)	
3.38	RAIDERS OF THE LOST ARK (pg **393**)	
3.39	SEE YOU ONE, RAISE YOU ONE (pg **395**)	
3.40	LOST IN SPACE (pg **397**)	
3.41	DUCKS IN A ROW (pg **405**)	
3.42	THE IMPORTANCE OF BEING EARNEST (pg **408**)	
3.43	RUSES ARE RED (pg **413**)	
3.44	THE RIDE OF THE VALKYRIES (pg **419**)	
3.45	YOU CAN'T PICK YOUR RELATIVES (pg **432**)	
3.46	I MET A GIRL WHO SANG THE BLUES (pg **434**)	
3.47	NIGHTS IN WHITE SATIN (pg **448**)	
3.48	MEMORIES LIGHT THE CORNERS OF MY MIND (pg **449**)	
3.49	IT WAS THE BEST OF TIMES (pg **455**)	
3.50	HEY LITTLE GIRL IS YOUR DADDY HOME (pg **468**)	
3.51	IT WAS THE WORST OF TIMES (pg **479**)	
3.52	LET YE WHO IS WITHOUT SIN... (pg **483**)	
3.53	FAR FROM THE SHALLOW NOW (pg **486**)	
3.54	YOU DON'T ALWAYS GET WHAT YOU WANT (pg **488**)	
3.55	SNAP! (pg **490**)	
3.56	RIDERS ON THE STORM (pg **492**)	
3.57	NO GUTS NO GLORY (pg **493**)	
3.58	THE WEDDING CRASHER (pg **495**)	

PART 4 - **AND**

- 4.1 SUNSET (pg **529**)
- 4.2 VIOLENCE ARE BLUE (pg **535**)
- 4.3 BREAKING UP IS HARD TO DO (pg **539**)
- 4.4 HELEN MAYER (pg **542**)
- 4.5 OH YEAH LIFE GOES ON (pg **543**)
- 4.6 KNOCK KNOCK KNOCKIN' (pg **548**)
- 4.7 THE HEART IS A LONESOME HUNTER (pg **554**)
- 4.8 SUNRISE (pg **556**)
- 4.9 BLUE SKIES (pg **558**)
- 4.10 ASHES TO ASHES (pg **562**)
- 4.11 SOMEWHERE OVER THE RAINBOW (pg **570**)

1

CRIME

1.1 THROUGH THE LOOKING GLASS

From a buried moment in time, there was a rustic, off-the-grid mountain cabin in northern California where a woman who called herself Bonnie Lass stood in her nightgown, lost in the eyes of her person.

She might have still been in her teens, but that was doubtful. She was pregnant. Not very much, but enough that she was starting to show.

She spoke with a calm, penetrating peace. And Doctor Green was giving her his finely tuned and undivided focus of attention.

At that same moment, and about 600 miles south of where Bonnie Lass stood, a young Nashville transplant to Los Angeles was appreciating her slightly more than middle-aged entertainment lawyer husband because of a new sign of hope.

"I bought a great lot in Pacifica Palisades today," as he was taking off his business suit before a nightly shower. "On a clear day, it has a long and broad view of the ocean. I have an architect meeting next week."

Nancy Grant had become Nancy Burlesconi less than a year earlier. She had doubts then, but the dream of becoming a star singer had petered out into the no-hope zone. Peter Berlesconi was rich and thus, to Nancy in her time of despair, he represented the appearance of security.

Peter had met Nancy in the course of her trying to find a record deal, and he had promised to open a few doors for her. The only door he ended up opening for her was the door to her bedroom.

At first, she didn't resent being the pretty young girl on his arm. But a year was a long time to never feel intimate personal engagement from the person who beds you, so she took the news about building a house as a possible sign that he actually *did* care about her.

Nancy couldn't remember the last time she was wide-eyed. "I can't wait to share some of my ideas with the architect! This sounds exciting!"

"Yeah, honey," as he threw his tie over his jacket on the chair back. "I can't get you into that meeting...but I'll let you know what we come up with."

Nancy's disappointment was distracted by the faint whiff of a strange perfume in the room as Peter threw aside his shirt and underclothes and headed toward the shower.

But all that was a long, long time ago.

1.2 THE MOUSE TRAP

On one fine and fateful Fall day in rural southern Middle Tennessee, Scott McNally didn't miss a beat in his daily routine. At 11:30AM, he drove his pickup out of his 1/2-mile long chert driveway to the only two mailboxes on the Little Buffalo River Road to check his mail and the mail of his elderly neighbor, Miss Dolly.

There was a day when Miss Dolly had to drive to the main road to retrieve her mail from amongst the rows of other mailboxes serving other rural dwellers whose access roads had been deemed unfit for safe passage by the U.S. Postal Service. But in a small town, even the U.S. Postal Service can be known to look the other way at its own regulations. When it became a hardship for Miss Dolly to make the daily trip, a decision was made to allow her to set a post in the ground at the end of her own driveway.

"Scottie," as Miss Dolly and the other couple of people who knew him referred to him, saw an opportunity to glom onto Miss Dolly's good fortune with the mail service and planted his own post next to hers. To assuage the guilt of his good fortune, Scottie began bringing her mail to her house, about a quarter mile up a rut-carved path of a driveway that tested the integrity of every vehicle that attempted it.

Scott McNally was an invisible person. He was the average height of every male in America, standing five feet, eight inches in his stocking feet. His facial features were not handsome in any way, but he was not unattractive enough for that to be noticed either. If he walked through a crowd at a store or a mall, nobody would be able to remember that they had ever seen him. Scott McNally, and everything about him, was nondescript. If he could have planned it that way, he would have.

It was a point of comfort to Scott McNally that he had lived for several decades in his rural community that had a small town attached to it, many miles away, and that he only knew three people. More important to him was that only three people knew *him*.

While Scottie stood at the mailboxes pulling out the receipts of the day, a shiny and familiar Cadillac Escalade, that was grotesquely out of place in that dusty rural setting, came down the hill and pulled up along side Scottie. The driver's side window glided down. The vehicle contained the only two other people who knew him besides Miss Dolly.

"Hey, Scottie! Good to see you out and about."

"Hello, Dr. Higginbotham. Are you just pulling into town?" The doctor's wife leaned forward from the passengers seat to add her greeting with a wave.

Scottie bent a little forward and waved.

Mrs. Higginbotham spoke up so her words could be heard past her husband. "Yes. We're just arriving. Can we entice you into supper at six?

I brought lobster tails."

"That sounds delicious. I'll look forward to catching up."

As Dr. Higginbotham's window was gliding up, he added, "Bring your appetite *and* your cholesterol pills, Scottie. We'll have plenty of melted butter on hand."

Miss Dolly's driveway circled around to the back porch of her house. When Scottie drove up that day in his nondescript, not-too-new, not-too-old pickup truck, there sat an old and rusty Dodge Caravan with a backwards baby seat inside and with Michigan plates on the outside. It was taking up his usual parking spot. 'A visit from the relatives,' thought Scottie. He parked behind it and walked to Miss Dolly's door.

Seated at Miss Dolly's dining room table was a young woman with a little baby. The baby looked like she was less than six months old. Miss Dolly introduced the young woman as her granddaughter and the little baby as her *great*-granddaughter.

"Now I got me seven great-grandkids, Scottie. Ain't that sumpin'? Maybe I'll be around to see a great-great one-a-deez days." Miss Dolly was exercising her gums while her welfare dentures soaked in a glass next to the kitchen sink. "You up to no good, Scottie?"

"I just had a brief visit from Dr. Higginbotham and his wife. They're at their cabin down the creek. I'm going over for supper tonight."

"I cain't figure why city folk want to come out to these here woods," Miss Dolly said, as the granddaughter bounced the pacified baby on her knee.

"Same reason as you and me, Miss Dolly. Peace and quiet."

Scottie set the mail down and turned to the granddaughter. "How's your visit going? Comfortable? Got everything you need?"

The granddaughter smiled while still bouncing the baby. "We've got a mouse. I set a trap, but all we're doing is just feeding the dang thang. They eat at the bait, but the trap never springs own them." The granddaughter liked to talk Southern when she visited. She thought it helped Miss Dolly understand her better.

Scottie was deliberate to respond with polite bland conversation. "Just listen for the sound of the 'snap!' That's probably all you can do."

The granddaughter nodded her head in rhythm to the baby bouncing. She changed the subject.

"With all the family up in Michigan and Granny Dolly wantin' to stay down here, we were thinkin' of gittin' her a cellphone so we could do Face Chat with her. That old landline don't help to remind her of what we all look like. Especially as the young-ins grow."

Scottie nodded his head in understanding. "There's no signal here."

"Oh...so much fir *that* i-dee."

"Well, I've got to back to my labor." Scottie rubbed the back of his finger on the baby's cheek. The baby smiled and cooed, then watched him with big eyes as he left.

There would come a day when Scott McNally would hear the sound of the 'snap!' in Miss Dolly's house. But it wasn't *that* day.

1.3 CALL OF DUTY

The Fall sun was still above the ocean horizon, out from Pacific Palisades, California, when Nancy Washington saw a call come in on her phone. It was from her childhood friend in Nashville, Tennessee.

Nancy would see Susan when Nancy would take her own daughter, and then added her granddaughter, on annual trips to visit Nancy's elderly parents in Nashville.

Susan, Nancy's childhood friend in Nashville, had a daughter and a granddaughter the same ages as Nancy's daughter and granddaughter. They had all become a second family to each other over the decades. Other than to make summer or holiday plans, Nancy never talked to Susan over the phone.

"Susie?" Nancy could hear Susan trying to breathe through her whimpering. "Susie? What's wrong?"

Susan couldn't compose herself. Nancy tried again.

"Susie?...Susie?...Tell me what's going on?...Susie?...Talk to me or I'm going to call 9-1-1."

Susan was trying to talk. "It's Cathy." Susan was still trying to inhale.

"What about Cathy, Susie? What's wrong with Cathy?"

Cathy was Susan's granddaughter. Over a year earlier, Nancy's daughter and granddaughter had accompanied Nancy to Nashville for young Cathy's wedding. It was right after young Cathy's High School graduation.

Nancy was beginning to panic. "Speak to me, Susie. What's wrong with Cathy? Is she OK?" Nancy became stern. "Susie...what is wrong with Cathy?"

Susan finally got enough air in her lungs to say, "Her husband...Mark...was killed this afternoon."

Nancy sat down and tried to process the moment. "Cathy?...Her husband?...He's dead?"

Susan just said 'yes' between each breath that she could gulp down.

"Sit tight, Susie. I'm going to see if I get on a plane tonight."

Nancy cut off her call in order to call her own daughter, Charleen.

"Char? I just got a barely intelligible call from Susie."

"I know, Mom. I know. I just off the phone with Jenn-Jenn to take your call."

Jennifer was the daughter of Susan in Nashville and the mother of young Cathy.

Charleen continued. "She said Mark was killed by two kids this afternoon outside the Walmart in Mt. Juliet. She said Cathy was with him. Mark wasn't in uniform. They were just walking out to their car with groceries."

As reality started to sink in for Charleen, she said, "Oh, gawd, Mom. This can't be real. This just can't be."

Nancy tried to calm her daughter. "Just try and relax, Charleen.

We'll find out what's going on. Then we'll make sure all of our Nashville girls get what they need."

"Mom?" Nancy's daughter paused. "Mom? Do you think it had to do with that kid that Mark shot a few months ago?"

"I don't know, Char. I just don't know. I've got to tell your father I need a ride to LAX for a red-eye to Nashville. I'll call you when I know more."

"OK, Mom. I'll call Christine. She doesn't have any classes this evening. She should be in her dorm room by now. I don't want to freak her out. She'll want to call Cathy. It's probably too soon. I'll just tell her that you're flying to Nashville to help Susie with some unknown family problem."

"Come on, Charleen. You know that won't flush. Just call her and tell her what we know…and that I'm flying out tonight."

"Christine?"

"Mom? What the hell?…CNN is showing a breaking news banner. It says a Nashville cop who was involved in the shooting of a fleeing teenager in July was murdered this afternoon outside a Walmart. What the hell, Mom? What the hell? Is that Cathy's husband they're talking about? What's going on?"

"Grammi just got a call from Susie who told her about it."

"What the hell, Mom? This can't be happening. How is Cathy doing? I feel like I need to be there for her. What the hell, Mom? What the hell? I can't just sit here and do nothing." Christine's normally flawlessly controlled demeanor was frazzled.

Christine's mother continued. "Grampi is driving Grammi down to LAX now."

Christine started crying. "I want to go with Grammi. Call her and tell her to pick me up on the way."

Charleen tried to talk her down. "Cathy has her mother and her

Grandma Susie. Give her time to get her feet under her."

"I'm scared for Cathy, Mom. I'm coming home. Take me to go stay with Grampi until Grammi comes home."

Earlier that afternoon, John Watkins had slipped out of his Memphis, Tennessee, office so he could bake a cake for his daughter's birthday. The Nashville 'Officer Down' news was all the buzz when he left. He was hoping the Nashville Metro boys would get a same-day roundup of the assailants.

MaryLou could smell her cake baking from her upstairs bedroom where she was getting her homework finished. A party with girlfriends was set for Saturday with a homework sleepover, plus to do more prep for their third round of SAT's, plus madrigal practice of the songs on the Winter concert list, plus to rehearse lines for the Thespians Winter Play Competition between the Freshmen, Sophomores, Juniors and Seniors in her High School. The Watkins were very supportive of their daughter's college preparations, but MaryLou knew her Mom and Dad wouldn't let her actual special day end without a celebration.

Her Dad had finished frosting the cake and was putting the two candles on top - the number 1 and the number 8 - while her mother set MaryLou's favorite supper on the table.

"Come on down for supper, Lou," her mom called out.

When MaryLou got to the bottom of the stairs, her father came out from the kitchen with a burning-candles cake in hand and started singing "Happy Birthday to you..." Her mom joined in.

MaryLou was beaming. She walked up to the cake in her father's hands and blew out the candles. "Thanks, Mom and Dad. I love you so much."

John replied, "You know you're our daystar, Lou. Happy Eighteenth! You're now, legally, an adult. But we know better, don't we?" Her Dad wanted her to stay a child her whole life.

MaryLou's mother, Jackie, always the practical one, said, "OK, you two. Let's eat the fixin's while they're hot. We can dig into that cake after."

Just then, the ominous sound of the first four notes of Beethoven's Fifth Symphony echoed out from the kitchen. John deflated. "Damn. Err, I mean, darn."

John had chosen that ringtone for his Assistant Director In Charge because John knew that whenever *he* called, it was never about anything good.

"Yeah, Boss?"

"Hey, John. That 'Officer Down' in Nashville isn't under control yet. They I.D.'d the perps from unreleased video. It was an ambush. The killers are cousins of the kid who was shot back in July. The cop was just released from desk duty. Was at the store picking up groceries with his wife. In his civvies. She saw the whole thing."

"So, we're in?"

"TBI and Metro just used S.W.A.T. for a ram breach at the two cousins' house. They're gone. No cooperation in the house. Possible out-of-state getaway. You know the sht's about to hit the fan, right? Make sure you're surgically attached to the Metro Chief and whomever TBI assigns as Field Investigations Agent in Charge. Call your crew and make sure they're in Nashville with you in three hours."

"It's a three-hour drive, Boss."

"Then you'd better giddy-up."

Special Agent In Charge John Watkins was charged up about his assignment, but he was dejected about having to leave his daughter's birthday celebration. The dejection part showed in his walk.

MaryLou knew her Dad had been called in to work. She tried to lighten the moment.

"Well, Daddy, like you always say, 'Work is the physical manifestation of love.' So go to work to prove that you love me." She was cranking out a broad, all-teeth smile to try and disguise her disappointment.

John bent over his daughter and kissed her on the cheek. "Then it's off to love I go...err, I mean work."

He kissed his wife, then he dragged himself into his study to collect his briefcase and his gun.

1.4 LAST DOLLAR LOTTERY TICKET

During supper at Dr. and Mrs. Higginbotham's cabin, down river from his own place, Scott McNally learned of the Nashville cop murder.

His hosts were outraged at the brazen act that was all over the news. They spent the evening talking about the ways the police needed to clamp down stronger on the lawless Blacks who were getting more and more out of control. "We need judges who will put more of them in jail. Otherwise, none of us will be safe."

After the meal, Scottie rolled slowly down his driveway toward his house. He thought driving slowly on the chert helped keep the dust down.

His front porch light showed dimly that someone and a car was there. Scottie never had visitors. Most country folk kept a gun nearby for occasions like this, but Scottie never felt the need.

Instead of hitting the garage door button on his visor, he pulled up next to his unknown visitors. He allowed for it being someone who was lost, even though nobody that was lost had ever ventured down his long driveway.

Before he got out of his truck, he recognized the woman standing by her front fender. Scottie had trouble with Black names, but he remembered how to pronounce hers by saying, 'swing *LOW* sweet chariot...unlock the door with your *KEY*...and the song *SHA*-na-na-na-hey-hey-goodbye.'

Loquisha Davis walked around the front of Scottie's truck to his window. He lowered it and turned the engine off. She spoke with firm purpose.

"Mr. McNally, you had strongly expressed a desire to support the issues of my community. I'm here to say I'm sorry for rejecting your kind offers...and because I've come across a situation in which you *can* help."

Scottie waited for the ask.

"I have two boys with me who, if their whereabouts become known, will be dead before they have a chance to defend themselves. I'm well aware of the grave implications involved in what I'm about to ask you, but I need time to think of a more long-term option."

Scottie looked over into her car and saw the outline of two young men's wild hairdos.

"If I can leave them here for a day or two until I can figure out what to do with them, it could save their lives."

Scottie stepped out his truck, closed the door behind him, and walked around Loquisha to the front of his truck to get a better look at her cargo.

"These the kids who killed that cop?"

Loquisha answered with a less strong strength-of-purpose than her initial presentation. "It's too soon for me to say that."

Scottie walked over to the front of Loquisha's car and stared in through the windshield to get a better look at her troubled youths. He could see they were staring back at him.

The one in the front passenger seat had a full beard that made him look older than he was. His hair was a wild assortment of knappy pool noodles sticking out in every direction. The noodles on top were tied together so that, to Scottie, it looked like a pineapple. The young man looked stocky and muscular, and the furrow in his brow was meant to intimidate.

The one in the back seat looked skinnier and younger. He had tightly braided cornrows that moved to the back of his head where they became a large group of individual strands of braided hair that disappeared to somewhere down his back.

The front seat muscular looking bearded fellow was wearing a black tee-shirt. Though wrinkled from his sitting position, Scottie could tell it had a large fist printed on the front.

Scottie could see that the skinnier passenger in the back seat was wearing, though the porch light was not great, a short sleeve, collared, buttoned-front Hawaiian shirt that appeared to be bright pink with large flowers on it.

"These the kids who killed that cop?" he asked again without breaking his stare.

Loquisha's head bent a little more. "Yes."

Scottie kept staring at the two figures through the windshield.

"So you came to my house to ask me to be an accessory to murder?"

"Murder is a crime for which they have not been convicted."

Scottie's stare was becoming threatening to the boys in the car. They started fidgeting and mumbling things to each other. Scottie was unfazed. His eyes were on the boys, but he was no longer looking at them. He was looking at his situation.

Finally, Scottie turned to Loquisha. "I have to take a leak."

Loquisha thought he was going to go into his house to make the dreaded phone call, but Scottie walked away from Loquisha and her car to behind a giant Ironwood tree on the rim of the hollow next to his house. Loquisha thought, 'Good gawd, he's going to urinate outdoors.' She looked into the car at the boys and shrugged her shoulders.

Behind the tree, Scottie leaned his back on it and slid down to a squatting position. He placed his hands over his face and called on a practiced technique to quiet his inner noise. Less than ten seconds later he had quieted himself. A few moments later, he started sobbing uncontrollably into his hands.

When he returned to the present, he tried to subdue his sniveling noises in the hope that his visitors had not heard him. Within another minute, he cleared his nose and used his sleeve to wipe the tears from his eyes.

The boys had gotten out of the car to stand with Loquisha. As Scottie emerged from behind the tree, they were pleading with her. "Come own, Miss Loquisha. Let's be gettin' outta this honky cracker bllsht hell place. We know you be tryin' to do us good, but this ain't gonna be happnin'. We ain't *wantin'* it to be happenin'. Come own. We be needin' to yonder own outta this bad white-devil hell."

When Loquisha saw Scottie walking toward them, she put her hand on the chest of the skinnier boy who was talking.

Scottie stayed a distance from them with his back to the porch light because he didn't want them to see his swollen eyes. His three visitors silently stared at him.

While he bided his time, Scottie noticed that both youths were slightly taller than he. He estimated they were both about, plus or minus, five feet, nine inches with shoes on. Scottie was waiting for his composure to more fully return. His visitors could not interpret the silence.

Finally, he looked at the two youths and firmly said, "I will help you."

1.5 THE PUNISHMENT

Special Agent in Charge John Watkins arrived at Nashville's Metro Police Headquarters and introduced himself to the Chief.

"I have a team of five agents, plus me. Two are over there. The other three are parking their cars as we speak."

The Chief called the small briefing auditorium to order. "Our FBI brothers and sisters are here. Everybody take a seat and we'll get them up to speed."

The Chief proceeded to speak. He would use the screen that was high on the front wall behind him for visuals.

"Officer Mark Johnson...rookie with a little over a year in service...DA announced no charges being filed against him in an officer involved shooting from three months ago, back in July...the DA's decision was released to the media two days ago...Officer Johnson was notified yesterday that he would take up patrol assignments again, beginning next week...he was relieved about being cleared in the shooting...and to get off desk duty."

A 'here! here!' murmur went out from the Metro officers in the room.

The Chief continued. "Officer Johnson was on an off-duty trip to the grocery store in his hometown of Mt. Juliet, accompanied by his wife. Here is the video of the Walmart parking lot surveillance camera...it is *not* high-definition."

The Chief turned on his laser pointer. "Here's Officer Johnson and his wife leaving the store and entering the parking lot with their bags in hand.

"Follow this car, right here, as it passes by Officer Johnson and his wife, to its parking spot...watch two gang-bangers get out of the car and approach Officer Johnson and his wife...you can see the wife is scared by the way she leans away from her husband and takes a couple steps back...here, Officer Johnson drops his grocery sacks and starts fighting this assailant in the black tee-shirt...then you see the second assailant jump on Officer Johnson's back, but doesn't appear to be very effective...here, the first assailant breaks free while second assailant is still on Officer Johnson's back...look here, as the first assailant appears to reach into his pocket for what we now know is a knife...the wound indicates it was likely a boxcutter...now the first assailant re-engages Officer Johnson and swings his knife hand like he's punching Officer Johnson in the neck...here you see Mrs. Johnson drop her grocery sacks and run back toward the store.

"Now you see Officer Johnson holding his neck…then the second assailant gets off Officer Johnson's back…now Officer Johnson falls to the ground…see the two assailants run back to their car…Officer Johnson's legs show movement for a few seconds…see the thugs are getting in their car…here, a couple of concerned citizens stand over Officer Johnson…here, Officer Johnson's kicking stops, but his upper body still shows movement…here you see the hoodlums' car pulling away…here, one of the concerned citizens looks over at the fleeing car while the second concerned citizen kneels down beside Officer Johnson…here we see the standing concerned citizen pull out his cell phone and calls 9-1-1. We have that recording…15 seconds after the punch to the neck, we see no more movement in Officer Johnson's body."

Chief Rand turned away from the screen to look at his audience. "When paramedics arrived, they waded into the pool of blood, checked for vitals, and didn't even bother with a resuscitation attempt…because of the blood loss."

Special Agent in Charge John Watkins spoke up. "I heard on a radio report on the way up here that you've I.D.'d the assailants…but this video isn't clear enough to see facial details."

The Chief told the room, "Officer Johnson's wife reported that the boys were screaming profanities at Officer Johnson when they approached, and that in-between all the profanities, they were accusing Officer Johnson of murdering their Cousin Jimmy. And that he, meaning Officer Johnson, wasn't going to get away with it.

"Cousin Jimmy would be James Jefferson, a 17-year old Black male whom Officer Johnson had shot and killed during a crime-in-progress shooting back in July.

"We know that Mr. Jefferson lived with his two cousins, a Black male by the name of Jamal Ali Jefferson, age 19, and Muhammad Dogg Jefferson, age 21, along with all three of the young males' mothers, as well as with the grandmother of the three young males. The mothers of the three young males are all daughters of the grandmother, Ms. Jacinda Jefferson."

Agent Watkins then asked, "How is it that they're all named Jefferson?" The other Metro officers in the briefing start chuckling amongst themselves.

The Chief told his officers to settle down. "The three daughters of Mrs. Jacinda Jefferson are all believed to have different fathers. That's based on neighborhood hearsay. And Ms. Jefferson never revealed the fathers' identities to any family services agencies. The three daughters each gave birth to one son, and none of those mothers named the fathers of each of their three boys. We've gotten to know a lot about this family since the July incident involving Jimmy Jefferson."

The Chief went back to his video briefing. "The grainy video shows two very distinctive hairstyles of the assailants. These hairstyles are consistent with the hairstyles of the two cousins, Jamal and Muhammad Jefferson. We told the media that we had video and that we had I.D.'d the assailants. We never said we I.D.'d them from the video. We needed to assure the public that we know who the perps are, and that we're pursuing them with the full range of resources available to the Department."

Agent Watkins asked another question. "In the video, you described the two Black males as 'gang-bangers.' What is their gang affiliation, and does that gang extend beyond Nashville?"

The Chief answered to the room. "Getting to know this family over the past few months, there is no doubt that they all have strong militant attitudes. We haven't been able to establish a known gang connection as yet, but just look at the hairdos."

Agent Watkins had a follow-up. "How often do you see a gang-banger in a Hawaiian party shirt around here?"

A Metro officer in the briefing leaned close to Agent Watkins' ear and said, "Don't make it look like you're choosing the wrong side."

Agent Watkins pulled back from the officer and looked down his nose at him. Then he redirected his attention to the Chief.

The Chief continued. "The SWAT team executed a ram breach of the Jefferson apartment a few of hours ago. There was no sign of the young thugs. All the women were home, and there was aggressive antagonism toward the officers. Read that to mean 'no cooperation.'

"We believe there is a strong possibility that the thugs have fled outside our jurisdiction. Your best help to us in this moment, Special Agent Watkins, would be to marshal your resources to find those two cop-killing murderers who may, now, be beyond our reach."

John Watkins made a mental list of all the racially charged terms used during the briefing.

After the briefing had concluded, the officer who had leaned in to advise Watkins about choosing the 'right side' walked up to Special Agent Watkins with the Chief at his side. The Chief made the introduction.

"Agent Watkins, I'd like you to meet Officer Neal Knopfler. He's the Union Rep for all the Metro Officers, and I'm assigning him to be the liaison between your efforts and my department."

Special Agent Watkins was taken aback. "Chief, I've never used an intermediary. I need a direct and private line of communication with you, personally. My bosses require that, also."

The Chief clarified, "I didn't mean to imply that Officer Knopfler would be a liaison between you and me. My Metro officers..."

Officer Knopfler interjected, "And *my* Metro Officers..."

The Chief frowned at Knopfler and continued, "...need regular updates on our progress. You know how personally we all take it when one of our own goes down."

Officer Knopfler spoke directly to Special Agent Watkins. "They trust *me*."

John Watkins inferred Knopfler meant the officers wouldn't trust the FBI, or specifically, perhaps, Special Agent Watkins, himself.

Officer Knopfler continued. "Plus, I trained Mark Johnson. Took him under my wing. This is way more personal to me than any other case could be."

The Chief added, "Officer Knopfler, because of his relationship with our slain officer, will also be the primary conduit of information to Officer Johnson's widow."

Special Agent in Charge Watkins thought that task would be more appropriate for a female officer...but this was not Agent Watkins' home turf.

Special Agent in Charge John Watkins pulled his team into an interrogation room where he gave them the plan outline for the team fanning out for interviews.

"Don't stay up tonight. We need to hit the ground running first thing. We have a communications room given to us here at HQ. Be there, ready to go, at 6:00AM. We're going to find these perps and bring them in. One way or another."

All the agents were charged up. This is what they lived for.

John Watkins stood at the door with the palm of his hand turned open at his side and below his belt. Each of the agents slapped Agent Watkins' hand down low on their way out the door. The feeling in the room was that of opening day for baseball season.

1.6 MY WAY OR THE HIGHWAY

Scottie took a wide berth around his three visitors, climbed back into his truck, started it, backed up to turn it toward the front of his garage, pressed the button to open the garage door, and left the garage while pressing the button to close the garage door. He walked back to his guests who were still assembled in front of Loquisha's car.

Scottie spoke to Loquisha. "Do you have your cell phone with you?"

"Yes. It's in the car."

Scottie pondered a moment. "How long before they figure out you're the one who got the boys out of town?"

"I..."

"How do you know these kids?"

"They're part of my community. I know *all* the kids in my community."

"So, you'll be one of the first persons the FBI looks at as a possible mule?"

"FBI?"

"The presumption will be that you took them out of state...or any one of a number of other rationalizations. Whatever it takes to get the resources of the FBI in on the case.

"They'll have a warrant to search your phone before lunch tomorrow. The GPS location data will lead them right to this spot at this time. They could be here by tomorrow afternoon."

The boys were looking back and forth at each other.

Loquisha said, "I can shut my phone off and think of another place to take them. I'm feeling like I shouldn't have involved you."

Scottie's head was in high gear. "Too late for that." He thought another second. "Who knows you have the boys or could have seen you leave with the boys?"

"Their mothers and their grandmother called me and asked for my help. They told me where I could find them."

"No. That's *not* why the women called you. They called you to say the boys were missing, and did you hear anything about where they might be."

"OK."

"Who could have seen the boys get in your car?"

"No-one. They were hiding up in the underside of the Jefferson Street Bridge. That's where I picked them up. There were no cars. It was after working hours, and only commuters use Jefferson Street in and out of State offices and nine-to-five businesses. Both boys laid down in the car before I drove out from under the bridge."

"Police cameras?"

"Maybe at a distance. There aren't any on the bridge."

"Listen closely and make a mental picture of everything I say. Don't alter a single picture: Their grandmother called you to see if you had seen them. You went driving around town looking for them. You were frustrated that you couldn't find them or know where to look. You stopped under the bridge to collect your thoughts. You were angry about getting sucked into their problems. You remembered the materials I had sent you that were sitting next to you on the passenger's seat, so you decided to relieve your frustration by deciding to come here to confront me about butting in where I don't belong...all because of your need to distance yourself from trying to find where the troubled boys might have run off to.

"You put my address from my materials that you had in hand into your phone's Google Maps and followed the route here. You waited a long time for me here because I wasn't home. When I pulled in, we had a late night confrontation about the materials. You threw them in my face and told me to never contact you, or anyone in your community, ever again. You left."

"OK."

"Which is what you will do now."

"What about the boys?"

"Your story must be based on an underlying motive. The real purpose of your trip, here, was to distance yourself as far as possible from wherever the boys were, and whatever they were doing...that your community work doesn't include being an accomplice or an accessory to crimes...that you don't appreciate friends taking advantage of you, exposing you to legal jeopardy. Got it?"

"Yes."

"Say goodbye. Don't deviate in any way from the story. Don't elaborate. Don't tell it more than once. Tell the grandmother and mothers you couldn't find the boys."

The stocky boy with the beard shouted, "Hey, mthrfker, my grandma needs to know we be OK."

Scottie looked at him. "You're *not* OK. You're dead. Your grandmother will never see you again unless you're in a casket or in a jail cell."

The skinnier boy stepped forward, angry also. "What the fck, mthrfker? You think your gonna be ninety-sixin' us?" He turned to his companion, "Cut that mthrfker."

The other one stuck his hand in his pocket. That made Loquisha step in between the boys and Scottie.

"What are you doing, telling these boys they're dead?"

Scottie answered her without passion. "I know what I'm doing. You don't. They don't.

"You said you brought them here because you want them to live. I know how to give them the best chance of that happening. You don't. They don't.

"I promise you and them this: they will never be prisoners here. They will be free to leave at any time if that's what they choose. But you will never see them again..nor they you. They will never contact you again, nor you them. Just like you will never contact me again."

The skinnier one of her charges spoke pleadingly to Loquisha. "This be bllsht, Miss Loquisha. Let's be gittin' in the car and be gone."

Loquisha looked to Scottie for the next move.

Scottie looked at her but was talking to all of them. "The cops are going to be in a mad hunt for two living beings. And nothing excites the blood that flows through these guys' veins more than a hunt. It may take some time, but I know how to get the hound dogs off the scent.

"Would I be right to say these boys have no experience outside their neighborhood?"

Loquisha wavered, not knowing why he was asking. "Maybe."

"Do you think the cops will find that out? That these boys have never been outside their neighborhood?"

"Probably."

"So, long term, where do you think the cops will look? An environment familiar to the kids? Like somewhere in the city? Any city? A city with relatives, perhaps?...Or do you think they'll suspect a place where they'll stick out like sore thumbs, such as KKK country in rural Tennessee?"

"OK."

"What I can do for them is their best shot. It's probably their *only* shot. The sooner everybody understands that, then the sooner they can die."

The more aggressive of the two stepped forward again. 'WTF, man. Stop goin' on about us dying or I'm gunna cut chew."

Scottie was nonplussed. Loquisha came between them, again, and said to the boys, "I think he's talking about giving you a new identity."

Scottie said flatly to both boys, "Someone's going to come along and take your place...someone with a different name and a different face."

Again, from the more aggressive one. "No fucking way am I bein' someone I ain't."

Scottie motioned his hand for the kid to go ahead and get back into Loquisha's car. "The door's open, but the ride ain't free. If you're willing to pay the price, step back into her car."

Loquisha spoke again. "Muhammad, I have to make a quick decision that I might regret...but you and Jamal might be standing where your only chance is. You know what's going down if they get a holt of you."

The other one, Jamal, put his hand on Muhammad's arm.

"Com'own, man. You heard the mthrfkr. We can be leavin' when we wants to." Muhammad shook the hand off his arm and turned his back to the group.

Scottie looked at Loquisha. "You've been here too long. When they show up here, I'll let them know it was a venomous argument in which we were lucky that it didn't turn violent."

Loquisha turned to get in her car. "That's not far from the truth."

1.7 I JUST NEED SOMEONE TO LOVE

The events that had led up to Scott McNally making the fateful acquaintance of Loquisha Davis had evolved from a number of converging circumstances.

When property cleanup chores had reached the point of requiring a lighter schedule of maintenance, Scottie's newfound free time had left him with a feeling of lack of purpose.

He could only find spotty entertainment by watching the evening Nashville news with his spotty TV reception, but during several stories about issues that were impacting the predominantly Black neighborhood of North Nashville, Scottie had seen a spokesperson who appeared both articulate and passionate. He finally made a note on a piece of paper that her name was Loquisha Davis.

Loquisha Davis and her passion reminded him of his own mother getting verklempt, even sobbing at times, over civil rights issues from the 1950's and '60's.

Those incidents had clearly had an impact on shaping the development of his soul, so it seemed a natural fit to him that he could devote his free time to being helpful to the causes of the TV's recurring civil rights champion, Loquisha Davis.

At his first opportunity, Scottie went to his satellite internet connection and found Ms. Davis' indirect contact information. His initial idea was that he could contribute some messaging improvements. He wrote her a letter offering to help.

He had no way of knowing that his letter of introduction would be received as being clearly written by a White person, and that his return address was so far away that it was interpreted as coming from a different universe altogether. A purely *White* universe.

Scottie could not have predicted that his letter would be met with something worse than indifference. It had been received, and instantly rejected, with aggressive disgust.

Scottie suffered through six weeks of anticipation about hearing from Ms. Davis. After those six weeks, he drove out to a hill where he could get a cell phone signal and attempted to call her.

His call went to someone who wasn't her, but whose voice was clearly Black. After a couple of 'please hold' shuffles, he was told that his number would be given to Ms. Davis.

Scottie was about to drive away from his hillside signal when an unknown number showed up on his phone. He answered. It was Loquisha Davis.

"Who are you with?"
"What do you mean? I'm not with anybody."
"Well, then, who are you? Who are you connected with?"
"I'm no-one. I'm not connected with anybody."
"So you're just an individual concerned citizen who wants to help?"
"Yes, M'am."
"No, thank you."
"If we meet, you might see I can help."
"Like I'm incompetent to know my own needs?"
"I have a strong desire and ability to contribute."

When he said that, Scottie thought he might be misinterpreted as wanting to make a financial contribution. Money. For her part, Ms.

Davis thought he was bragging about his White communication skills that she had gleaned from his letter.

"You might find this hard to believe, but we have a treasure trove of skilled communicators up here…who actually have Black skin."

"Why are you being so dismissive?"

"We have to be careful. We get all kinds of calls. Infiltrators…usually the police or their White Supremacist partners."

"Well, Ms. Davis, I'm neither…"

Scottie saw the 'call ended' message when he was mid-sentence.

Scottie was more capable of dedication to purpose than what appeared on his amiable surface. He spent the next six weeks working on some print mailing pieces that were meant to persuade and enlighten politicians that they were on the wrong side of history. The wrong side of humanity.

When he got one that he thought was hard-hitting enough to be worthy of use, he decided to drive to Nashville to see if he could find Ms. Davis at a Community Center where he'd seen her on TV.

"We talked on the phone several weeks ago. I have a sample piece I'd like to show you."

Loquisha was put off by his assertive behavior, but she took the piece from him and looked it over. After reading it, she set it down on the table next to her.

"You White folk are not dependable. At end of day, you go home with your White skin to your safe and comfortable homes. We go home with our Black skin to our homes that are known to police as targets for forceful and unannounced invasion.

"On the way back to our unsafe homes, we live in a constant state of fear of being seen by a White cop who isn't from our neighborhood and who we don't know. We have *every*thing at stake. You just have your

White guilt at stake.

"Instead of trying to assuage your White guilt by 'helping,' just go get some of that good ole expensive White counseling. The more it costs you, the better you'll feel about yourself."

Scottie wasn't deterred. "This is not some guilt-of-the-moment. I grew up watching and feeling my mother's pain as we watched the aftermath of Rosa Parks, the open casket of Emmet Till, the KKK and the 16th Street Baptist Church bombing in Birmingham, and the pictures of those four little Alabama Sunday School girls. Bull Conner and the firehose cannons, and the attacks of the biting police dogs. The lynching photos. The voting intimidation and suppression. The Edmund Pettus Bridge. The March on Washington. The Memphis Sanitation Workers' strike. The murder of Martin.

"I'm not trying to assuage my own guilt. I recognize the insidious effects of White Supremacy in my country...and I want to contribute to it's dismantling and demise."

Loquisha shook her head and started to walk away.

Scottie made on last desperate plea. "I'm a combat veteran. I wasn't putting my life on the line for a country where justice and equal opportunity are a joke. I fought for a country that I knew could only be strong by all of us living with equal opportunity. A country that would be strengthened by people getting jobs based on the merit that came from equal opportunity in education and housing...and social treatment in general. That's what I fought for. That's what I put my life on the line for. That's what I want to join the fight for, now."

"Go home, White boy. You don't have a dog in this fight. So, take your White guilt and get outta here. Nobody's gonna win this fight but those of us who are willing to die for it. And let's not bllsht each other. That ain't chew. We don't need no White Knight. And even if we did...that ain't chew."

"Please take my contact information. If you have a change a heart, call me."

She wouldn't touch the piece of paper, so Scottie just set it on the table.

"On your way home, White boy, every time you see a cop on the road, axe yourself if you're afraid...and if you have to cower to not be seen by him. And if you have to cower if you *are* seen by him.

"Then, when you get home without incident, fix yourself a slice of warm apple pie. Put a scoop of vanilla ice cream on top. Add a cherry right in the middle of the ice cream. Then put your feet up and try to convince yourself you care by watching a Black sit-com on TV. And try to remember that somewhere, way back in your history, you had a Black friend somewhere, somehow. And that that means you're not a racist."

With that, she walked away from Scottie and started greeting others that they both had thought were too far away to hear.

Scottie walked toward the door to leave and found himself surrounded by a group of five or six menacing looking young Black men. When he started to walk through them, they closed in tighter to hinder his exit.

It bothered Scottie that his mind still went...reflexively...to the sequence of pictures of what to do to neutralize a close-contact, multiple-person threat. But consciously he didn't want to be a lethal person anymore...unless it was in the defense of somebody else. And even in that circumstance, he wanted to will himself the patience to hold out until it was a last resort.

So, Scottie wasn't scared. But he was patient. He was saddened that these boys were using the same intimidation tactics imposed on them by the police their whole lives. Having spent decades keeping his lethality in a safe place, he had no intention of letting the dogs out in that moment. So he waited them out so they could have the freedom to live...and so he could have his freedom of passage without damage to his acquired values. That's when he felt an arm encircle his waist from behind.

He turned his head to see Loquisha standing beside him. It was her arm around his waist.

The boys started looking at each and nodding, saying things like 'Oh...he be coo,' and 'OK, man. We ain't gut no problem wit chew.'

When the circle of boys opened up, Loquisha walked back to from whence she had come.

Scottie walked out to his car to return to from whence he had come.

1.8 THE SECRET OF NIMH

When Loquisha got in her car and was ready to leave, she said to her contraband, "Do what he says until you cain't."

The three remaining co-conspirators watched in silence as her car kicked up a cloud of chert dust, barely visible in the reflected porch light...like stardust.

When they could no longer hear Loquisha's car, Scottie motioned for the boys to follow him. "Come into the house. You'll need a good night's rest. We begin first thing in the morning."

Jamal, the skinnier one, said to Muhammad, "I ain't going in that cracker-mthrfkr's house. He say he be goin' to off us."

Scottie turned back to them and offered, "The side door to the garage is open if that works better for you. It won't be comfortable, but you can sleep in the bed of the truck...if you don't mind sore bones in the morning."

Scottie walked toward the front door of his house but turned back before he got there. "Nothing's locked around here. If you change your mind, come in and get as comfortable as you can."

The boys looked at each other and headed for the side garage door.

Scottie gave them a half-hour to get cold and, when they didn't come in, he brought out his own two blankets for warmth. Plus he brought out two sofa cushions for them to use as pillows.

They didn't take the comforts from him. They waited for him to just lay them in the truck bed. Nor did they express thanks. But after Scottie returned to his house, they wrapped their cold bodies with the blankets and laid their heads on the cushions.

MORNING ONE

Scottie walked into the garage at 5:30AM. It was still too soon for dawn's early light. A whole cage full of roosters had begun crowing from an unseeable property across the river.

He rousted the two young men that were semi-sleeping in the truck bed. The rousting was not difficult considering neither one of them was really asleep.

The stocky one was cranky. "WTF is that noise, man?"

The skinnier one piped in with his scratchy morning voice, "Is that what a murder goin' down sounds like out here?"

The stocky one added, "Why don't someone shoot dem dumb mthrfckrs?"

Scottie coaxed them out of the bed of the truck. "Let's go fellas. The day waits for no man."

The two followed Scottie into the house with their blankets still draped over their shoulders. As they all walked together, Scottie told them, "That sound is roosters crowing. Whomever lives across the river over there raises roosters for cock fights. That's a sound you'll hear every morning that you're here. It will enhance the pleasure of your stay if you can learn to enjoy it."

Both the boys mumbled with grumbles.

Once inside the house, Scottie directed them into his bathroom while he grabbed a notepad and pen, and a wooden ruler from the kitchen drawer.

In the bathroom, he had each of the boys step on the Physician's Scale. Scottie adjusted the counterweights, measured the height of each, then had each step on the wooden ruler, heel against the baseboard.

Scottie made cryptic notes: M - 5' 8-1/4" 168 lb size 9; J - 5' 8-3/4" 138 lb size 8-1/2". "Use the toilet if you have to." He knew they would.

Once they were inside the inner sanctum, Scottie placed three glasses on the kitchen counter and poured from a plastic gallon jug of room temperature mineral water. He instructed them to take a glass.

Once they all had a glass in hand, Scottie instructed that they all three drink slowly. Scottie demonstrated the pace. The boys kept looking at each other with apprehension, but followed.

Scottie then had each of them clean their glass at the sink with a lightly soaped sponge. They all three then rinsed their glass under the faucet's running water. They all three then wiped their glass dry with a dish towel taken from a hook on the front edge of the counter. Then they each placed their glass back in the overhead cabinet from which it had come.

"Whenever you eat or drink, immediately wash, dry, and put away your dishes. Always keep in mind what a person will see when they walk in here. Why would I, a single solitary man, have dishes for three people laying around?"

The boys looked at each other to decide whether or not they would comply. So far, they understood how this instruction would safeguard them.

Jamal, the skinnier one, asked, "So you says yuuz ain't bein' married?"

Scottie nodded and then had them each stand in place in the living room area. He led them in arm stretches, then body stretches. The boys were semi-compliant.

Then they were shown how to stand on one leg. Then alternate to the other. The boys started making noises about how 'stupid-ass this bllsht' was.

Scottie offered, "For the human brain to allow a sustained balance, it must clear itself of other noise. This exercise is meant to help clear your mind."

Then Scottie led them in shaking their hands and fingers at their sides. When he saw they were getting impatient with all that non-sense, he said, "Do it like somebody's watching you and you want to make them nervous about you." They couldn't understand how this was a superior alternative to furrowing your brow with a mean look in your eye. They would later learn that 'crazy' and 'scary' can be interchangeable.

"Now, we're going to make breakfast."

Muhammad, the stocky one, said, "We ain't eatin' yo cracker food, foo. Take us to Mack Donald's."

Jamal, the skinny one, piped in, "Or at least go *git* us some Mack Donald's."

Scottie said, "Follow me," and started handing them bowls and plates and glasses from the cupboards, including a hand-juicer, and mixing and eating utensils from drawers.

Scottie interspersed the breakfast chore with some guidance about their desire for Mack Donald's. "The 'you'...the *person* that you are...is different from your body. Your body is physical and can be physically seen and touched by other people with their physical bodies. But the 'you'...the person that you are...is spirit.

our body, or physical being, is the house that your spirit-being, which is called your 'soul,' lives in. Your soul is you.

"It is unusual for your body and your soul to be separated from each other. It usually requires the death of your body.

"Because the bond between your body and your soul is so unbreakable, it might make sense to you that things that happen to your body affect your soul. And the things that happen to your soul...in your thoughts, for example...affect your body.

"Food is the most common thing that 'happens' to your body. To nourish your body with food that is good for it can only serve to healthen your soul.

"The moral of this story is that the thing we call 'fast food,' or 'prepared foods,' should generally be regarded as *not good* for your body and, hence, *not good* for your soul."

The boys were looking back and forth at each other with a look on their faces that said to Scottie, 'Uh-oh. This guy's a looney.' Scottie directed them in setting the oven temperature.

Scottie then showed them how to squeeze his last six oranges into a small bit of orange juice for each of them, then adding all the pulp that stuck to the juicer. Then he had them measure and mix the biscuits ingredients.

While the biscuits were baking, he showed them now to warm two frying pans, how to peel bacon strips, and how to crack eggs.

The skinny one said, "We ain't stupid, man. We already knowed how to bein' this here sht."

Scottie said, "Now you know where to find everything you need to do it...here."

BREAKFAST BRIEFING

When the boys started wolfing down the chow, Scottie said, "Eat slowly. Fast eating shocks your body and makes your food more difficult to digest."

The boys looked at him with a defiant 'don't be tellin' us what to do' look, but each slowed their pace to somewhat match Scottie's. Scottie added, "Eating slowly takes practice. It has to be done on purpose. Think about it while you're doing it. Tell yourself it's to make your body happy."

As they proceeded, Scottie adjusted himself into command mode.

"This is where we're at fellas. All three of us.

"As long as you are willing and able to stay here, and as long as I am willing and able to put up with you staying here, the goal is make you into different people than you are now."

Jamal objected, "We don't need to be no different-ass people, man. We be bein' who we be."

Scottie continued, "If you become a different person, you will no longer need to hide. Hiding is temporary and is the opposite of living. If you want to live, there is a long-term commitment that must be made, and the commitment includes adhering to disciplines that are different from the ones that got you here, today."

Muhammad said, "That's bllsht, man. We know how to hide from the pigs. We ain't be needin' to be no diffrent than what we is."

Scottie replied, "I know about a lot of people who thought they could hide. They all got caught or turned themselves in. And the one thing they all had in common was that not one of them was able to fully kill their old self and create a brand new person. And I know of one case of someone who was able to fully kill her old self...and she was never discovered by the people who might have been hunting her.

"In the case of you two, whether you get found or whether you turn yourselves in, you know full well what the next thing that will happen will be.

"You murdered a cop. If you're not tortured and killed before you even get to prison, you'll be murdered in prison while being supervised by the guards. And that's the merciful alternative. The other way it happens is you're tortured daily for their amusement. And then, when it's no fun for the guards or your fellow inmates who ingratiate themselves to the guards...you're done."

Muhammad was leery. "Why ain't chew wantin' to help that pig? He be wantin' us to pay for what we done to his ass. The way we made him pay for what he done. Nobody be gettin' outta dare sht foe free."

"Justice is always in the eye of the beholder. You will always have the option to turn yourself in. But you were brought here because of a view that there is no justice for you in the White Supremacy system. People who hold that view, like Miss Loquisha, hold that justice for you lies outside of that system. So, commit to having the parts of you that define you being stripped away, including all family and all friends, or I'll release you to your own ways…the way of certain physical death."

The boys weren't fully buying it that Scottie was in this for their interests. But for the moment, they said nothing.

"My job is *not* to convince you of anything. My job is to show you the way…once you've convinced yourself that I am *capable* to show you the way…to your best hope for your own sense of justice."

Scottie added, "I've lived underground before, staying below the radar from law enforcement. I know what I'm doing. It was a randomly unpredictable coincidence that Miss Loquisha brought you here, probably the only place on earth where your challenge can be accomplished. We never know how or why some doors in this life get opened for us. But it's always our choice whether or not to walk through those open doors. It's not up to me whether or not you stay here. It's only up to you."

Jamal, the skinny one, said, "You bin hidin' out from the law? So you wuz what? A gangsta? You murder somebody, too?"

Muhammad interjected, "You in dis wit us, foo. We get caught, chew goin' down wit us."

Jamal asked, "Why woot chew do dat, man? Wudever you be thinkin'? It look like dis ain't that good fir yo ass. Wuzz you game, man? You makin' me nervous about chew."

Scottie said, "My sole job is to prepare you for the opposite of jail and all that that represents for you. You'll have a little time to think it over. But there will come a point when you have to choose…to commit to my plan, or to choose your own plan and leave."

After the boys finished breakfast in their day-old murder clothes, all three cleaned and restored the dining table and kitchen to order.

Scottie showed them all the scraps that were compostable versus those that weren't. Then he showed them the compost pile out behind the house.

"Why doan' you jess be puttin' it in the trash, man?"

Scottie showed them how to cover the scraps from a pile of grass clippings and a pile of dead leaves. "This makes dirt. Dirt is useful around here. Plus, we help to save our home from trash piles."

"Home? I ain't seen no trash piles around here."

Scottie said, "Our home is the earth."

When the meal clean-up was complete, Scottie said, "I'm going out for the day. Pay close attention to what I'm about to show you."

He led them over to a wall bookcase at the dining table end of the inner sanctum.

"Watch where my hand goes and what I do." He then reached over a section of books at eye level at the end of the bookcase and pushed the upper right hand corner of the wood backing panel. The boys heard a latch sound, then the entire bookcase moved out a little at an angle. The far-end, back-side stayed against the wall, and the near-end that was tight to the end wall of the inner sanctum dining area sprung open about a foot.

"Feel behind this open end for a finger-catch carved into the wood." He had them each feel for it. Then he instructed the stocky one, Muhammad, "Pull lightly on the finger catch."

When he did, the entire bookcase floated effortlessly away from the wall at an angle. It was rolling silently on silicone rubber wheels that were hidden behind the bookcase's baseboard trim. "Now, look behind."

Each of the boys took a turn looking inside, and each came back with their mouth open. The skinny one, Jamal, said in awe, "It's stairs!"

Scottie flipped a light switch at the top of the stairs and led the boys down.

It was a giant basement of all concrete that had pipes and partitions and utility lights throughout. There was a concrete counter with a kitchen sink, a propane kitchen stove, and a bathroom and shower with a mini washer/dryer combo. There were no windows.

There were also no beds, no linens, no tableware, nor pots and pans. There wasn't even any toilet paper. It was as sterile as the buried ruins of Pompeii.

Scottie said, "These pipes along the top corners provide air circulation. They have small fans inside them that bring in fresh air from hidden, camouflaged 'U' shaped pipes from the woods in the hollow." Scottie then led the boys back to the stairway.

"This chain is to unlatch the bookcase from down here so that it will open. And the wheel is to close and latch the bookcase from down here.

"Stay here and close the bookcase by turning this wheel until you here the latch catch. Then open it using the pull-chain. Then come back up."

When they were all back upstairs, Scottie said, "I'm going to show you the driveway alarm. When it sounds, go to the front picture window outside this inner sanctum. The black solar shades over the window will allow you to see out, but people outside can't see in.

"If you see a car coming down the drive that is not my truck, glance around to make sure no sign of you is left behind, then go down the stairs and close the bookcase from below by using the wheel until you hear the latch sound. Stay down there until I return.

"It's very soundproof down there, so you won't know I'm back. If you're not up here, I'll open the bookcase so you know it's safe to come up. Do *NOT* come up on your own. Someone might be here. Then the worst part of your nightmare comes back."

The boys were too awestruck to object, though they were both far from comfortable with this new living arrangement...and the unknown that lay ahead.

1.9 GANG VIOLENCE

The Metro police had five times the normal number of officers in the neighborhoods of North Nashville. Their goal was to collect intelligence about the movements of Muhammed and Jamal Jefferson. Their methods were less than cordial.

Agent Watkins had requested a Justice Department attorney to work side-by-side with the Tennessee Attorney General and the Davidson County District Attorney. That team included an on-call judge who would sign off on all requested warrants.

The first search warrant was for the land-line phone of Ms. Jacinda Jefferson, the grandmother of Jamal and Muhammad. Agent Watkins was interested in the list of numbers, incoming and outgoing, from the day of Officer Johnson's murder to the present.

The list was all local calls. Long distance calls were not allowed on State-provided land-line telephones. Metro detectives and FBI agents were paired up and each given a number to investigate.

The second search warrant issued was for the residence of Ms. Jacinda Jefferson. The SWAT team, an array of patrol officers, and three detectives were given that assignment.

A dozen patrol cars formed a circle in the street in front of the residence as well as blocking the streets beside and behind. Each patrol car had an officer standing by their vehicle with their hand gun at the ready.

The SWAT armored vehicle pulled directly up to the front door steps of the apartment. Then a swarm of robo-cop clad, army-looking commandos exited the vehicle and surrounded the perimeter of the building. They were followed by two SWAT members who approached the front door with a battering ram.

The door was already in splinters and could not be closed as a result of the previous evening's ram breach, so the SWAT officers pushed the splinters aside and entered the apartment. They were screaming the announcement of themselves with their rifles in the aim-and-fire position. A line of Metro uniformed officers followed with guns drawn.

All four Jefferson women were inside and were screaming with their hands held above their heads. They were each violently spun against the wall, roughly hand-cuffed, and then had their legs swept out from under them so that they slammed down against the floor.

The grandmother, Jacinda, who was only fifty-three years old, though extremely stiff-jointed for her age, was violently tripped to the floor while cuffed. That caused her to scream in pain from smashing the side of her face on the floor.

An individual officer had his boot on the back of each woman to keep them down, while another line of officers entered the house, each taking a room, and began tearing things apart and throwing every item they broke into heaps on the floor.

Trinkets were smashed and lamps were shattered into pieces. Drawers were broken into splinters, and dishes were reduced to ceramic shards, thrown against walls like frisbees. Then knives were used to rip open every piece of furniture in the apartment, including bedding.

Nobody was 'looking' for anything. These Jefferson women had an open lawsuit against the department and specific officers, and they lived off of the welfare system. The 'Family Services' system. The higher-ups in the department knew these people didn't have the money to do anything about this home invasion. And an action that has no consequences has trouble finding its own boundaries.

As the rampage was ending, after the legion of officers leaving the building had made their point, Officer Neal Knopfler went to each of the women, one by one, and lifted them off the floor by their hand-cuffed wrists behind their backs, stretching their shoulder muscles into excruciating pain and doing some irreparable damage that would make shoulder movement limited for the rest of two of the women's lives. It wasn't an accident.

One by one, Officer Knopler asked each woman, his face so close to theirs that he was spitting into their mouths when he spoke, "Care to share any information about where your nggr boys are?" The only officers that had entered the residents were White, and they were personally known to Knopfler. Knopfler had made sure of that by hand-selecting all the entry officers, himself.

When he picked the grandmother off the floor by her cuffed wrists, her loud whimpering became a blood-curdling shriek as her shoulders snapped. He looked at her bloody and swollen face and dropped her back down to the floor.

Knopfler left the apartment. The two remaining officers un-cuffed the four weeping women. Then they left the women alone.

The search warrant lessened the chances of the Jeffersons securing a conviction for Breaking and Entering, Assault and Battery, Abuse of Power, etcetera, etcetera.

Jacinda's injuries would need emergency room medical attention. She had a thought that rose above her pain. 'Would the world be any different if the criminal gangs were in charge...?'

Back at Metro Headquarters, Agent Watkins and his team were being briefed on the list of numbers from the Jefferson land-line warrant.

When they got to a 4:17PM outgoing call, the briefer said, "Outgoing call to Loquisha Davis. Duration, one minute." Then he looked up to tell Watkins the profile of the receiver of the call.

"Loquisha Davis is a community activist. She's reported as being militant in her guidance of the neighborhood youth. Everybody knows her...parents and youth alike. She's highly respected in the neighborhood. She's been the spokesperson to the media for the neighborhood for years.

"She retired from the Metro Schools System as a guidance counselor on a dubious disability. She was a classmate in school of the grandmother to the boys, Jacinda Jefferson, who did not graduate.

"Loquisha Davis does not have a degree. She was hired into the school system before a degree was required for a teaching certificate."

Just then, Officer Neal Knopfler walked into the briefing. "If there's gonna be a race war, she's gonna be the General for the enemy."

Knopfler walked over and stood next to Agent Watkins. Watkins could smell the adrenaline that had oozed out of his pores during his Jefferson women's assault.

Watkins said quietly to the hyped-up officer, "That was a lot of hardware...for a house full of girls?"

All of Special Agent in Charge John Watkins' fellow FBI agents had turned to look at Knopfler who appeared to coming down from a roid-rage incident.

Knopfler worked to keep from exploding. He leaned even closer to Watkins. "You don't want to get on my bad side."

Agent Watkins thought, 'Too late,' and turned back to the busyness at hand.

All the agents had one common thought. 'What is *wrong* with that guy?' All the Metro officers already knew.

1.10 TIL DEATH SO US PART

After that first morning's breakfast and instructions to the boys, Scott McNally drove to Columbia in search of a Black cemetery.

Before he reached the city limits, he saw a Black groundskeeper was in the cemetery of the old Polk family Episcopal Church that had been built by their slaves. He stopped for some guidance.

When Scottie first walked inside the masterpiece, slave-built stonewall that encircled the graveyard, he walked slowly toward the groundskeeper, stopping at each magnificent stone memorial to read the names and dates.

Many of the names were familiar to Scottie as names pulled directly from the Tennessee history books and the Civil War. The Polk family name was prominent, they being the family that gave America their eleventh president.

When he finally got to the groundskeeper, who turned off his string trimmer on Scottie's approach, Scottie pointedly asked, "Sorry to stop your work. I'm in search of a Black cemetery here in Columbia. I see all these names are quite White."

The groundskeeper gave Scottie a quiet and contemptuous laugh. "A Black cemetery? Like we don't belong to be buried wit chew White folk?"

Scottie didn't want to get sucked into an argument. "For instance, I know these White names in this graveyard are names I've heard of. The Polks were slave owners. Where are their slaves buried?" thinking that the groundskeeper could lead him to a modern-day Black cemetery.

"You jokin' wit me, ain chew?"

"No. Why would you think I'm joking? I'm asking a serious question."

The groundskeeper rolled his eyes back into his head. "Look across the street, there."

Scottie looked over the two-lane that had just brought him to this church and cemetery. All he could see was an expansive harvested cornfield. "Yeah? I see that cornfield."

"That's no cornfield, my man."

Scottie was puzzled. He knew the difference between corn and sorghum. Sorghum would still be green in the middle of October. He was looking at the sand-colored, bent and cut stalks of the past summer's corn. "Not corn? Then what?"

"That's a graveyard, my man."

"C'mon. I know what I'm looking at. There aren't any headstones over there. In a cornfield?"

"That's where all a deez White people's slaves is buried."

Scottie took a new look at the property across the street.

"You lookin' for a *Black* cemetery? There you go. Have at it, cracker."

Scottie could feel the ire of the groundskeeper rising, so he excused himself and continued on into Columbia.

While Scottie was absent to do his day's chores, the boys saw his phone in one of the kitchen drawers. They turned it on, discovered it was unlocked, and tried to call home.

"I don't know the number by heart. I jess press a button on my cell phone. You know it, doan chew, Muhammad? You knows it by heart?"

Muhammad pressed the keypad numbers and got the graphic message, "No Service Available."

Jamal saw the message. "Do you think Grandma disconnected it so we cain't call?"

Muhammad responded, "The cops probably pulled it right out da wall."

Once in Columbia, Scottie changed his strategy. He would find a Black neighborhood, identifiable by the smaller, less renewed houses that are emblematic of lower income earners, plus by the distinctive accessories on the cars in the un-garaged driveways. Then he would start driving around in ever widening circles until he came across a cemetery.

It didn't take long to find a well-kept acreage of headstones behind a wrought-iron fence. He parked and entered with a notepad in hand.

After a long time of searching, he found one that met his criteria...a White sounding name with a birth date from about twenty years ago, and a death date before the age of thirteen. 'Michael Dean. Born at the right time. Died at age nine. Perfect.'

It took Scottie an hour and a half to review each and every headstone in the cemetery, but he couldn't come up with a second match, so he drove around other parts of Columbia until he knew he was in another Black neighborhood. Then he started widening his driving pattern.

Again, it wasn't long before he came to another cemetery established on the backside of a distinctively Black neighborhood. An hour later, there was nothing Scottie could use.

His third try had taken him in the direction of Mt. Pleasant, and it payed off. 'Robert Smith. Born nineteen years ago. Died at age four.'

Scottie closed his notebook and headed to the retail shopping district of Columbia proper.

When Scottie returned to the house, he triggered the driveway alarm which didn't cause a strong reaction from the boys who had spent most of the day going to the window to see if anyone was coming. It would always turn out to be a false alarm. Their routine of looking out the window caused them to perk up when they saw Scottie's truck coming down toward the house from over the rise.

After Scottie pulled into the garage, the boys left the house via the side door to tell him the G.D. driveway alarm had been going off all day. As Scottie was dropping the tailgate on the truck so the boys could grab bags and packages to bring into the house, he said, "Lions and tigers and bears! Oh, my!"

The boys continued to think he was crazy.

"I should have told you that the wildlife around here trips the alarm all the time. Deer, coyote, rabbits, squirrels. Even birds can set it off. And there's a lot more wildlife than that for you to see.

"But I get the problem. The answer will be a video surveillance system, camouflaged enough to not be seen by visitors, and triggered by an infra-red trip instead of a motion detector. That'll be the next shopping trip."

The boys unloaded the truck while Scottie monitored the driveway.

The boys carried in blankets, pillows, sheets and other bed linens, two twin mattresses, and two unfinished pinewood twin bed frames. Plus bar soap, hand soap, washcloths, towels, bathmats, toothbrushes, toothpaste, plastic reusable bathroom cups, razors, shaving cream, big fingernail clippers, tweezers, toilet paper, paper towels. Plus underwear, pullover hoody sweatshirts and tee-shirts, and several pajama styles for each.

Plus, there was food, including ingredients for cooked breakfasts, dry cereals, sandwich meats, condiments, chips, ingredients for cooked suppers, fruits & vegetables, milk, oranges to make own orange juice, and herb teas. Absent from the haul was coffee.

Plus, there were several books, three of each title. Plus pads of lined paper, a box of pencils, a wall-mount pencil sharpener, and two positionable desk lamps...with LED, warm-glow bulbs.

After the truck was empty of all its bags and packages, Scottie saw that his phone had been moved from where he left it.

"The phone stores lots of information. We live in a place that cannot make or receive phone calls, but everything you put into it is stored...which means somebody can go into the phone and get that information. The phone number you dialed was to whom?"

Jamal said, "Grandma and our Mammas."

"Did you know that if you don't enter in the area code of the number you call, the phone will only look for your number in the area code in which you're standing?"

Jamal, again. "What area code?"

"The first three numbers before the actual phone number. You boys have never been outside Nashville? You've never called anybody outside Nashville?"

Muhammad didn't like this talk. "Hey, fck you, man. I know what a area code be. So, juss be lettin' that sht go."

"There will come a day, maybe tonight or tomorrow, when the cops will come here. They will take my phone and copy everything in it. Everywhere I've been. Every call I've made. What do you think they'll do if they see that a number was entered, even if it comes back 'no such number' for this area code? They might recognize it as your home number, even if it didn't have the right area code. Then what?

"Then they know you were here.

"This phone will be available to you every time I leave. At some point, you will know where you have to go to get a signal. But know this: every time you touch this phone, you're inviting a raid from the cops. But it will always be your choice to do that.

"I leave the phone here when I run errands for you so they have no way where to check the video of places I went. And everything I buy for you, I pay cash.

"But I will make separate trips to buy 'my' stuff, for which I will take the phone, and I will pay with a bank card…just so the only record they have is a record of me buying things only for me.

"Everything around here is unlocked. You can touch or take anything, including this phone. But until you get smarter about what will snare you in a trap…best to not touch anything you haven't figured out, yet. And that will take time. Include the computer on the list of things that represent a danger to your safety, here. Use it once, and your activity will be available and recognizable to the cops. So, make a decision in your own minds, right now, about your computer use, also."

Jamal said, "You shouldn't a bought all that sht, man."

Scottie mirrored his statement. "I shouldn't have bought all that merchandise?"

Muhammad took over the conversation. "We ain't staying. We leavin' jess as soon as it be dark."

"You still have some time before dark, so use that time to help me get all this merchandise put away downstairs."

The boys looked at each other, shaking their heads and rolling their eyes. But they knew they couldn't leave for a while.

Scottie led them in setting up the beds, the bathroom, separating clothes between the two, all of which he had them try on for sizing.

"All the packaging trash will stay down here until I can make a run to the landfill. All the cardboard stays here for burning, and nothing goes in the landfill bags except non-recyclable plastic packaging."

When the clean-up was finished, Scottie instructed them, "Take showers and put on whatever new clothes you want to run away in. When you strip off your murder clothes, put them all in the bag with the burnable cardboard."

The boys had been stinking up a storm in their murder clothes, but Scottie knew the fire would be the next day.

Wearing their new clothes, fresh from their showers, Scottie announced it was time to make supper. "Pork chops and apple sauce and mashed potatoes and green beans, all topped off with a healthy dose of milk fat. That means 'whole milk.' You're both still young enough for whole milk."

While cooking and eating and cleaning up, Scottie used every free breath to tell them about their new names, their new birth dates, and introduced them to the concept of being 'born again.'

After cleanup, and after saying their new names to them each and every time he spoke to them, they had both become fed up. "No new names. We ain't buyin' in own that bllsht."

Scottie retorted, "Jamal and Muhammad only exist to go to

prison...if they'd even make it that far."

When Scottie said that, it had been dark for some time. The boys looked at each other and started to head out.

They had not gone five steps beyond the front door when Scottie heard Muhammad say, "Go back down and git our hoodies."

Scottie turned the outside porch light on for them. He left it on as they headed up the driveway in their brand new, fleece-lined, hooded sweatshirts.

There was no moon that night, and the sky was crystal clear. Scottie knew that meant it would cool down fast.

At end of driveway, the boys had to make a blind decision whether to go left or to go right. They couldn't even see the road, and they didn't know what lay to the left nor to the right. That was the 'blind' decision they had to make.

Sure enough, a chill came into the air, quickly. The boys stood in silence, each waiting for the other to make a random direction choice. And the boys kept hearing rustlings in the bushes and in the woods.

Finally, Muhammad/Michael said to Jamal/Robert, "Fck it, man. Deez cracker hillbilly's ain't got no streetlights. We be havin' to do diss in the daylight."

As they made their way back down the driveway toward the porch light that Scottie had left on for them, they were both thinking of those new mattresses with new sheets, and blankets, and pillows.

Scottie didn't say a word when they entered the house and went straight down behind the bookcase to have their first decent night's sleep since the day Mark Johnson was murdered. They were so tired that their legs were like rubber and their eyes were trying to close on their own. It was only 8:30 at night. That was too early for Scottie to let them sleep.

Scottie followed them downstairs and took two pads of paper and two pencils that were sitting on the concrete countertop next to the kitchen sink.

Scottie said to Jamal, "Robert Smith. Write your name and your birth date over and over, enough times to fill one page of this pad. And *no* excessively large letters." He then said the same thing to Muhammad as Michael Dean.

The boys were humbled enough from their 'outing' that they complied. But they both struggled.

Scottie took each pad, one at a time, and wrote on a fresh piece of paper, darkly, their name and their birth date. Then he slipped the printed paper under a fresh piece.

"There. Trace it until you get used to doing it on your own. Say it out loud every time you finish a line."

Scottie supervised until he could see that they were doing it. Then he started rummaging through their piles of new merchandise to pull out three copies of the same book. Scottie read through the book until the boys finished their name-writing exercise.

Scottie told the boys to change into pajamas and to climb under the covers on their mattresses. While they did that, Scottie set up the two desk lamps on the floor next to their mattresses.

Once the boys were in bed, Scottie handed them each a copy of the same book. "Turn to Chapter 17, and follow along while I read." The boys mumbled that 'this is all bllsht.'

Michael's protest came out as, "We can tell by the way you talk you a gddmnd Yankee. Yankees always be thinkin' they gots sompin' over us. This all bllsht, man! If you cain't be treatin' us like weez equal to you, then stay the fck outta are face. We be greater than you bah-cuz we survive against all odds while you jess be coastin' along in a world that greases yo way *foe* you."

Scottie answered, "Are you telling me that you can tell where a person's from by their accent? By the way they talk? Do you want the people you meet in your next life to know where you came from? So they can track you back and find out who you are...and what you did? Then listen closely to the way I talk. Not because it's right nor because it's better. But because it's different. And you're going to be needing 'different.'

"Everything about me is different from you. So, do you think it's better for your new life to hate the way I am?...or do you think it's better for your new life to be like everything about me that's *different* from you?

"Copy the way I talk with a Yankee accent. Copy the words I use. Copy the way I make sentences. Make it a game - which one of you can do the best impression of me. The better you can impersonate me, the better you'll do in the afterlife."

Robert/Jamal piped up, "We can talk White when we be needin' to."

Scottie replied, as he cracked open his book, "You need to. All the time."

Scottie started reading from *The Adventures of Tom Sawyer and Huckleberry Finn*, but he saw the boys didn't turn the page at the right time.

"You boys aren't following along with the words?"

Michael/Muhammad erupted, "Hey, fck you, man! What'da ya think yur doin'?"

Scottie jumped right in. "I'm not sorry that you're embarrassed about your reading ability. However, I *am* sorry that you are unable to control your anger.

"You felt embarrassed because your pride was assaulted when something you wanted to keep secret was revealed. A fake part of you was exposed into reality. Embarrassment opened the door to anger. Anger opens the door to self-destruction by doing things like fighting or committing murder. It all starts with pride. The definition of pride is trying to present a delusion of yourself to yourself and to others.

"You want people to think you're better than you are? That's just an act to inflate your pride. Do you want to destroy yourselves by fighting or committing murder?...If you don't, then get rid of the pride.

"How do you get rid of pride, you ask? Learn to laugh at yourself *with* others when your deficiencies are exposed."

Scottie looked at the pages of their books with them and showed them how to recognize a paragraph beginning and ending. Then when he read, he would announce each new paragraph.

Robert/Jamal objected. "We ain't needin' to be doin' no readin'."

Scotties said, "If I'm going to read, you're going to know what the bunches of words I'm reading look like...and I'm *going* to read."

When Scottie finished reading at the end of Chapter 17, he said, "Tom and Huck rose from the dead to be celebrated for their new life."

Robert/Jamal said, "But according to you, we ain't gonna be seein' are family again. You changin' that by reading this story?"

Scottie answered, "The family that celebrates you will be the new family you have in the afterlife."

Michael/Muhammad said, "So *not* like in the story you jess be readin'?"

Scottie said, "The story isn't meant to be literal, but to be a metaphor."

Michael/Muhammad, "You sayin' sht like that don't mean nothin'."

Scottie said, "A metaphor is when you use one thing to instructively support another thing. The thing this story has in common with you is...attending your own funeral."

Robert/Jamal said, "You talk too much, man."

Scottie answered him with, "Repeat after me. Mark Twain...Tom Sawyer...Huckleberry Finn...attend their own funeral...like Jamal and Muhammad." They wouldn't repeat the last part.

Scottie closed his book and set it aside. "Congratulations. You just gave your first book report."

Scottie went upstairs to go to bed. He left the books behind.

1.11 THE CANVASS CAN DO MIRACLES

Special Agent in Charge John Watkins gave his team of FBI agent investigators, and Metro Nashville officers, a pep talk before they set out on their cold calls and interviews.

"Never forget the basics, team. The perps need food, shelter, and clothing. Repeat after me, 'Food, shelter, clothing...food, shelter, clothing.'

"Metro, work all your snitches. Somebody knows something about these perps. Put the circular snitches method to use. Just do whatever it takes to get our action info.

"Now get out there and find these kids. There's a free lobster dinner with me and my Assistant Director to anybody holding the handcuffs while walking one or both of the perps in."

Agent Watkins immediately called the league of high-ranking political lawyers at his disposal and asked for a warrant on the phone of Loquisha Davis...based on the timing of a call she received from the grandmother's phone shortly after the murder. The need for the warrant was supported by all the soft information about her relationship to the boys' grandmother and her activism in the community.

In less time than it took for Agent Watkins to hang up and get into position to supervise information as it came in from the field, the search warrant on Loquisha Davis' phone was approved. Watkins liked the purr of a humming machine.

An immediate call to AT&T and a secure data connection was all it took for Loquisha Davis' call data to be transferred to the task force. And before the download was complete, a call was placed to the canvassing officers, along with an electronic search warrant authentication, authorizing them to seize her phone and do a data dump.

The canvassing law enforcement representatives were two females. One, an FBI agent who was White. The other, a Metro Police officer who was Black.

Agent Watkins felt sending two females to interview and seize the phone data of a female was simply smart. And it was. There would be no phone calls to Metro HQ with any form of complaint from Ms. Davis.

The data download from Loquisha Davis' phone revealed her mapped travel on the night of the murder...the briefly lost signal under the Jefferson Street Bridge...and then the travel almost two hours south into the hinterlands.

There was a scramble to identify the property. Once it was Google-mapped, a phone call to the Registrar of Deeds office showed the property was owned by a Trust, and that the Trustee was a Nashville law firm. A high-priced Nashville law firm.

Agent Watkins asked the Tennessee Attorney General if he had any contacts in that law firm. "Of course."

About forty-five minutes after it had been requested, the Attorney General hand-walked the requested information to Agent Watkins in person.

Very privately, the AG explained to Agent Watkins, "This is privileged information that cost me big time. Me getting it violated the fiduciary responsibility of the giver. I will disavow any knowledge of ever having received it, if asked. Are we clear, Agent Watkins?"

"We're clear, Sir."

"The person living on the property is the original and anonymous Trustator. His name is Scott McNally. That's all I could get."

"Thank you, Sir. We can go forward with that information." Agent Watkins had the tip of the iceberg. "Oh, one more thing before you go, Sir. Are you close to the State Banking Commissioner? We could use all available financial information based on a name-only database search on the person tied to the address."

The AG humpffed and hawed. "You're pushing the envelope. The normal search warrant channels would be the way to do that."

Agent Watkins pled his case. "It's all about the clock ticking, Sir. The perps might be there as we speak. We need to do an in-person interview at the property with as soft an approach as possible. But when we go in, we need to know who we're dealing with. You're an attorney, Sir. Never ask a question you don't already know the answer to?"

The AG was sympathetic. "Your only issue for not doing it right...is the time it will take?"

"Yes, Sir."

"I can't do it. We all need to keep our noses clean as best we can. And I've already dirtied my nose for you, once."

Agent Watkins was ready to accept the time delay involved in getting the warrant to get the background information on McNally. Then the AG finished his thought. "But I can hand walk it or talk it to all the parties. Warrant and requests for information from Banking, Motor Vehicles, etcetera. One condition?"

Watkins said, "Yes?"

The AG said, "If I have the warrant and the database info in less than two hours, you buy me a Filet Mignon at Morton's...out of your own pocket."

Watkins pulled his wallet out of his pants pocket and opened it as though he was looking for how much cash he had. He looked back up at the AG and said,

"Sorry Sir, I don't have enough...oh, wait..." and he pulled out a Visa credit card. "Look at that, will ya? My wife left her credit card in my wallet." Both men were smiling.

"OK, Sir. It's a deal. As long as you don't mind if get their cheeseburger. I mean...if I'm buying..."

Agent Watkins hated small talk and banter, though he had learned to do it.

While he waited to hear if the AG could produce meaningful results, Watkins was handed the recording of the Loquisha Davis interview on his interviewing-agent's phone.

"I got a call from a former schoolmate, Ms. Jacinda Jefferson. She asked me if I had heard anything on the whereabouts of her missing grandsons. They had been implicated in the cop attack by then.

"When I told her I had not, she asked me if I could find them and either bring them home, or make them safe for a while. I didn't agree to do that, but I did tell her I would see if anybody knew where they were.

"I drove around the city for a while. I was banging my head against my steering wheel for not telling Jacinda that I could not get involved in a potential crime.

"I took a break to consider what to do next, stopping under the Jefferson Street Bridge. I decided in that moment that the only way I could get out of helping my old friend was to leave town so I could tell her I had business to take care of outside of Nashville.

"That's when I saw some flyer samples a White guy who doesn't live around here had mailed to me. He sent me the stuff even after I told him I wanted nothing to do with him.

"It made me mad when I thought about how pushy he was, like 'here was another White fool thinking that Black folk can't take care of themselves.'

"Then I thought it would make me feel better if I could just throw those things in his face…and that it would get me out of the city as well.

"So, I put his address info from the flyers into my phone and made the long drive. The truth is, I was fit to be tied. I didn't like this White boy the day he just showed up out of nowhere to tell me wanted to help our community. *He* was coming to *me*, and we didn't never get along.

I don't know what made him think I'd receive his unwanted help after that.

"I cussed him that first time he came to me...just for being White. White people are historically horrible partners to the Black community. When they go home, they're still White in a White-run world. When we go home, we're still Black in a White-run world.

"I was all worked up about surprising him with a night visit and putting a nail in the coffin of our non-relationship. If he can show up unannounced and uninvited on my doorstep, why couldn't I do the same? White people don't like being treated the way they treat us. So, I went down there looking forward to it. Looking for a fight. Anything to get the frustration of Jacinda asking me to help her boys out of my system.

"When I got there, he wasn't home. So, I waited for a long time. I figured he was coming back because his porch light was on. When I was about to leave, he came down the driveway.

"I cussed him out for sending me the flyers uninvited...and threw them in his face. He didn't hardly say a thing. I got it off my chest and came back home."

The AG was on the phone to Watkins an hour and forty-five minutes after their last conversation.

"Got a pencil?...bank balance seems to remain steady from cash deposits. Never has more than a couple thousand dollars in there. Spends less than five hundred a month. All on bank debit card transactions. Ten to twelve small transactions per month. Looks like mostly grocery store purchases. No other bank or investment accounts listed to him in Tennessee.

"Owns two motor vehicles. A seven year old Ford F150 pickup truck that he registered and insured four years ago. No associated bank transaction for the purchase. And a six year old Toyota Camry that he registered and insured three years ago. No associated bank transaction for that purchase, either.

"I, personally, have never been asked to look into a guy like this before. You've got one real life 'poor bastard' that you're looking into. I can't believe he's not on any kind of welfare. No food stamps. No nothing. Not even any U.S. Treasury money from Social Security or anywhere else going into his bank account. I've never even heard of anybody like this. I guess it's true what they say about me. I don't have any friends in low places."

"That information is a great help, Sir. Especially the timeliness of your effort. I look forward to paying off my debt to you."

"Wear a bib, Agent Watkins. I've heard their cheeseburgers are juicy." There was a pause. "Oh, and by the way, Agent Watkins...don't ever ask me to be your secretary ever again."

Both men hung up chuckling.

When Watkins finished his polite banter chuckling, he thought to himself, 'I don't like how small this guy's footprint is. Unless he's selling used stuff on Craigslist, how does he live? Doesn't life require more than just food and utilities? And what's with the property being in Trust without his name attached to it? That sounds like something rich people do. How can I find out more about this guy before I meet him?'

Watkins turned his thinking to his next meeting with the task force where he would share the profile work-up on the two boys.

That's when it came to him. 'Ah, yes! Social Security records on the McNally guy. Earnings history would be a deep dive into employment history...but why isn't he collecting?'

With McNally's Social Security Number in hand from the AG, Watkins called his go-to pool secretary back in Memphis and asked her to work out getting the earnings history, pronto, by having the Assistant Director make the request directly to the SSA for a verbal readout.

1.12 WILMA !!!

Agent Watkins took it as his personal task to interview this McNally person who had been visited by Loquisha Davis late in the night of the murder. Before setting up the face-to-face, he wanted to know more about the mystery of McNally not having any money.

Watkins got a call back from the pool secretary in Memphis.

"Our Assistant Director made a personal high-level request at the Social Security Administration for the McNally earnings records. He got a verbal that it came back blank. He was told that, other than this case being some kind of fraud case, the only other place to seek earnings info is if the target had earnings from the Department of Defense. Military pay records or retirement income don't show up at SSA.

"Our Assistant Director then called the Pentagon and made an urgent-action request for information. He was told that there was no retirement benefits records for the target, but that service records of personnel in Mr. McNally's age group have not been photo-digitized yet, so they're stored off-line.

"A request must be submitted to St. Louis where a physical data storage device, which is government-speak for a filing cabinet, must by located, so the record, if it exists, can be physically retrieved and physically photocopied and physically mailed to the data requestor. Our Assistant Director has instructed that you request this file search, yourself."

Watkins was frustrated. "Sounds like Fred Flintstone."

"Yes, John. And it could take two or three days to make all those things happen…even under an emergency request from a 'Political Influence' person. Which you are not."

"Thanks, Sandra. I'll start pushing my bare feet along the ground so my stone-wheeled car can take me over to St. Louis."

Watkins felt he was more blind than he wanted to be for a McNally property visit. 'I don't like this guy. Nobody has no earnings record.'

1.13 MY MONA LISA

Agent Watkins, along side Chief Rand, had the Task Force assembled in the Metro briefing auditorium.

"We have worked up a profile on the two perpetrators that will guide our efforts going forward. Please take notes.

"First, the perpetrators will stay together. They have lived together in harmony for their whole lives and don't have a lot of outside friendships that we've been able to discover.

"They will not stay in their neighborhood. This is based on their mothers' and grandmother's knowledge or expectation of being surveilled. The mothers and the grandmother appear to be street savvy.

"They will look for a Black neighborhood or home in which to stay hidden. They have only known their own segregated neighborhood their whole lives, and we can't find any history of either suspect interacting with White people, or in White businesses, or in White neighborhoods. We could uncover no information revealing any White friends.

"They will seek out family. We have not been able to determine any family connections outside their home. But if one exists, that will probably be their first choice for refuge. We will continue to dig in that direction for a connection. For now, there are no leads in that direction.

"If a family connection brings them to an inner-city environment, that will be our best chance of finding them. 'Snitch' networks are effective in the cities, and cities with concentrated Black neighborhoods have already been put on alert with this profile.

"Pride is a primary motivator for both youths, so we would expect conflict to erupt between our suspects and any alphas in their new environment. So, listen for stories of challenges to, or conflicts between, new arrivals and existing social power structures.

"Pride will also influence them to keep their hairdos. So look at the age-progressed portraits taken from young childhood photos. Add to the physical distinctions the hairdos and the gold grilles of teeth and these two should stand out in a crowd.

"In the case of fear of imminent arrest, their first instinct will be to run. They've already exhibited that behavior. If they cannot run, we expect they will kill, again. So...when they're found, call in the cavalry. When it comes to an arrest, remember the phrase, 'armed and dangerous.'

"We will update this profile as new information comes in.

"Good luck. And stay safe."

Watkins called his team together along with Chief Rand. Neal Knopfler, the Union Rep and Liaison Officer, insisted on attending.

"Our primary aid-and-abet suspect is the community activist by the name of Loquisha Davis. She made a long drive out of the city the night of Officer Johnson's murder. I'm leaving Nashville as soon as an on-site interview at her destination can be coordinated."

One of his agents interjected, "With all that's going on in Nashville, Boss, do you think it's a good idea for you to go? Can one of us go, instead?"

"There are many dynamics at play in my decision. One is that I've profiled Ms. Davis as being a 'passive on the outside, aggressive on the inside' Black militant. She told a story in her field interview that the property owner is a White guy with whom she had a conflict. But the audio recording gave me hints that there were lies in her story.

"If he *is* White, a conflict would fit her profile. But I suspect the person she visited is Black. Ms. Davis only associates with Black people.

"If the property owner *is* Black, then me being Black will make the approach more soft. I've been informed that the target area has very few Blacks. A Black officer showing up unannounced on his property might lower the tension. The lower the tension, the lower the risk of an incident...as well as the higher the probability of cooperation.

"One possibility, maybe even probability, is that our suspects are being housed there...or have *been* housed there. So, there is also a risk of ambush.

"I want to go in without any weapons showing to reinforce the idea that we're just there on routine information gathering. No weapons-on-the-hip increases the risk to our persons in the event of an ambush. I would never ask any of you to expose yourselves to such a risk."

The team was humbled into submission. And they were proud they had an Agent In Charge who knew what he was doing.

1.14 CAN A BROTHER GET A FAVOR?

Agent John Watkins consulted with TBI Special Agent Ben Waters about doing an in-person interview on the rural address that was discovered as having been visited the night of the murder of Officer Mark Johnson. They were both perplexed that, whom they suspected was a Black man, would be living in the heart of KKK country in rural Middle Tennessee. The two law enforcement professionals agreed that a low-key, general information seeking interview with the subject would be their door opener.

Neither Agent Watkins nor TBI Agent Waters wanted any show of force to accompany their interest. An introduction by the local Sheriff would be their most disarming approach.

"Sheriff Brewer? This is Special Agent In Charge John Watkins with the Memphis Field Office. Ben Waters has been designated Special Agent of the TBI's Field Investigation Unit for a case we're investigating, jointly. Officer Waters gave me your name and number in the hope that I could ask you a few questions about a person of interest we have in that case. The person of interest lives in your jurisdiction. Do yo have a minute?"

"Sure. We love Ben around here. We love it when he comes to visit. We're all part of the same family."

"Yes. Officer Waters has told me as much.

"Our person of interest is a Scott McNally who lives off of the Little Buffalo River Road. Do you know him?"

"I know most everyone around here, but that name doesn't sound familiar. Who's he kin to?"

"We don't know. We were hoping you would."

"Let me ask around. Maybe he's paid his taxes, or registered his car in person, or recorded a deed, or something like that. I'll call you back."

"One more thing, Sheriff. My beginnings with the FBI were as a profiler. I'm interested to know, before we visit, if he's Black."

"Black? I'd say whoever he is, he's not Black. People around here keep a pretty close watch on the Blacks that come through these parts. Don't get me wrong. We're a welcoming community. We have us a couple a Black folk that get along just fine, here. Good folk. We're glad to have 'em. But there's a feeling on the part of some that, if you get too many of 'em in a group, it turns into a whole different kind of problem. So, I think I'd know if this feller was Black, or even Mexican for that matter. We keep a pretty close eye on them, too. People get crazy when they get scared. We're all about keeping the peace."

Watkins thought it was a good time to end this conversation. "OK. Let me know what you find out about our person."

"I checked with our Clerk and our Assessor and our Registrar. I even called the Superintendent at the landfill and the Constable for your person's district. Nobody's heard of him. That's a bit odd. We're a pretty tight knit group. Everybody's either related to, or knows, everybody else, one way or another."

Agent Watkins got straight to the point. "I'd like to meet our person face to face, but I don't want to make it look like 'the Feds' swooped in. No visible weapons or accessory belts. One single car. No appearance of an invasion."

"Real friendly-like? That's fine. That's the way I've always run my department, anyway. I don't even wear a gun."

"So could you drive me and Agent Waters in your car so we don't raise any alarms?"

"Sure thing. The Constable for that district wants to come, too. His job is to know who all his neighbors are. Can you tell me what your interest is in our resident? I mean, he's *our* neighbor. He doesn't pose a threat, does he?"

"He's just a guy we have to scratch off a list. You know…grunt work. Shoe leather."

The Sheriff thought to himself, 'That's a lot of high pay-grade doin' shoe leather just to scratch someone off a list.'

1.15 BORN AGAIN: LABOR

MORNING TWO

Scottie woke the boys out of bed and walked them up the secret stairs at 5:00AM. He had them each pour themselves a glass of mineral water. At Scottie's instruction, all three drank slowly at Scottie's pace.

Scottie then led them in a stretch, then standing on one leg while doing their arms in wide swings, then had them repeat how to shake their hands and fingers at their side.

This morning, Scottie added sticking their tongue down their chin as far as possible. "Do it like you're trying to scare somebody."

Now say these words, "Kee-ah ree-tay."

Robert/Jamal asked, "What doze word mean, man?"

Scottie repeated the words. "Kee-ah ree-tay."

Robert/Jamal didn't like being ignored. "I ain't sayin' no words I doe know."

Scottie repeated the words.

Michael/Muhammad had an early morning outburst. "WTF, man? Cain't you hear nothin'? We ain't saying no words we doe know what it means."

Scottie said, "The words are a foreign language."

Robert/Jamal said, "I still ain't sayin' 'em."

Scottie repeated the words.

Michael/Muhammad said, "What language?"

Scottie repeated the words.

Michael/Muhammad got a little hotter. "You doan wanna be pissin' us off, you White fckn' scarecrow."

Scottie repeated the words. "Say the words and I'll tell you the name of the language." Scottie then repeated the words again.

Robert/Jamal shook his head.

Michael/Muhammad looked at Robert/Jamal. "Kee-ah ree-tay."

Scottie said to both the boys, "Make this sound - mah...Now make this sound - mow...Now combine those sounds into one sound - mao...Now make this sound - ree...Now put it all together. Maori."

Michael/Muhammad said flippantly, "Ain't never heard of it."

Scottie asked, "What languages have you heard of?"

Michael/Muhammad said, "Spanish."

"OK. Then you probably know that Spanish is spoken all over the world, from Spain to Mexico to South America. Maori is spoken all over Polynesia in the South Pacific."

Both boys knew if they looked at each other, it would give away that they had no idea what Polynesia and the South Pacific were.

Scottie repeated, "Kee-ah ree-tay."

Michael/Muhammad repeated it.

Scottie repeated it.

Robert/Jamal whispered the words under his breath, while Muhammad repeated it out loud.

Scottie repeated.

Robert/Jamal said it a little louder.

Scottie repeated.

Both boys said it out loud.

Scottie then said, "Start shaking your hands and fingers at your side. C'mon. Do it like I told you yesterday. Do it like somebody's watching you, and you want to make them nervous.

"Now say loudly, 'kee-ah ree-tay,' and stick your tongue down your chin as far as possible, like you're trying to scare somebody."

"Good. Now, stop and turn around and be instantly normal."

The boys did it but were convinced they were in the care of an insane person like they had never heard about before...not even in horror movies.

Scottie told the boys to only use their new names from now on. "I will try and catch you responding to your old names from time to time. Don't be fooled."

Robert/Jamal said, "We doan like this new name sht, man. An why you be tryin' to trick us wit our real names?"

"A smart cop will test his suspicion that you might be who he thinks you are by calling out your old name. If you respond or flinch...game over.

"It's common in sports for an athlete to practice something so many times that his brain doesn't have to think about it any more. Like taking shots from all kinds of positions on the basketball court."

Robert/Jamal interrupted, "Hey, man. I know you think we be Black an all, but we ain't into sports. So, chill on the basketball story."

"Muscle memory is the same in your tongue as in your body muscles. When you repeat something often enough with intention, your brain can do it without thinking about it. It becomes automatic.

"This information is useful to you because repetition is how your brain is going to not have to think about you being called by your old name...and *only* by your new name."

Muhammad/Michael Dean said, "Muscle memory? You mean like I practiced my neck move befoe I laid it on that cracker piece-o-shit blue devil piglet...and then I could do it in my sleep?"

Scottie went backwards. "Cop, pig, etcetera, are words that will not take you where you want to go. Always use 'police officer' to take the edge off of others' fears. Every time you use a pejorative to describe a police officer, you add one more straw to the bale of hay that will eventually crush you."

Robert/Jamal said, "Pejora- what?"

"A pejorative is a word used to cast a negative feeling about someone or something. Now repeat 'police officer' out loud 21 times."

Michael/Muhammad said, "You're fckd, man, if you think I be doin' that."

Scottie spoke to both in a flat tone. "It's a life or death choice. Anything you allow to remain from your former selves presents the risk of revealing you, and that takes away your one remaining shot at turning your remaining life into something that works *for* you.

"If your only remaining shot is taken from you, then good luck with the perp walk to jail. You'll never make it to jail. And if you do, you'll have the opportunity to evaluate torture as a quality of life."

The boys had repeated 'police officer' seven times under their breath when Scottie determined they'd had enough of that for now.

Scottie said to Michael/Muhammad, "Michael, you must get rid of the box blade in your pocket. It makes noise and it's an identifiable bulge for a police officer to see...and they will be looking...it defines who you were, and so it can no longer exist."

Michael/Muhammad didn't say anything, but he didn't remove it from his pocket, either.

Scottie tried persuasive argument. "You've already demonstrated that you act with passion. But if you cannot channel that into *positive* passion...it will be the difference between a possible good life and a certain bad life."

Michael/Muhammad's body language was as though Scottie was talking to a wall.

Scottie changed the subject. "I notice you boys are sniffling."

Robert/Jamal said, "Yeah, man. We probblee got a cold from not having the heat on enough."

Scottie said, "It's likely to be allergies. You're not used to being in the country, and every green thing you see around here puts out it's own fertilizer for it's own seeds. Until the human body develops antibodies in the blood for those new things, your nose is going to drip, your eyes are going to water, you'll sneeze a lot, and the thing that could actually hurt you, if you ignore it, is a sore throat.

"Follow me. We can help your body adapt to this environment."

Scottie brought them to the kitchen where he had them make their own cups of an allergy symptoms tea. It was a concoction of a mint tea/lemon/cayenne/ginger/honey/cinnamon mix.

Then he showed them how to do a nasal flush with a Neti pot and a saline solution. They were grossed out, but did it.

Then he showed them how to measure salt with water and how to gargle to kill anything growing in their throats.

After lunch, Scottie told them about the affect that appearance has on the inner-racist in people.

"A shaved head is necessary to change the most distinctive part of your appearance...your haircuts. Plus, those haircuts, while cool in your neighborhood, are a draw for a White person to make conclusions about you before they know you.

"Answer? The hair must go."

The boys looked at each other and were shaking their heads.

"White people with whom you will interact will make a first impression of you based on the fact that you're a young Black male. Eyeglass frames take away some of the threat-response."

Scottie took both boys outdoors and had them look at various objects at various distances with one eye covered, and then the other. Then he took them inside and had them do the same with various distances of near objects with detail. He determined that both had close to 20/20 vision.

"I'm going to bring you each a pair of glasses frames with non-prescription lenses. Just get used to wearing them. It will be part of your 'different' look than the one you used to have."

Robert/Jamal said, "Glasses that don't do nothin'? You be crazy."

Scottie explained, "Even in the short term, if by some chance...a chance that we're going to try and avoid...a cop who is looking for you...which is *all* cops right now...sees you with glasses on, and bald, do you stand a better chance of not drawings attention for who you used to be?" He waited to see if they were getting it.

"Another trick to reduce fear in White people..."

Michael/Muhammad cut in, "Is to be White, mthrfker. That's what all this be about."

Scottie continued, "is a clean shaven face."

Michael/Muhammad changed from being a funnyman to being serious. "My beard is part of my faith-identity as a Muslim man. I ain't shaving this off."

Scottie said, "The Muhammad you used to be was Muslim and had a beard. That's the person they're looking for, right?"

Micahel/Muhammad, "I'll fck you up before I'm giving up my

faith."

Scottie went on to his next point. "Country club clothes reduce the threat factor, also. Sagging pants and showing your undershorts increase the perceived threat level of you. Dressing like an Abercrombie and Fitch model is very different from the old you. Get ready to look like Chad and Biff just coming into the clubhouse from a round of golf at their daddy's country club."

Later, Scottie brought up an important security concern.

"Watch the crows and learn from them. They stay spread out and they signal each other about any abnormalities. Paranoia is a disease. Awareness is a virtue. Learn what both are so you can tell the difference.

"All these planes you see flying over all the time? It's air traffic between government air bases in Memphis and Smyrna.

"If there becomes the slightest hint that you boys might be here, those planes and helicopters are going to have high-definition cameras on them…taking pictures of all of us.

"Know the things that will identify you from above. We'll deal with each of them in time…but for now, be thinking of hats and gloves, masks and skin coverings.

"We'll deal with dimming down identifiers for the cameras, but the first, most obvious identifier from above, is your hair. It must go. Here are the clippers. You can do it to yourself if you like. Or I will do it. There is no other option."

Michael/Muhammad ran straight at Scottie.

Scottie had an instantaneous flashback to his judo training to disable and kill an attacker. Then he came instantly back from his flashback to allow himself to be slammed into the ground.

Both boys were on top of Scottie trying to punch him. But the punching died as the kids realized Scottie was limp with no resistance.

Michael/Muhammad got up.

Then Scottie got up and said calmly, "You're in charge of you, and I'm in charge of me."

When boiling blood had settled down, Scottie said, "Let's collect some tools from the shed and do some trimming in the woods around the bluff."

1.16 VISITORS OUT OF THE BLUE

While TBI Special Agent Ben Waters was driving Agent Watkins to a small town Sheriff's Office to do a ride-out to the home of one Scott McNally, Waters informed Watkins that Scott McNally had no criminal record in the State of Tennessee, and that his name didn't show up in any law enforcement databases.

Agent Watkins asked Waters to take the questioning lead once they arrived at the McNally property. Watkins wanted to observe.

At the Sheriff's Office, TBI Agent Ben Waters initiated introductions all around. The Sheriff clearly had a look of horror on his face when he saw that Agent Watkins was Black. He shook hands with Watkins, but it took him a little longer to wipe the horror off his face.

At his first opportunity, the Sheriff pulled TBI Agent Waters aside. "Why didn't you say something about him being Black, Ben? I said some things to him on the phone that I wouldn't of if I'd known."

Ben Waters spoke lowly, "That's true for all of us, Dwayne. He was standing right next to me when he called you. It wasn't like I could have pulled the phone out of his hand and given you a heads-up."

The Sheriff then privately expressed his apologies to the Constable, Jonathan Price. "I had no idea the FBI guy was Black. He didn't sound Black when I talked to him on the phone."

All four men got into Sheriff Dwayne Brewer's cruiser and headed out to the country. John Watkins sat in the back with the Constable, and there was no conversation between the two. Sheriff Brewer and TBI Agent Waters were chatty in the front.

John Watkins noticed Confederate flags on houses starting in town, then all along the twenty-five minute ride. Plus, he kept seeing front license plate Confederate flags on much of the oncoming traffic. Then he noticed several pickup trucks with rear window confederate flags and rifles in rifle racks. He thought to himself, 'We're not in Kansas anymore.' Then he thought, 'Rural Kansas isn't much different.'

When the Sheriff's taxi service pulled into the McNally driveway, the alarm inside the house went off. But the boys and Scottie were working out on the bluff behind the house.

Muhammad/Michael heard car tires on the chert driveway and called to the others. They stopped and saw a cloud of chert dust coming from below the rise in the driveway. Scottie's instructions came immediately.

"Take your tools and make your way into a crevasse or a cave in the bluff. Split up for deeper hiding. And make sure of your footing. I'll find you when they're gone. Is the bookcase closed?...Who closed the bookcase?"

Robert turned back as he was quickening his pace to the bluff's edge. "I did."

Scottie wiped his brow in relief as he took his rake in hand to see who was coming.

The loaded Sheriff's car was all the way up to the house when Scottie got to the driveway. He waved with his free hand.

The Sheriff introduced everybody. McNally looked for something in Agent John Watkins' eyes as they shook hands, but concluded, 'He doesn't remember me.' Then TBI Agent Ben Waters took over.

"Mr. McNally, we asked your Sheriff to bring us here so we could ask you some questions regarding a case we're working. Are you alone here?"

Scottie didn't want to seem too defensive...nor too compliant. "Why do you ask? You'll make me feel better about talking to you...on my own property, I might add...if you can take some of the mystery out of your team approach."

Agent Watkins thought, 'He's not timid.' John wanted to guide Agent Waters with, 'We'd better play him straight up.' Scottie noticed the look on Agent Watkins face and concluded that Agent Watkins was actually the person in charge of this visit.

TBI's Ben Waters said, "We're here because we've been assigned to an ongoing investigation that shows that a Loquisha Davis came here to your residence on the night of the Nashville cop murder. Did you hear about the cop murder?"

Scottie wanted to show he was forthcoming...by being forthcoming. "I have an antenna TV that I hardly turn on, mostly because it's hit or miss if I get a picture. But I did see some local news stories about it. What does that have to do with Ms. Davis?"

Agent Watkins thought, 'He knows why we're here. He's cool as a cucumber.'

TBI Agent Waters said, "That's what we're trying to find out."

Scottie continued with his forthcomingness. "I don't know what day it was, but yes. I *do* know Miss Davis...and she *did* come by here a short time back. Some days ago. But she didn't say anything about the cop murder.

"I only know her as an angry Black woman who works very hard around White people to not show just how angry and how Black she is. And frankly, we never got along.

"But as much or as little as I know her, I can't see her being involved in something like that. And besides, what I heard on the news was that it was two young men, not an angry Black woman. There was videotape, the TV said."

Agent Watkins thought, 'He nailed it with the angry Black women assessment.' Then he thought, 'They both said they didn't like each other. Corroboration that neither one of them had anything to do with the two boys?...or cooperation in dovetailing their stories?'

TBI Agent Waters asked, "Did she have anybody with her when she came here?"

"Just herself. I'm sure the reason she came alone is because her reason for coming here was best handled without any witnesses."

Agent Watkins thought, 'It's good that he's talking a lot. Let's see if he can talk himself into some inconsistencies.'

TBI's Waters asked, "Why would it be important that there were no witnesses?"

"She came here hotter than a blacksmith's iron fresh out of the furnace. Come into the house and I'll show you why she came here."

Agent Watkins held a stop sign with his hand out to the Sheriff and the Constable. "Keep an eye on things out here. We don't want to be ambushed." He got a nod from the Sheriff and the Constable who split to opposite ends of the house.

Scottie led the two agents through his front door and into the inner sanctum where he rummaged through his kitchen trash can until he got to the bottom. He came up with a wad of crumpled up papers. He removed them, wet and dirty from food and other kitchen scraps, and spread them all out on the kitchen counter.

"Here is a communications piece she came here to throw in my face after lambasting me in front of a group of people in her Community Center. Apparently that public tongue-lashing was not enough. I guess she had to drive down here to get it all out of her system." He handed Agent Watkins the wet, dirty, smelly, old-food-laden flyer as Agent Waters looked on.

Watkins reviewed the flyer that was getting sticky and smelly on his hands and thought, 'So far, matches everything she said, including the animosity. Nice touch of authenticity with the soiled trash can retrieval.'

Watkins read the flyer and passed it over to Agent Waters...so Waters would have to get his hands dirty, also. Watkins kept repeating in his thoughts, 'Who is this guy?'

TBI Special Agent Ben Waters asked, "Why was she so hateful to you?"

"Basically?...because I'm White. She said White people are bad partners because they lack a self-interest. At the end of the day, the Blacks go home still Black and are subject to broken-windows-policing designed to support Black mass incarceration. White people go home without molestation to have their crumpets and tea."

Agent Watkins thought, 'Ahh, the old reverse racism argument. I wonder if it's real. And would Loquisha Davis use the phrase, 'crumpets and tea?'

TBI Agent Waters asked, "Why would she drive all the way down here just to cuss you out?"

"I was motivated to help her cause, and I just couldn't accept that she was rejecting something that I was sure was going to help her."

Agent Watkins wondered, 'Is he playing the misunderstood White person trying to relieve his own White guilt? Is this an act of deception that's going to get bigger and bigger?' Then he thought, 'Keep going bigger. If this a play, we want to see all three acts.'

TBI Agent Waters asked, "What was it you were going to do to help her?"

"I thought I could help put together some communications pieces...like the one in your hands...the ones she threw in my face that I dug out of the trash for you to see.

"I had some ideas that I thought would improve the effectiveness of her message about changing the way her community was being mistreated, particularly around policing. But she had budget gripes, as well.

"What I sent her was sort of like advertising. I thought I had a better way to express the message than what I saw her doing on TV."

Agent Watkins thought, 'Hmpf. Educated. Conjugates his verbs properly. Knows which pronoun to use. Self-inflated about having a better idea.' Then he thought, 'The deeper and more detailed the story, the less likely that it's true.' At that point, Watkins took over the interview. "And what was in it for you, Mr. McNally?"

Scottie turned his head to look at Agent Watkins. He knew the real show was about to begin. "Relief."

Agent Watkins played along. "Relief from what?"

"Boredom, I guess. After years…decades…of tending to this place, I finally got it pretty well under control. Then I didn't have a full day's work, anymore. A feller needs to do *some*thing lest his only remaining purpose in life is to die."

Agent Watkins thought, 'The guy's a philosopher, too?' but didn't want McNally's hucksterism to distract from the point of this interview.

Watkins continued the questioning. "But why a Black community? Why her?"

"On a rare occasion when I got an antenna TV picture, I saw her on TV. I felt her pain. I used to see my mother cry when all the civil rights battles played out on the TV in the 1950's and '60's. Maybe I felt the need to avenge my mother's pain. Plus, I finally had the time…and in case our good Sheriff and Constable didn't tell you, 'we ain't gut no Blacks in these parts.' I had to go outside my neighborhood if I wanted to help."

Agent Watkins asked, "Your mother was White?"

Scottie got a little smart-alecky with him. "Yes. I'm referring to my *biological* mother."

"And she was crying over Black people being beaten down?"

"Surely she wasn't the only White person in America affected by the

TV images of the day? Bull Conner's dogs and water cannons and such after the KKK bombings of those little Black girls at Church in Birmingham."

Agent Watkins wanted to see if he could find some buttons to push. "Affected enough to *do* something? Or just to cry?"

Scottie thought he should display his ability to defend his territory. "Go easy there, Agent Watkins. You don't throw shade on my mother, and I won't throw shade on yours."

Watkins thought, 'The guy's a hipster to boot?' Then he spoke out loud. "So, maybe you were trying to fulfill her unfulfilled intentions?"

Scottie wanted to show his back getting up a bit. "Pretty deep. Are you going to charge me your hourly rate for this therapy session? Sounds like you're schooled in psychology?"

Agent Watkins laid out his thoughts. "It sounds to me like *you're* the one who's schooled in psychology. You've laid out all the dynamics pretty neatly. A thorough explanation. Are you, Mr. McNally? Schooled in psychology?"

Scottie didn't like that Watkins was digging deeper. "Like a farmer's schooled in botany." Scottie saw Agent Watkins was trying to wrap his head around that one, so Scottie added, "Farmer's don't necessarily learn plant and soil sciences from a textbook."

"Yes. I got your meaning." Watkins shifted. "The property is beautiful...a lot for one person."

"I just finished telling you...I don't have much else to do. Occasionally, I'll pay a local kid or two that needs the money to do some lightweight help. Mowing or trimming. Things like that. But I live on a budget, so it's mostly me."

Watkins wanted to set a trap. "What do you do for a telephone out here?"

"I live in danger. I don't have a landline, and there is no cell service out here." Scottie assumed that Watkins could have researched his mobile account with AT&T. "But I do have an iPhone for when I go out on errands." Scottie did a quick review in his mind that he had no call record on his phone...that Michael's attempted call to his Grandma wouldn't show up on his call history. He also knew the phone would show all his movements via Google maps. He instantly concluded that there was only benign data there. And by 'benign,' he meant 'misleading.'

"Do you mind if I take a look at your phone?"

"The FBI wouldn't let you loose out on the streets if you didn't know that you're asking for something that would require a search warrant." Scottie said that while he was digging his phone out of a kitchen drawer. Scottie booted it up and handed it to him. "Like everything around here, it's unlocked."

Agent Watkins scrolled through the phone call history. Scant. Watkins thought, 'Could have cleared his history. But he can't clear it from AT&T's records...but that *would* require a search warrant.' "Do you mind if I download your phone info so I can review it at a later time."

Scottie calculated that this was a level of compliance that would be convincing. He motioned with his hand toward a kitchen countertop electrical outlet and said, "Be my guest."

Agent Watkins reached into the inner pocket of his suit jacket and pulled out a small device with a couple of cables hanging off it. He plugged one cable into the outlet and the other into McNally's phone. "This should just take a few minutes."

After a few minutes of everybody watching the device work, and Watkins trying to notice any fear or concern in McNally, the download was complete. Watkins moved the group into the hallway outside the walled sanctuary. Watkins thought, 'McNally's folksy details and compliance were out of character for who I think he is,' which kept Watkins' flag of suspicion flying.

Once out of the inner sanctum, Watkins looked at the covered windows and, even though he could see out through them, asked, "What are the blackout shades on these windows for?"

"Oh, I couldn't live with blackout shades. I need sunlight. Sunlight disinfects everything. Including the soul, I believe. No, these are solar shades. They keep the summer sun from turning this place into an oven."

Scottie didn't mention the second set of shades that pulled down from the same recess above the picture window. Those *were* blackout shades. Those *did* stop all light.

"I built the inner sanctum as a relaxing space where the temperature is always 72 degrees year round. I can't control the rest of the house that fully, but the solar shades help. I don't have a central air conditioning unit common to most houses in this part of the country. I can't afford a high power bill. I rely on more sustainable solutions."

At that moment, the Constable walked in and asked if he could use the bathroom. Scottie wanted to keep his country-boy affect up. "You came in from the biggest toilet in the world...the great outdoors...to use a toilet?" He laughed with the Constable and pointed him to the bathroom.

Agent Watkins and TBI Special Agent Ben Waters walked out of the house with Mr. McNally. As the Sheriff came over and joined the TBI detective on their walk back to the Sheriff's car, Agent Watkins held Scottie back.

"I feel like you don't fit with Miss Davis. It's all too random. Investigators don't like random. We like order. When everything fits...that's order. These fine fellows who accompanied me here are going to drop you off their list. I can tell that they're sold. 'Hook, line, and sinker' I believe is the 'folksy' phrase. Right? But it doesn't feel right to me."

Scottie assumed the stance of a fencer in his mind. 'En garde!' "It seems to me that I agree in every way that Miss Davis and I don't fit. I think I told you that, directly. That's why we never had a relationship.

"Look, Agent Watkins, I know you have to do your job thoroughly…you need to be the smartest guy in your class. But there's a difference between being thorough versus forcing something that you know is not true.

"I do a lot of mechanical repair work around here. When I try to make a part fit where it doesn't fit, I can actually make things worse than when I started. Maybe it's the same in your business."

Agent Watkins wasn't used to being schooled in his 'business.' And he knew that there was a whole lot more to Mr. McNally than what was being presented.

Scottie didn't like the probing of his psyche that he felt coming from Agent Watkins, and he felt it was being done because Watkins wasn't buying appearances. Scottie decided to take the offense and try to jamb Agent Watkins…to see if he could draw out the *real* John Watkins.

"Now that you know I have a heart for the struggle of Black people in this country of White Supremacy, you'll know where I'm coming from when I say that I respect that you've made it as far as you have in the FBI." John Watkins tried to figure out the 'why' behind this speech before it was even finished. Scottie concluded, "I just hope you're not their Helen Mayer."

Watkins got his back up a little. "Do you mean you respect me for achieving a high position because I'm Black?" Watkins was feeling better about ending their meeting with some antagonism. But then he thought, 'Who in the *world* is Helen Mayer?' He walked to get into the passenger seat of the Sheriff's car and thought, 'If this guy *is* involved…he's good.' John Watkins was always motivated by a challenge.

Scottie returned to his house and met the Constable coming out. The Constable stretched out his hand to shake Scottie's hand. Scottie hoped the Constable had washed it.

"This a beautiful place you got out here. I'm glad to know we're neighbors. Sorry about that FBI guy. Ain't it wonderful to live in peace with no nggrs around to ruin things?" He leaned into Scottie with a little hand pat on Scottie's arm and said in a more quiet voice, "But then, I guess that's why God gave us White folk such good trigger fingers."

The Constable chuckled at his own cleverness and started to walk toward the Sheriff's car. Then he leaned back in toward Scottie for one last word.

"I ain't sure about a nggr *cop* huntin' a nggr cop *killer*. When it comes down to it, they all stick together." He then raised his eyebrows at Scottie as if to say, 'You *know* what I'm sayin' is the truth.'

Scottie found himself consciously holding back a snarl. 'It's no accident that we live in a beautiful and peaceful place? You're the White trash that litters these country roads.'

But he kept his mouth shut. After all, Scottie never knew when he might need a neighbor for something.

On the drive out, the Constable said to the rest of the car, "What a fine citizen. Beyond that he was harassed by a Black lady, I don't know what your interest in him could be. But if everyone in this country was like him, we Officers of the Peace'd be out of a job."

The Sheriff looked in his rear view mirror and said, "That's enough, Jonathan."

John Watkins kept quiet.

On the ride back to Nashville with TBI Agent Waters, Ben said, "There's nothing going on there. If Loquisha Davis *did* bring those boys down to drop them off, I think she either hit a brick wall with that McNally fellow, or he took the boys and got rid of them...passed them on, or whatever. But truth be told? I just can't see that guy having anything to do with a couple of murdering teenagers...of *any* color. I believe his story. Loquisha Davis is just an angry Black woman who needed to take her frustrations over her community's bad behavior out on a White guy."

Watkins said, "I'm going to have my people dig deeper on this guy. Such as, whom does McNally know that he could have passed them off to. And even if that comes up blank and the boys *were* in the car with Miss Davis, is there any reason he'd cover up for her? Discovering motive can be the trickiest, but most meaningful, part of our business."

TBI Agent Waters added to his summary thoughts. "I hear what you're saying, John. But actual evidence can be pretty meaningful, also. What about money? He said he don't have no money. And look around. His house is the oddest looking house I've ever seen…"

Watkins jumped in, "But *extremely* well built. And that took *some* money. People who don't have money don't spend money. He spent some at one time."

Ben Waters continued, "…but it's not fancy by any means. Plain and simple. A one bedroom, one bath, with a detached garage. That all points to him not having extra money for things like food and clothing for a couple of dependent fugitives. And where would they stay? A hut in the woods? City boys? I just can't see it."

Agent Watkins added his knowledge to the analysis. "According to the IRS, the second biggest indicator of secret money is order. And no-one can deny that Mr. McNally lives an orderly life. He's a neat-nick. Everything's in its place. And in addition to his house, the entire property is better groomed than any State Park *I've* ever seen.

"For right now, we both know his and Davis' stories match up like a mirror image. What's that old saying? If it's too good to be true…?"

Ben Waters said, "I hear you. This door seems pretty well shut, but we're not ready to hear it latch. Don't lock it for at least another day."

Watkins concluded, "*Now* we're singing from the same hymnal."

Scottie waited for the lawmen to be gone for over an hour before he went looking for the boys...just in case the men in blue circled back.

From his perch along the top of the bluff, Scottie was disturbed that he found one of the boys by seeing the handle of a rake.

"Hey, Robert. I see your rake handle from up here. Find Michael and come on back to the house."

When both boys entered the house, Robert said, "How did you know that rake handle was mine?"

Scottie just looked back and forth between the two of them. The boys knew he was saying, 'Do yo think I don't you both and each by now?'

Michael piped up, "What'd the cops want?"

Scottie looked back and forth at them both, again. "You."

Once back in Nashville, Agent Watkins inventoried his thoughts.

He believed the Davis/McNally relationship story as it was told, but it didn't feel it was complete. Watkins felt a need to know the part of the story that *wasn't* told. *And*, most importantly, if those missing pieces had anything to do with his 'Officer Down' murder suspects.

Agent Watkins also knew he had to keep himself in check by not allowing himself to overanalyze and get tunnel vision down a tube that didn't allow for alternative explanations.

He resolved to re-focus on eliminating all other leads...when he got an email notification on his phone.

"DoD St. Louis." Watkins was amazed it came in on email.

"re: Service Member: Scott McNally

"Branch: US Air Force

"Service Dates: April 21, 1971 - April 20, 1975

"Discharge Status: Honorable

"Discharge Rank: E-5, Technical Sergeant

"Training Record: Para Rescue, 2 years, see detail

"Duty Stations: Vietnam, 2 tours

"Citations: National Defense, Outstanding Unit x 2, Vietnam Service x 2, Purple Heart, Silver Star."

John Watkins tried to never swear. 'Holy sht! A Silver Star? This guy's a war hero…who's never had a job?'

He pondered the new information. Then he added to his summary. 'I was right. This guy is not what he appears.'

1.17 SIGNS THAT MIGHT BE OMENS

After the visitors had left and the boys were settled back into the last conversation they had had inside the house, Michael/Muhammad still had some anger and rage in his blood about having to cut his hair. But he was also deeply embarrassed by his urge to assault…by his assault. His embarrassment made him feel like he had to leave.

Scottie spoke to Michael/Muhammad as he walked away. "Watch out for wild animals. You'll recognize them by their Confederate flags."

As Michael/Muhammad got smaller and smaller in the distance, Scottie needed to have a serious conversation with Robert/Jamal about strategies.

"Michael will get caught. His apprehension will lead authorities straight back here to you."

Robert said, "And to you."

Scottie replied, "That's not a consideration. But we must come up with a plan to move you on. Otherwise, you're just a sitting duck for the duck hunters."

Robert said, "Let's wait till morning to see what happens. I'm willing to take a risk for that long."

Scottie was taken aback by Robert's ability to speak the King's English when Michael wasn't around.

At the end of Scottie's driveway, Michael/Muhammad randomly chose to turn left in the direction that the Little Buffalo River Road went up a steep hill. Michael/Muhammad figured he could hear a car coming from the other side of the hill before it could see him. And walking up the hill would give him a long view in the other direction for any coming traffic.

Michael was already starting to think like Muhammad-the-fugitive. Scottie had been trying to communicate the benefits of being Michael-the-person-who-doesn't-need-to-run-from-anything-because-he'd-never-done-anything-to-need-to-run-from.

When Michael/Muhammad heard a truck coming from the other side of the hill, he made a jump into the brush and woods. He watched from hiding as a pickup with a rifle in the rear window and a Confederate flag for a front license plate drove by.

When the second vehicle to come by had all the same accessories….that was all it took to drive Michael back to Scottie's driveway.

When he got back to Scottie's house, Scottie and Robert came out from the inner sanctum to greet him. Michael/Muhammad couldn't hide that he had had a sight that frightened him.

Scottie said to both boys, "Anger is a reaction that you have when you feel provoked. Rage is your reaction to the anger. Resentment is the memory of your anger and rage. You fear letting go of resentment as though holding onto it will protect you from future people who will provoke you.

"That's a lie we tell ourselves in order to allow resentment to stay in us. In reality, all resentments that we harbor are just a way to let someone else live in our head…without paying any rent. And that should sound foolish to you.

"Remember this summary to all that: 'I'm in charge of me, and you're in charge of you.'

"When you feel rage taking over within you, do a slow-count to ten before you take any action. That's all it usually takes."

Scottie finished by saying, "We make our own heaven on this earth...and we make our own hell. You've proven to be pretty good at doing one of those things. Now let's see if you can do the other."

Scottie told the boys to shower and dress for bed.

While they were tucking themselves in, Scottie pulled out another book in triplicate. A book of poems by Robert Frost.

Open your books to page 28. Scottie read *The Road Not Taken*.

"...Two roads diverged in a yellow wood...I took the one less traveled by, And that has made all the difference."

As his way of saying goodnight, Scottie summarized their nightly reading. "You boys are on a road less traveled. Let's see if it will make a difference...*all* the difference."

1.18 A FRIEND IN NEED

The next day, Scottie brought the mail to Miss Dolly. He broached a subject to both her and her granddaughter.

"I've been thinking about what you said...you and the family wanting to be able to see your grandmother when you talk to her."

The granddaughter was nodding as she sipped her coffee.

"I know some people at the State level who have been talking about setting up a program to help some of their clients with technology. If it's OK with you, Miss Dolly, I'd like to ask them if they could use you for a test case. It would mean an all expenses paid computer and internet connection so you could stay in touch with family using Face Chat technology."

Miss Dolly said, "That's sounds wonderful to me, Scottie. Ain't you a peach."

"OK, then. Let me see what I can do to make that happen. Are you in favor of this?" he asked the granddaughter, knowing her cooperation would be instrumental.

"Oh, yes, Mr. Scottie. This sounds like a dream come true for *all* of us!"

Enthusiasm was what Scottie was hoping for.

1.19 BELOW THE RADAR

The boys had been dropped off at Scott McNally's late on Monday night. After Thursday morning's morning routine, McNally was having concerns about the boys buying into the program. Over breakfast, Scottie brought up the need for the boys' hair to go to the burn pile.

Robert was not resolved that it was necessary. "My cornrows make me me. I ain't gonna do away wit dat so quick."

Michael chimed in, "Our style defines who we be. Our age. Our time. It make us who we be. If we be changin' it, then we be stickin' out for not looking like our time."

Scottie was shaking his head. "You think you're original? That your hair defines your age or your time? Ha! You don't even know your own culture. Your knowledge of Black culture doesn't go beyond five square city blocks. You know the why of your existence like the rocks at the bottom of a high waterfall know why they're smooth. You've been shaped by a world that you don't even know exists. And it came along before you. Tracy Chapman has had your hair since the 1980's."

Robert looked over at Michael and then back at Scottie. "Who's Tracy Chapman?"

Scottie shook his head again. "She came before you. She predicted you. She's a singer. She sang, 'One fine day all our problems will be solved. Bang. Bang. Bang. We shot him down."

Michael was incensed. "We ain't be shootin' that mfkg pig piece a sht."

Scottie said, "I was talking about her hair. But you should know that she also predicted your time by writing about the past...that *still* hasn't been fixed. What she wrote about all those years ago should still be an anthem, today. For *your* time. About *your* world."

Michael asked, "Yeah? What was that? That she wrote? Back when our mamas was still babies."

Scottie laid it out. "Bang. Bang. Bang. They shoot us down."

Michael and Robert started looking back and forth at each other.? Scottie had a proposal. "People are what they were when.' That's a phrase that means we're all influenced by outside things like music or happenings in our world differently...based on how old we were when the music or the events happened. I have a set of headphones that has music playlists grouped by decades."

Michael said, "We ain't hearin' no cracker music."

Robert added, "Yeah, man. You tryin' to make us crazy?"

"I want you to use those headphones when you're outside mowing. The headphones will protect your ears from the noise of the mower...and will give you something that will help you relate to all ages of people. That could be a useful tool in your afterlife. And it will expose you to Tracy Chapman...among others."

The boys just looked at each other like this was one more harebrained idea.

Scottie thought to himself, 'This is gonna be a massive task.'

While they were cleaning up after breakfast, Scottie wanted to make them aware of some of the more subtle ways they could be discovered.

"I want to give you some extreme examples of how you and our operation here can be traced. One example is an overzealous investigator taking samples from the septic tank to get some DNA profiles from our solid waste. That's why we use the Rid-X. It accelerates the bacteria eating the solid waste, hence eating the DNA evidence.

"Also, our electric usage will show an increase from you being here. We're using more water, so the electric well pump will use more electricity. The stove and water heater are run off of replaceable propane tanks which I fill with cash payment. So that's not an issue. Electric lights won't be significant because of LED's. So just be aware of unusual electricity usage. Turn lights off that are not in immediate use.

"If an investigator thinks you're using outdoor equipment or tools, they might try to steal in and wipe a sample for touch DNA. So wear neoprene or nitrile gloves when you can. If your hands are sweaty, there are baby powder containers in all our work areas that will absorb the sweat off your hands so the gloves will slide on. Remember to wipe touch surfaces with anti-bacterial wipes when gloves aren't practical.

"Clean the toilet rim after every pee. Your pee droplets have your DNA in them. Plus, it will make you a favorite of future housemates if you're in the habit of keeping a clean toilet. And always put the toilet seat down after every use. Nothings shouts 'boys' like a raised toilet seat.

"Burn all paper trash in the outdoor water heater furnace.

"Cut all plastic recycling to mini pieces for lesser volume and to make DNA detection more difficult. The low volume will keep recycling trips to the landfill from raising any eyebrows.

"I make cash purchases for you on separate trips from the debit card household buying I do for me." The boys didn't know if it was a bad sign the Scottie had already told them that.

After the breakfast cleanup, Scottie led the duo out to the garage.

"You know the pickup truck from having slept in it. This vehicle, under the dustcover, is just for rare occasions." He removed the dustcover. "I rarely use it because people identify you by what you drive. If I need to run an errand that I want to be as private as possible, I take this car. Notice that it is nondescript in style and color. If you walk around it, you will notice the color changes depending on the angle that you're looking at it from.

"Plus, I always sweep the vehicle I'm driving for a GPS tracking device before every cash trip...but if I find one, I'll make sure it's reinstalled for all debit card purchase trips so there's a record of me coming and going for my own errands."

Robert asked, "How could someone put a device on it?"

"We could have a device inserted without us even knowing someone had been here. That's why I always check."

Michael piped up, "You sound like you be paranoid, man."

"Paranoia is a mental illness. Caution and preparedness are the tools of successful people. Learn the difference."

The boys didn't know if it was a bad sign the Scottie had already told them that.

Scottie re-covered the little car with the dustcover and led the boys on a tour of the property.

"These are the driveway alarms. They're motion activated which is why we get alerts whenever an animal passes by. We will be replacing these with infrared trip-wire detectors with night vision video. We'll add some in the woods around the house. We'll get an alert and a video pop-up on the computer every time one is activated. That should cut down on the false alarms."

Scottie walked them through the woods to the bottom field. "Keeping this field cut with the finish mower is a chore I'll pass off to you two while you're here. But look up at the open sky. This property is on a flight path from Memphis to Smyrna, two cities that have National Guard military bases and active civilian airports. That's why you always see and hear aircraft overhead. And, maybe you've already noticed the helicopters and the small planes fly very low."

The boys didn't know if it was a bad sign the Scottie had already told them that.

Michael wondered out loud, "This field is totally hidden from the world. Nobody could ever find this place. Why you keep it so golf-course looking?"

Scottie turned to walk out of the bottom field and disappeared into himself for a moment. He spoke so quietly as though he was speaking only to himself. But the boys heard him. "It's for the children." The boys looked at each other as though Scottie had lost his mind.

Returning to the task at hand, Scottie continued. "If suspicions arise about you being here, some of those aircraft will take high resolution pictures of what's going on here. Before you mow, you will be outfitted with masks and hats and beige gloves. Plus, you'll have the headphones on to keep the mask tight to your face. Plus, you'll mow with white long-sleeved shirts that have a collar. With no black skin exposed, you'll never have to worry about airplanes or helicopters overhead."

Then Scottie walked around the woods line to the farthest corner of the bottom field and onto the downstream end of the riverwalk.

"It's very rare, but every once in a while a fisherman walks down this river. We'll be down here swimming quite a bit, plus this trail we're on along the bank of the river will be your responsibility. So be vigilant about who might be wandering by."

Michael said that neither of the boys swim. Scottie kept walking. "You will."

Scottie stopped the boys at the rapids below the dog's leg turn in the river. Scottie pointed out a backwater pool that was still. He pointed out a school of little small-mouth bass.

"Let's walk down to their pool and watch what happens."

As they approached, all the little fish scampered out of the pool and out of sight.

"They felt our footsteps through vibrations from the ground into the water. Investigator cops know this lesson. That's why the good ones tread softly. You must learn to do the same. The loud and the proud end up in a frying pan.

"The fish hang out in all the same places...places where they can relax because there's no current. And places where they're shaded from the sun. With this knowledge, you can predict where you're going to find the fish. Don't be a fish. Try not be predicable.

"When feeding, fish expose themselves because they usually enter the current to eat nutrition that is flowing in the open current from upstream. They let the food come to them. Seems smart. But what does that tell you about where to find fish?"

Robert said, "Find fish where they eat."

"So, if a fish doesn't want to end up in a frying pan, what should the fish know?"

Michael said, "Don't eat in the same place all the time."

"Fish like to travel and gather in groups. Whether it's minnows or adult fish, they think they're hiding in the crowd. But the truth is, the crowd attracts the attention of fish-eaters.

"Look here for fish in the river." The boys couldn't see any fish until the fish moved. "They're camouflaged against the rock bottom of the creek. They give themselves away when they show movement.

"Look upstream at that giant bird standing in the water. It's a Great Blue Heron. It will stand perfectly still until the fish don't even realize it's there. Then it eats.

"Are we talking about fish?"

Robert answered. "No. You be talkin' 'bout people. Like us and the cops."

After they had walked the entire length of the riverwalk, Scottie said, "This is as far as the riverwalk goes. The bluff goes directly into the river from here all the way to the bridge."

Robert said, "So this is the end of the line?"

Scottie nodded and led the boys back to where they could climb the edge of the bluff through the woods back toward the house.

On the upward climb along the edge of the bluff, Robert pointed at a sprawling growth at the base of a tree. "Hey, man. Has this tree got a disease?"

Scottie and Michael walked over to it. Scottie said, "That's a mushroom. There are mushrooms all over these woods. Learn to identify them. Some are edible and some are poisonous. The edible ones are a delicacy we can cook in our food or put in our salads. But the poisonous ones can make you sick…even kill you. There's a book on mushrooms in the dining room bookcase. Learn your mushrooms."

When they got to the top of the bluff behind the house, there was a circle of turkey buzzards floating the thermals to look for dead or wounded animals on which to feast. Scottie pointed up to the giant birds. "Watch the way hunting animals hunt. They're patient. They don't waste a lot of energy on finding their prey. They just wait and watch. Investigator cops hunt the same way. They sit and wait for their prey to make themselves known. Unless you want to be pounced upon, it will behoove you to take pains to not make yourselves known."

Robert and Michael were looking back and forth at each other, again. Robert said, "Don't be using fake words on us, man. Talk right so we know what chew sayin'."

Scottie was careful to not visibly shake his head.

When they got back to the house, they prepared lunch. Michael went to the bathroom and, when he came out, he turned to the right instead of walking back to the kitchen. He opened double sliding closet doors on the coat closet. He dug behind the hanging coats and jackets to find a long plastic case. He pulled it out and laid it on the floor. He opened it.

Inside, he saw a long rifle with a mounted scope. His eyes got wide. He closed the case and carried it back to the kitchen.

With the rifle case in hand, Michael spoke to Scottie. "Hey, man. Chew ain't said nothin' 'bout no guns. I wanna be shootin' this thing. You need to be showin' us how."

Scottie looked down at the case, as did Robert. "Guns, or knowledge of them, cannot be a part of your life. Let people think you're anti-gun by saying things like 'guns kill people, so I want nothing to do with them.' It will diminish fear in people about your Black skin.

"You're holding something you don't ever want your fingerprints or DNA found on, so...you've had your look. But don't ever touch it, again. This is a non-fingerprint case, but let's get rid of any 'touch' DNA."

Scottie then took the case from him and wiped it all down with antibacterial wipes. "Did you touch the gun inside the case?"

Michael dejectedly said, "No."

Robert asked, "Why you got it?"

Scottie answered, "It's a relic of days gone by. It's a model we were trained on in the military."

Robert asked, "You mean you was in the Army?"

Scottie just tilted his head with a quick and shallow up and down.

Michael asked, "What was that like? Bein' a fighter with a license to kill. I mean, that's what the Army is, right? Like the cops?"

Scottie liked hearing Michael conjugate 'to be' properly, but he didn't want to share details about his military background. "I did the minimum. If I had someone to give it to, I would. Sniper rifles don't have much legitimate use outside a war zone. Even hunters only need so much firepower."

Robert quipped, "We might be goin' to a war zone. Maybe you could give it me..."

Michael argued, "I'm the one who found it. If he be givin' it to anybody, he be givin' it to me."

Scottie picked up the case to walk it back to the closet. "I'm working to help fine-tune the tools of life for you. Not the tools of death. To some people, war is necessary. But never mistake it for what it is."

Robert asked, "What is it?"

Scottie noticed Robert's grammar, also. "The guy who led the invention of the atomic bomb went to the desert in New Mexico to see the first test explosion. When he saw the mushroom cloud reach into the sky…and then when the blast wave reached him…he quoted a Hindu Sanskrit writing. 'I am become death, the destroyer of worlds.' That should answer your question about what war is."

Michael said, "Yeah. We know. War is death. Remember why we here? Our cousin, Jimmy?"

Robert spoke to Scottie as Scottie was walking away. "I feel better that chew have it. Just in case the cops surround us. You can pick 'em off one at a time."

The boys laughed together and shared a high-five.

After lunch was cleaned up, Scottie sent the boys back out to the property to retrace their steps from earlier in the day. "If you're going to be here for a while, it would behoove you to learn all the nooks and crannies, all the hollows and ridges, all the trees and rocks of this place." It was the first time the boys had been turned loose on the outer grounds. "But be aware of your surroundings at all times."

The boys looked at each other. As he was rolling his eyes at Michael, Robert said under his breath, "Behoove. Ha!"

The boys started out down the driveway, but they stayed off the roadway itself. They started pointing out familiar landmarks to each other. They discussed what they remembered being beyond visible landmarks and then proceeded to confirm their memories.

After walking the creek bank on the riverwalk, they got where the bluff dropped into the river. Michael said to Robert, "This is 'The End Of The Line."

Robert tried to sound like Scottie. "So you have said it. So may it be so." They both had a good laugh as they took a seat on the bent ironwood tree that marked their first named property landmark.

As they were resting, Michael asked Robert, "Do you think this White mthrfckr be for real?"

Robert said, "I know he be gettin' put out witt us. I ain't knowin' how long he can last."

Michael said, "I wish I knowed why he was doing this. I mean, would you take a chance on goin' to jail for the rest of your life for someone you ain't never knowed?"

Robert contemplated Michael's thought. "You got a point there, Michael."

"Don't be callin' me 'Michael.'"

"OK. Muhammad. But I git what chew sayin'. I'd be feelin' better if I knowed why he was puttin' hisself through all a dis."

Michael was feeling troubled. "I ain't trustin' him. If it was me, I'd be turnin' us in at the first sign a trouble."

Robert agreed.

On their way back to the house, the boys entered the finely trimmed bottom field. Michael asked Robert, "D'jew hear what he say about this field being cut so nice?"

Robert answered, 'Yeah. I hear-ed him."

Michael became agitated. "What's witt that talk about children? He say he ain't married. There ain't no pictures a kids nowhere."

Robert added, "There ain't no toys for kids, neither."

Michael wondered, "So what chew think that mean? 'For the children.' There ain't a soul that could find this place without havin' a map."

Robert said, "Somethin' ain't right witt him."

Michael echoed the sentiment. "He ain't all there."

Robert added, "The elevator don't go all the way to the top floor."

Michael kept it going. "He ain't holdin' a full deck a cards."

Robert continued it. "The lights be on, but ain't nobody home."

That got Michael giggling. Then Robert joined him. They both had to sit down to laugh it out. It took long enough that they both had to start wiping their eyes before they could compose themselves.

It was evening before the boys got back to the house. Scottie congratulated them on finding their way back home. He said they must have come in because it was supper time.

Robert stopped him. "You gonna turn us in over to the cops whenever we be too much trouble for you?"

"Yeah," Michael agreed. Mockingly, he added, "It would *behoove* you."

Scottie felt a triumph.

Michael continued. Scottie could see something rising up within Michael. "You jess gonna be like every other White piece a sht mthrfckr. If it come down to you or us...you gonna turn us over to the pigs."

Scottie turned his back on Michael to get supper started. He turned back when he heard Michael's footsteps running at him.

Just as Scottie turned, he saw the steam coming out of Michael's face. Scottie relaxed and prepared to go limp.

Just before he got there, Micheal knew that Scottie was going limp. He stopped at Scottie's nose and stared with angry eyes. He whispered close to Scottie's lips, "I be in charge of my own self." He slowly pulled away from Scottie and said as he turned away, "It was a mistake last time."

As Michael retreated, Scottie asked, "If a mistake leads you to the right answer...was it a mistake?"

Robert knew Michael was too angry to answer. "Only if it hurt another person."

Scottie tried to comfort Michael with his tone of voice...but he had to keep his words honest. "You *are* going to get turned over to the cops. But the one that's gonna do it is you. And I'd prefer that you *not* do that, because when you do, you're turning Robert and me over to them, too." That kept Michael's anger level up.

Scottie said to both boys, "Get supper started. I'll be back shortly."

With that, Scottie left the house.

The boys started pulling pots and pans and dishes. Robert went downstairs and retrieved the food.

Scottie returned to the kitchen as the boys were putting supper on the table. They all ate in silence.

They washed the dishes in silence.

The boys were about to retreat to the basement in silence when Scottie stopped them and told them to sit back down at the dining room table.

Before Scottie sat down, he pulled out a mustard-colored, banded stack of money from each pocket. He threw one stack in front of each one of them. Neither one of them touched it, but stared in wonderment.

Scottie explained. "There's $10,000 in each band. One for each of you. If you need to leave, take this...or whatever part of it you think you might need to go as far as you think you'll go. But if you decide to stay here until you're ready to go, it will be the starter money for your new life. And what to do with starter money, and lots of other knowledge about money, will be part of your preparedness training here."

Scottie left the room to go to his bedroom. When he came back, the boys had still not touched the money but were still staring at it.

Scottie set a black zippered bag on the table and unzipped it. "Now...here are the hair clippers and razors. It's time."

1.20 THE CRIME

Agent John Watkins asked the Metro Chief to brief the Task Force on the incident that clearly motivated the murder of Officer Mark Johnson.

When the whole of the Task Force was assembled, the Chief began.

"I have prepared the interview recording of Officer Johnson that he gave to our Internal Affairs personnel. It will inform you in your investigative efforts to know the alleged motive behind the murder of our brother officer, Mark Johnson.

"The preliminary testimony is that Officer Johnson and his partner had stopped for a 'courtesy coffee' at a friendly coffee shop in North Nashville. We all know where I'm talking about.

"After Johnson's partner exited the patrol vehicle to retrieve a couple of coulee lattes for himself and Officer Johnson, that's when the incident began. From that point in time, I'll just run the tape. It speaks for itself."

Officer Johnson: "I saw a Black kid with one of those 'African hairdos' acting suspiciously around a parked car. While waiting for my partner to return with our coffees, I exited the patrol vehicle to confront the perpetrator."

Interviewer: "What did you perceive him to be 'perpetrating?'"

Officer Johnson: "The theft or vandalism of a vehicle."

Interviewer: "Are you aware that the vehicle is registered to the deceased's grandmother?"

Officer Johnson: "There is no way I could have known that at the time of the incident."

Interviewer: "What happened after you exited your patrol vehicle?"

Officer Johnson: "I called out to him and asked him what he was doing. He looked over at me and ran. I ordered him to stop. When he ran, it was reasonable for me to presume that he had been in the act of committing a crime...and he *did*, in fact, commit a crime by failing to follow my commands. So I gave chase.

"He ran between a couple of houses and I pursued.

"The suspect turned with something in his hand that I recognized to be a gun. Fearing for my life, I shot him until he hit the ground and was no longer a threat."

Interviewer: "What verbal commands had you issued to the deceased back at the car?"

Officer Johnson, "I told him to stop what he was doing and to place both his hands on the roof of the car in a leaning position...that I was going to pat him down."

Interviewer: "He then fled?"

Officer Johnson: "Yes."

Interviewer: "Why were you going to pat him down?"

Officer Johnson: "To protect myself from the possibility that he had a gun on him before I investigated his suspicious activity around the car."

Interviewer: "Did you issue any verbal commands to the deceased as he fled?"

Officer Johnson: "I commanded him to stop several times. He ignored my lawful commands."

Interviewer: "How many times did you discharge your service weapon at him?"

Officer Johnson: "I have since been told that I shot three times. When a person sees that their life is in danger, and that the aggressive party is attempting to terminate my lawful execution of a law enforcement action...and my life, then I have a responsibility to the citizenry, which we serve, to take all reasonable and necessary action to stop the threat."

Watkins thought, 'Lawful execution' sounds like the right words, so far.'

Interviewer: "And are you now aware that all three of your service weapon discharges found their target in the back of the deceased?"

Officer Johnson: "I have since been informed of that."

Interviewer: "Have you been coached by an attorney or by any Police Union representative on how to describe your incident involving the deceased?"

Officer Johnson: "No."

Watkins looked over at Neal Knopler to see him crack a subtle smile.

Interviewer: "A neighbor's security camera, though grainy, doesn't show the suspect turning, nor does it show any indication of anything in his hand."

Officer Johnson: "The key word there is 'grainy.' What I saw wasn't 'grainy.' I have 20/20 vision."

Interviewer: "The security camera doesn't show any indication of you recovering anything off the ground after the takedown. It just shows a body that doesn't have any movement."

Officer Johnson: "I was told, later, that the investigating officers on the scene found the gun after the paramedics had left with the body."

Interviewer: "The security camera shows that you stood over the body while apparently talking into your radio. There in no indication that you rendered any medical attention, whatsoever."

Officer Johnson: "It was clear to me that he was dead. I haven't received any medical training on how to bring someone back from the dead."

Agent Watkins thought, 'The arc of justice has a strange way of turning chaos into order…if we can wait long enough.'

1.21 NO JUSTICE NO PIECE

The photo of the gun recovered from the James "Jimmy" Jefferson takedown was shown on the briefing screen. The handle had blue spray paint on it indicating that it was now the property of the evidence room at Metro police.

Agent Watkins noted that the gun was photographed *after* the evidence room had tagged it with their paint. Watkins knew it happened in that order sometimes, but it still caught his attention.

Watkins leaned over to Agent Brenda O'Malley and whispered in her ear, "You have a photographic memory, right?...Go to the evidence room and ask to see that gun. Look it over, closely. Take a snapshot in your photographic mind of the serial number. After you leave the evidence room, write the number down and give it to me. Keep it quiet."

Agent O'Malley reported back. "The serial number had been filed off, but in the right reflection of light, I could make out the whole thing."

Watkins looked at her, eyes wide, and with a cock to his head. "A photographic memory *and* superhuman vision? Looks like the FBI knew what they were doing when they hired you."

Agent O'Malley smiled and handed Watkins a slip of paper with the number written on it."

Agent Watkins copied the number onto another piece of paper and called Agent Bradley Summers over to his side. Watkins whispered in his ear, "Run this serial number through the database. Bring me the results. Keep it quiet."

Agent Summers came back with nothing in writing. He spoke privately to Agent Watkins. "It's a weapon in the custody of the Metro Nashville Police evidence room. It was recovered as an unregistered weapon from a 'stop and frisk' four years ago."

Watkins nodded his head to Agent Summers and said, "Thanks."

Agent Watkins kept it quiet.

1.22 CHANGE YOUR TUNE

After a long day of fighting over hair, that was now gone, and trying to absorb all the changes needed to live a secret life, the two boys were sitting at the table at the lookout picture window. Robert/Jamal was trying to keep his crying quiet. Michael/Muhammad was trying to not pay attention.

Scottie stood over Robert and started softly patting his shoulder. "You're crying because you miss your mother, and your grandmother, and all your familiar surroundings. It will help if, when those feelings come...and they will come again...it will help if you picture yourself crying with someone who is crying for the same reasons as you."

While still keeping his face hidden in his hands, Robert quietly said, "You mean, Muhammed, err, I mean Michael Dean? Or do you mean my Mama and my Grandma?"

Scottie stopped patting his shoulder but left his hand in place. "I mean the widow, Mrs. Johnson. The wife of the cop you murdered."

Robert Smith blew-up. "I'm glad the mthrfckr's dead. I'm pissed that we're the ones who had to do it. Who gave that White-ass-cracker-piece-a-sht the right to murder us? To murder Cousin Jimmy? I'll tell you the answer. That pig-cop mthrfckr Johnson thought it was OK cuz that's just the way it is. The White-ass cracker mthrfckrs who let him get away with it be all the White-ass cracker mthrfckrs who make the rules. They give the cops permission. It's the system, man. That's just the way it is."

Scottie removed his hand from Robert's shoulder and pulled out a chair to sit down with the boys. "There's an important thing to do in life that takes a lot of practice for most people. It's an act that takes place within you. In your person. In your soul. But the evidence of the act will show up in your actions. Your behavior. The things you actually do.

"The act in your person is the recognition, the acknowledgment, that something you did was wrong…that it was not consistent with what is right. This recognition and acknowledgment has to come from your own definition of right and wrong. Not somebody else's. You do that within yourself. It's private. It only has meaningful meaning to you. Within you.

"The evidence that you have been honest with yourself is your growth away from that thing you called 'wrong.' You will know if you're growing away from that thing you call 'wrong' by how you deal with the opportunities to do it again.

"The whole process is a skill. An art. It needs the same kind of attention as something you're making that you want to come out beautiful. It doesn't happen on its own. There's a time commitment involved."

Michael Dean saw where Scottie was going, and he didn't like it. "We dun the right thing, killing that murdering cop who was never gonna get justice for murdering Jimmy."

Scottie sensed they needed to talk it out. "How did you find him?"

Robert had stopped crying. "When the DA announcement came over the TV that there was gonna be no charges on the pig-cop, we was hyper. We axed Grandma for the keys to her car and took off with Muhammad driving. He drove to a liquor store. He bought a bottle a Jack and we started sharing it. It was to calm us down, but we wasn't calmin' down. We wanted to kill the mthrfckr. The Jack becum our liquid courage. We decided to drive to his hometown even though we gut no idee where that mthrfckr's house was at."

Michael picked up the story. "We never bin to White towns. Too much danger for a nggr. So, we be jess cruisin' around, tryin' to be invisible, when we seen a Walmart store. We pulled in thinkin' we wiz gonna steal something...jew know...jess to pay Whitey back."

Robert took over. "We was drivin' by the doors to get a parking spot when I seen the mthrfckr coming out. I hit Muhammad in the arm, 'Hey, ain't that the mthrfkr?' Muhammad looked over and said, 'Yeah. That be that racist nggr-killer.' So, I be sayin', 'What we do?' and Muhammad say, 'Park and walk past him like we be goin' in...and don't be lookin' at him. Then when he goes by, that be when we got to jump that cracker pig."

Michael picked up the narrative. "We parked the car and walked at the mthrfckr. When we walked by him an his ole lady, his ole lady says to the mthrfckr, 'What are they doing here?' At first I be thinkin' she knowed who we wuz. But then I knowed she was jess axin' what a couple a nggrs was doin' in their neighborhood.

"As soon as they walk past us, we turned and jumped that pig mthrfckr...like we was wantin' to take him down. Jamal jumped on his back, and we be punchin' him in the head, over and over. He turn over and be fightin' back when I pulled my blade. I punched that mthrfckr in his neck.

"His ole lady be screamin' for help, and White people be turnin' and lookin'. We then run back to Grandma's car. We took off back to our car an be headin' home. But we be knowin' we had to hide."

Scottie asked, "When did you feel like you had done the right thing?"

Robert answered. "Jest as soon as we be makin' our getaway."

Michael added, "The whole way back home. We know we dun the right thing."

Scottie asked, "When did the first doubts about it being the right thing come into your minds?"

Robert sad, "The moment we met chew."

Michael was nodding, "That night...when Miss Loquisha be droppin' us off here. If what we done be what bring us here...that be proof we messed up. You ain't where we was needin' to be."

Scottie was pointed in his assessment. "You said you needed to drink some Jack. You said it gave you liquid courage. Have you ever considered that if you need to drink some liquor in order to have courage...that you never had any courage to begin with?"

Michael didn't like that. "What chew be knowin' about courage, man? You jess a old White foo hidin' in the woods from yur own self. Cuz you scared a sumptin'."

Scottie rarely gave into the allure of bait. "It's been a long day. Get showered and into bed. I have a reading picked out."

When Scottie could hear that the boys were settled, he headed downstairs.

"This book," as he handed copies to Robert and Michael, "has a poem by the important poet named Robert Frost to whom you've already been introduced. He's important because his poems are part of the collective consciousness of Americans. Turn to page 36 to the poem entitled *Stopping by Woods on a Snowy Evening*."

Michael wanted to derail Scottie's planned poetry reading. "I think I know who my father is. He go by the name a Rico Teardrop. He ain't a Rican. He be a banger that everyone respect."

Scottie asked, "By 'respect,' do you mean everyone fears him?"

Michael said, "Same thing."

Scottie asked, "Have you ever talked to him?"

"No, man. I seen him around. He don't act like he know he be my father. But I hear Mama saying something to my aunt one time. Made me believe it. Plus, everyone knows Rico makes trouble cuz he got no chance to make it in a world that shut him out cuz the color a his skin. People in my neighborhood respect that sht."

Scottie asked Robert, "Robert? Do you know who your father is?"

"No, man. I never hear nothin'. Our Mama's never say who our Daddy's be cuz they jess be needin' a chile to love. Namin' the daddy is jess a way to open the door for Whitey to crush a nggr."

Scottie had compassion on both boys. "The memories and the feelings from when you were Muhammad and Jamal may never fully disappear. But the sufferings of the present will fade as you bloom more and more into your new lives. To have those feelings and memories is a good thing...as long as they don't trip you up into making a mistake. As long as they don't fool you into thinking they're still you.

"It's a healthy human trait to mourn the loss of dead people. That's why I've told you that you must go through the process of mourning the death of your former selves. When you nostalgically remember, treat your memories as mourning for a dead person.

"Now, onto page 36..."

> "...The woods are lovely, dark and deep,
> But I have promises to keep,
> And miles to go before I sleep,
> And miles to go before I sleep."

"The 'woods' are your life here. 'Promises to keep' is the promise of your afterlife. 'And miles to go before I sleep' is your training...your orientation. 'Sleep' is the death of your former selves for you to have a successful afterlife."

Robert asked, "Wha chew be doin' with a room down here like this? It ain't like you was jess waitin' on us to be showin' up."

Scottie collected the Robert Frost books from the boys. "Have either of you ever heard of the Underground Railroad?"

Robert said, "Chew mean where slaves was hidin'?"

Scottie filled in the blanks. "Runaway slaves were hidden by people on their property or in their houses, often in secret hiding places within the house. When it was safe, the runaway slaves would be moved to another house or property closer to their destination of freedom.

"The whole process was a high risk proposition because, not unlike your own situation, they would be hunted long after they arrived safely at their freedom destination.

"Do both of you know our National Anthem?"

Michael said, "Don't be callin' it *our* National Anthem. You be livin' in a different country than we be livin' in."

Scottie agreed with half of that. "You would be right to say our National Anthem is not *your* National Anthem...but you would be wrong to think we live in separate countries...that we're not all Americans.

"Do either of you know the words to the National Anthem of The United States of America?"

Robert offered, "Maybe."

Scottie continued. "Most people who think they know the words only know the first verse. But the person who wrote the song was a Pro Slavery White Supremacist. He used the song to exalt the goodness and virtue of this America by writing that we...yes, We the People of the United States of America...are a great country because we hunt runaway slaves and bring them to justice. And justice meant a public hanging...a lynching...or returning the captured slave to their owner, the Master of the Plantation from which they had escaped for a flesh-removing punishment that awaited them there... in front of all the other slaves. A lesson for all who might want to cast off their chains of subservience and humiliation."

Michael commented, "So that's why White people be lovin' that song so much?..."

Scottie continued, "The vast majority of White people who know what the song says are repulsed by it being our National Anthem."

Robert asked, "Then why is it the National Anthem?"

Scottie was plainspoken. "Because our White Supremacist Congress passed a law saying it was our National Anthem."

Robert asked, "You White folk are still in charge. If White people are 'repulsed' by it, why is still the law?"

Michael added, "Yeah, man. If Whitey feel bad, why don't Whitey *do* somethin' 'bout it?"

Scottie editorialized. "The majority of the Congress of the United States of America is still White Supremacists. Most of them keep it a secret…many of them keep it a secret from themselves. But when it comes time to write a law…or to abolish a law…they can't hide their stripes.

"Every day that a United State Senator or Congressperson goes to work, they see a painting on the high and lofty ceiling of the Rotunda in the Capitol Building of George Washington depicted as sitting on a throne as God.

"When I was in school, we were taught a lie. The lie was that George Washington was such a perfect person the he could not tell a lie. But the truth is that, in addition to being the General who oversaw the Colonial Army, George Washington was a whore monger who lost all his teeth from contracting the Syphilis sexual disease, and he had teeth pulled from his slaves to have dentures made for himself.

"George Washington also promised his slaves that he would free them in his Will. Which he did not.

"Why do men and women in Congress leave a racist National Anthem in place? For the same reason they leave a painting of George Washington as God on their ceiling. None of them have the backbone to lead goodness over evil."

Michael just got confirmation about what he already knew. "See? That be what we sayin'. Whitey still keepin' the nggr down…no matter how clean and Christian they pretend to be on the outside."

Robert added his two cents. "Wha chew gonna do about it, man? You say you wanna help? Wha chew gonna do about it?"

Scottie voiced his sentiment. "Change it."

Michael said, "Wha chew gonna change it to, man? Gangsta's Paradise?"

Scottie felt it was time to wrap things up. "Somebody has to have a suggestion. What would your suggestion be? I'm confident that *Gangsters' Paradise*, fine a song and anthem as it may be, wouldn't be broadly supported."

The boys just looked at each other. Scottie gave them a minute to come up with something installable.

Finally, Scottie said, "Good night. Sleep tight. Don't let the bedbugs bite."

Scottie turned to walk back upstairs and started singing in his normal, slightly off-key way, "O beautiful for spacious skies, For amber waves of grain..."

Michael whispered to Robert, "He can carry a tune like you can carry a bucket of water with holes in it."

"...For purple mountains majesty above the fruited plain..."

When Scottie got to the top of the stairs, he turned into the dining area but listened from above. He heard Michael say to Robert, "I think that song he was singin' was his idea for the National Anthem."

Then he heard Robert respond, doing an impression of Scottie. "After a thorough and convincing analysis, I do believe you're beginning to figure him out...Mr. Michael Dean."

As Scottie pulled away from the stair opening to go to his bedroom, he heard Robert whisper to Michael, "Wuz bedbugs?"

1.23 TECH SOLUTIONS

On his third "accessory supplies" shopping trip, Scott McNally purchased a linchpin piece of technology on which the success of his mission hinged. A large-screen Apple desktop computer. It was for Miss Dolly's house.

Miss Dolly's granddaughter and great-granddaughter from Michigan were near the end of their visit. It was crucial for Scottie to execute his plan while the Michigan granddaughter was still there.

When Scottie entered Miss Dolly's house to deliver her mail that day, he said to the two women, "I've been getting a lot of information from higher-up people in the Department of Human Services, and they've come up with a way to funnel money around the normal system so you can communicate with your family in Michigan, Miss Dolly." Miss Dolly just loved the welfare system...as long as it was *her* who was benefitting. Otherwise, it was a waste of taxpayer dollars.

"A bank account must be set up in the name of one of the out-of-state people who will benefit from this arrangement."

The granddaughter raised her hand and piped up, "That could be me." Scotty acknowledged her volunteerism with a head nod.

"The purpose of the bank account will be to have a place where the State can deposit the funds for this project. Then those funds can be distributed to the satellite internet company. This is a trial program, and the Family Services higher-ups who are testing it insisted they can only keep it going if the local Family Services don't know about it. The higher-ups are afraid that if word got out, everybody would want to participate before the program is fully tested."

Miss Dolly and her granddaughter were both nodding their heads in agreement to the terms.

To the granddaughter, Scottie said, "You'll have to accompany me to the bank to set up the bank account. You have a valid driver's license on you?...And you know your social security number?"

The granddaughter retrieved both items from her purse.

Scottie looked over the two cards. "OK. Good. The State has given me an initial deposit in cash to open the account, and then they will fund it monthly to keep your service in operation. I will hold the debit card issued with the account so funds can be dispersed according to the State's instructions."

Both women were nodding and smiling at each other.

Scottie continued. "It will take a couple of weeks to get everything set up and rolling. By that time, I'm sure you'll be back home," looking at the granddaughter who was nodding her head.

"If you can get all the names, email addresses, and phone numbers from all the relatives who agree to having video chats with Miss Dolly, then I'll make sure they each get an email of what day and time they can go online for their Face Call. I'll be sure to be here on those days to help Miss Dolly with the technology end of things."

Less than two weeks later, Miss Dolly's guests had gone home. Scottie oversaw the satellite installation and set up the computer and the internet connection. For inexplicable yet unquestioned reasons, a printer with a supply of ink and paper was also part of the installation.

The first thing Scottie did was to have Miss Dolly try a video chat with the granddaughter. Miss Dolly loved it...as long as she didn't have to do anything.

The second thing Scottie did was to order copies of two birth certificates of dead children be mailed to Miss Dolly's address. He had the supporting data for his request on a pad of paper. Date of Birth. Parents' names. He paid with the debit card from the "Family Services" bank account. Scottie would keep that account well funded.

1.24 GANG-BANGING IN NORTH NASHVILLE

A secret cash kitty had been organized and collected by the Metro Police Union Representative, Officer Neal Knopfler. The terms for collection were that whomever brought either of two named bodies in would collect the pot. If the bodies were brought in separately, then the pot would be split. Knowledge of this pot was limited to officers deemed trustworthy by Knopfler. Seven hundred fifty four dollars was not exactly incentive money, but Knopfler knew it was the thought that counts.

By the forth day after the murder of Officer Mark Johnson, there were more cops on the streets of North Nashville than citizens. That meant it was not a good time to be a citizen of North Nashville. 'Stop and frisk' was way too mild an expression to describe what was going on.

The goal was confessions of knowledge.

The police radio airwaves would be filled with urgent revelations from many roughly induced street confessions. It would take a few days for the Task Force to figure out that the calls produced a perfect record. 'Batting a thousand' was the baseball term applied to the effort. Not a single confession turned out to be useful or true.

A group of three teenage Black youth were conspicuously suspicious looking because of them being a group, because of them being male, because of them being teenagers...and because they had an inflammatory skin color.

They were cuffed and taken in three separate Metro cars to the Headquarters station. They were not booked. They were led to the furthest back cell in the empty jail holding area.

A gang of thugs made their way to the isolated cell while a wall of lookouts guarded the jail hallway.

The gang of thugs walked into the cell while slapping their batons into the palms of their hands in order to appear menacing.

"You boys have an opportunity to leave this jail cell right now...if you so choose."

The officers in the cell had formed a wall between the boys and the open cell door while continuing to slap their palms with their batons. The boys were trembling in fear.

After thirty seconds, the wall of blue had a conversation amongst themselves.

"Looks like these little nggr street rats want to stay here for a while..."

After some intimidating banter between the cops, the questioning turned to the boys.

"You know Jamal and Muhammad Jefferson?"

One of the boys nodded, while the other two shook their heads in fear.

"So, we'll take that to mean that you *all* know them. Which one of you is going to save himself by telling us where we can find your nggr friends?"

All three boys indicated they didn't know where the fugitive pair was.

One of the officers raised his baton over his head as if to strike one of the boys. His baton strike was held up by one of his fellow officers. "No blood," was all he said.

At that point, all three officers sheathed their batons, then removed their handcuffs from their equipment belts. Then each officer, one at a time, cuffed the ankles of each boy to the steel pipes that supported the bench that the boys were sitting on. It was a technique learned through the grapevine from their fellow officers in New York City and Baltimore.

Once all the boys were cuffed at the ankles with their legs splayed open, the focused questioning began.

News of the boys rendition spread quickly through the neighborhood. That brought Loquisha Davis to appear before the Desk Sergeant at Metro HQ.

"We have no record of any boys by those names being booked in here."

While he was talking, Loquisha could hear the screams and the moans and the pleading echoing from some unidentifiable direction.

But she knew where the holding cells were.

"Buzz me in so I can inspect your jail cells. I hear my boys back there."

No chance.

Loquisha unsheathed her phone and pressed a button for one Brian Sommerset. Attorney Sommerset was part of an ACLU team that focused on police civil rights violations.

"...Yes. They're being held by Metro, and I can hear sounds of their torture while I'm talking to you." Loquisha made sure her conversation was in the presence of the Desk Sergeant.

The Desk Sergeant removed himself from his desk and disappeared into the walled-off office space behind him.

Within one minute, the sounds of torture had ceased.

Within two minutes, the Desk Sergeant returned to report the he had personally inspected the holding area and that none of the cells had occupants.

Loquisha rushed out the front door of the station and ran around to the back of the expansive building. Just as she got to the back of the building, she saw a Metro squad car fleeing the scene. She could make out three heads in the back seat, all three of those heads lifelessly resting on each other's shoulders.

Loquisha found her car and headed back to the neighborhood where it didn't take long to find the three boys in the house of one of their aunts. Loquisha and the aunt and an uncle helped all three boys into Loquisha's car. She drove them to the emergency room at Vanderblane Medical Center. Loquisha told the admitting nurse that she wanted documentation on the nature of the boys' injuries.

After two hours in the public waiting area, and after two hours of phone calls to attorneys and television contacts, Loquisha saw the boys coming out of the E.R. exam rooms corridor, two on crutches and one in a wheel chair. There was a white-coat with a stethoscope opening the door for them.

"I have examined their injuries. They all appear to have conspired to make up a story about a police beating. But my conclusion is that their injuries are consistent with some rough sex play the three boys had with each other, perhaps in conjunction with a fall or impact crash from a physical activity such as skateboarding. That's the conclusion that is detailed in my report, and that will be part of their permanent medical record at this facility."

When the doctor released the boys into Loquisha's custody, he opened the door to return to the corridor of medical exam rooms. There, standing in the hallway, Loquisha saw someone she knew well. The Metro Union Representative, Officer Neal Knoplfler. He nodded his head in recognition to Loquisha...and added a smirk.

Loquisha didn't make it in time for the Six O'clock News, but she did get on the Ten O'clock News.

With the beleaguered and still energy-drained boys flanking her, she detailed the torture they had survived, as well as the complicity of the doctor at the E.R.

"Do your White children get secretly and unlawfully kidnapped to be taken to a secret holding cell for torture? These boys hardly know the suspects the police are after. So, they were kidnapped and tortured, not for useful information, but to send a message to the neighborhood of what is coming for anyone who fails to comply in a cowering and subservient manner.

"So, to my White fellow citizens, I ask you to consider this: If this kind of police authority can go unchecked in *my* neighborhood, when will it be in *your* neighborhood?"

The White folk who got her unsolicited diatribe over their TV's that night had no concerns about unlawful police actions coming to their neighborhoods...because *they* were law abiding citizens who didn't pose a threat to society. Because 'we *are* the society.'

1.25 DISCIPLINE TAKES DISCIPLINE

As Scottie was about to pull out of Miss Dolly's driveway from delivering her mail and fiddling with her computer, he had to stop for a familiar car coming down the hill. It was Dr. Higginbotham and his wife on their way to their cabin. Mrs. Higginbotham was driving. She stopped in front of Scottie's truck to block him in so Dr. Higginbotham could get out.

"Hey, Scottie. We're just getting into town. The Mrs. and I would like you to come over for supper tomorrow night if you're free."

Scottie had to remind himself that his old self was never busy. "I'd love to see you both. A man needs to be jolted out of his boredom from time to time."

Back at the house, Scottie didn't pull his truck into the garage. He walked in in a hurry and told the boys they needed to get him fed so he could go out on another shopping venture. "You fellas have plenty more basic needs to acquire so you can settle in for the long haul."

It was suppertime before Scottie returned to the house. His pickup was overflowing with goods that had been strapped down to keep any of it from sailing or bouncing out.

He parked in the garage, but left the garage door open so the boys could help parade the new merch downstairs.

The goods included desks and swivel chairs, bookcases, and dresser drawers, all in unfinished bare pine.

Robert asked, "You gonna leave dis new furniture wit no paint on it? Ain't chew gonna protect the money you spent on it?"

Scottie answered, "If everything works out, all these things will be turned into ashes. Paint doesn't burn as well as bare wood."

They carried down a new physician's scale, a wardrobe of clothing for each of them from Abercrombie and Fitch, two pair of non-prescription eyeglasses, and another bunch of reading books...in triplicate.

Night-vision video cameras and several driveway infra-red trip lights were left on the upstairs table under the picture window, outside the inner-sanctum. Batteries and mounting hardware we also left upstairs.

While they were preparing supper, Scottie played a 1928 series of songs by Billie Holiday on the computer. Robert commented, "That sounds like crap, man."

Michael continued that thought. "Yeah, man. You trying to torture us?"

While they continued with the food prep, Scottie responded, "Can you hear past the scratchy sound and low recording quality? Once you can, you'll hear as beautiful a singing voice as there is...or has ever existed."

Robert asked, "Beautiful singing voices are everywhere. Why her?"

Scottie went into teaching mode. "It's not really about her. It's about internalizing the discipline of seeing beyond the scratches and the low production value. Learning to hear below the noise isn't about music. It's about people. It's a discipline that you can train yourself to do. But it takes discipline to exercise that discipline."

Michael refuted, "Whada we gotta look below the surface for. If someone show you they nasty, then they nasty."

As they put the meal on the table, Scottie responded, "Nasty is a defensive mechanism. Looking below the 'nasty' will help you to see the real person. To know who a person really is is to know how to best work with them. You can't know who the person really is unless you can see below the scratches and the low production value...the nasty."

After cleanup, the rest of the night was spent setting up the new furniture in the boys' space and filling dresser drawers with new clothing. It was predictable to Scottie that the boys would object to their new fashion accessories. But when they handled the quality, especially the cashmere sweaters, their objections petered out.

"Tomorrow we install all the driveway hardware and do the software connections and testing. Then I have a supper appointment with a neighbor."

Once the boys were settled into their new beds, Scottie began reading *Old Yeller*. They were both asleep before he finished the first page. To Scottie, that was always a positive sign. A tired body and a tired mind. Proof of a good day's work.

1.26 BENCHED

On Friday afternoon, Agent Watkins wanted to revise his 'Mona Lisa' profile that he had given to the troops on Tuesday. He wanted to add the possibility that an old recluse White backwoodsman who lives in KKK country with no money could have been, or is, an agent for the fugitive boys. But when he said it out loud, his instinctual reaction was that he would be committing career suicide. So, when he called the FBI and Metro Task Force together, he kept the strength of his gut feelings to himself.

"We're at a 'watch and wait' crossroads at this point. All of our surveillance warrants and apparati are in place. All of you detectives are on your sources, listening for new leads. My team and I have the next level of digging to do on all possibilities for leads outside Nashville and outside Tennessee. Chief Rand and I will be updating each other on all new information or sustainable theories as they arise...so let's all stay on it until we get these killers. Let's never forget why we do this. It's all about justice for Officer Mark Johnson and his wife and family."

In the middle of the dense evening rush hour traffic back to Memphis, Agent John Watkins had private and quiet time to plan the next step if no other leads emerged: dig deeper into this McNally guy.

To Watkins, McNally still didn't add up to being a neatly sealed box with a pretty bow on top. McNally was rubbing a sensitive sore on Watkins' investigative instincts.

1.27 BLACK IS THE NEW WHITE

John Watkins grew up as, what is commonly referred to as, 'an Army brat.' However, his father was a career Air Force man.

His father had figured out early in his career that the path to a more comfortable retirement included playing the real estate game.

About every two years throughout his career, his father would be transferred to a new Air Force base. His father had figured out that, wherever there was a military base, there was a reliable source of turnover in the civilian housing market. So, instead of living in Base housing, he would buy a home in a community near the base. Flipping houses was all about using his capital gains to invest in his next house. And the houses got nicer and nicer with every transfer.

When John Watkins' father had crossed over the twenty year mark of service, making him eligible for retirement, he asked a favor of his newest Base Commander: "Could I be given the courtesy of not getting transferred until my retirement so my son can attend the same High School for all four years?" That last assignment had been to an Air Force base that was tangent to a small and wealthy suburb outside Boston named Lexington, Massachusetts.

The Watkins' would be one of the only Black families in the town...which had always worked out well for the Watkins. A Black military family, as long as there was only one, had always been welcomed in the previous towns in which the Watkins had lived. *One* Black family made many of the citizens proud to be considered inclusive. And *only* one Black family made the threat of their neighborhoods becoming overrun non-consequential.

John Watkins had been raised with a very supportive homework ethic from his parents. It had always resulted in him being considered the 'smartest kid in the class.' At Lexington High School it would be no different.

John was the only Black student in his High School and was well respected by the Honors students. That made him mythically untouchable by the few who had been raised to be small-minded about race.

Also, John, in his Freshman year at Lexington, had run for and had won the election to be President of his Class. He would get re-elected the three years following, all the way through his Senior year.

That, combined with his perfect grade point average, along with his extra-curricular activities, none of which were sports, made him a shoe-in to be named Valedictorian of his graduating Class. When he gave his speech at graduation, he had already been accepted by, and had accepted, a full scholarship at nearby Harvard College.

One of the factors that made John so easily received was that he was, other than the color of his skin, indistinguishable from all the White people around him. That's the way it had always been. A chameleon doesn't choose to blend in with its surroundings. It just happens naturally.

His Valedictorian speech was pleasing to his audience. It gave them an opportunity to relish the fact that they were so evolved so as to accept a Black in their all White community, even going so far as to allow him to be a role model...as long as there was only one of him.

John's parents were easy to pick out in the crowd. He also knew many of his classmates' parents. He was comforted by the scene of parents and families coming together to celebrate this last event in the lives of their loved ones before the big launch into adulthood. Semi-adulthood.

As John peppered his audience with eye contact while he recited his memorized speech, his practiced scanning came across one picture that didn't fit.

A man, maybe in his mid thirties, too young to be the parent of a graduate, and dressed as though he had just come off the factory floor...even though Lexington didn't have any factories...was in stark contrast to the formal and Sunday-go-to-meeting attire of the rest of the crowd. The man was sitting in the bleachers in the midst of the more respectable-looking attendees, and he was giving sporadic attention to a dollop of ice cream in an ice-cream cone. John had been trained since his days as a toddler to spot 'what doesn't belong in this picture.' John didn't like the boldness of a person who wasn't afraid to not fit in.

When John noticed that the man noticed John staring at him, Watkins had a flash of recognition that it was the man he had met while he was talking to the Principal about his graduation speech one afternoon. John noticed their mutual recognition. Then John looked away from him and resumed his practiced moving-eye-contact across the crowd.

When John moved into a four person suite in a dorm building in Harvard Yard, he had never considered the meaning of his own race. His three White roommates and he got along fine. Their common goal of academic achievement was their main focus.

But as John crisscrossed the campus for classes and study sanctuaries, he was repeatedly approached by Black students who wanted to meet him. Actually, they didn't just want to meet him, they wanted him to associate with them. To affiliate with them. For John to be one of them.

Their pitch was, 'we need to stick together...we're all in the struggle together...they're gonna start picking us off, one at a time, if we let them...'

All this was news to John. But it did have an impact on him. John grew his hair out into an Afro and would be sought out by, then sought out himself, other Black students for things as simple as cross-campus walks.

Those walks often morphed into deep dives into the American history of White brutality on Blacks for the purpose of sustaining the subjugation and servitude of slavey, having lost the convenience of keeping them housed on the Plantation.

The long and the short of it was that John, who never went so far as to attend 'meetings,' became aware that he was Black. And that made him start to notice some differences in racial attitudes that he had never noticed and, therefore, had never contemplated before.

John's undergraduate major was English Literature, to which he added a minor in Psychology. He saw the two as being related in that a writer had to know the motives of his characters.

His undergraduate academic fidelity and focus paid a big dividend for John. He was accepted by, and offered a full scholarship to, Harvard Law. He thought that being an 'academic' lawyer was a pretty low-stress way to make a living. And the bookwork part of it was already comfortable and familiar territory to him.

The summer before the Harvard Law paper chase, John wrote a letter-to-the-editor of the Boston Globe about a legislative proposal submitted in Congress by the newly minted Freshman Congressman from a district that included John's own address of residence, Lexington, Massachusetts.

The letter lauded the Congressman for proposing a progressive piece of legislation that would match environmental cleanup funds to profits made by the oil and gas industries from government contracts, and from profits made off government lands, and from the dollar value of government subsidies.

The Globe sent John a check for fifty dollars along with a letter that explained that his letter was printed on their Op/Ed page.

The Congressman's office called John to say the Congressman wanted to meet John to speak to him about a speechwriting and communications job.

John showed up at the Congressman's local office to witness the visible shock of the Congressman when he saw that John was Black. John was now able to recognize the reaction, but he also recognized the Congressman shaking it off.

The Congressman shook John's hand, and said, "Sorry if I looked shocked. I didn't know ahead of time that you're Black."

John said, "Yes. I'm probably more used to it than you are."

The Congressman was pleased about John's sense of humor and his easy manner, so he offered John a summer job as a speech and general communications writer.

That would be John's summer job for the three years he was in law school.

The year that John graduated from Harvard Law, he decided that sitting in an office writing briefs and opinions to some panel of Appeals Court judges that he would never meet was not how he wanted to die...he was sure it would lead to an early death...from boredom...and petitioned his Congressman boss for a recommendation to get into FBI Training School in Quantico, Virginia. It would help that the Congressman was a Junior Member on the Judiciary Committee which oversaw the Department of Justice and, hence, the FBI.

John Watkins made it through a hellishly challenging period of Basic Training at Quantico and was assigned to his chosen field...he got to work as a Profiler alongside some of the legends of the trade.

John's first field assignment was being attached to an office in Kansas

City, Missouri, where he met an office worker named Jackie Trumbolt. They would marry.

Jackie would later give birth to their daughter, MaryLou.

In his first twelve years with the FBI, John had gotten to work on several high profile cases. As the Profiler, he would work hand-in-glove with field Special Agents in Charge as well as with Assistant Directors.

John's ability to dissect and take the lead on cases made the recommendation that he be promoted to become a Special Agent in Charge well received.

Becoming a Special Agent in Charge meant that John now *carried* a gun. Although he never actually carried a gun, just having it in his briefcase added to his career pride.

Part of John's career training included the FBI's history of using deadly force. John paid particularly close attention to the statistics on the number of cases in which the FBI had used deadly force on people in their custody.

It all contributed to John's hope that he would retire someday, never having shot his weapon outside the shooting range. He was aware that his view was in direct contrast to the view of most of his fellow agents. The common comments he heard from them was their pride in having earned 'a righteous license to kill.'

John knew that the statistics proved that 'righteous' was the right word. In the entire history of the FBI, no agent had ever been charged or disciplined for using deadly force on a subject in custody. All FBI custody homicides had been stamped, "JUSTIFIED."

1.28 THE HYPOCRITIC OATH

At Saturday night supper, Scottie was asked by the Higginbothams why he was so obviously tired.

"Property management. Am I getting too old for this game if I fall asleep at supper just because I've been holding a set of loppers over my head all day?"

Mrs. Higginbotham commented that they were happy to just be able to do what little yard work they did to keep their country property up.

Dr. Higginbotham asked Scottie if he had heard that crazy Black lady on TV going on about the heavy-handed abuse of some of the friends of the cop killers.

"The E.R. Doc that was supervising the shift that afternoon was a former practice partner of mine. I heard the statement he released to the press about those kids who were brought in by that crazy Black lady. His statement said the injuries were consistent with the kind of roughhousing and horseplay that often goes on between teenage boys."

Scottie said that he had not seen any TV in the past couple of days.

"Well, the inside story from the Doc, himself, is that none of those boys will ever have children…if you know what I mean. The Doc didn't report the abuse in order to support police keeping the hooligans out of our neighborhoods. You know as well as I do, Scottie, that those kind just don't learn from being talked to. Something has to be *done* to them to get their attention."

Scottie started nodding his head with an internal, diametrically opposed skepticism. "It's important to get a person's attention."

Dr. Higginbotham summarized. "It'll be a good thing for society if those ruffians never have kids. Eugenics at work."

Mrs. Higginbotham served a Strawberry Shortcake with homemade whipped cream for dessert. While enjoying the sweet end of their time together, Scottie had a question for Dr. Higginbotham about plastic surgery.

"I have a deviated septum that inhibits me breathing through my nose. When I'm in the throes of hard labor, my Yoga experience tells me that I should be breathing through my nose. I'm considering having it operated on to open up the septum, but I thought while I was at it I might have my nose fixed. You can see it's slightly crooked from a break during my military training.

"My question is, what should I anticipate for recovery time if I get the plastic surgery? And is it all outpatient or should I plan on some kind of stay?"

Dr. Higginbotham was happy to share his knowledge. "Depending on how extensively the surgeon has to re-break your nose will determine your recovery time. But the procedure would be out-patient. He'll put a protective cast over your nose until the swelling and bruising resolves. But the whole thing should be pretty straight forward and low key."

Scottie was curious. "What about it being off-the-books? Plastic surgeons must do most of their work in cash because insurance doesn't cover the cosmetic procedures. If I don't want the procedure to show up on my medical record, is there a guideline cash incentive to keep it between me and the Doc?"

Dr. Higginbotham was skeptical. "The surgeon would always have a record for his own for liability issues. But why would you care about it going on your medical record?"

Scottie got all he needed. "Privacy, I guess. I don't like living in this information age where a computer hacker can get access to anything they want. My nose isn't important. It's just the principal."

Dr. and Mrs. Higginbotham nodded their heads in agreement.

Scottie returned home to start *Old Yeller*, again. As he watched the boys silently reading along, he thought, 'Your obstacles are great.' The Higginbotham report on the E.R. doc story was still on his mind.

As he allowed a sliver of pity for the boys' plight...and the plight of their former playmates...Scottie's thoughts went to that Vanderbilt E.R. doctor...

'Do no harm.'

1.29 SAY CAN I HAVE SOME OF YOUR PURPLE BERRIES

Two decades before the killing of Nashville Police Officer Mark Johnson, Dr. and Mrs. Higginbotham bought their cabin downstream from Scott McNally's place. Their second meeting was a curious coincidence to Scottie.

One hot summer day, Dr. and Mrs. Higginbotham decided they would cool off by taking a walk upstream in the river water and the shade of all the overhanging trees. She had suggested, "Let's walk upstream so the walk home is easier."

Scottie was picnicking at the swimming hole and could hear them coming over the babbling sound of the running water. He was stretched out on a blanket on the soft sand deposited on the beach by the cycle of receding flood waters.

When she noticed Scottie, Mrs. Higginbotham was startled in mid-conversation. She poked Dr. Higginbotham to look. The couple stopped their conversation but continued walking against the flow of water while not taking their suspicious eyes off Scottie.

Scottie recognized them both immediately. He held up his wine glass as the couple got along side the sandy beach. "Please stop to take a rest and join me."

The couple looked at each other for confirmation to take him up on his offer and made their way out of the water. Scottie realized they had no idea who he was.

Dr. Higginbotham surveyed the picnic scene and asked with a chuckle, "An extra wine glass and plates and utensils and food? Were you expecting us?...or are you waiting on someone?"

Scottie stood up with his wine glass and shook the doctor's hand. "My name's Scott McNally. I like to come down here in the shade to escape a hot day. It's like natural air conditioning. Will you rest here and have a glass of wine with me? And a plate of food if you're hungry?"

Mrs. Higginbotham asked, "We don't want to interfere. Are you waiting on somebody?"

Scottie explained that his grandmother, who used to own the property, would always set an extra plate at the dinner table for unexpected company. "And here you are."

The Higginbothams were convinced Scottie was 'good people.' The Higginbothams sat and nibbled and shared sips, between the two of them, from a common wine glass.

The wine made sharing their life story easier. At one point, they explained that they lived in the dream home of their own design. That it was up in a very secluded and upscale part of Nashville, but that one evening they came home from eating out and there were two youths who had broken into their house..and were still in there. That Dr. Higginbotham started shouting to try and scare them as he made his way to their gun safe. By the time he had opened the gun safe, the two youths were gone.

Dr. Higginbotham went on to explain the impact the event had on them. "When that happened, we knew the city was losing control of its Black youth and that we had better find a nice and secluded 'bug-out' house in the country. It's the cabin we have downstream from here. It's our Apocalypse Escape House."

Scottie wondered…'if the youth in there had been White, would they have felt the need to buy a second property?' But the Higginbothams answered that question for him.

"Just because they were nggrs isn't why we bought down here. We're not racist, after all. I should tell you that I have a Black friend.

"Besides, down here in the country, danger is even *more* uncertain because everybody's White. And stupid people, no matter what their skin color, are always dangerous. At least if someone's Black, their Black, and you know right up front. But with White folk, it takes a while to find out if they're stupid enough to be dangerous. So, it's not a question of race. Dangerous people are dangerous people. It's just easier to know in advance when they're Black."

Mrs. Higginbotham was in total agreement. "We always keep a pistol-grip shotgun at the ready by our front door down here. We're so far out in the country that it makes no sense to try and call 9-1-1."

As the couple was getting more comfortable with Scottie's apparent level of education, Dr. Higginbotham asked, "Were you ever in the Army, Scott? I mean for firearms training? Do you keep an arsenal at the ready out here in your country home?"

Scottie nodded his head while he sipped his wine. He didn't want to go into any detail.

Dr. Higginbotham pressed him. "You old enough for Vietnam? I was in the Tennessee guard medical corps during Vietnam…at the ready on a moment's notice. But we never got called up to serve in-country."

Scottie just nodded his head. "I was in the Air Force at that time. We all know about the Air Force, right? It's like wearing a suit to work every day. Sometimes it made you feel like a draft dodger."

Dr. Higginbotham agreed. "I know what you mean. Being in The Guard was used for draft dodging by many."

Their conversation went on for a good long while. When Mrs. Higginbotham decided they'd better head home, Dr. Higginbotham expressed that meeting Scottie made them feel better about coming down to this part of the country. "We'll let you know when we get down here for a visit. We'd love to have a dinner-friend in the neighborhood."

1.30 SENT DOWN TO THE MINORS

Agent John Watkins had returned to his office in Memphis in that last week of October. Every day he would wait for his phone to ring or his computer to ding with a fresh lead from Nashville or from one of his agents assigned to the Mark Johnson case. It was now Christmas. Crickets.

After some cookies and cake and eggnog, the office was closing at noon on Christmas Eve. Watkins had just snapped his briefcase closed for an early departure when the first four ominous sounding notes of Beethoven's Fifth Symphony sounded from his phone.

..."Yeah, Boss. Merry Christmas to you, too."..."Nothing new to report on that case."..."Well, I'd like to devote more resources into the McNally guy out in the country."

Watkins' Boss got perturbed. "All of the data show that that guy is where he says he was, when he says he was. His internet history is nothing but news and weather. He doesn't even have an email account, John."

"But, Boss. He clicks on every news story on his news feed page. Don't you see? Nobody reads every news story that's printed. The reason he does that is so nobody, including Google, can profile him. Staying hidden is his highest priority in life. Nobody puts that much effort into being unseen unless they're doing something that's nefarious."

"C'mon, John. You're way deep into the weeds on that analysis. The facts are that you haven't shown a single inconsistency in anything he has said or done."

Watkins countered, "He could have a second phone."

The Boss' temperature rose another degree. "Figure out how he does that, John. We have all his financial records. There is no second phone. It appears that he doesn't even need the one he has."

Watkins was getting a bit combative. "My point, exactly. Who in America doesn't need a phone? He could be using a friend's phone. The data we need to expose his involvement could be on the friend's phone."

The Boss was getting exasperated. "Who *are* his friends, John?"

Watkins was about out of gas. "He doesn't have any...that we know of."

The Boss was ready to hang up. "See what I mean, John?"

"Yes, Sir. We need to redirect resources while we wait."..."Then, am I still a Special Agent In Charge if I don't have any agents who are in my charge?"..."Yes, Sir. I'll have a re-prioritized case list for you after the first of the year."..."Yes, Sir. You have a Happy New Year, too."

2

...AND PUNISHMENT

2.1 TEACH YOUR CHILDREN WELL

For that first Winter with Scottie, Michael and Robert had been outfitted with all the necessary cold-weather clothing. Equipment and building maintenance were their most frequent cold weather outdoor chores. Outdoor nature chores were minimal. There was no mowing. In the woods, Scottie liked to trim growing growth, so there wasn't a lot to do in the woods.

The backyard wood stove was built to be a circulating water heater. A year's supply of firewood was neatly stacked next to it. All paper and cardboard trash was burned before it accumulated. The hot water from the outdoor stove fed pipes buried in the concrete floors of the main floor, as well as the basement floor. A Winter of walking around in stocking feet to enjoy the penetrating warmth made for a comfortable cold weather stay.

Scottie had stocked the bookcase in the dining area, as well as the boys' bookcases in the secret basement, with a broad range of books. Most were Coffee Table type books. Most had excellent visual aids in the form of photographs or paintings. The number of subjects covered was wide-ranging.

Science and Technology, Nature and Outdoors, Earth and Space, Food and Exercise and Health, some Popular Culture books that chronicled current events or Biographies on important historical figures. All the Audubon books on Plants and Birds and Mammals and Insects and Reptiles and Trees. Plus many historically important novels and poetry. The novels and poetry were largely reserved for bedtime, out-loud reading.

A consistent behavior on Scottie's part, whether indoors or out, was that he never shut up. There was a method to his madness. Nonetheless, it drove the boys to distraction throughout that first Winter.

The night and day before the full moon in January, there had fallen a rare snow. It accumulated to an even more rare four or five inches. Scottie knew it wouldn't last more than a couple of days.

"We're going to do a winter camping sleep outside."

The boys objected.

Scottie retorted, "Fear of the cold is as debilitating as fear of anything else."

They traipsed out beyond the drive to the clearing that was pretty much the front yard. There, they laid out a plastic tarp held down by their sleeping bags, and pillows, and extra blankets. They all climbed into their sleeping bags fully clothed, including wool hats and mittens. The insulating properties of goose-down and man-made Thermolite were discussed and compared.

As the moon rose from behind the house, they were all three lying in their sleeping bags. Scottie said, "Bend your heads backwards by stretching your necks until you can see the full moon…

"Now, hold your heads still and fix the moon against something like a leafless tree branch.

"Now, see if you can detect the movement of the moon."

In less than one minute, Michael and Robert were both ooo-ing and ahh-ing that they could see the moon moving.

Then Scottie asked them, "Are you seeing the moon moving?...or is the moon only *appearing* to move because the earth is rotating?"

Once they all agreed that the earth was rotating, Scottie said, "Then spread your fingers straight out, and move your hand in the direction the earth must be rotating in order to make the moon appear to be moving in the direction you are watching it move."

There was a half-hour of debate and conjecture. Michael picked up on it first. Finally, Robert got the whole concept.

"You'll notice the sun moving across the sky in the same direction as the moon and the stars. Now you know that it's not the celestial objects moving. It's the earth turning.

"The earth moves toward the East and away from the West. So once you've figured out what direction the earth moves, you'll know where East and West are, which means you'll know North and South."

Scottie then sang them the favorite song of a friend of his, *You Can Close Your Eyes*, because it referenced the sun setting and the moon rising. The boys cringed at his not-quite-in-tune singing, which made them focus more on the words.

After an hour of stargazing and talking constellations and their apparent direction of movement being the opposite direction of the earth moving, Robert was the first to complain that he was hot. Even that he was getting sweaty.

Scottie said, "Let's all get out of our sleeping bags to cool off."

While they were all standing, Scottie said, "Look at the moonlight on the snow."

Both Michael and Robert commented on what a beautiful color it was.

Scottie asked, "What color is it?"

Robert said, "It's kinda white. But I see some blue in it."

Michael added, "And it sparkles. Plus, when I relax my mind, I feel some grey...and I feel some oranges and yellows and greens are somewhere in there. In the sparkle."

They all absorbed the color for a long time.

Finally, Robert asked, "So what color is it, Scottie?"

Scottie unveiled a truth. "Our brains don't think in words. Our brains think in pictures. The purpose of language is to make a word for every picture that can exist in our minds. That way, we can share those pictures with others. But here's a great mystery. We've been exhilarated for the past half hour by the most beautiful, most magical color any of us has ever seen."

Michael impatiently asked, "So what's the name of the color, Scottie?"

Scottie said, "The most beautiful and most magical color on earth has never been given a name."

Robert said, "Then maybe we should give it a name."

Scottie said, "Give it a try. Pick a name that does it justice."

The silence lasted minutes.

Finally, Michael said, "Hey, I'm all cooled down. I'm getting back in my sleeping bag."

Scottie said, "You'll only get hot, again. Take off all your clothes, then climb back in. Put your clothes in with you to keep them warm."

Robert said, "You nuts, man. I'm not doin' that."

Scottie said, while stripping out of his clothes, "Tell me in the morning if I was wrong."

In the months of night sky watching, Scottie rehearsed the boys in identifying the four brightest stars in the sky by name, and that they were brighter than any stars in the unseen Southern Hemisphere.

He would cover topics like satellites that they had seen moving across the sky in the early darkness of evening, and geostationary satellites that masquerade as stars, and the International Space Station, and shooting stars, and the visible planets, and constellations, and nebulae.

He had them observe how the night side of the earth showed the whole universe over the course of one revolution around the sun...a year. And how their view of the Milky Way changed through the seasons so they could tell where their solar system...their earth...their home...was located in the outstretches of one arm of their own galaxy.

The boys became proficient in identifying the Big Dipper. They learned how to use The Big Dipper to find the North Star...The Great Compass In The Sky...and Cassiopeia, and Orion, and Orion's Belt. And, how none of what they see can be seen in the Southern Hemisphere. And that people in the Southern Hemisphere couldn't see the things they were seeing.

Scottie's plan of continually talking would allow for the introduction of a broad range of topics.

2.2 HOMEWARD BOUND

A decade or so after Scott McNally got out of the Air Force, he thought it was time to make the long drive back East to settle his parents' estate.

From Mattole Beach in northern California, he chose the more scenic route of staying along the coast. He drove up through Oregon and Washington, then headed East on I-90 all the way back to Lexington, Massachusetts.

He had left California in October and arrived in Lexington in May. So, he had also chosen the route upon which Winter had hindered his progress. He didn't care. If the roads were bad, he'd stay in a hotel for a week. In Chicago, he had rented a hotel room for six weeks. He enjoyed the view of the Lake out his window, but he never used room service. Even in the windy winter of downtown Chicago, he chose to venture out every day for meals and for catching up on what had been going on in the world for the previous decade. His favorite end to a day was to order and eat his supper while sitting at the hotel bar.

He made similar stops in Detroit and Cleveland to mirror some shorter stops he had made in Montana, Minnesota, and Wisconsin.

Spring had fully sprung by the time he arrived in Lexington. He found a modest motel away from the town center.

Scottie's father had come from the backwoods of rural middle Tennessee to earn a PhD in Electrical Engineering from a trade school in Cambridge called M.I.T. His father used his brilliance to become a middle manager over top secret government contracts at Draper Laboratories. He had suffered from depression all of Scottie's life, but had gone to work every day.

Scottie's mother had grown up in Lexington and had decided she wanted to live in the same zip code that her parents had...even though it was before there was such a thing as a zip code. After marrying Scottie's father, she took a job as a secretary at Lexington High School. She worked there beyond retirement age...until she got sick.

Scottie stopped in at a couple of funeral homes until he found the one that had his parents' death certificates. He paid for a stack of copies and asked if there was any payment due on the cremations. He was informed that Probate Court had distributed funds from the pending estate, and that the ashes had been spread respectfully after three years of not being claimed.

With Death Certificates in hand, Scottie found the courthouse that housed Probate Court. He laid out his purpose to the Clerk and Master. He was informed that a California Driver's License was not sufficient I.D. He'd have to at least get a birth certificate. In a small town like Lexington, he was told that a visit to Lexington High School might loosen the knots of progress. A personal identification by a former High School official would ease the Court's wariness and shore up their I.D. documentation.

Scottie went to Lexington High School to see if anybody was still there from his alumnus days who would remember him...perhaps from remembering his mother.

He had a long chat with the Dean of Administration. He had been his mother's boss. She was well remembered and sadly missed. Plus, he remembered Scottie, if only vaguely and in passing. Many of the details of their conversation confirmed Scottie's identity to the Administrator.

"Shannon Doherty, over at Probate Court, suggested I ask you to call her to confirm my identity for settling my parents' estate." He was happy to do it with a phone call, right then, as they were speaking.

When the Administrator walked Scottie out of the office, a Black student was standing in the doorway of the Principal's office. He was engaged in a conversation with the Principal. When Scottie had been a student, he didn't even know what Black people looked like. Scottie must have had a physical reaction.

The Administrator must have noticed Scottie's reaction, so he introduced Scottie to the student. "Ah, John, if I might interrupt...I'd like to introduce you to an alumnus of Lexington High School. His name is Mr. McNally. His mother, Mrs. McNally, was our school secretary before your time."

The student turned and shook the hand of Scottie. "Nice to meet you, Sir. My name is John Watkins. I was just discussing my Valedictorian Graduation speech with the Principal."

Scottie shook his hand as their eyeballs locked on to each other, each taking the measure of the other.

"It's nice to meet you, Mr. Watkins. Good luck with your speech. And your continuing education."

When the Administrator walked Scottie out to the front door, he added, "John Watkins is going to represent our school at Harvard this fall. He really is a once in a decade type of student. He'll make us all proud."

By the time all the paperwork had been collected and filed, Scottie had been in Lexington more than a month.

The remaining estate amounted to just under $100,000 in cash. Scottie had grown up in a very modest home that still had a mortgage balance at the time of his parents' deaths. After three years, and after no heir had come forward, the house had been released by the Probate Court for sale.

The estate also included a deed to his father's childhood home in rural middle Tennessee. Scottie remembered it being a couple hours south of Nashville from a visit he made there when he was a kid. The Clerk and Master told Scottie he would have to take the deed to Tennessee to find out if it had been auctioned off for back taxes by the County down there.

Scottie remembered the Tennessee farm from a childhood visit. Scottie was eight at the time.

He vividly remembered his grandfather giving him a nickel on that visit. Scottie had seen some TV Westerns where the cowboy would bite on a coin to see if it was real gold, so Scottie amused himself by biting on the coin when it was handed to him.

When Scottie bit on the coin, his grandmother reached over and slapped him across his face. Stunned into a full body freeze, Scottie then heard his grandmother say, "Don't be puttin' that in yer mouth. A filthy nggr might a touched it."

Scottie had no idea what a 'nggr' was, but it must have been bad, because they were filthy...and they warranted a hard slap across the face. At the time, a picture formed in Scottie's mind that it must be some kind of animal in the woods, down there, that gave people diseases...like a mouse or a mole.

As Scottie sat on the edge of the front porch waiting for the sting to leave his face, and listening to the sound of his grandfather rocking behind him, he heard another sound that made him look to the woods...and then up to the sky.

"Granddad? Do you hear what I hear?"

"Yes, son. Many, many years ago, back when the fire fell, the country folk in these parts all put together to build the Methodist Church...up in the oak grove, headin' toward town. The story is that a fella named Ray Brewer couldn't help bah-cuz a his city job, but he knowed a place to get some old church bells that wuz stored in some barn up near where he worked. So, that was Mr. Brewer's contribution. He brung them church bells down here, and the people built a tower for 'em.

"The Methodist Church is seven miles from here, but the hollers make like a hollered out bull horn for hearin'. Fer as I know, this is the only place in the County that can hear 'em, other than at the church, proper."

Young Scottie's enchantment by the pure and distant harmony helped to mask the pain of his grandmother's slap. "It's beautiful."

His grandfather continued. "With every blessing comes a curse, son. Them same hollers brung the sound a killin' all the way here from Nggr Holler, every time they strung one a them filthy nggrs up."

One day Scottie saw a ground hog digging a hole in the ground and spraying lots of dirt out from under itself. Scottie thought, 'Oh, that must be a filthy nggr.' He could imagine the squealing noise associated with stringing one up, but thought it was a lot of trouble just to kill a varmint. Scottie knew there was a stack of loaded rifles behind the front door for just such a purpose.

Adult Scottie thought he would make the trip to Tennessee to clean up any final legal issues associated with the deed to the old, rocky scrub farm of 65 acres...if it hadn't been auctioned off already. But he had every intention of getting in and getting out as fast as possible. Just from that one summer when he was eight, Scottie didn't have altogether positive memories of the place.

On the last night of his stay in Lexington, Scottie took a stroll across the Lexington Common. He visited the familiar and iconic statue of the farmer/minuteman...the citizen/soldier. A musket in one hand. A plow in the other. He re-read the plaque honoring Prince Estabrook, the first wounded combatant of the Revolutionary War. The fact that Prince Estabrook was a Black slave seemed to have been buried in the details of America's fight for freedom. Scottie enjoyed the irony. 'A Black slave fighting for his White master's freedom. Ha! What a way to create a country.'

The June evening was perfect in temperature and humidity, so Scottie bought himself an ice cream cone at his favorite childhood ice cream window. Then he extended his walk toward all the traffic and parked cars.

Scottie found a seat in the football field bleachers. From there, he could finish enjoying his ice cream and watch the spectacle of an outdoor High School graduation.

Scottie listened to the speech of the young Black man he had met at the Principal's office. It was full of the standard fare...find your passion...set goals...stand firmly...overcome the odds...never quit. But Scottie thought it had been eloquently assembled and delivered.

As the Valedictorian was exercising his oration skills, which included making moving-head eye contact with the crowd, Scottie noticed the speaker had stopped his moving-head eye-contact on him while Scottie was licking his ice cream cone. Scottie could tell by the facial expression that the speaker felt it was a gesture of disrespect to be eating an ice cream cone in the middle of his speech. The fact that all the parents and families were dressed in their Sunday best, and that Scottie was wearing his old navy blue work shirt and his navy blue work pants, went right over Scottie's head.

After John Watkins had frozen on the disrespectful attendee for a second, Scottie saw the look of recognition come over the speaker. Scottie thought, 'That's right, son. I'm the guy you met, before. Now, move on."

When young Watkins realized they were locked together in eye contact, he bowed his head in acknowledgment and continued in the cadence of his speech.

Having put a bow on all his errands in Lexington, Scottie made the long drive down to Tennessee. As he had done in Lexington, he got a room. It was at the only motel in the little town of his destination.

The next day, Scottie went to the courthouse with the deed and the Massachusetts Probate paperwork in hand. The Registrar of Deeds looked up the deed. It was in regular order. The taxes had been paid in advance eleven years earlier. "The money on file will have covered the taxes until next year."

Scottie figured that he had to put the property in his name in order to sell it, but he wanted to see it before committing too much energy into the selling effort. He got a map from the Registrar and headed twenty-five minutes out of town into the deep country.

Scottie remembered the long and rolling chert driveway. He drove over the unimproved dusty rubble to its end. There, he parked in front of a dilapidated building that had caved in on itself. He remembered it as the house his grandparents had lived in…and that he had stayed in…during that summer back when he was eight years old.

Scottie got out of his truck and started walking around the old home place. The nearby barn had also fallen in on itself, as had both the smoke house and the outhouse. His walk took him out to a bluff overlooking a beautiful river, 120 feet below. He found a spot between the trees where he could sit down and listen to the gurgling water through the country silence.

After absorbing the ambience, he made a wide circle to view some of the other upper property features. It was all a jumbled tangled mess, but

Scottie could see through the distracting noise of chaos to what lay beneath. And he liked what he saw. Potential.

Scottie returned to the property every day for the rest of that week and weekend. On Sunday, he made a point of sitting on the edge of the dilapidated porch. He made plans in his head all day as he listened. By nightfall, he never heard the sound of the bells from the Methodist Church. 'They must have fallen into disrepair.'

Upon waking the next morning, Scottie made a decision. 'I will make this place my home.'

The following week, Scottie made a trip to Nashville and rented a room at The Wyatt Regal Hotel. He spent a week learning the city.

On the Saturday night of his week, Scottie bellied up to the hotel bar and ordered his late night supper. While he was eating, a crowd of tuxedoed and well-dressed couples streamed into the bar, all of whom appeared to be well inebriated.

A man, who appeared to be one of the most drunk of the celebrators, wobbled up to the bar with his equally drunk wife at his side. He made a hard bump into Scottie without appearing to notice it. He raised his hand to the bartender and ordered two Vodka Martini's. The bartender said, "Right away, Dr. Higginbotham," as he turned to make the drinks.

While waiting, the inebriated patron took notice of Scottie eating his late-night supper at the bar. He drunkenly asked, "Wife kick you out?"

Scottie responded while chewing. "Yes."

The drunk patron slurringly said, "Gimme her name and number. I'll talk some sense into her. I'm the President of *The Nashville Club*. That'll make her listen to sense."

Dr. Higgnbotham's wife gave her husband a sharp elbow to the ribs. "Stop it, Darling."

Dr. Higginbotham shook his head to try and make himself one level less drunk. "You got a good lawyer, friend? That's all it'll take."

Scottie saw the door of opportunity open. "Actually, I'm in Nashville to find a lawyer..."

Dr. Higginbotham could only handle one sentence at a time, so he interrupted, "I just brought a house full of lawyers into the bar with me." He turned to see if he could signal one of them.

Scottie said, "No introductions tonight, please."

Dr. Higginbotham turned his foggy head back to Scottie. "Then tell me what you're looking for."

Scottie took an improbable chance. "I'm looking for the most politically connected law firm in Nashville that has only the most wealthy as their clients. A law firm chosen by the most wealthy...because of the firm's discretion."

Mrs. Higginbotham had turned to gaggle with another wife who had bellied up to the bar next to her. Dr. Higginbotham leaned on Scottie's shoulder and whispered a name in his ear. Then the Doctor/President was pulled away by the delivery of two Vodka martinis.

On Monday morning, with a name in hand, Scottie found the right door. Though not 'dressed,' he got an introductory meeting with a curious partner. In a very private and well appointed conference room, Scottie went straight to the point.

"I have inherited a small piece of acreage in the country. I want to establish ownership control without my name showing up anywhere in any public records. And I need a relationship with a law firm with whom I can conduct this and all my future business with equal discretion."

The partner appreciated Scottie's directness. The partner was accustomed to serving the needs of wealthy farmers who made it their *modus operandi* to dress down to feign poverty. "Money is all it takes."

It was a brief meeting. Scottie handed over the deed and the Lexington Probate Court paperwork. "I have no phone, so tell me when to come back and how much cash to bring to sign what I need to sign."

Both parties appreciated doing business the easy way. A relationship of trust was their mutual understanding. And, as it would turn out, it would be a long lasting relationship. Scottie was learning how to turn green money into results with minimal questions. Win. Win.

Scottie set up a four-season tent on the property from which he would design and build his house. The house was designed to require minimal grid electricity usage...and ultimate internal privacy.

Construction was split into phases so the whole of the plan was never known by any one contractor. And all contractors were brought in from outside the area with minimal size crews. And all contractors were paid in green money. Scottie communicated clearly that part of the *quid pro quo* was no records and a short memory. The contractors who agreed to do the work all thought they were doing business with a drug dealer.

The most unique feature of the house was a large, underground, ventilated room, designed specifically to grow all things green. In the event of the Apocalypse...vegetables. In the event of an economic crisis...marijuana or some other illicit drug. Scottie like to keep his options open by designing multipurpose uses. And all of it was designed to hinder prying eyes.

Scottie had ingrained the importance of privacy into his being over the previous decade. Or however long it had been.

2.3 MINING FOR GOLD

Scottie extended one of his February shopping trips to Muscle Shoals, Alabama, for a face-to-face with a Black dentist he had found on the internet...from Miss Dolly's house...while he was doing service maintenance and updates on her computer.

"My nephew is marrying a Black woman out in California this summer. It's a second marriage for both of them. She has a twenty-something son who is coming to my house to stay for a couple weeks this month.

"Her son has a grille of gold that his mother said she doesn't want in the wedding pictures. Her son is going to be a groomsman. I thought that as a wedding gift, I would have a dentist remove the gold and replace it with caps that are more ivory looking…"

The dentist said it would take six visits and it would be expensive. He added that he could reduce the cost by the value of the gold if he, the dentist, got to keep the gold.

Scottie said that wouldn't be necessary…that he wanted the gold to have a ring band made for his future great-nephew-in-law.

Scottie asked if the number of visits could be reduced to two visits on Saturdays. "I appreciate that the cost of overtime will be reflected in your quote. I know that putting a full day into one patient will require a relaxing vacation to the Islands next winter."

Scottie then asked if the whole procedure could be done under the table with no medical record. "My nephew said his future wife thinks the boy is going to be a famous rap artist one day, and that she coaches him, all the time, to keep anything about himself out of social media so nobody can throw shade on him when he's famous."

The dentist said he had to create a medical record for liability reasons.

Scottie said, "I'm planning on paying for this gift in green cash. I won't need a record from you…if you won't need to create a record for him."

The dentist shook his head as though this was the first time anybody had ever suggested such a thing.

Scottie said, "Take a look in his mouth to give me a firm quote. Figure the cost of not creating a medical record into your quote."

By the beginning of March, Robert had no more gold grille...plus a new rack of white teeth like a movie star. All porcelain. One all-day Saturday to remove the gold and prepare his existing teeth for the porcelain caps and the dentist taking a mold, then the second Saturday to have the new caps installed.

Robert had shown up to both his all-day appointments, in addition to his 'price-quote' appointment, with a 'broken nose' cast taped to his face. Scottie didn't want there to be any physical recognition issues.

After the second Saturday appointment, the dentist asked Scottie, "Shouldn't his nose be healed by now?"

Scottie put his finger to his lip to indicate silence. "Remember...his mother doesn't want any recognition of past deeds for when he's famous."

The dentist, with his technician standing next to him, said, "We know who he is..." causing an adrenaline rush to surge through Scottie's body.

Then the dentist added, "But we have no desire to know anything about who *you* are." The technician gave Scottie what he interpreted to be an approving smile. Scottie thought, 'The Underground Railroad is alive and well.'

In the month of March, Scottie used his experience with the dentist in Muscle Shoals to propose a like transaction with a dentist in Memphis that Scottie had also found on-line. The dentist's office was on the same road as the Memphis FBI office. Scottie was not afraid to use the 'nobody would be stupid enough' disguise. Except for the one-way, three-and-one-half hour car trip via State Highways, it all went the same as Robert's procedure. Except there was no recognition through the 'broken nose' cast.

In the first week of April, Scottie drove two baggies containing a group of gold alloy nuggets to a jeweler in Nashville. He gave the jeweler two ring sizes and asked that the initials 'MD' and 'RS' be stamped into the outside of the respective bands. Scottie was told he could pick them up in a week.

When Scottie drove to Nashville to pick up the finished ring bands, he thought, 'The boys should have *one* reminder of the life they are growing away from.' Scottie knew his gesture had a potential downside.

2.4 FATHER KNOWS BEST

"Loquisha" Davis was known to be a take-charge leader by the time she was in the First Grade.

It started out with Loquisha calling it out when the teacher would show favoritism to the boys. She was exiled to the hallway regularly, and she was left out there long enough that all teacher and administration traffic in the hallway would take notice.

The hallway punishment worked. Her reputation became known by all the adults in her North Nashville school, as well as by all the students.

By the end of that First Grade year, she was calling out the teacher for subtle cues given to those same boys in her class...cues that were undermining their self-esteem. Cues that were subtle reminders that the boys were Black, as if Black was a deficiency or handicap of some kind. Loquisha was also calling out the teacher for those same cues the teacher was communicating to the girls.

One of the girls in her First Grade class was Jacinda Jefferson. Jacinda would grow up to have a very famous household in North Nashville.

As an adult, Loquisha had become the go-to person by the television and radio media whenever a North Nashville issue was deemed worthy of wider attention. She was often titled by the media as a 'Black Organizer' or a 'Black Community Activist' or a 'Black Community Leader.' One of the wonders of television was the redundancy of showing a Black person on camera...and then referring to them as 'Black.'

By the time she became well known on Middle Tennessee television, she became referred to as 'an activist for her community.'

It seemed fitting that she became locally famous via the same medium that had made her aware of the treatment of Black people who wanted to rise above the slavery that continued into her lifetime...one hundred years after slavery was supposedly declared 'abolished.'

The first television image that would get her attention was not police dogs, nor water canons, nor baton beatings, nor lunch counter beatings. It was something that happened the Fall before her first year of school, before that First Grade class, when she was at her next door neighbor's house. And it came from the TV that was left constantly on.

Music replacing talk on the television was what got her attention. The playing of the National Anthem got her to turn away from her playtime to look at the little black-and-white screen.

What she saw created questions, which created feelings, which created action. It was Tommie Smith and John Carlos clothed in USA jackets. They were bowing their heads with medals hanging from their necks. Their black-gloved fists were raised above their bowed heads.

Her motivation to support the unsupported, to help the helpless, to do for those who could not or would not do for themselves, all started with that image on a little black and white television. And all the questions that came from it.

"Loquisha" was *not* Loquisha's birth name. The birth name her single mother gave her was 'Jane Wyatt Davis.' As a small child, everyone called her 'Jane.'

Loquisha's first objection to her own name was when she got exposed to *Tarzan the Ape Man* television shows, and a *Tarzan* movie in the movie theater.

She dissected, with no adult help, that Tarzan was a White man living among depictions of Black men...the Apes. She felt a visceral objection to Black men, the Apes who supported Tarzan's heroics, being depicted as lesser beings...only capable of showing awe for the superior feats and intelligence of their more evolved friend.

But the White-man/Black-man dissection was not her first objection. Her first objection was Jane needing to be rescued and protected by a man. Loquisha believed the story should be that Jane could defend and save herself.

The 'Jane' objection first turned to action when Loquisha told her First Grade teacher to call her 'Loquisha' and not 'Jane.'

The teacher wouldn't do it. So, Loquisha marched into the principal's office to request a compliance mandate on her teacher.

When Loquisha was told that she had to go by the name on her school record card, Loquisha told them to change her name on the school record card.

When the office wouldn't do it, Loquisha created and participated in her first sit-in strike. She wouldn't leave the office. The office called her mother in for a conference.

The White principal told Loquisha's mother about 'Jane's' obstinance. In his presence, Loquisha's mother patronized Jane by bending over to her and telling her in a little girl's voice, "Just do what the nice principal wants, honey." Then she added, "Father knows best."

The principal cleared his throat in discomfort. Loquisha folded her arms over her chest and remained silent.

The principal told Loquisha's mother, "Jane's school record can only list her officially legal name. If no alternative resolution arises, you can go over to the courthouse and file a name-change form. Then we can change it on her school record." That was the start of negotiations at home.

After a week of back and forth, Loquisha's mother finally came home with a name-change form from the courthouse. Her mother had filled it out, "Lowkeesha Jane Wyatt Davis."

Loquisha looked at the filled in form and said, "No. That's not right."

So, Loquisha's mother went around to the neighborhood asking how to spell Loquisha. She got many variations, but the one she settled on was L-o-q-u-i-s-h-a because it was the weirdest. Her mother thought that was Loquisha's motive. The 'more different,' the better.

She came home with a new name-change form from the courthouse and filled it out in Loquisha's presence. 'Loquisha Jane Wyatt Davis.'

Loquisha looked at the form and said, "No."

Her mother had a conniption fit. Loquisha had no problem with the 'Loquisha' part. She never did. It was the 'Jane Wyatt' part that she would not abide.

Her mother went into manipulate-with-tenderness mode. "But, Jane, sweetie, I named you after the person I wanted you to be. Jane Wyatt had it all. A good husband. A happy family that had no problems. A pretty face. She lived in a nice house. I watched her every week while I was pregnant with you. She was the star of my favorite TV show, *Father Knows Best*."

Loquisha, at six years old, thought that her mother chose the name based on what she, her mother, wanted for herself. It would be decades before Loquisha realized that her mother wanted Loquisha to grow up to *be* Jane Wyatt. That her mother wanted Loquisha to grow up to be White.

Loquisha still said, "No." Her mother asked for a compromise...to leave the initials 'J.W.' and not spell out the name.

Loquisha demonstrated that she was capable of compromise and acceded to the initials being part of her official legal name. Her First Grade teacher would hate on her for the rest of that school year for having triumphed.

Loquisha's mother was concerned about her daughter's obstinance, so she talked to the Pastor about it.

The Pastor told Loquisha that the reason she's a Christian is so she can be more like Jesus. He gave her examples like "caring for sick people, and feeding hungry people, and making sure people have enough clothes and warmth for the winter, Jane."

Jane rebuked him. "Don't call me 'Jane.' My name is Loquisha."

The Pastor continued. "You seem angry, Loquisha. Jesus didn't get angry."

Loquisha rebuked him again. "Oh, yes he did, Pastor. He hated people who acted religious, such as praying in public. And he hated fig trees that didn't produce fruit." Apparently, Loquisha had been listening in Sunday School.

The Pastor pastorally rebuked her. "Jesus didn't hate *anybody*, Child."

The last private words that Loquisha would ever have with her Pastor were, "Tell that to the religious people burning in hell. And tell that to the fig tree that he killed."

Loquisha then demonstrated that, even from her young age, she knew how to leave a room.

Loquisha's activism took on public displays of protest from her teen years.

She hated that Henry David Thoreau was White, but his writing became written in her soul. *Civil Disobedience*. With a dictionary by her side, she first read it in Middle School. It became the foundation of her appreciation for writers, and those written about whom she admired more, like Angela Davis, and Malcolm X, and Huey P. Newton, and

Bobby Seale. She appreciated the heart and methodology of Martin, but she wanted to see change in her lifetime.

Loquisha became a preacher in her community on issues that included civil-rights-demand techniques and strategies, rough policing and over-policing by White cops in Black neighborhoods, rejecting the slavery mindset of 'go along to get along,' stopping 'broken-windows' policing for getting Blacks into the court system as a way to effect the mass incarceration of Blacks, the subjugation of Blacks through employment loopholes such as underemployment in relation to Black education and skill-sets, and resumé rejections based on Black name recognition…to name a few.

Loquisha's rhetoric and her demanding actions would keep most people from seeing the underlying content of her character. Were it not for her skin color and that her truths were an affront to Whites and the White Supremacist mindset, she would have been recognized as the embodiment of Jesus Christ, Himself. 'But then,' she would reason, 'people who call themselves Christians wouldn't still be in church unless it was because they didn't know who Jesus was, yet.'

"I ain't gonna be no fig tree that don't produce no fruit. Come hell or high water, I'm gonna get results." Her best hope for being 'nearer my God to Thee' would become, "What you did for the least of these…"

2.5 CHASING RABBITS

After a winter spent largely indoors, plus a mostly rainy introduction to Spring, Michael and Robert were getting restless. They watched as the rabbits got cautiously close to the outer room picture window to nibble on the fresh green popping up between the rocks in the driveway and in the front yard area.

Scottie was aware of the boys' need to stretch their legs. He knew it would help them get back into the groove for the coming season of property maintenance.

"Why don't you two get out and get some air? It's getting to be time to be outdoor workers again. Keep a watchful eye out for people."

Michael and Robert checked the temperature and retrieved a couple of light Spring jackets. Robert complained to Scottie that his arms stuck way outside the sleeves of the jacket that had fit perfectly four months earlier when it was bought.

Once outside, they saw the rabbits continuing to eat their new-shoot greens while keeping a wary eye on the boys' movements. Robert threw down a challenge to Michael. "Think you can catch one?"

Michael returned the challenge. "Think *you* can?"

The boys started circling the rabbits to come at them from opposite directions. They had not accounted for the rabbits' escape route to the sides of the boys' encirclement, nor had they ever gotten a close-up look at the speed of a rabbit.

When the rabbits made their escape in opposite directions, Michael said, "To the woods!" as he followed the several that headed in that direction. Robert was in tow.

By the time the boys got to the woods and into the hollow, they had lost sight of their prey. Robert said, "Maybe they have a hole in the ground. Look around for where they could have gone down into a hole."

Both boys started wandering around, in no particular pattern, looking for a rabbit hole. That's when Robert called over to Michael. "Hey, man. Com-ear. Look at this."

Michael came to Robert's side. They were both staring down at a new-growth fungus on the ground. Michael said to Robert, "Edible or poisonous?"

Robert said, "I dunno. Maybe we should ask Scottie."

Michael said, "If it tastes bad, it's poison. If it tastes good, it can be ett."

Robert said, "Try it and see."

Michael said, "*You* try it and see."

Robert reached down and pulled the unrooted fungus off the soil's surface from beneath the dead leaves that carpeted all of the woods. He looked at Michael. Michael looked back at him as if to say, '*You're* the one who found it.'

Robert looked at it in his hand. "If it tastes bad, I'm spittin' it out." Michael nodded his head as he watched with anticipation.

Robert nibbled at the edge of the cap. He worked the sample around in his mouth. Then, looking at Michael, he swallowed. "Doesn't taste bad."

Michael reached out to take it from Robert's hand. "Then it must be the kind you can eat." With that, Michael nibbled off a slightly bigger sample than Robert. He nibbled while he looked to the sky, waiting for a taste verdict. Then he swallowed and said, "Edible."

The boys passed the mushroom back and forth between each other until there was no cap left. Then they looked at each other about eating the stem. Michael shook his head. Robert discarded the stem into the leaves. The boys resumed their hunt for the rabbit hole.

After fifteen minutes or so, the boys were separated by twenty yards with their heads focused on the ground. But they were both losing focus on the task at hand.

Michael looked up to see where Robert had gotten off to. Robert seemed much farther away than he actually was, so Michael shouted to him. "Hey, man! It might be poisonous!"

Robert thought Michael's voice was coming to him from the ground, so he shouted back into the ground, "Why?"

Michael squinted his eyes and said in a normal voice, "There's a stem growing out of your skin with leaves growing out of the stem…fast. Quick! Pull it out!"

Robert looked at his arms and legs and body. "You're crazy, man.

There's nothing growing out of my body." Then he saw a knight in a full suit of armor. He had a giant sword. He was looking around the base of a tree. "Hey, look, man. We gotta go tell Scottie. There's a knight in the woods."

Michael looked all around, but all he saw was the Sun resting on the ground, half in the ground in the hollow. "Hey, man! Look at the Sun! It ain't burning the trees down, man. Whadaya make a that?"

Robert was watching the foraging knight, but turned away to make a circular scan for the Sun. "I don't see the Sun, man. Where you looking?" Robert then saw plants growing, right before his eyes, out of the ground and around tree trunks, then talking to each other. "Hey, man, let's get outta here. There's some weird sht happening. We gotta go tell Scottie."

Michael was already running in fear. He was heading straight back to the house. Robert was on Michael's heels, but he wasn't running. He was riding on the back of a rhinoceros. The rhinoceros kept turning its head back to Robert, saying, "Faster, Robert! Faster!"

Scottie was returning to the house from the sheds when he saw the boys running. He assumed they saw a trespasser in the woods and were rushing back to the house to hide. Scottie ran to meet them at the door. Scottie asked worriedly to both boys, "Is there someone in the woods?"? Robert said to Scottie, "You saw him, too?"

Scottie said, "Whom? Saw whom? Whom did you see in the woods? Who's coming?"

Michael was being held up by a giant, slimy slug, moving up one side of his body, and a talking tree on the other side. "Help me, Scottie! Help me! Get these things off me!"

Scottie looked at Michael to try and answer his concerns. "What things?"

Robert said, "Scottie, climb on board, man. This buzzard is cool to ride. Get on man. We're flying over the earth. I see oceans and islands.

Get on man. It's cool."

Scottie realized the boys were hallucinating. "Did you boys find some mushrooms in the woods? Did you eat some mushrooms?"

Michael said, "Here, Scottie. You have some, too." He reached his arm toward Scottie to offer him some slithering worms that he had taken out of his mouth, but were now squirmingly emerging from deep inside the palm of his hand. "Eat these, Scottie."

Scottie took Michael by the arm and led him in to the couch in the inner sanctum. He covered Michael in a blanket and set his head under a cushion. "Just lie here and relax. Don't be afraid. I'll be right here if you need help." He then went out to retrieve Robert.

He led Robert by the arm into his bedroom. There, he peeled back the blanket. He helped Robert rest his head on Scottie's pillow. Then he covered him with the blanket. "Just relax, Robert. I'm not going anywhere. I'm here for you. Everything's gonna be alright." Then he went back to check on Michael.

For the next two hours, Scottie made trips between the two boys. He was taking their temperatures and using a cool washcloth to wipe away any sweat that would develop on their foreheads. And he listened to them.

When Robert would say he was scared, Scottie would say, "You're OK, Robert. I'm right here. Even if you can't see me, I'm here. You're not going anywhere. I'm not going anywhere. Nothing bad is going to happen to you. You'll be fine. Everything's gonna be alright."

When Michael would snap his body back like he was trying to get away from something or someone, Scottie would put a gentle but firm hand on his shoulder. "I'm right here, Michael. Tell whatever you see that it can't hurt you. Nothing can hurt you unless you let it. Don't pay attention to any fear. I'm here with you. Tell whatever you see that you're not scared."

When Michael would change to being in awe and wonder, Scottie would say, "If it's beautiful, enjoy it. I'm right here, Michael. Fully enjoy it. Just relax and enjoy it as long as it stays with you."

When Robert would be in awe and wonder, Scottie would share the same assurances as he had shared with Michael.

The boys' visions stopped coming after those two hours. Later, they recounted their hallucinations to Scottie.

Scottie said, "The psychedelics in the mushroom opened some doors in your mind that you don't usually get to see into. And don't fear the psychedelics. There's no psychedelic on earth that is addicting…that will make you feel the physical need to do it again.

"Everything your brain did in presenting these things to you, whether it was inspiring or fear-inducing, was there for you to accept as it is. Don't try to analyze. Just know that everything you saw, whether good or bad, whether happy or frightening, was there for you to acknowledge and accept."

Robert was reticent. "Why would I accept something that was scary and couldn't have come from my own brain? My own brain has never seen those things…or even known they exist."

Scottie said, "Contributions to your brain can come from far beyond your personal experience. Both of you have an opportunity to grow and heal from the good and the bad. If you reject something you didn't like, you'll miss the opportunity to be healed by it and to grow from it."

Robert was still skeptical. "How am I going to be healed by seeing some being that is trying to kill me…that's holding my wrist at the edge of a cliff and trying to find a way to throw me into spikes bigger than trees…a mile below me?"

Scottie shook his head. "I don't know. I only know that accepting what is is how you get past it controlling you. The ultimate fear for many people, especially young people, is death. If someone were trying to kill you and you accept that, can they control you anymore with your fear of death? If they're going to kill you, that's not about you. That's about them. The thing that's about you is whether or not you're going to let them make you fear something. Try these ideas: What is, is...Whatever will be will be...I will put no energy into the things I cannot control."

Robert was nodding his head in understanding and agreement, but Michael had an objection. "I ain't doing it, man. If someone's trying to kill me, then I ain't gonna let 'em. If it's me or them, it's gonna be them."

Scottie had to end their talk. "Just be careful, Michael. Killing the other person would only be because you fear them or have anger toward them. And anger is rooted in fear. Killing them doesn't end your fear or your anger. Your fear or your anger will just wait for the next person to feed it. Acting on your own fear or anger will just bring what you fear or what you're angry about *to* you. In your example, it's your own death."

Scottie could see he wasn't going to enlighten Michael in that moment, so he said to both boys, "It's coming up time for bedtime reading, so let me just end with this saying: 'Be not afraid.'"

The origins of the whole ordeal made Scottie think of a more developmentally useful way for the boys to chase rabbits. He would save it for a later stage of their preparedness.

That night, they began reading Lewis Carroll's 1871 classic *Through The Looking Glass*. The boys were gobsmacked by its relevance. There was comfort in knowing they weren't the only ones who hallucinated. Also, they had never been aware of how much they wanted, or needed, a little sister. But now they felt they had one. Even if just imaginarily.

'Goodnight, Alice.'

2.6 ON THE ROAD AGAIN

Loquisha Davis had daily assaults from the likes of her former classmate, Jacinda Jefferson, and two of Jacinda's daughters, the mothers of Jamal and Muhammad. The assaults went from being whiny in nature to being pathetic inquiries into their children's and grandchildren's whereabouts and well-being.

Loquisha Davis printed an area roadmap on which she used yellow highlighter to mark road turn-off directions. Manual. No electronics.

Loquisha then, knowing she was under surveillance, stashed a wig in her purse that matched the hairdo of a friend of hers, along with sunglasses that were the same as her friend's.

She drove to her friend's house and parked off the driveway, next to her friend's car. She knocked on the door.

The surveillance officer had followed Loquisha and positioned himself out and away from Loquisha's friend's house.

Ten minutes later, a woman, who appeared to be the woman whom the surveillance officer had seen answer the door, left the house and got into her own car. The surveillance officer maintained his position to surveil Ms. Davis who, he believed, was inside the house.

While surveilling the house, the officer saw a woman appear outside the corner of the house, in the backyard, to tend to a small dog. He thought he recognized her as the woman who answered the door when Loquisha had arrived, but she was dressed differently. He called it in.

By the time the disguised Loquisha had passed by Franklin, going South on Interstate 65, a BOLO (Be-On-The-Lookout) had alerted a State Trooper to the car. He dropped way back until an unmarked State Trooper could get into position. The unmarked Trooper stayed several cars back and in the same lane so as to maintain the secrecy of his presence.

Loquisha turned off the Interstate onto several more connecting highways until she made a turn onto Highway 20 in Summertown. The unmarked Trooper remained several cars back on her tail. He was familiar with all the roads in the area to which Loquisha had driven.

Still keeping his distance, the unmarked Trooper saw her turn onto the single lane, unimproved Railroad Bed Road. The Trooper knew the road would normally have no other traffic on it in her direction of travel, and, that if he followed her, she would 'make' him.

The Trooper drove past the Railroad Bed Road and radioed it in.

Scott McNally and the boys heard the driveway alarm go off inside the house. They dashed to the video monitor to get multiple angles of the progressing visitor. None of them recognized the car.

By the time she had entered the fourth camera, Michael Dean said, "That's Miss Loquisha in a wig!"

Scottie said to both boys, "Prepare to disappear. There may be a cop passenger hiding on the floorboards or in the trunk. I'll greet her, myself. Watch from behind the solar shades. And stay on the driveway monitor in case she was followed. If she's alone, I'll wave you out.

"This is a chance to find out if you've made any progress away from your former selves...if you're on the path to life...if you're fully dead. If she notices a difference, then you're on your way to being converted from the dead to the living."

By the time the boys had received the 'wave' signal, Loquisha was in high gear. "...Taming of the shrews?...Teach the lowland silverback to type?...Fix the problem?...Their culture?...Their upbringing?"

McNally presented reason. "Your racism has reared its ugly head. The goal is to make them unrecognizable...untraceable. Cops will look for where the boys are comfortable. Relatives...familiar neighborhoods...the urban jungle from which they emerged.

"If they're to stay unfound, they'll have to fit in where they're *not* currently comfortable. Why is it so hard for you to accept help from someone who shares a common goal with you? Does my White skin blind you from being able to discern what's in your best interest?...their best interest?"

Loquisha looked the almost unrecognizable boys over and insisted that they each come in for a hug. She hugged Muhammad without comment, but when she hugged Jamal, she turned to Scottie and said, "What have you been feeding this boy?" Then she went back into high gear. "Ain't it like Whitey to think the way to fix a Black man is turn him White."

McNally wasn't going to beat a dead horse. "You didn't hear me."

Loquisha was still hot. "You didn't have to say a word. I can see it with my own eyes."

Scottie entreated her. "If my goal were to make them White, I would have taught them that their culture was bad...that being Black was bad. Because thinking like that is what it takes to be supremely White. Ask them for yourself if that's what I've done to them?"

Loquisha started to come down a little. "We love these boys for who they are, not for who you think they *ought* to be. If I had the ability, I'd take you down and skin you right here and now...and see how you like having to change the way you were born."

Scottie said, "They weren't born the way you love them. You love them for who they developed into being. They're still developing. Can you not love them anymore? Or did they have to freeze in time in order to keep earning your love?"

Loquisha had dropped her head and was shaking it. "You make me sorry that I ever brought them here. I'm sick over it. I want a do-over. And that's what I'm gonna get."

Loquisha looked at the boys. "Why are you just standing there? Come on. I'm sorry I did this to you. I'm gonna save you from this hell-hole...this concentration camp...this brainwashing experiment of this madman."

The boys looked at each other and took some false half-steps forward, and then back, still looking back and forth at each other.

Loquisha asked, "Has he weakened you so much that you can't do what's good for you? Muhammed? You coming? Jamal?"

Michael was the first to speak. "I'm sorry, Miss Loquisha. We've come too far to go back."

Loquisha looked at Robert. "What about you, Jamal? You under his spell, too?"

Robert answered her. "Jamal is not my name anymore, Miss Loquisha." Then he couldn't look at her anymore. He dropped his head toward the ground. He still couldn't look at her. He started slowly and sadly shaking his head. Then everyone heard him mumble, "Too far."

Loquisha turned to McNally. "You *are* the devil."

Scottie allowed that. "Perhaps that's true. But I've never heard of the devil having good intentions...which would make neither one of us the devil."

Loquisha would not be swayed. "The road to hell is paved with good intentions."

Scottie said, "You're on a mission for their grandma...for their mothers. You've come to get answers for the women who raised them and love them. The answer you must bring back to them is that the boys are gone. Dead. Otherwise, they *will* be gone. Dead."

The boys had tears rolling down their cheeks and were squeezing their eyes to try and make it stop.

Loquisha said sternly, "Why are you boys cryin'? You've made your choice."

McNally responded to Loquisha. "They're crying at their own funeral. They're afraid that you're going home to give them away. How much do you think they want a new life if they're willing to never see the ones they love the most, ever again?"

Loquisha said, "I wasted a day and a trip. And who knows if anyone was onto me."

McNally told her, "If they were close on you, they'd have been here by now. You did well with the friend's car and the disguise. But if they've figured out the direction of your journey, then I have to be like the angel of God that said to the Three Wisemen, 'Go home a different way."

Scottie retrieved a pad of paper and a pencil. Then he drew directions, including distances between turns.

"This will take you out of here toward the south on The Trace. Then you'll turn off the Trace and take a right onto the 64 Highway ramp *after* the bridge. That will get you going East. Don't turn off 64 East until you get to Interstate 65 North. Stay on that until you recognize where you are, back in Nashville."

2.7 PRIDE AND PREJUDICE

During her Senior of High School, MaryLou Watkins' was in a Winter play that won the Tournament of Classes. She had also been named 'Best Actor' from that Tournament. Then she had been given an individual bow after her solo performance in a piece performed by the Madrigal during the Winter Choir Concert.

Those recognitions, plus her audition performance, made the choice easy for the Casting Committee on the Spring Musical. They selected MaryLou Watkins to play the lead character of Eliza Doolittle in the Werner and Lowe Broadway classic, *My Fair Lady*.

April was the perfect month for the last big act of MayLou's Senior year. On the final night of the performances of *My Fair Lady,* John and Jackie Watkins had been pinned with rose boutonnieres before they entered the auditorium. That was after they had spent a couple of months listening to MaryLou practice her songs and her lines up in her bedroom, sometimes accompanied by other cast members. John and Jackie Watkins thought they might have more anticipation for this final performance than even MaryLou.

After the performance, for which the crowd had gone wild, and who had made especially loud whoops and hollers, then a long standing ovation when MaryLou took her individual bow, John and Jackie were waiting outside the auditorium for their daughter. Among the congratulateers were fellow parents, the Croftons and the Mayberrys.

To his congratulations, Eric Crofton added, "Lowe and Werner did a great job reconstructing George Bernard Shaw's *Pygmalion*. And, let's face it, if Shaw could convince us that a statue can come to life and be human, then no-one should have a problem with Eliza Doolittle becoming White."

Then Don Mayberry added, "MaryLou was fantastic. She was not only convincing that a poor beggar can be trained to fit into high society, but that a *Black* poor beggar can be trained to be *White* to fit into high society. You both should be very proud."

Both John and Jackie had the social graces to not show their disdain for those two parents seeing the whole play...and their daughter...in racial terms.

For John Watkins' part, the opining parents had created an echo that began etching a permanent mark into his brain. 'A poor *Black* beggar can be trained to be *White* to fit into high society...a poor *Black* beggar can be trained to be *White* to fit into high society...'

John's echo was interrupted when MaryLou came out from the classrooms behind the stage that had been used as dressing rooms. She made her way to her parents through a sea of other parents complimenting her on her performance. Her parents were aglow from their beaming-with-pride delight.

After all the hugs and gushing from her parents, MaryLou said, "I'm going to ride with Margeaux Littlefield to the cast party, and she can give me a ride home. So, you don't need to wait up for me. I love you so much for being here. Now go home and get a good night's sleep."

Jackie gave MaryLou a shoulder-hug and said, "OK, Lou. Have fun."

John interjected, "Be safe, Lou. And watch out for paparazzi and autograph hunters."

MaryLou had a little laugh of delight to herself. 'Autograph hunters? *There's* one of the joys of having old parents.'

The ringtone for Metro Nashville sounded on Watkins' phone. 'Pretty late on a Saturday night for a call from *them*.'

Watkins directed the State Police Special Agent. "Put out a BOLO for the car and the license plate, as well as for the McNally vehicles and license plates. If McNally's smart, he'll send her back to Nashville a different way than she went. There's a straight line, from South to North, from McNally's place to Nashville. It's the route through Centerville. Give our boys on that route a special encouragement."

While Agent Watkins and Jackie were driving home above the speed limit, John was thinking that the racially charged comments from his two fellow parent-neighbors displayed some respectable knowledge of the cross between literary playwrights and popular culture. Then he thought, 'I should have expected nothing less from my neighbors. A college education exposes people to information other people don't usually get...and our upscale, White suburban town is *filled* with college graduates.'

The thought of their literary knowledge made Watkins' mind turn to reviewing his memory of all the books on Scott McNally's bookshelf. Watkins had the pictures emblazoned onto the visual cortex of his brain:

The Complete works of William Shakespeare;
Atlases, including a photo album of The World From Above;
Audubon books on flora, fauna, birds, reptiles, and minerals;
The Power of Mathematics;
Electrical Engineering and Fundamentals;
Auto and Auto-Body repair;
Mechanical Devices and How They Work;
Incredible Cross-Sections of Machines;
Mark Twain;
The Great poets;
Moby Dick;
Mutiny on the Bounty;
Pygmalion..."

That echo was still pinging off the envelope of John Watkins' mind. 'A poor *Black* beggar can be trained to be *White* to fit into high society...a poor *Black* beggar can be trained to be *White* to fit into high society...a poor *Black* beggar can be trained to be *White* to fit into high society...'

The etch of the echo was getting deeper with every ping.

The town of Collinwood was twenty minutes South, using the Trace, from McNally's house. John Watkins had told the head State Trooper to put extra attention on the *North* route back to Nashville.

Collinwood had an access road to The Trace that was a frequent meeting place for Park Rangers, and State Police, and Wayne County Sheriff and Police cars for donuts and coffee and conversation.

When the BOLO came over the radio, there were three police vehicles parked at the Collinwood entrance to The Trace. A Tennessee State Trooper, a Wayne County Deputy Sheriff, and the Park Ranger. They were all parked side-by-each with their windows down so they could have conversation with each other. They all listened attentively as the BOLO announced the person's description, then all the vehicles and plate numbers.

The Deputy said, "Three plates and vehicle descriptions? That's a little like scrambled eggs."

The State Trooper said back to him through their open windows, "Don't worry about it. We're looking for a Black lady to drive by. The vehicle doesn't matter."

The Park Ranger laughed. "That's true. It'll make an I.D. easier. If there's a Black lady driving down this stretch of The Trace, it'll have to be her."

As the Law Enforcement Officers were bantering about her, Loquisha Davis was driving South on The Trace and was about five minutes from that meeting of the Brotherhood.

The band of brothers stopped every conversation they were having whenever a car approached from the North. "Nope. White. Not her."

Scottie knew The Trace like the back of his hand. Loquisha turned off The Trace and onto the 64 Highway one exit before she would have encountered the socializing guardians of a well-ordered society.

When Loquisha pulled into her friend's driveway to return the friend's car, she noticed an unmarked stake-out car watching. Not a minute after she had walked into the friend's front door, the surveillance car and two Metro patrol cars blocked the driveway from Loquisha's car leaving.

Loquisha closed the door behind her, took off her wig, and traded clothes back with her friend...all before her friend answered the knocks at the door that were accompanied by a loud voice shouting, "Police! Open up!"

Loquisha was still in the friend's bedroom freshening up when her friend opened the front door. "Yes, Officer? How may I help you?"

"We want to talk to Ms. Loquisha Davis." The surveillance cop was looking up and down the friend with a disturbed look on his face. "Did you just pull in the driveway from taking a trip in your car?"

"Why, yes, I did Officer. And to what do I owe the honor of you stalking me? Looking for a Black lady friend, are you? You kinky little thing?"

Loquisha walked to the door from the bedroom. "Your dog, Sasha, didn't give me a bit of trouble while you were gone, Honey." Loquisha kissed her on the cheek. "Call me tomorrow and tell me how things worked out with your boyfriends, here."

Loquisha walked out between the officers. As they watched her approach her car, she turned back to them and said, "Could you boys move your cars for me. I'm needing to get back to my own house to feed my own pet cat. Her name is *Tabitha*...if any of you are interested in that kind of information for your report."

It was 2AM on Sunday morning when Agent Watkins joined TBI Special Agent Ben Waters in debriefing the Metro surveillance team leader and the Tennessee State Police undercover boss.

The Tennessee State Police undercover Officer in Charge explained, "If my man had followed her down the Railroad Bed Road...that road is so rural and under-travelled...my man would have been 'made' right away. And that would have led to the target diverting away from her intended destination. By choosing to not pursue down the Railroad Bed Road, we kept our surveillance secret. It is clear that we would have lost the intended destination of the target no matter which course of action we chose. My undercover made the right choice...in that he preserved the integrity of our secret surveillance."

Watkins asked the nearby Metro Task Force Officer, "Has your surveillance been re-set at the Loquisha Davis house?"

"Yes, Sir."

Agent Watkins turned to TBI Agent Waters. "She outsmarted us."

All TBI Agent Waters could say at that early hour was, "*Damn* it!"

Watkins saw the connection between the proximity of the Railroad Bed Road to the McNally property. Watkins assumed she went to McNally's house to pick up the boys, or to trade information with McNally about the boys, or that the visit had *something* to do with the boys. 'Surely, she didn't go there to cuss him out again.' Watkins felt that he knew his unknowns. The pride of his 'gut feeling' having been right about McNally was welling up inside him.

Watkins turned to TBI Agent Waters and patted him on the shoulder. "Don't worry about her outsmarting us. We just got our justification for a search warrant on our friend, McNally's, property."

The next day, Loquisha made a circuitous trip near Jacinda's Jefferson's apartment. She stealthily made her way to, and entered through, the back door. After turning the volume up on the TV in the house, she spoke below the volume of the TV to all the women.

"The man I had brought them to said the boys took off on their own six months ago, right after I dropped them off, and he hasn't heard a thing about them since."

2.8 PEEPING TOMS

After the suspected trip of Loquisha Davis to the McNally property, Agent Watkins worked through the night with the Task Force on defining the scope of their search warrant. Watkins was waiting for his FBI Boss to return his call.

"Boss, we have probable cause for a search warrant on the person and the property of the guy I interviewed about receiving a visit from the Black Community Activist lady the night of the Mark Johnson murder.

We believe she visited him again, yesterday. That's the probable cause to search McNally's property to see if we can uncover why she traveled there."

His boss challenged him. "You *believe* she visited him?"

"Yes, Sir. Surveillance spotted her absence from where she was supposed to be, and car tracking surveillance followed to within twenty minutes of the target property."

"Twenty minutes of drive-time, John? How many possible destinations are there in a twenty minute circle from where she was dropped by surveillance?"

"I get your point, Sir. But that circle is extremely rural. Not many choices of where to go. And she's a person who never leaves Nashville."

"OK. Good enough. I need some movement on this case as much as you do."

Watkins continued with his original purpose. "My instant access to all the people I need to push this through has evaporated over time. I'm calling to ask you to get our DOJ lawyer back on the case, and for him to re-energize the Tennessee Attorney General. The sooner we can get this approved and back from the judge, the better."

Watkins had told his Task Force team that he believed "this McNally guy is way smarter than he appears, which is why we need to focus on the details of this comprehensive warrant.

"If he's housing the perps, he's got to buy groceries, make other purchases, such as clothing. We'll get new bank records so we can track down receipts to see how many people he's buying for.

"Phone location history can be matched up with receipts to see if he's doing any 'off the debit card' purchases. Trips and purchase receipt locations should all match up."

The team worked out a schedule of warrant targets:

    any and all bank accounts;

open-ended telephone data for numbers and locations visited;

computer hard-drive download;

voice monitoring of any and all telephones found to be associated with the target;

a thorough and complete search of house contents...;

the physical structures on the property...;

the whole of the property acreage;

arial surveillance resources for pre-raid intelligence;

and GPS device tracking for both vehicles.

At the end of their strategy session, Watkins told the team, "We have to be smarter than a smart guy. And the smartest thing about him is his desire to make us think he's not smart.

"When we get the arial surveillance resources in place, maybe we can get a good idea of how many people are traveling in and out...or around...that property."

Watkins and Waters briefed the physical warrant-service-team that every inch and every nook and cranny of that place was to be photographed with High Definition video cameras. "We don't want to suffer eye strain when we review the evidence. And we want *all* the evidence.

"Once all the 'pristine' photo and video evidence in collected, tear the place apart. There is no clue too small. There is no item that is not of interest. There is no back corner of any back draw of any cabinet that does not warrant your enthusiasm."

When the search warrant approval came back 'Authorized,' Watkins called his Boss.

"Thanks, Boss. We're moving on it. Fingers crossed that this guy is the Mastermind."

His boss responded, "If we can't do better than 'fingers crossed,' John, then we shouldn't be in this business."

2.9 SYMPATHY FOR THE DEVIL

After things had settled down from Loquisha Davis' tumultuous visit to the McNally back-country, Robert asked Scottie, "Is what Miss Loquisha said true? Are you turning us White? Is that your whole plan, here?"

With Michael paying close attention, Scottie answered. "When Miss Loquisha made her ill-advised visit, you heard that her primary objection to the seven or eight months that you've been here, so far, was that I was changing you from who you were into someone who she didn't like. She liked you before. She doesn't now. I hate to say it so plainly, but that's the proof that we're on the right track."

Michael said, "What about the 'turning us White' stuff? I do feel like I'm not as Black as I used to be. Like I might not be welcomed back into my own neighborhood."

Scottie said, "You're using the language about a dead person as though that person is still living. Your concern about 'changing' is the proof that we're heading in the right direction. If your old neighborhood wouldn't welcome you back, it would be because they don't recognize you...which is our goal.

"Look. You're Black. You're always going to be Black. The way you speak or the things you can converse about will never change that you're Black. You'll know that for sure when you start driving again.

"The fundamental question is whether or not you're recognizable as the former Black man you once were, or if you're *unrecognizable* because of the new Black man that you've become.

"Both of you...sit down. I want to tell you about why you'll always be Black."

All three of them took their seats around the dining room table.

"White people have thought they are in charge of Black people for four hundred years, ever since White people started packing Black people into the cargo hold of ships in the most inhumane conditions imaginable. You should know that America is named for the slave trader, America Vespucci.

"That gross act of anti-Christ inhumanity called slavery is what established the Whites as Supreme over Blacks.

"It took 250 years, but good and decent folk finally put their lives on the line to stop the inhumane and anti-Christ institution of slavery.

"In that war, which is called the Civil War, the good and decent folk declared victory. But the forces of evil were't erased. They were allowed to re-establish their evil empire. That should be a lesson for the future.

"The very definition of a Confederate…as in Confederate soldiers and their supporters, even into today…is a Pro-Slavery White Supremacist. It's the *definition* of a Confederate. And they exist and flourish, today. Right now, while we're talking.

"Up until Lyndon Johnson signed two major civil rights laws, they were called the 'Dixecrats.' As in Dixie Democrats. They were the ones who continued slavery after it had been outlawed. They were the ones who wrote the Jim Crow laws. They were the ones who erected Confederate statues all over the country to honor inhumane and anti-Christ behavior. Full-throated White Supremacy.

"But when they got mad at Lyndon Johnson, they left the Democratic Party and infiltrated the Republican Party. And the Republicans welcomed them in. And you, today, suffer under the jackboot of White Supremacy because adding new party members was more important to the Republicans than making them pass a morality test.

"That's why, today, the Republican party is the White Supremacist Party. If they *allow* it…they *are* it.

"Human beings honor what they respect. They honor what they

strive in their hearts to be. In our very own state of Tennessee, the White lawmakers and the White governors have established state laws saying that we have to honor Pro-Slavery White Supremacist Confederate leaders four times a year...and that the Governor has to sign the proclamations honoring those anti-Christers four times every year...while the Governor and his White Supremacist Legislators call themselves Christian. Being *Christian* is one of their campaign slogans.

"So, we in America have an entire State that officially...by the Government...honors Pro-Slavery White Supremacists. That means we respect Pro-Slavery White Supremacists. In actuality, it means we strive to *be* Pro-Slavery White Supremacists in our hearts...because we honor them."

Michael and Robert appeared engaged in this topic.

"So, your next question should be...with Whites in charge for four hundred years, how have they done?

"On the surface, the answer is 'pretty well'...*if* you're White. But if money is not the only measurement, then the answer becomes...deplorably.

"Whites have weakened our own country by debilitating entire ethnicities of people. How many medical cures have *not* been found because our system of White Supremacy has held back a Black person from becoming a doctor? How many energy solutions remain undiscovered because a Latin person has been held back from the education needed for a lucrative field of study such as engineering? How many ergonomic designs have been missed because Native Americans have been relegated to the trash heap of progress?...relegated by White Supremacist genocidal maniacs to un-funded reservations in the most inhospitable parts of our country.

"Did you know that the person who invented the blood transfusion was a Black man? And did you know that he died from not being allowed a blood transfusion at a White hospital after a traffic accident?

"That's what White Supremacy looks like. It's just a continuation of slavery. 'We'll use your contributions to our benefit, but we won't allow you to benefit from them, yourself.' I'm talking about a system that is in place today, as well as for the past four hundred years. Today.

"Whites, because they are, and always have been, in charge, are responsible for fossil fuels assaulting the air that protects our earth from being uninhabitable. America is five percent of the world population. But we put *twenty*-five percent of the world's pollution into the air. Congratulations to White Supremacy. We are Supreme in air pollution.

Whites think their interests will be eroded if they give up their Supremacy, yet by polluting our home, they use their Supremacy to commit genocide, which ultimately becomes suicide, by destroying the only home they…we…have to live in.

"Whites have been in charge of establishing a political system that is not owned by the voters of the democracy, but is owned by whoever has the most money…which is White people. In particular, the top one percent of White people.

"Good or evil means nothing. It's all about the money. You and I both, here in the State of Tennessee, sent a woman to Congress who claims she was once a welfare-receiving single mother. Today, she's moving toward being worth one hundred million dollars. And nobody asks how that happened?

"It's a result of the White Supremacy 'laws-are-for-sale' system, still in tact and thriving as we speak. And the White Supremacy politicians won't change it. Why? Because they're getting Marie-Antoinette-rich off that system. The system they created so they can get stinking rich. They are the new Plantation owners. White Supremacy in action. It's always been good for the Plantation owner. It still is."

Robert and Michael looked at each other because this definition of 'the new Plantation owner' was new to them.

"You might have to be White to have heard this, but did you know that Whites quote I.Q. score data to prove that Whites have superior intellect? What they don't tell you is that the I.Q. test, itself, was developed and is maintained by White people who come from families that have multiple generations of college graduates. Studies have found that the I.Q. test doesn't measure a person's capacity to learn. It measures the probability that the test taker is White, and that he or she is from a multi-generational family of White college graduates. The college route, by the way, which, statistically, has a wall of White Supremacy around it.

"White Supremacy is the Achilles Heel of America...and White people can't even see it."

Michael was paying attention. "What's that 'Heel' thing?"

Scottie explained, "Achilles was the greatest warrior in the war between the Greeks and the City-State of Troy. Homer. *The Illiad*.

"But Achilles had one weakness...one vulnerability that would expose him to defeat. It was a tendon on the bottom of his foot. If his enemies could attack him there, he wouldn't be able to defend himself or his countrymen. And, so, his enemies *did* attack him there. And Achilles *was* defeated...not able to protect or save his countrymen or his country.

"That's what White Supremacy is to America. An enemy could take us down in short order if they knew where to attack. And the place to attack is our national racial divisions...established and maintained by White people who fear not being in charge. White Supremacy. America's Achilles Heel."

Robert was also paying attention. "But I heard all my life that America is the most powerful country on earth. That nobody could ever beat us at war or destroy us."

Scottie was glad to hear Robert say 'us' in referring to America. "If the measure of power is missiles and bombs, that's true as of today. But the art of war is based on attacking your enemy where they're weak. Not where they're strong. And America's greatest weakness is our racial

Caste system that's been set up and is maintained by scared White people. White Supremacists. At the core of our political system. Plus, it's more likely that our Achilles Heel will be exploited from within, not from without.

"Is the definition of racism 'attributing the characteristics of a few to an entire race...ethnicity?'"

Michael and Robert looked at each other and were nodding their heads in acceptance.

"You should know that America elected a President of the United States who announced his run for the Presidency with these words: 'Mexicans are rapists and murders.'

"Those words are the *exact* definition of racism. And did his political party, as any good and decent person would have done, bar him from running because of that racist assault on humanity?

"The answer is, 'No.' His political party recognized that he was creating a special tingle in the genitals of White Supremacists. And his political party needed that special tingle in those people in order to win an election. And winning was more important than humanity, decency, or what that President would do to our country...bring it to the edge of the cliff of becoming a dictatorship...by calling for an armed assault by his White Supremacist followers.

"White Supremacy brought us to the edge of having our democracy destroyed...all to maintain our racial Caste system where they are the kings based on nothing more qualifying than the color of their skin.

"Could a child entering the First Grade understand the stupidity of that thinking? Having been a First Grader, I know the answer to be, 'Yes.' First Graders know skin color has nothing to do with ability.

"So, pity the handicapped thinker. But don't allow them to be in charge of anything. We've seen how that works out. We *all* become at risk.

"What about you two? What would either one of you call a person who insists on maintaining a system that ensures their own ultimate destruction?"

Robert answered first. "Not that smart?"

Michael chimed in, "Not the brightest light bulb in the package?"

Scottie agreed. "You're both right. We're talking about people who can't see the forest because the trees are getting in the way. They have a tragic gap in their brain function. And so, on the one hand, you must feel sorry for them for their handicap. But on the other hand, you must restore goodness by taking political power away from stupid people. Even if they can't see their own stupidity. Even if, in their stupidity, they think they're right.

"The toddler throws a tantrum when he can't have what he wants. But the adults have to be in charge of the toddlers. We need the adults to be in charge. And the toddlers need a permanent time-out."

Robert innocently asked, "So how do you end racism?"

"Here's the key to the whole debacle: Nobody is born a racist. A human being has to be *taught* to be a racist. So the question is: who's teaching everyone to be racist?

"The answer falls primarily at the feet of parents. Today's racists learned to be racist from their parents. Their parents learned it from their parents. And their parents learned it from their parents, ad infinitum.

"Sometimes, it's direct instruction. More often, it's hints and prodding for children to give the right answer to racist questions. Sometimes, it's the conversations the children overhear between the adults. And sometimes, it's as simple as the choices a parent makes about where to send their children to school, or where to go to church...or whatever other social-fraternal group with whom the parents choose to associate."

Robert broke in. "What's 'ad infinitum?'"

Scottie took a break. "'Ad,' as in additional, like one plus one plus one. 'Infinitum,' as in infinity. Put them together and it means something that keeps adding onto itself into infinity. Language has a code. Learn the code and you can decode the meaning of any word."

Michael asked, "All White people can't be White Supremacists. So, why don't the 'good and decent folk,' as you called them, tell their neighbors and their friends to stop being that way? And why don't they elect good and decent people into office instead of electing the White Supremacists?"

Scottie was visibly saddened by his answer before he spoke it. "White people who are not White Supremacists fail to realize that their silence and their failure to take political action against the morally depraved makes them White Supremacists, themselves. 'If you *allow* it…you *are* it.' Their silence makes them complicit. Their silence makes them accessories to the crime. Their silence makes them Fake Christians."

For some reason, that answer saddened Robert, also.

Then Michael broke in. "You've said that we're racist just like White people. How can that be?"

Scottie corrected him. "I never said you're racist just like White people. I said that you and White people are both racist. The key difference is that your racism is less consequential than White racism. That's because Whites are in charge of the systems of government. That means they can use the levers of political power to inflict meaningful pain with their racism. As a minority, all you can do with your racism is be a nuisance.

"A famous movie had a famous line in it. 'The greatest trick of the Devil was convincing everybody that he doesn't exist.' It's no coincidence that in this analogy the Devil and White Supremacy are the same thing. And the greatest trick of White Supremacists is their constant effort to tell people that White Supremacy doesn't exist. I mean, why would anybody fight something that doesn't exist? Why would anybody write laws to abolish something that doesn't exist? It's the greatest trick of the Devil. And today, this very day, we live in a system set up by and administered by the Devil. Which is the White Supremacists. Which, they will tell you, doesn't exist, even though here in Tennessee, we are required to honor the Devil four times per year. And it's our Christian Governor and our Christian Legislators who are the Devil's handmaidens.

"And if you need examples of White Supremacy being real in America, look to a 1909 court case in which a Lebanese immigrant saw that opportunities were only open to Whites, so he sued in Federal Court to have Lebanese people legally declared White. The court agreed to legally define people of Lebanese decent to be White.

"Then, in that same year of 1909, an Armenian immigrant sued in a *different* Federal Court for *Armenians* to be legally declared White. He won his case, thus legally making people of Armenian decent White.

"Why would people go through all that trouble in court unless not being White was the consequential excluder of one's ability to be successful in America?"

Robert broke in. "Then maybe Black people should sue to be legally declared White." Michael laughed out loud.

Scottie ignored the comic relief. "Today, right now, this very day, people in Black families who can pass for White are considered having won the Golden Ticket. And in many cases, they venture out into White society, keeping their Black roots a secret so they can enjoy the privileges and freedoms of being White. That's real. How clear does it have to be that it's only the Devil or a stupid person who will tell you that White Supremacy doesn't exist today? Right now. This very minute.

"When slavery was so-called 'abolished,' White Supremacists weren't going to stand for it. Jim Crow laws were established by the Confederates and their descendants. Those laws allowed for every human indignity to be visited upon Black Americans without consequence to the White criminals that hid behind Jim Crow laws. Jim Crow is how White

Supremacists said, 'We can make you wish you were never set free. We can make you believe you had it better when you were a slave.

"Right here, in the very town where you're being domiciled, the local newspaper publishes pictures of meetings of the Sons of the Confederacy and the Daughters of the Confederacy throughout the year. Over and over, again. The newspaper goes so far as to quote participants as saying, 'It's a fact that many slaves said their life was better when they were slaves.'

"How much proof does a person with a functioning brain need in order to see that White Supremacy is not some secret society the hides in secret meetings. White Supremacy is put on display and celebrated right up front...right in public...for all to see...just like lynchings.

"Pity the fool who says White Supremacy doesn't exist. But don't let the fool be in charge.

"And the Jim Crow laws of the White Supremacists went far beyond indignities such as riding only in the back of the bus, or not being allowed to drink from White-Only public drinking fountains, or not being able to use White-Only public restrooms, or not being able to eat in White-Only public restaurants, or not being able to swim in White-Only public swimming pools.

"White Supremacy went *far* beyond defining public amenities and recreational opportunities as White-Only. It made it legal to torture and mutilate Emmett Till, and to publicly hang and have your picture taken with the hanging corpse of thousands of Blacks, including Thomas Shipp, Abram Smith, Will Brown, and Jesse Washington.

"The photography parties that accompanied those lynchings included Sheriffs, and Mayors, and all the City Leaders dressed in their fine suits to be in the photos with the swinging corpses.

"There are over 14,000 documented cases of lynchings of Blacks in America. And that's only the *documented* number. The real number would be thousands upon thousands higher.

"Then came the likes of Ronald Reagan who, as Governor of California, ran the whole state as a White Supremacy police state. He was responsible for policies using the police to 'stop and frisk' every Black male who dared show his face on a public street. And it wasn't a gentle 'stop and frisk.' It was done to intimidate and make subservient every Black male in California.

"Ronald Reagan can be given credit for being a primary cause for the rise of the Black Panthers. The Black Panthers formed their social fraternal organization for the purpose of providing community services to their community...because the White Supremacy government of Ronald Reagan wouldn't take care of the neediest Californians if they were Black.

"Then, when Reagan was President, Nancy Reagan added her hand of White Supremacy into the national scene by championing a War on Drugs that was designed to round up and incarcerate massive and disproportionately huge numbers of Black people. And *that* White Supremacy strategy of mass incarceration of Blacks was continued and strengthened before Reagan by the likes of Richard Nixon, and after Reagan by the likes of George H.W. Bush, both of whom championed the same kind of laws to put as many Blacks in prison as possible. 'Law and order.' Of course none of those Presidents were racist...because they were all friends with Sammy Davis, Jr."

Robert and Michael looked at each other. Robert spoke up. "Who is Sammy Davis, Jr?"

"He was a Black entertainer who was elevated as a token to show America that we are not a White Supremacist country. 'See? We got us one who is friends with the President.'

"To move on, there is a White Supremacy narrative that Black single mothers exist because Black men are deadbeat philanderers. Nobody seems to acknowledge that the largest group of welfare-supported poor in America is single White mothers. But why ruin a good narrative with the facts.

"One of the effective tools of White Supremacy is the denial of employment opportunities to Blacks...or to only allow them to be one-dollar-per-hour garbage collectors. See the history of Memphis, Tennessee, for that truth.

"Under-employment and denial of employment is where the cycle of Black single mothers begins. With no job, a man can't support a family. *With* a husband, a mother can't collect support benefits from their government. The White Supremacy system is set up so, that to feed her children, a Black woman must *not* have a husband.

"The cycle of White Supremacy says not to employ a Black because they're uneducated. Yet education is denied to Blacks as a result of keeping Blacks segregated in their own communities...communities that are kept poor by job exclusion. And a poor community has no tax revenue for schools. See how the White Supremacy system is kept in place? It's a cycle. How educated do you have to be to see it?

"The White Supremacy mantra says that Blacks are just animals. Their proof is that 87% of violence on Blacks is committed by other Blacks. But they fail to tell you that 90% of violence on White people is committed by White people. Who's the animal now?

"White Supremacy arguments for the rightness of White Supremacy are all false. And yet there is an entire eco-system of media that exists for the purpose of perpetuating these false arguments. And the most ignorant Americans flock to those media sources because it reinforces their own willful ignorance. 'It can't be wrong if all my friends believe it.'

"When I was a kid, my mother used to ask me, 'Would you jump off a cliff just because Johnny is doing it?' At age five, I completely understood the logic behind that question. And yet a huge mass of Americans jump off the cliff every day by following media liars. And the lies become self-reinforcing.

"The lies work because a person without knowledge is not armed to call them false. In the words of a famous White capitalist, 'In all thy getting, get understanding.' Do you understand? Do you understand that ignorance is the only thing that allows White Supremacy to be sustained?

"Pity the ignorant. But don't follow them off the cliff.

"In the 1968 Summer Olympics in Mexico City, Tommie Smith won the Gold Medal in Track and Field, and John Carlos won the Bronze. After having their medals hung around their necks on the awards platform, they both bowed their heads and raised their fists during the playing of America's National Anthem. It was a protest against America's system of White Supremacy. They knew they were taking their medals home to a place where they could be killed or imprisoned at the hands of those who were being paid to protect and serve them. Over all the decades between then and now, has the White Supremacy system in America been dismantled?...or properly outlawed to the point of its vanishment?

"No. The lawmakers of this country don't denounce White Supremacy. Instead, they *elevate* White Supremacists.

"On his last day in office, a Secretary of State of the United States of America sent a message out to America via social media: 'AMERICA IS *NOT* A MULTI-CULTURAL COUNTRY!'

"He sent that message out to please his White Supremacist boss, the President...but he also sent it out because he, himself, is a White Supremacist. His message was a clarion call to all White Supremacist to come to his aid so he can achieve high elected office, himself...in order to represent the White Supremacists! As an elected office holder. In the Unites States Government.

"People cling to and reinforce their White Supremacy by communicating with other White Supremacists with words that tells who they are. The word 'heritage' is a common code word. 'I'm not going to call the Pro-Slavery White Supremacist Confederacy wrong. It's my heritage.' People then encode communications with the same language. 'If your *heritage* is important to you, then I'll marry you.' That's a way of saying, 'If you're a Pro-Slavery White Supremacist, then I will marry you.' The word 'heritage' is a dog-whistle. It's meant to secretly communicate that the user is a White Supremacist.

"A dog-whistle is a sound that only dogs can hear. Other common dog-whistles include *law & order*, *thugs*, and *gangs*, the *thin blue line*, *blue lives matter*.

"Blue Lives Matter' is a phrase invented by White Supremacists to express their support for police brutality against Blacks. They deny it with 'right-wing-media, George-Orwellian' double-speak. But it's plain for anybody who is not willfully ignorant to see.

"Just listen to a rally speech by a White Supremacist President of The United States. It's replete with dog-whistles. One of the scores of dog whistles he uses to stir up his base is when he starts chanting, 'Blue Live Matter.' And the dogs all gather 'round. And they all chant, 'Blue Lives Matter!'

"Look at the pictures of all that angry and ignorant chanting. When they chant it, they are saying, 'Support the police to use violence in order to keep our White Supremacy in place.'

"A denier of the fact that 'Blue lives matter' is used as a White Supremacy dog whistle is willfully ignorant. In the First Grade, I was introduced to the concept that 'one plus one equals two.' And at six years old, I fully understood it. Pity the ignorant fool who denies that one plus one equals two...or re-install them back into the First Grade for continuing education.

"Then there's the issue of Fake Christianity.

"Christianity has been used for centuries to support slavery. Even today, the most ardent and vocal White Supremacists are found in certain so-called 'Christian' churches."

Robert tried to stop Scottie by holding his hand out. "Wait a minute, there, Scottie. When you say 'Fake Christian,' you're going against what you told us about the poet, Maya Angelou.

"You told us the story of her being approached by someone who said they were a Christian, and she said, 'Already?' And that that meant she was saying that everybody is evolving into what they will become, but that nobody is there, yet."

Scottie had to pause at Robert's grammatically impressive memory. He then gently revisited the Maya Angelou conversation.

"Maya Angelou was saying that nobody should be so audacious so as to call themselves a Christian until their life is a mirror-image of Jesus, himself. That just walking down the aisle and proclaiming Jesus as their Lord and Savior is no awarding of the badge. That the badge is freely available to all, but is constructed over time and is not given by self-proclamation. And that nobody has to have ever even *heard* the name of Jesus in order for the construction of the badge to take place. Please open your Bibles to Matthew, Chapter 25."

Michael and Robert started looking at each other like Scottie was being weird.

"I'm pretending to be a preacher, fellas. You're not the only ones who can be funny."

The boys relaxed back into their state of listening.

"So-called Christians have maintained that slavery was justifiable because Blacks were only three-fifths of a human being, the other two-fifths of a Black person being a guerrilla. This was the supposed rationale for justifying enslaving them...it was because the Blacks weren't human beings. It was meant to hide the *true* reason for enslaving them...greed. Gimme more money. Gimme more money. I need unpaid people to do my work for me. Gimme more. Gimme more. Gimme more.

"So, let's get back to the so-called Christian rationale that Black enslavement is OK because Blacks are two-fifths animal.

"One of the privileges of owning a Black person was to use the women and little girls for sex-at-will. Just ask Thomas Jefferson.

"The word in the English language for that is 'rape.' Of course, it wasn't rape when it was a little Black girl because she wasn't really human, and besides...the little Black girl was the *property* of the rapist. And we all know that a person can do whatever they want with their own property.

"And the rape of Black women slaves had the same justifications. And the fact that those Black women slaves had husbands was irrelevant…because animals can't get married. There was no such thing as an official slave marriage. Animals can't marry.

"So, the Fake Christian slave owners maintained that it was OK to rape Black girls whenever the spirit moved them to do it. Because they were slaves, because they were not humans, because they were animals. This rationale seems to be ignorant of the *Christian* fact that if a person engages in sex with a non-human, it's a sex act called beastiality. Beastiality is defined as a human performing a sex act with an animal. And the Christian Bible forbids it.

"So, all these self-professed Christian White Supremacists were not only rapists, but were also performers of beastiality…according to their own definitions. They really knew how to make Jesus proud. They really *know* how to make Jesus proud.

"Today, this very day, the White Supremacists, who are Fake Christians, still think they're making Jesus proud. They think they have *already* become Christians.

"So, to say that a White Supremacist is a Christian can never be a true statement. Under *any* circumstances. The definition of a White Supremacist and the definition of a Christian makes those two things mutually exclusive. If you're one, you can't be the other.

"The only true way a White Supremacist can be called a Christian is if they add the word 'Fake' to the word 'Christian.' The true statement is said this way: 'A White Supremacist is a Fake Christian.' So, in acknowledgment that Maya Angelou was saying that we're all 'under construction,' White Supremacists calling themselves Christian is like the person who has taken an entrance exam to get into med school, then starts calling himself a doctor."

Scottie wanted to make sure Robert understood that using the term 'Fake Christian' was not a contradiction to Maya Angelou. Robert was nodding his head.

"White Supremacists like to hold up examples of a Black person who has beat the system that's rigged against them and have 'made it' in America. They use the exception as though it's the rule. These statistically rare successful Black folk are used as tokens to say, 'See? If the system were rigged, they never would have made it.' Remember Sammy Davis Jr.?

"But here is the great historical lesson of being used as a token. In 1936, Hitler was in peril of having key countries exclude themselves from his showpiece Olympic Games. The Jewish communities in the United State and Great Britain, as well as some other countries, put pressure on their governments to not participate in the German Olympics because of Hitler's threatening words against German Jews. The Jews knew that words have consequences...that words are how tyrants signal what they're going to do. And words are how tyrants amass their cult followers to do tyrannical things. This truth has been on display in America, as well.

"Hitler outsmarted them all by finding a Jewish athlete...*one* Jewish athlete...to participate in the games so he could say, 'See. We have nothing against Jews. Here's one right here on our very own Olympic team.' He was using an exception as though it was the rule. And stupid people bought it.

"The token Jew that Hitler found was a woman Fencer named Helen Mayer. And it turned out that she was no ordinary Fencer. She won the Silver Medal for Germany.

"At her awards ceremony, when the Silver Medal was hung around her neck, she stood straight up and gave the Nazi salute for the crowd and the cameras...and for her Fuhrer. Six million dead Jews later, her role as a token Jew for Nazi Germany could not be taken back.

"So, what does this mean to you?

"On the one hand, never allow a White Supremacist to use a token example as proof that White Supremacy doesn't exist.

"On the other and more personal hand, it means never allow yourself to be used as a token. The price goes far beyond what you or your fellow prisoners could possibly pay.

"If you 'make it in America,' use your success to help abolish White Supremacy. And never allow yourself to be used as a token…as an example of why White Supremacy doesn't really exist. I had to say it twice. Did you get it the second time?"

Michael was unimpressed. "We heard it the first time you said it."

"And speaking of six million dead Jews, the history of the United States has a long train of Black soldiers who laid their lives down for their country…no matter how bad their country was to them. The White Supremacist always has said that a Black person can die for their country, but if they make it home, they're still subject to the inhumanity of White Supremacy. 'To the victor goes the spoils' doesn't apply to Black Americans.

"The largest cycle of lynchings in America happened after Black soldiers returned from the nasty chemical warfare of World War I. White Supremacists felt the need to beat the pride of Blacks for having fought and died for their country back down into cowering subservience.

Another way that Black Americans have been useful to their country is by being the subjects of medical experimentation. The most famous case went from 1932 to 1972. It involved infecting healthy Black men with the Syphilis disease in order to track the long-term affects it had on the human body's organs. These men were promised 'free health care' in exchange for their participation in a 'medical study.' But the cure for Syphilis was a simple penicillin treatment. It was withheld from all the men to their deaths.

"It's harder to document the lore in the Black community about White doctors withholding curative treatments…or giving treatments to do harm to Black patients. But the response is that Black Americans, statistically, get professional health care at minuscule rates compared to White Americans. And it's not just about money. It's about fear. Fear of the White Devil. Fear of the White Supremacist. Fear of the White Supremacist doctor.

"Who would have guessed that there is an entire race of Americans who fear being seen by a doctor? A 'do no harm' doctor? Yet, that's where we are. And the data...the data...the data...says that the fear is real.

"Today, the mass incarceration of Blacks is executed via a policy made famous by Rude Giuliani. It's called 'Broken Windows Policing.' In this White Supremacists' ploy, police are used to bring as many Blacks into the court system as possible by arresting them for the most minor or for made-up crimes. And to do it as repeatedly and as dastardly as possible. It's a practice that doesn't exist in White neighborhoods. That's one of the benefits of 'Segregation now, segregation forever!' It makes it easier for the White Supremacists to know where to target their sadistic rage at someone who dares to have a different skin color than them.

"When a person appears before a judge, the introduction always includes how many times, prior to this appearance, the person has been arrested. And the judge uses the number of prior arrests as justification to send the minor offender to jail. Another Black off the streets of America. Another Black woman without a helpmate. Another Black child without a person to provide for them. And so the cycle goes.

"And there are White Supremacists who lobby for those kind of judges to be appointed...to perpetuate the system. White Supremacist organizations established to get White Supremacist judges appointed. That's how the system is self-sustaining. That's how the system is self-perpetuating.

"Then there's the issues of the great wealth of great entertainers. White people who have appropriated Black artistry as though it's their own are too numerous to list, but the list includes Elvis stealing from Check Berry. Elvis was greatly talented. But what made Elvis Elvis was the moves and the rhythms of a Black man. Which of those two men died rich?

"Tupac was an authentic Black voice. The honesty and pain of his anti-cop songs were too much for the White Supremacists. So, Robert Dole and his conservative Republican cohorts, including his White Supremacist wife, tried to outlaw Tupac's music. 'It's morally repugnant.'

"It was like living in a country where starving children who have flesh hanging off their skeletons get a response from their government that says, 'Let's criminalize people who are undernourished. Then we can get them out of our sight by putting them in jail. Out of sight, out of mind.' White Supremacy at its finest."

To Scottie's surprise, both Michael and Robert were wide-eyedly riveted by a rambling speech that Scottie thought would have ended with both boys snoring.

Robert asked, "Is there any hope for being Black in America?"

The late hour told Scottie that he had to wrap things up. "Gains have been made. Gains are being made. But until America realizes the weakness it suffers for not allowing all the cream to rise to the top, your ultimate hope is that they can't kill all of you. If there's only one of you left…there's still hope.

"But the beginning of hope comes from recognizing the system that your Black skin will have to deal with. Why else would White Supremacists deny that White Supremacy exists? The Devil's greatest trick.

"That thing that 'doesn't exist' is the system of White Supremacy that is hunting you for executing the justice that the police, and the District Attorney, and the judges, and the elected politicians refused to execute, themselves. If they find you, they will kill you for doing the job that they chose not to do."

Robert asked, "So what can we do about it?" Michael was nodding his head in mutual wonder.

Scottie saw his opportunity to lay out the solution. "Elect people who have eyes to see. Ensure judges are elected who have ears to hear.

Elect District Attorneys who serve the public good of humanity when human dignity is in conflict with actions taken by their partners, the police. Require elected officials to hire police from the neighborhoods they live in, or elect people who will do that."

Michael was shaking his head. "How can we do all that? It's too much."

Scottie defined the consequences. "If it's too much, then you accept that your fate is to be determined by people who pre-judge you by the color of your skin...you accept living in a heightened state of tension every time you or your children get in a car to run an errand...every time someone with a gun knows the person who lives in your house has Black skin." Scottie had to end the long talk. "You choose."

Robert and Michael were in introspective thought. Then Scottie snapped them out of it.

"You were both Black the day you arrived here. You'll both *still* be Black the day you leave. And if you ever doubt it...just go out into public. That's where White Supremacy reigns supreme."

Scottie stood up from the dining room table. "No bedtime reading tonight. Go to bed. We have a busy day tomorrow."

None of them knew just how busy tomorrow would be.

2.10 TIME FOR A LOOKEY-LOOK

The calendar was freshly May when Scott McNally, along with Michael and Robert, were clearing underbrush and cleaning up dead branches in the woods. Michael kept looking up through the canopy to see if he could make out the low-flying, slow-flying airplane.

The tree canopy dappled his view, but he called out to Scottie and Robert, "Hey! That plane is the State camera plane. And that's the second pass I've seen it make since we've been out here."

Scottie answered, "Don't worry about it, Michael. We can't be seen through the tree branches."

Scottie then noticed the sound of a low-flying helicopter traveling from East to West over the North side of the property. But it was out of sight. He kept on with his work.

Ten minutes later, Scottie heard the sound of that same helicopter at the same elevation. Only this time, it was flying West to East over the South side of the property. Scottie alerted the boys. "Drop your tools. We need to make a run to the house. Somebody's watching."

All three ran to the edge of the woods, searched the sky for sound, then searched the high blue sky for any sign of an aircraft or drone. When they were satisfied there was nothing overhead, they all made a dash to the back door of the house.

When they got inside the house, the driveway alarm sounded. All three hurried to the monitor. There was an armada of vehicles making their way down the driveway toward the house. They were all law enforcement vehicles from various agencies.

Michael and Robert followed Scottie to the bookshelf. Scottie reached in and pushed the release panel. The bookcase bounced out of position. Robert reached into the end panel for the finger latch. He pulled on it and released the bookcase to be fully opened. The boys hurried down the stairs.

Scottie closed and re-latched the bookcase. Then he went to the pantry and grabbed the whisk broom. He swept all the woods debris in hurried motions toward the back door. He opened the back door, then swept the debris to the outside.

He returned the broom to the pantry, then he ran to the front hall to look out through the solar shades. The armada was in sight and making its way down the final stretch of his driveway.

Scottie ran through the sanctuary, out the back door, and straight for the bluff, knowing that the house would block any view of his escape.

Once at the bluff, Scottie jumped down to the rocks below yard level, then he carefully made his way back to the area of the woods where they had all been working.

He placed the tools in an organized pattern that made them all easily accessible to himself. Then went back to work on the underbrush and the dead branches.

Scottie could easily hear and partially see the armada pull into his front yard and make a wall facing his house.

The SWAT team entered the unlocked house and went room by room, weapons at the ready, to clear the house. When they found no persons, they moved to the unlocked garage and did another full clearing inspection. Then to the sheds.

The SWAT team then set up a perimeter around the buildings while the camera operators entered, followed by Agent Watkins.

Watkins showed the camera operators to each area, and then stood back like a movie director, supervising the high-definition recording of every detail of every room from every angle.

Watkins had all the rooms filmed except the dining area and the bookcase. He was saving that for last.

After the first camera operator was dismissed and the second camera operator was sent out to the garage, Watkins had the third operator film the dining area and the bookcase in slow detail.

Watkins moved the operator to approach from multiple angles on the bookcase. "Get the whole thing, shelf by shelf."

Once the filming was done, Watkins called in a squadron of detectives and told them, "If there's a spider that looks suspicious, bring it to my attention."

Then the tearing apart of Scottie's house commenced.

Every drawer, every closet, his bed mattress and box spring, everything that wasn't nailed to a wall was heaved into scattered piles throughout.

The bookcase was a target of particular detailed interest. Every book was removed, one by one, so that its pages could be fanned and shaken for anything that might be in the books. Once inspected, the books made a heaping pile of their own on the dining area floor.

While the house was being scrutinized, part of the SWAT team had been dispatched to search the outside area of the property. In short order, they came across McNally doing his cleanup chore. Every SWAT member had a body camera on.

The SWAT members ordered McNally to the ground, had him spread his legs so he couldn't jump up, then instructed him to place his hands behind his head. Then one member approached McNally's prone body, leaned the full weight of his knee into McNally's back, and cuffed him.

Once cuffed, the SWAT officers walked Scottie back to the house.

Once back to the driveway, two members guarded him as he stood between two vehicles.

While standing there, Scottie saw Agent Watkins exit the side door of the house and walk around the front of the garage to its side door, which he entered.

In the garage, Agents Watkins instructed one of his team of agents to pull the dustcover off the car. Watkins walked around it, followed by other agents.

Watkins instructed one of the agents, "Tag that thing. It's the Batmobile."

The agents looked at each other in surprise. "Boss, this thing is a run-of-the-mill car you buy for your daughter for her Senior year of High School." The other agent added, "And that she doesn't want anyone to see her driving."

Watkins looked at the two agents. "Do you keep your daughter's run-of-the-mill, first car protected with a dustcover?"

The agents looked at each other and dropped it.

Watkins repeated his instructions to one of the agents. "Tag this thing. When this car leaves this garage, it's important."

An agent opened one of the boxes they had brought in. He got down on his knees and inspected under the vehicle. He found a good hiding spot on top of the rear axle that was hidden by the suspension system. There, he attached the GPS tracking device.

The other agent said, "Hey, Boss, look at this. The trunk has a Toyota emblem on it, but the hood has a *Nissan* emblem on it. So which is it?"

Watkins couldn't remember the registration details, but he said, "It's a Toyota. If he gets pulled over and the plates are run, the Toyota emblem on the trunk will match what comes back. But if cops are looking for a Toyota and drive past him from the front, they'll I.D. it as a Nissan and disregard it."

The agent asked, "Do you think he's that smart? That devious? That would be a criminal mind at work."

Watkins answered, "I think he's like a Boy Scout. 'Be Prepared.' I hope he's not a criminal, because he's smarter than most criminals. And the smartest thing about him is that he doesn't appear to think he's smart...or at least to let us think he's smart. But if he is a criminal...all of that will make him a worthy opponent.

"Has the pickup truck been tagged, yet?"

"Yes, Sir."

When Watkins exited the garage, he walked directly over to McNally. McNally was nonplussed.

"Are you here for a search warrant?...or with an *arrest* warrant? Because I'd be interested to know your probable cause for keeping me in cuffs. Technically, I'm under arrest. I want to know the charge."

Watkins nodded to one of the SWAT members guarding McNally. The SWAT officer stepped behind McNally and unlocked his handcuffs. McNally rubbed his wrist to stimulate the blood flow.

"I was shown the search warrant. Looking for two young Black men who fit a certain description? Somewhere in all of this there's a joke...right? But my problem is that I'm not laughing. I'm not a lawyer...and I don't know anything about the law...but isn't there a requirement for probable cause for an action like this?"

Watkins was getting everything McNally said on body cams...just for the record.

"We have reason to believe Loquisha Davis came here three days ago. Based on our previous interviews with both you and her, she would never...*ever*...show up here again. That you two hated each other. But...then she came here. So there you have it, Mr. McNally. Probable cause to investigate if she was here to pick up and move the boys...or to communicate with one or both of them in some way...or to communicate with you about the boys. So which is it, Mr. McNally?

hy was she here?"

McNally countered for the record. "If you weren't so reckless, Agent Watkins, you'd know there is no basis for your assumption that she was here three days ago. I haven't seen her or heard from her since the first time you were here. And...what boys?"

Watkins was still confident. "The FBI has more lawyers than the moon has craters. If we're here, it's because people way above my paygrade have deemed it a legal action. We don't make legal mistakes."

Scottie was ready to end this reparté. "Yeah, right. I don't think you're the one who gets to decide that."

A radio call came in from the members scouring the outer reaches of the property. "No other persons."

Watkins told McNally, "The search inside revealed you have a sniper rifle with enough ammunition to take down a small army. Stay out here until we're all reloaded and gone. It'll just keep everyone from getting jittery."

McNally waited patiently for everyone to get loaded and to pull out.

Once the last vehicle crested the rise in his driveway, Scottie went back into the house and scoured through the mess. He finally spotted what he was looking for. It was a small, thin local phone book.

Scottie started fanning the pages until he got to a yellow colored page that said, 'Lawyers.' There was only one listing.

Scottie thought, 'If a lawyer has to put an ad in the Yellow Pages in a town this small…where everybody is related to, or went to school with, everybody else…then he must not be that good of a lawyer.' Scottie closed the book and thought to himself, 'Perfect. He's my guy.'

Scottie detached the GPS tracker from underneath his pickup truck. He then drove it up the hill above Miss Dolly's house. That's where he could get a cell phone signal.

The lawyer answered the phone. Scottie thought, 'Just as I suspected. No secretary. Not busy.'

When Scottie returned from his Yellow Pages phone call, he walked around the mess to come up with a cleanup plan.

The first thing he noticed was that all the contents of the refrigerator and the freezer had been thrown on the floor. So, he opened the door to the freezer and restocked those items first. Some minor thawing was evident, 'but nothing too serious,' he thought.

Then he rummaged through the piles to find as many of the refrigerator items as he could. He restocked the fridge.

Then he took his sweet time to restock the bookshelves with all of the books piled up on the floor. There was a particular order in which he liked to display them. That took an additional couple of hours.

When dark had set in, he went to the front hall and pulled down the blackout shades. Then he returned to the bookcase to open it and call to the boys. They walked up the stairs. They looked a bit apprehensive.

When they came out of the stairwell, they both started wandering around the house. It was like a minefield. Piles everywhere. No place to walk. They were wide-eyed at the mess that was so thick that they had to lift their feet to move anywhere. The floor in front of the bookcase was the only clear floor space. Scottie gave the boys a chance to take in all the chaos and destruction. When they appeared to have seen everything, he asked them, "What do you say we eat in the basement tonight?" They all needed some positive energy from some good food...away from the piles and strewn clutter.

The boys headed back into the basement ahead of Scottie. When Scottie got to the top of the stairs, he heard Robert say...in his Whitest voice yet, "I'm deeply impressed that we were not discovered."

Then he heard Michael mockingly and Whitely answer him. "Well put, Professor Smith. I am in total agreement with your assessment."

2.11 CHANGE IS GONNA COME

After the home invasion, supper was pretty quiet. Scottie was making mental notes to himself. One was, 'Remove the GPS tracker from the truck when I go to Miss Dolly's to do computer work.'

After supper, the boys got their showers and climbed into bed for their nightly reading. However, when Scottie came downstairs, he was not in the mood to read from a book for the second night in a row.

"All cultures depend on the successful growing of food in order to survive. Historically, the greatest threat to food has not been invading armies. Nor has it been the failure of peoples to cultivate their own food. What do you think was the greatest threat to their food supply?"

Robert and Michael looked at each other. Neither one offered an answer.

"It has been the unpredictability of rain.

"This has given rise to one person being the most important person in the community. Do you know who that person is?"

Michael and Robert looked at each other and shrugged their shoulders.

Scottie said, "It's the Rainmaker."

Both Michael and Robert nodded their heads as if to say, 'Of course.'

"The Rainmaker is the person who puts their heart and soul into calling on the forces of nature to produce rain. We know the Rainmaker isn't responsible for the rain coming. But the Rainmaker is responsible for creating hope. And hope is necessary to carry people through despair.

"Someday, you will leave here and enter a world where you have none of the traditional support people around you. You must become your own Rainmaker. Everything we say and do here is meant to make you both, and each, a Rainmaker.

"Do you like a system of so-called justice that doesn't serve you? I mean, you're in this predicament because your cousin Jimmy was not going to get justice. Am I right?"

Both boys nodded in agreement, knowing that another long explanation of something was about to come.

"Have you ever heard that America is 'a nation of laws?"

Both mumbled in the affirmative.

"Are you aware that all laws are enforced at the end of the barrel of a gun?"

Michael said, "Whataya mean, man? Are you saying that if someone gets a parking ticket, someone's going to point a gun at them to pay it?"

"Yes. Ultimately. If a person gets a parking ticket and doesn't pay it, they get a summons to appear in court. If they don't appear in court, a summons for their arrest is issued by that judge. If the citizen doesn't submit to the arresting police officers, the guns come out. Make no mistake about it. All laws, even the most insignificant, are ultimately enforced at the end of the barrel of a gun."

Robert asked, "So, if the cop isn't right to arrest us, what a we do? Get a bigger gun than him?"

Scottie continued. "The cops are not the problem. The cops are nothing more than employees doing what their employer wants them to do. And who is the cops' employer?"

Robert guessed, "The judge?"

Scottie answered, "The judge is one of his bosses. So are the cop's supervisors. Ultimately, the boss of all the cops is the elected official who appoints the people who hire the cops. So, if you want change from the cops' behavior, should you go to the cop? Or should you go to the person who decides to *hire* the cop?"

Michael said, "Hire."

Scottie went on. "So what if the person who hires the cops won't weed out the bad ones?"

Michael said, "Fire the person who hires the cops."

Scottie asked, "And who can fire the person who hires the cops?"

Michael said, "The elected guy."

"So if the elected guy won't fire the person who hires the cop, what can you do about it?"

Michael said, "Kill the elected guy."

Robert quickly interjected, "Vote the elected guy out."

Scottie pointed to Robert. "That's the answer. So, if you're not registered to vote...or if you don't vote...can you change the behavior of the cops?"

The boys got it, so they didn't answer out loud.

Finally, Robert said, "How do you know who to vote for? How do you know who will do the right thing?"

"You'll never know who will do the right thing until you know what the right thing is. Let me tell you a short story that should help you to know what the right thing is.

"Rural cops are community cops in that they live in and have family in the community in which they police. The number of adrenaline-producing threats from another human is very low for rural cops. Partly, that's because most all of the people in rural communities are not 'different' from the cop, himself. The citizens are mostly the same skin color, and mostly they use the same words in the same accent.

"But skin color and speech are not the overriding issues that make rural policing so much safer than city policing. The overriding issue is that cops know, if not all the citizens directly, then he knows them by their family name...or he knows someone who knows the family of the citizen.

"I heard from a neighbor of ours that the Sheriff, right here where you've been living with me, had an incident where a man went into the courthouse through a back employees' door, and he went into a room of clerks, holding them all at gunpoint. He was deranged.

"When the call went out, the Sheriff, himself, who was not wearing a gun...which is his normal practice...knocked on the clerk-room door and announced that he was coming in to talk to the gun wielder. They had gone to High School together.

"The Sheriff talked the guy down. Then he walked his former classmate out of the building, not even putting him in handcuffs. He ask the man to sit in the front seat of his Sheriff's car, next to him, and drove the man down the street to the police station, supervised his booking, and told his former classmate, 'I'll put in a good word for you when we go in front of the judge.' Can you imagine how that would have played out differently in the city? SWAT teams and hundreds of officers at the ready? That's the formula for a bad ending.

"So, the point is that rural cops have a better opportunity to police the citizens based on personally *knowing* the citizens...or maybe the family of a citizen. Or a neighbor of the citizen.

"A city cop often lives outside the community they police. All people resent being policed by someone they don't know. The level of fear from lack of trust is huge on both sides of that equation. Fear leads to adrenaline-producing encounters. Adrenaline-producing encounters lead to bad endings. Like with your cousin, Jimmy. So, what do you think a person who hires the cops should know about policing?"

Robert answered, "That the cops should be people who come from the community that they're policing."

"That's right, Robert. So who should you vote for?"

Michael answered. "People who know to hire people who hire the cops...who all agree that cops should come from the community they're policing."

"That's right, Michael. And when that happens, the bad cops who think it's their job to dominate and subdue will be replaced by cops who know their job is to protect and serve.

"And how do you know if a person sees that simple wisdom and will carry it out?"

Robert said, "You ask them."

"That's right. You ask them. And what if there is no-one running for office who will commit to affecting that simple wisdom?"

Neither of the boys could answer, so Scottie waited.

When it was clear that no response was coming, Scottie finally said, "You run for the office, yourself."

Michael and Robert looked at each other and began nodding their heads in understanding.

Scottie turned to walk up the stairs. Then he turned back to the boys and said, "When you run for the office, yourself, you have become the Rainmaker."

2.12 DRESSED IN A LAW SUIT

The next day, Robert and Michael and Scottie all worked diligently to re-sort and put everything back in its place. Some of the mess went into landfill trash bags. Some went into burn piles. Some were sorted out to go the sheds for repair. But for the most part, everything was returned to some semblance of normal.

As Scottie let the boys handle the final details of clean-up, he recovered the small telephone book, folded it in half, and stuck it in his back pocket. Then he told the boys, "I have to run to town. I should be back in a couple of hours."

When he left the property, he had put a small gym bag in the front seat of his car. He liked to use gym bags. Gym bags and money. Gym bags and money. There was something familiar about that combination to him.

When Scottie got to town, he found the lawyer he was looking for. He had no secretary and didn't appear to be in the middle of anything. When he walked in, Scottie wondered if the guy was playing a computer game at his desk.

Scottie's first order of business was to size the guy up. Scottie ended up having a long meeting with him.

Scottie determined that the guy had a clear, if unused, mind. That he could absorb details. That he could follow directions. And, lastly, that had always wanted to have some things that his fledging law practice had not yet provided him.

Oddly, it was Scottie who was taking notes during the meeting. Then Scottie would pass the notes to the lawyer. All the notes were written in pencil on flash paper.

The notes included things like names and phone numbers of some Nashville lawyers at a particular Nashville law firm. Notes about legal issues around search warrant law. Names and associated agencies of certain individuals.

Scottie left the small gym bag with the lawyer. He also gave a final set of instructions. "No phone calls. I'll come to you, you don't come to me. And fraud is the number one cause for disbarment, including tax fraud cases. We have a mutual interest in you retaining your license to practice law, so...loose lips sink ships."

The lawyer was smiling while nodding his head.

Scottie was satisfied that his new intermediary could handle the job.

2.13 MICROSCOPIC PEP TALK

A month after Agent Watkins had received the go-ahead on his comprehensive search warrant application and had executed it flawlessly…though without immediate results…his phone sounded with the ominous sounding first four notes of Beethoven's Fifth Symphony.

"Yeah, Boss?"

"John, you're getting a lot of good press up the line. Reports are coming in about what a bang-up job you're doing in reviving this case. Reports from Nashville, the State of Tennessee, and our own DOJ bosses."

"That's nice, Boss. But surely you didn't call just to tell me about whispers in the wind?"

"You're right. I called you to give you a heads up."

"What's the heads up, Boss?"

"Getting warm air blown up your dress isn't procreative sex. Even if it feels like it."

"I get that, Boss. I've never been a fan of getting warm air blown up my dress."

"Look, John. Becoming 'high profile' can be a stepping stone to career advancement…but's it's a double-edged sword. When one person wants to elevate you, there always seems to be another who wants to prove you're not worthy."

"I get all that, Boss. I'm closer to retirement than a promotion. A promotion isn't even on my radar. Is this supposed to be some kind of pep talk? Because, if it is, I think you've lost the meaning of the word 'pep."

"You know I look out for you whenever I can, John. Right now, I just want your antenna to be sensitive about some of the extra attention you're getting outside your normal channels. You're getting good reviews from people who don't even know you. Those are the kind who show up out of nowhere and then tend to disappear just as fast. Or, worse yet, lead the charge against you."

"You're speaking in code to me, Sir. Can you be a little more direct?"

"Keep your eye on all the details, John. The higher the profile of your case, the more scrutiny you get. If someone decides to stick a microscope up your ass, they're *going* to find some fecal matter. That's just the plain truth about everybody."

"OK, Boss. I think I got it."

Watkins concluded that his Boss called him to tell him to make sure he was doing a good and thorough job. Watkins didn't know whether or not to feel insulted.

After he had disconnected the call, Watkins started to feel an increasing sense of suffocation from an enveloping dark fog...that the call had been some kind of an omen.

2.14 DAMAGE ASSESSMENT

The heat and humidity of July was making everybody cranky. The Bureau lawyers in D.C. had finished reviewing the complaint with DOJ lawyers.

"How is it that a bumpkin lawyer from some Podunk town in the middle of nowhere knows how to use this legal language and how to lay out the structure of this complaint? Columbia State Junior College? Middle Tennessee State University? Nashville School of Law? It's a night-school where working people get their law degree, for heaven's sake. Let's put some investigators on this guy. We'll play the lawyer, not the complaint."

"He's a wills-and-divorce small town attorney who owes money. Owed money. Debts are now resolved. His life seems to be incrementally upgraded all around...in barely visible ways.

"Our contract-investigator got into his general ledger in his desk drawer. It shows one cash payment from a guy on a divorce case. It was filing fee money. All other receipts are by check and show up in his meager bank account. McNally's name didn't even show up.

"He just replaced his twelve year old car for a two year old car from a used car lot in town. Paid cash.

"He eats a sandwich at the diner across from the courthouse every day that he's in his office. He'a added a daily dessert to his lunchtime routine.

"He goes home at night to his rental house and watches game shows on his newly installed satellite TV, with a DVR, making the antenna on his roof obsolete.

"He does internet searches for pornography on his newly purchased computer that's connected to his new high-speed internet account. He had no internet connection before the McNally incident.

"When we had everything we could get, we sent our most goon-looking contract-investigator in for a face-to-face. The lawyer told our goon that he's representing McNally pro bono. He added a question to our guy. 'You do know he's a poor bastard with no money, don't you?"

Watkins got the report and made another call to his boss. "Cash. McNally has a cash stash that we didn't find in the search. That would not only explain the lawyer, but it would also explain how the fugitives are being supported."

Watkins' Assistant Director Boss was getting impatient. "What fugitives? Are you withholding evidence from me, John? Did you find something to indicate the boys were there?...or had ever *been* there?"

Watkins loaded the search warrant videos, including all of the body cam videos. He began reviewing all of it. The house *and* the property.

From a body cam video, Watkins took note that, of the assortment of tools that McNally had with him out in the woods, 'why did he have two pairs of bypass loppers? Two loppers indicates he was not alone at the time of the raid.'

Watkins had to think like a defense attorney. 'A dull pair for small branches. A sharp pair for bigger branches.' Watkins was trying to get his brain to fire on all cylinders. He kept thinking. He was trying to energize the necessary pros-and-cons arguments.

Watkins stayed in defense attorney mode. 'What evidence is there that more than one person was in the woods on that day? What *evidence*? What *evidence*?...'

Watkins' District Agent in Charge got a call from the D.C. FBI staff lawyer who was coordinating with DOJ lawyers.

"There are flaws in the search warrant. You're going to have to personally answer for that, which I assume means Watkins, too. Aside from a projected loss in court if the thing gets that far, Justice feels it's a bad image case for the Bureau. After all, we're here to investigate civil rights violations, not violate them, ourselves. Get ready for some heat. Assignments, if not jobs, might be on the line."

Watkins turned to his phone at the sound of the first four ominous sounding notes of Beethoven's Fifth Symphony.

"Yeah, Boss."

"Things aren't looking good on the raid lawsuit. They're talking some kind of settlement to keep the thing out of court."

"That's a shame, Boss. You know we had probable cause."

"John. This applies to both of us. Things look a certain way on one day. Then on another day…the same thing can look totally different."

"Are our jobs at stake?"

"That discussion is on the table. It doesn't help that this case has nothing new. I've already cut you back to two agents to help with your total case load. There's pressure to re-assign them. Possibly to re-assign you, also."

"OK. I can take over the shoe-leather work. But this case is far from cold. I didn't work Profiling for most of my career for nothing. The McNally guy is the key. I know it. I just need to nail it down."

"Evidence, John. Evidence. We can't sell gut feelings anymore. We need evidence. Plan on being re-prioritized into your other cases. Just hope they don't 'Cease and Desist' you from the 'Nashville Officer Down' case."

2.15 YOU'RE SO VAIN

Scottie used his 'computer maintenance technician' time at Miss Dolly's to do all his necessary homework, as well as to 'test' Miss Dolly's Face Chat system. She was never suspicious. She was never even curious.

Scottie looked up and researched the profiles of a dozen plastic surgeons within a day's drive. One of his criteria was finding a plastic surgeon who didn't advertise. If the doctor had the desire to be 'known'…that was the opposite of what Scottie was looking for.

He felt good about one he had found in New Orleans and one he had found in St. Louis. He emailed them both about coordinating a Face Chat chat to discuss his needs.

The Face Chat chat turned out to be identical with both surgeons. "I have an old Vietnam War buddy who is Black and lives in California. He has a grandson who has great promise in the entertainment industry. The grandson wants to get a Michael Jackson nose job before he becomes famous. He wants it to be verifiably discreet so that it never has a chance of becoming part of his rise-to-fame narrative.

"My Vietnam buddy sends the grandson to my farm in the country every summer for the month of August. I'd like to do this favor for my buddy and his grandson while the grandson's here this month."

Objections were expressed by both surgeons about the need for record keeping for liability reasons. They both also said that upfront I.D. confirmation was necessary to prove the patient is a legal adult.

"You'll know when you meet him that he's of age. My buddy sent him out here with the cash to do the job. If it's not enough, I'll supplement, as a family favor, out of my own pocket. I'm needing for you to quote a price for me that includes me being with the grandson throughout the procedure...and no before and after pictures."

Both surgeons made comments about it sounding like a fugitive-from-the-law case. Scottie ignored that response with the encouragement, "Let your cash-price quote cover all the requirements I've stated from my end."

Scottie knew he was paying more than double in each case. But both surgeons' prices were nearly identical, so Scottie was satisfied.

The second week in August involved driving Micheal down to New Orleans and leaving Robert at home. The instructions to Robert were clear. "Stay in the house. Remain vigilant on the driveway monitors. Be prepared to disappear downstairs on a moment's notice...And the same goes for you, Michael, when I take Robert for his cosmetic makeover."

Scottie and Michael stayed in the same hotel and in the same room. That negated the need for Michael to produce I.D. and a credit card. Scottie secured both rooms with his own I.D., and had prepaid for the rooms with a debit card with a woman's name on it...who lived in Michigan.

The day after check-in, they drove to the surgeon's office. The surgeon's suspicions about the case were assuaged by the extravagant vacation the surgeon was planning with the cash. It would go the same for Robert in St. Louis. Tax-free money. Win. Win.

By the first week of September, Michael's black-and-blue had healed and his nose cast was discarded into the burn pile. By the middle of September, all the same was true for Robert's surgery. It would take a month of everyone in the household doing double-takes at each other before they all got used to the new looks.

Scottie started breathing easier about the eventual fledge.

2.16 THE THUNDER ROLLS

Scottie had spent a lot of time on the subject of health and hygiene with the boys. Part of it was for general knowledge. Part of it was a response to issues the boys required being nursed through.

Scottie had shown the body assembly in the Grays's Illustrated Anatomy book from the bookshelf. At one point, he focused on the relationship between the eyes-ears-nose-and-throat and how that was all part of the same system when it came to illnesses.

Scottie had used the blood pressure cuff to demonstrate how biofeedback was useful in controlling biometrics. He noted to the boys that high blood pressure was a common malady in Blacks. "If I had to live in constant tension, I'd have high blood pressure, too. Hyper-*tension* is another name for high blood pressure."

Chemical foods had been discussed. "Fast-food orange juice is made from chemicals. It doesn't have one iota of the orange that comes from a tree. The same is true of fake whipped cream. Not an ounce of real cream."

Scottie had bought a container of fake whipped cream once and left the container unrefrigerated so the boys could see what it was made of. "See. It's nothing but a chemically derived soup of oil."

Scottie had talked a lot about sugar being a poison and how carbohydrates are converted into sugar by the body. He told them how the low sugar and the low carbohydrates in a healthy diet result in avoiding the onset of diabetes. He added that diabetes was not just an ailment common among Blacks, but among the poor in general. "People who don't have room in their budget for good food...or the time to do at-home food preparation...end up buying food based on quick, easy, and cheap. That's the formula for diabetes."

From day one, Scottie had the boys make menus and food shopping lists. The receipts were always reviewed so the boys could understand what it cost to eat properly. "Food is the number one contributor to a person's wellness. That's why it's a great mystery that doctors in America don't have one single required course in nutrition as part of them earning a medical degree."

Scottie taught them about fats and cholesterol. "Cooking with oil, which is fried food, changes most oils into saturated fat, which is the source of bad cholesterol. But there are oils that don't change into saturated fat until they get to temperatures higher than we cook with. Avocado oil is one. Grapeseed oil has the highest conversion temperature of any."

Hygiene as a necessary part of health was the source of many talks.

"Take cold showers. Avoid hot showers. Only use hot showers to recover from a low internal body temperature. That's not necessarily when you *feel* cold, but when your actual body temperature is below normal. Otherwise, stick with colder showers. It stimulates your blood and muscle systems, which in turn gives you more energy...and makes you feel great in general."

"Michael, when you shave, some of your facial hair becomes ingrown. Use the sharp tweezers to dig into the ingrown pimple and yank out the ingrown hair by its root. The hair will eventually grow back and become ingrown again, but in the mean time you will avoid infections."

"Wise people say to never put anything into your ear that's smaller than your elbow. Don't be afraid to get soap in your ear canal. It will loosen the wax so you can then rinse it with a baby nasal aerator. Clean outside your ear canal daily with a Q-tip, but never put it in your ear canal."

"Make sure your eyebrow and nose hair is always trimmed. Wild hairs will draw attention to you and cause people to make negative judgments about you. Judgements about you will make you more memorable to people than no judgements. And your goal is to *not* be remembered by people you meet in passing."

Over time, Scottie had treated the boys for every malady know to man. The list included insect bites, snake bites, colds, the flu, bee stings, burns, stomach ailments, diarrhea, and constipation.

Constipation allowed Scottie to teach the boys about drinking the highest volume of water as fast as possible to flush the blockage out. Scottie called it 'the water cure.' He also showed them how copious amounts of the watermelon could do the same thing.

"The cause of constipation is usually dehydration in your intestines. Or, it can be from the bacteria in your gut shutting down and not processing the food you sent them. Feed the microbes in your gut what they like. You can't be happy and healthy unless *they're* happy and healthy."

Scottie had also treated the boys for food allergies, a sprained ankle and a sprained wrist, pollen washes with a sinus flush and a tea mixture recipe, plus poison ivy and poison oak. He taught them how to identify the poisonous leaves. "Leaves of five...live and thrive. Leaves of three...better flee."

At the beginning of their stay, he had both boys rub tiny-to-increasing amounts of poisonous plant leaves on their wrists. It eventually made them immune. In the meantime, he taught them about calamine lotion.

Many of the outdoor chores had been exhausting. Scottie taught them sayings that were meant to weaken their arguments to quit. After being drenched to the bone in sweat while moving a large collection of dead branches to add to a dam meant to slow rushing water from eroding a hollow any further, Robert made a complaining whine to Scottie that it was time to quit. Scottie shouted to Michael, "Tell him the facts, Michael." Michael didn't break stride in his work and shouted over to Robert, "Nobody has ever died from drowning in their own sweat, Robert."

One of the outdoor work related lessons Scottie had taught the boys was, "The threat of rain has cancelled more work than actual rain ever has." He would add, "Never let the *threat* of rain stop a day's work."

On a hot day toward the end of September, after both boys had recovered from their plastic surgeries, a condensed effort of mowing was underway to compensate for the ever-encroaching grass growth from the weeks of plastic surgery neglect.

The day was hot, like a mid-summer day. The dark clouds of a summer-like thunderstorm were gathering over the bottom field. Michael had the chore of taking the overgrown grass down a notch that day. He repeated Scottie's words in his mind, 'Never let the threat of rain stop a day's work.'

As he mowed, the sky darkened. Scottie and Robert were working in the woods on the upper property. Just as the blast of wind from the cold front moved over them, a nearby crack of lightening made Scottie and Robert stop their work. The roll of thunder immediately vibrated their internal organs.

Scottie instructed Robert, "Let's get all our tools into the shed and open the tractor shed doors so Michael can drive straight in." The downpour had begun just after the flash of lightening.

Scottie and Robert stood, soaking wet, holding the two tractor shed doors open so the doors wouldn't be slammed shut by the wind. They stood there waiting in the wind and the rain for Michael to show up. They knew Michael was getting soaked, also. They waited to hear the sound of the mowing tractor coming up the steep and rugged tractor path.

After five minutes of no sign of Michael, Scottie said, "I'm going to go see what's taking Michael so long."

Robert let go of his door and said, "I'm going with you."

When they got to the opening to the bottom field, they could see the stopped mower in the middle of the field. Then, through the pouring rain, they made out Michael's body lying on the ground behind the tractor. They both sprinted to find out what happened.

Michael was unconscious on the ground. He had been removed from his work boots. There was smoke rising into the rain off his clothing. And there was a burned tear up the side of one of his pant legs.

Scottie and Robert got down on either side of Michael and tried to revive him. When there was no response, Scottie felt for a heartbeat. There was none.

Scottie started performing CPR with pumps to Michael's chest, interspersed with mouth-to-mouth breathing per his military first-aid training.

Finally, there was a gasp of air and a fast sitting up by Michael. His eyes were bugged out.

Scottie moved to the tractor to try and start it so they could use it to transport Michael back to the house. The tractor was dead.

Scottie and Robert picked Michael up, one under each of Michael's arms. Michael asked what happened. Scottie said, "That lightening bolt hit you."

Michael asked, "What lightening bolt?"

Michael didn't have the strength to walk, so Scottie and Robert walked him up the tractor path, back to the house, Michael's arms draped over their shoulders. None of them were wearing rain gear. Michael was in his stocking feet, but his feet barely touch the ground for being carried.

The flooding rain from the storm didn't let up until after they had Michael seated at the dining room table.

Scottie took Michael's temperature. His body was cold from the rain soaking. Then Scottie had Robert take his own temperature. He was also at 95.6 degrees. Then Scottie took his own. It, too, was below normal.

"Robert, follow Michael down the stairs and get him into a hot shower. Once he feels warm, tuck him into bed. Put all the blankets on him. Then you take a hot shower, yourself."

Scottie made sure the boys made it down the stairs safely, then took a hot shower of his own.

Scottie and Robert prepared a hot supper while Michael continued to rest. Just as they were putting the food on the table, Michael appeared from down below.

They all ate in uncommon silence. After eating, Michael finally spoke. He directed his words at Scottie.

"You told us, man, to never let the threat of rain stop us from doing a day's work."

Scottie was nodding in agreement. Robert was looking back and forth between Scottie and Michael. Then Michael said, "Of all the other things you been telling us...how much a *that* is bllsht, too?"

With that, Michael wiped his mouth, stood up, and went back downstairs. He climbed straight back under the pile of blankets.

Robert was contemplatively silent while he and Scottie cleaned up after supper. Scottie was contemplatively silent, also.

There was no bedtime reading that night.

2.17 DO YOU SEE WHAT I SEE

Michael's recovery from the lightening strike was faster than his recovery from ever trusting Scottie again. It was more than a month later, and past the one-year anniversary of the boys' arrival, that Scottie felt he regained some semblance of trust. At bedtime one night, Scottie skipped the book-reading he had planned.

"There are lots of ways to see. If you walk around with your eyes closed, soon you will be able to sense objects and distances by the way sound echoes back to you...like the way bats see. Or by different temperatures of objects, such as a person's body versus a cold ceramic statue.

"Mosquitoes and the deer flies that bother us while we're out working know we're around, not because they can see us, but because they can see the carbon dioxide that we exhale and that excretes and rises from our skin.

"Bees 'see' the flower because of the smell of the nectar that comes from the flower's stamen.

"Blind people can read using the feel from their fingertips.

"No matter what source of input we use, the result is the same: our brain creates a picture that tells us what's there. Everything we do and everything we remember is from a picture. Words are just an awkward way that we try to tell other people what the picture in our brain looks like.

"Learning to purposefully *create* your own pictures in your own brain...and not just have pictures created *for* you...is the key to having some level of control over your reality. Your life. Your future."

Robert asked, "Why should we care about this? How is this supposed to help us?"

Scottie answered, "Developing the ability to purposefully create visualizations in vivid detail is like anything else. It takes practice...repetition...to get good at it. Visualization is the key to creating accomplishments before they happen. You already do it all the time.

"When you're cooking, how do you know what pots and pans and utensils to get? You create the picture in your brain, then you do what's in the picture. As human beings, we are hard-wired to walk toward the pictures that are in our brain. So, it should make sense that, if we want to chose where we go...where we walk to...then we should control what pictures get put into our brains.

"So, visualization is the way you get from where you are right now to where you want to be. Without this tool, we're leaving everything to chance. And chance directs enough of where we go, as it is. Visualization that you create on purpose increases the odds of getting you where you want to go...instead of relying solely on a lucky wind to take you there.

Michael said, "Sometimes I wake up in the middle of the night with a picture in my mind. I always just thought of it as a dream."

Scottie said, "Sometimes a dream is just a way of getting something out of our brain that we didn't flush out, ourselves, during our day. Or dreams can be the way our brain answers a question for us that we haven't answered in our conscious mind.

"But if it's just a nagging image, that could be your brain making you aware of something that your conscious brain has overlooked...something that never made it to your conscious brain. That's why I always tell you to keep your pad of paper and a pen next to your bed. When you wake up in the middle of the night, write down the image that woke you up...because those images don't get well stored into the conscious memory part of your brain."

Robert said, "So a dream is not just some random thing? It's trying to tell us something?"

Scottie answered, "I know that to be true, sometimes."

Robert said, "Well, then I want to dream more. How do I do it? Make myself dream more?"

Scottie said, "The poison we call sugar is known to enhance dreaming. Or at least it's known to enhance remembering our dreams in more vivd detail."

Michael said, "This all sounds like hocus-pocus. What's a useful way to use what you're saying?"

Scottie asked both boys, "Did your mamas ever have baby pictures of you around the house? Either one of you?"

Both boys were nodding their heads and looking at each other. "When we were real little. Up to maybe Middle School."

Scottie asked, "Do you think your mothers ever looked at any of those pictures and visualized in their minds who and what you would become?"

Michael projected that thought and got his back up. "Hey, wait a minute, man. Why are you trying to take us there? That's not helping anything. We know what we become. Don't be puttin' that on our mamas."

Scottie said, "Pictures of young people are a great tool to open the door of visualizing what is possible. The future of a young person is all in front of them. It's unknown, but it can be created in advance of it actually happening.

"As far as your mamas go, there comes a day when a parent looking at that picture is not the one in charge of who that young person becomes. So now, today, the important question is less about what your mamas projected your future to be. Your mamas' work is done. The important question is what do *you* project that person will become."

Robert said, "Your talking crazy, Scottie. We can't go back in time and change what will happen to us."

Scottie said, "Both of you...close your eyes." He waited. "Now, each of you picture one of those pictures of you from before you were in Middle School." He gave them another minute. "Now picture what that person will become."

Michael opened his eyes and cut Scottie off. "We know what we become, man. We can't change any of that."

Scottie said, "At the moment, you have failed the exercise. You have failed all of our time together, so far. You're telling me that you know what a dead person became. But you said it in terms of who you are right now. That tells me you have a long way to go because you have not accomplished your core goal: to let the old man die."

Robert said, "I was thinking the same thing as Michael. So what now?"

Scottie said, "Both of you close your eyes again...Now, picture in your mind that picture of your younger self...before the person he grew up into died...But now you know that the younger you has grown into a new...a different person. But you don't know what's going to happen to the new person, yet. The new person has yet to walk into his brave new world. So, holding the image of the younger you in your mind, make a picture of what that younger you will become. In your upcoming life. In your afterlife."

When Scottie turned to make his way back upstairs, both boys were still silent with their eyes closed.

2.18 ALL IN A DREAM

For their second New Year's Eve together, Scottie and the boys made a cake from scratch. They also made a sour cream frosting from scratch.

While they were mixing the frosting, Scottie said, "Watch out for this huge amount of powdered sugar. An overload of sugar can interfere with a good night's rest."

Sugar treats were rare, so the boys binged. They couldn't get enough of the frosted delight on top of the sweet and moist vanilla cake.

On the morning of New Year's Day, Scottie went down below to roust the boys for their morning routine. He saw Michael's pad had some scribbling on it. "Did you have a creative thought last night, Michael?"

"No, man. I had a dream."

Robert broke in. "Wow, man! I had a dream last night, too. Like one

I never had before!"

Michael said, "What was it? I hope it wasn't the same one I had."

Robert said, "I was flying. It was indoors...like the inside of a large gym or a small basketball arena. And *I* was the one flying. I could see everything...like I was a bird. The weird thing about it was that I could feel the g-forces when I made sweeping turns. It lasted for several circles around and back and forth and swoops and turns. I woke up right in the middle of it. I've never felt more exhilarated in my life! Even after I went back to sleep and woke up just now...I feel great!"

Scottie asked, "You too, Michael?"

"No, man." And he got quiet. He picked up his pad with scribbles on it.

Scottie was curious. "Well?..."

Michael hesitated, but looked at his pad. Then he went ahead and read from it. "I dreamed I saw a child of God."

Scottie cocked his head at the familiarity of Michael's words.

Michael continued reading his notes. "She was walking along the road, and I asked her, 'Where are you going?'"

Scottie began half-chuckling. "You're making this up. That's a song I know. It was a favorite of a friend of mine."

Michael protested. "Hey, man, I'm telling you the way I heard it. The whole thing was creepy. That's why I wrote it all down when the dream woke me up.

"A voice in the dream was speaking to me, 'I dreamed I saw a child of God.' I was watching this beautiful White girl walking down a path in the woods. Not woods like here. It was more rolling ground. And the vegetation was less thick than it is here. There were no big trees like there are here. And this whole scene was being spoken about in the dream."

Michael looked back down at his pad. "The dream said, 'She was walking along the road.' So then I asked her in the dream, 'Where are you going?' and she told me, 'I'm going down to Eli's farm.'"

Scottie started to feel a separation from reality. He said in a challenging way, "And where'd you get that 'Eli's farm' thing? What is *that*?" Scottie was speaking in a shortness that the boys had never heard before.

Scottie felt his own agitation. He was fighting between the surreality of the moment and the reality of a memory. He was spiraling into the memory while trying to stay present.

Michael said, "I don't know where the 'Eli's farm' thing came from, but all of a sudden I was inside a house on what I somehow knew was Eli's farm. Don't ask me how I knew. Probably just because she had said it before.

"Then there was no more talking. And like in Robert's flying dream, it was like I was up above her with my back against the ceiling, looking down. But I wasn't moving or flying like in Robert's dream. Just watching."

Scottie was trying to concentrate on every word and inflection and muscle movement in Michael. His brain was having trouble distinguishing between Michael's story and the pictures that were flashing before him.

"So, I was looking down at her and…me and Jamal, err, I mean, Robert…no, man, I'm telling you it was Jamal. We were there. And so were you, Scottie. But you were different. I knew it was you, but you didn't look the same. And the child-of-God girl was your wife."

Scottie knew what question to ask next, but he was frozen.

Michael was getting more upset from the imagery of the dream. "It wasn't me, man, that was standing there…that I was looking down at. It was Muhammad." Scottie's head fell to his chin as he tried to dissipate an intensity within himself. "And I was just watching from above. And Muhammad…he killed her, man. I knew it was Muhammad because he killed her the same way I killed the pig cop that killed Jimmy. It was horrible. And then Muhammad and Jamal ran away."

Just as Michael was finishing that last sentence, Scottie had taken two steps toward Michael and grabbed him by the neck with both hands. He started squeezing hard enough to break Michael's trachea. "Stop talking!" as Michael's face began to turn red.

Robert jumped in and tried to pull Scottie's arms away. Scottie was about to kill Michael when Scottie raised his strained voice. "It's none of your business! Stop talking! It's none of your gddmnd business!"

Robert was still trying to pry Scottie's hands away from Michael's neck. "Hey, stop it, man! What are you doing?!. You're going to kill him, man!. Let him go!"

Scottie came into the moment from Robert tugging on him. He couldn't believe what he was doing. He immediately let go of Michael's throat and backed away. He tried to shake it off.

Michael bent over and was gasping for air. Then he started rubbing his throat. "WTF, mthrfckr! WTF was *that* bllsht? Huh? You crazy mthrfkr? Get the fck away from me, you sick bitch."

Michael was still rubbing his throat when he bowed his head and started crying. Through his sniffles he was saying, "WTF, man," over and over.

Scottie turned away in shame and climbed the stairs.

A few minutes later, Robert came upstairs to confront Scottie.

"What was that all about, man? You freaked Michael out. And me, too. Michael said if you ever call him Michael again, he's going to cut you. He said to call him Muhammad from now on. And he's taking his money and he's leaving."

"He's not ready. And neither are you."

"You're too dangerous for us to be around, man."

Scottie descended the stairs and Robert followed. Michael was still affected. He turned his back when he saw it was Scottie.

"I owe you both an explanation for my behavior. Please sit down." They begrudgingly complied.

"The things you were saying, Michael..."

"Don't you ever call me 'Michael' again, you sick mthrfckr," while he continued to rub his throat.

"The things you were saying...they brought back memories of a good time and a bad time. I got lost in those memories. My conscious brain stopped working. I wasn't meaning to attack you, Michael..."

"If you say 'Michael' one more time, I'm walking outta here."

"In my mind, I wasn't attacking you. I don't know how else to say this, but I was attacking a memory that I didn't want to come back. A wound. A loss. And I'm sorry. Me doing something like that has never happened before. That's the best I can offer for saying it will never happen again."

Scottie gave Michael a wide berth for the next three days. Every time Scottie saw him, he was spooked about Michael's dream. 'The song...Eli's farm...the child of God...'

Up until that point, Scottie had never believed in this kind of thing. But now he was wondering if he had been spoken to from another dimension. He tried to write it off as being some weird trick of the mind. His own mind. But the incident was creating a shift in Scottie to a different understanding of the metaphysical.

On Michael's part, it took three weeks for the pain and stiffness in his neck to go away. And that was how long it was before Scottie could have a peaceful word with him.

"Things are going to happen to you, Michael. I'm sorry I was one of those things. But it's not what happens to you that will decide the outcome for you. It's how you respond to the things that happen to you."

"You're just full of sht, man. You on the edge, man. You put on a face like yo sht don't stink. But you be one fckd up mthrfckr. Howz it yo cracker talk says it? You got issues, man. And whatever happened to that 'slow count to ten' bllsht, man?

"You always walk around here like you better than us, man. You're just full of sht, man. I killed that pig mthrfkr cop cuz he murdered

Jimmy. You tried to kill me for *no reason*. Which one of us is better now, man? Huh? Which one of us is the better person, now? At least I had a reason...at least I had a reason."

Michael wasn't looking at him, but Scottie was proud of him for having listened and learned some things over the previous year. 'That was the most clear construction of logic I've ever heard from either one of the boys. Michael might be more ready than I realized.'

"I don't want either one of you here any longer than is necessary, but neither one of you is ready, yet. All of this time, all of this effort will have been wasted if you go too soon. There's a life out there for you. And for Robert, too. Let's all commit to sticking with it through the final stretch."

Michael said, still not looking at him, 'What's 'the final stretch?"

"It's when runners are running a race and they're exhausted...and they feel like they have nothing left in them...and like they would rather be any other place than where they are in the race...but they dig deep within themselves for whatever it takes to make it across the finish line."

Michael felt he had one sharp stick left to poke into Scottie's eye. "You tried to kill me before I was finished telling you how the dream ended."

Scottie's interest shifted. "Yes?"

Michael said, "The room where it happened?"

Scottie said, "Yes?"

Michael told him, "The room became full of other people. They were all crowding around. There were so many people there that there wasn't room for one more person. And they were all saying things to each other, like, 'The Queen is dead...the Queen is dead.' And they were saying, 'The Princess is dead,' and 'The Princess is dead.' And then they were all saying, back and forth to each other, 'Long live the Queen,' while others were saying back and forth, 'Long live the Princess."

Scottie's mouth was open. He had become frozen. Without moving a muscle, he departed.

Robert had been listening from a distance. Michael walked over to Robert and the two boys walked down the stairs together.

Once out of sight of Scottie, the boys stopped at the bottom of the stairs. Michael said, "He's always saying that people are not what they say…they are what they *do*. And look at what he done. He attacked me…and worse than that, it was for no reason. We gotta get outta here."

Robert tried some encouragement. "If people are what they do, look what he does, man. He's made himself a criminal so we can have a chance out there. I think that's who he is because *that's* what he does. What he done to you was a mistake. A hiccup. Like what we done to that pig mthrfkr who murdered Jimmy. We ain't murderers, man, even though that's what we done one time. Same with Scottie. We ain't gonna finish here unless we can get past this bad thing he done to you."

Michael held his hand out for Robert. Robert clasped it like a twisted handshake. Michael said to Robert, "Let's finish this thing down 'the final stretch'…and then get the fck outta here."

Robert was nodding his head.

2.19 MAKING FRIENDS

When Scottie's assault on Michael had finally thawed, the ground was still frozen. February was the coldest month of the year, but it was a good time to start what Scottie knew would be a long and slow process.

"The animals in the woods are cold. When they need to eat, the pickins are slim. So it's a great time to start a friendship. There's something they want. You have to find out what it is and give it to them.

"Taming a wild animal…making it trust you as a friend…takes time. The skills you'll develop while learning how to do this will be one of the most useful skills for you in your new life. The first step is for each of you to choose an animal."

Michael spoke up first. "There's a hawk that I see perched in a tree over the upper field. I wanna get him to fly down and perch on my arm and eat out of my hand."

Scottie was skeptical, but said, "OK. What about you, Robert?"

Robert said, "I'd like to feed a deer out of my hand and pet her fur coat."

Scottie guided them throughout their individual quests. He started with, "The very first thing is be a regular presence to them so it's not unusual for them to see you. And then, be still when they come to expect you. And then, once they've come to expect you, disarm them by sitting on the ground…or even lying on the ground. Whatever it takes to *not* appear as though you could suddenly pounce on them."

The boys started spending more time in the places their animals hung out.

Robert could sense his familiarity to the deer over the month of February. Michael complained that his hawk would fly away when it was clear that Michael wasn't just passing through.

Scottie's advice to Robert was easier. "Take a cup of corn and a cup of salt to your spot. When your deer appears, let her watch you pour both foods onto the ground. Then walk slowly backwards away while watching her. She'll start to show movement when she thinks you're a safe distance away. Try to watch her eat. Wait for her to leave. Then go clean up the salt and the corn so she can't come back for more when you're not around.

"As you repeat this every day, you should see her come to the food while you're less far away. The goal is to have her start to approach before you empty the food."

Scottie's advice to Micheal was less detailed. "Michael, you have to become the hawk. Why is the hawk perched in that tree over the field every day? Be the hawk, Michael. Be the hawk."

Robert was amused. "Yeah, Michael. Be the hawk. You're the *Black* hawk, man. You're the Black hawk!"

Scottie tried to ignore Robert. "Why is the hawk in the tree, Michael?"

"He's waiting to see a mouse or a mole or a snake in the field."

Scottie brought him a little further. "So what could associate you with what he wants?"

Michael had an idea. "What if I made a fake mouse on a string and pulled it through the grass?"

The only encouragement that Scottie could come up with was, "Give it a try and see what happens."

By the end of March, Robert had measurably progressed in his quest. His deer was now waiting for him to come to the feed spot. But Michael was frustrated. None of his efforts and adjustments were endearing himself to the hawk.

Robert would chide Michael whenever Michael complained. "You've got to be the Black hawk, man. You've got to be the Black hawk."

Scottie would stop Robert, but Robert would just whisper under his breath, "Be the Black hawk. Be the Black hawk."

Throughout the year-and-a-half that the boys had been climbing their learning curves, they would bring bird feathers in for identification. They were long past identifying the feathers of three of the big birds...the Turkey Buzzard, the various owls, and the various hawks. But one day, Michael brought in a big feather that he had found at the base of a snag in one of the hollows.

Scottie looked it over. "Show Robert and me where you found this." Michael led them to the hollow.

Scottie said, "This bird makes a schedule of rounds every day. He's like clockwork. I'll sit out here tomorrow before dawn and wait to see what time he comes. Then the next day, we can all come out at the appointed time."

On the third morning, Scottie brought the boys out to an observation spot in the hollow. "It's nine o'clock. We should see what we've come here to see by nine-thirty. Let's sit still and be quiet."

A half-hour later, Scottie could hear the rhythm of the bird's uneven, wing-snapping flying pattern as it approached from deeper in the woods. He alerted the boys with a hand signal. Then they saw a giant black bird with a bright red tuft on its head, and a bright white chest, contrasting with it's shiny black wings and body feathers. The twenty inch bird stuck a landing onto the side of the snag.

They listened to it pound the tree and turn its head to listen for the insects inside to move. Then they watched it dig for its snack.

After it had dropped off the snag and beat it wings in its odd snap and float rhythm, Scottie told the awestruck boys what they had just seen.

"That, my friends, is a Pileated Woodpecker."

Robert said, "Whoa! That was the biggest woodpecker I've ever seen out here!"

Michael added, "And bright, contrasting colors."

As they all rose to return to the house, Scottie said, "That's the closest living thing to a dinosaur that you'll ever see."

After several steps, Michael asked, "What about those horny lizards we see all over the place?"

Scottie said, "OK."

Then Robert added, "So, you think we'll never see a crocodile or an alligator...or are you including things that are older than a dinosaur...like a great white shark? I guess that means you're not planning on sending us to Florida...or to any place with an ocean."

Scottie was proud of their acquired knowledge and observations. He gave them their victory. "OK, OK, OK." Scottie elevated his assessment to *both* boys being one step closer to ready.

By April, Robert's deer was not only waiting for him, but she would approach him when she saw him coming. She would stand about ten yards from the feed spot. Then she would wait for him to step away. Over the month of April, she would stand closer and closer to the feed spot and require Robert to retreat less and less before she would start eating.

But April brought a different result for Michael. "My hawk hasn't perched over the field for a week. I wait patiently, but he doesn't come. I think he thinks I've scared all his food away. Or if he did see a rodent in the grass, he's decided he wouldn't go after it anyway…as long as I'm lying in wait."

Scottie observed, "It sounds like you've learned a lot about your hawk's inner motivations and behavioral responses. So that's a victory in-and-of itself."

Robert couldn't let his own comparative success go unnoticed. "Maybe it's time for the Black hawk to choose another animal to make as his friend. Let's see now…what animal would like to be friends with a Black hawk?" Robert added a chuckle to the end of his musing.

Scottie said, "Robert might be right. Is there another animal for you to choose?"

Michael said, "I can't believe you want me to give up. To quit."

Scottie said, "There comes a time to let go. To move on. That's an important life skill, knowing when to let go and move on."

Michael wasn't happy, so Scottie made a suggestion. "The grey tree squirrels around the house are out and about. What if you tried one of them?"

By May, Robert was feeding his pet deer out of his hand, and she was allowing him to pet her. He named her 'Mary.' "Because I think she wants to marry me."

Michael had also made a focused and methodical effort with the grey squirrels and had one eating out of *his* hand, as well. He hadn't named it.

By June, Robert's girlfriend, Mary, wasn't coming around any more. Scottie explained that the herd had plenty to eat in the woods, and that they needed to start making themselves known to the bucks...to be available to be mated.

Michael continued to feed his squirrel every day, but then he came down with a bad case of the itch. On closer investigation, Scottie discovered that Michael had fleas. And he couldn't scratch or wash or wish them away.

By the time red bite marks covered his whole body, and most importantly, his private parts, he pleaded with Scottie for help. Both Scottie and Robert were now having to scratch the biting fleas from their own bodies.

The entire house and basement were sealed for the smoke bombs that would end what had become everybody's nightmare. Then came the cleanup after the smoke bombs.

At the end of the cleanup, Michael complained that he's never going near a wild animal ever again. "Another example of you giving us bad advice, Scottie."

Robert taunted him, "You shoulda stayed a Black hawk, man. I thought more of you when you were a Black hawk than when you became a rodent."

Scottie stepped in. "That's enough, Robert. Michael achieved the same goal as you. He tamed a wild animal into eating out of his hand. The patience and persistence that both of you showed over several months is a tool that will serve you both well."

Michael couldn't hold back a final quip. "Yeah, man. At least I didn't turn my pet into my girlfriend."

Robert just laughed. "I'd rather have a girlfriend than fleas. Way to make the wrong choice...Blackhawk."

2.20 NEGOTIATED SETTLEMENT

The wheels of Justice turn slowly. It had been a year since the fruitless search warrant on the McNally property had turned up nothing.

A Department of Justice lawyer placed a call to Agent Watkins' Assistant Director with the news of their negotiated settlement regarding the lawsuit brought by McNally over 'no probable cause' for the search warrant, the destruction of private property, etcetera. Watkins then got the call from his Boss.

"The DOJ has settled with McNally. The terms are Justice paying the Podunk lawyer's fees, for which the final bill was highly inflated...but not contested by DOJ. They figured they were getting off light for not letting the thing go to court. That was in exchange for McNally signing off on there being 'no wrongdoing' on the part of the Bureau or Justice. And *that* was in exchange for you getting demoted, a condition required by McNally in order for him to settle for the rest of the above."

"So, I'm getting demoted? To what?"

"Don't worry about it, John. The Justice lawyer said, 'Fck 'im. McNally can't see inside our walls.' But it means no direct communication between you and McNally. It's time to move on from this case, anyway. There haven't been any active leads to follow since before the search warrant. Take it off your desk so you can take it off your mind."

"That's not true, Boss. We can go deeper on McNally."

"John! Did you not hear a word I just said?! It's over between you and McNally. Until a new lead surfaces, it's time to move on to other business."

Watkins could be a good soldier. But he wasn't going to let go of McNally being the key to solving this case.

2.21 DENNIS RODMAN GROWTH SPURT

July was an odd month for Scottie to come home with heavy winter clothing in his shopping bags for the boys.

As they were sorting through the bags, Michael tried on the assortment of heavy winter wear that were his size. A heavy winter coat with a fur-lined hood. Thermite under jackets and under slacks. A pair of heavy mittens and a pair of heavy gloves. They all fit perfectly. Scottie had learned how to size the boys.

Robert asked, "Where's my winter stuff?"

Scottie tried to deflect his question. "You're too big. Nobody had your size in stock during the summer."

Over the past one-and-three-quarter years, Robert had experienced a phenomenon. He had grown seven inches in twenty months. When Robert had arrived, he was a little over five feet eighth inches tall. Now he was flirting with a towering six feet, four inches. It had been a challenge for Scottie to keep him in new clothes that fit.

Robert wanted assurance that he was not going to be left out. "So, my winter clothes are coming before the new year?"

Scottie was noncommittal. "We'll see. There's no indication that you've stopped growing."

Michael asked, "Why all the heavy-duty gear? Last winter's clothes weren't this hardcore. And they're still wearable."

Robert was also curious. "Are we expecting a deep freeze of some kind?"

All Scottie would say was, "It's better to be over-prepared than under-prepared."

2.22 I DON'T WANT TO BE LONELY TONIGHT?

Along and hot and humid day of September mowing brought Robert and Michael in for cool showers before making a light supper. They were both dragging their feet...dragging their whole bodies.

While assembling all the ingredients for a garden salad with crackers and mineral water, their droopy body language was accompanied by silence.

Scottie took note. "The last blast of summer has made you boys exhausted?"

There was a room full of silence.

Finally, Michael spoke. "I'm lonely, man. I'm sick of you two being the only people I ever see or talk to. I'm just sick of it."

Robert echoed Michael's feelings.

Scottie didn't respond until they were seated and eating. "You must know we're very near the end."

Both boys perked up. Robert asked, "Wha's that mean, man?"

"I'll be kicking both of you out of the nest after the last mow of the season."

Michael asked, "What makes you think we'll be ready?"

"You're ready when there's nothing more I can offer you." Both boys had stopped eating and were listening with interest. "You're ready when the need for change can be a source of fuel for you to create your new world." The boys didn't look at each other, but they were both absorbed in what Scottie's words meant to each of them, individually. "You're both within weeks of fledging."

Robert returned to his salad and spoke with his mouth full. "Why don't I feel real good about that?"

Scottie wiped his own mouth with his napkin and placed his hands on the table in preparation for a long explanation.

"You're both aware that your personal growth has slowed. You're both depressed from your learning curve flattening out. You both have anxiety about adapting to an unknown world. You both miss your mothers and your Grandma.

"Anxiety and loneliness and depression could make you fledge too soon. But we all need to wait until the stars align. Until everything falls into its proper place. Until circumstances say, 'Now!'

"When that happens, we have to strike while the iron's hot. Otherwise, you'll find yourself trying to beat a cold piece of steel into the shape you want it to be. When that happens, stop and recognize that finding the flow of the river, and getting in it, is a better use of your energy."

Robert smiled. "Shame on you, Scottie, for using a mixed metaphor."

If Scottie needed a confirmation that their time was near, that was it.

"Going underground has a mixed history of success and failure. Learn from both.

"Katherine Ann Power was a domestic terrorist who was 23 years underground. The FBI had closed her case file after 14 years. After 23 years, she was married with children. But she turned herself in to try and relieve her depression. She had failed to kill her former self. She wallowed in a pool of the past instead of celebrating the new and the free.

"Another example was Katherine Boudin, a Weather Underground actor who had also been involved in some violent domestic terrorism. She was a fugitive for eleven years. She was caught committing bank robbery, recommitting the crime of her past. Once again, she's an example of someone who failed to kill her former self.

"Then there was Abbie Hoffman. He had been a fugitive seven years. The FBI had 13,262 pages on him, but he was lost and gone forever. He turned himself in after having reinvented himself as a successful environmental activist. He had had face-to-face interactions with his U.S. Senator and his State's Governor. His new identity had been 100% successful.

"Mr. Hoffman's crimes were inciting to riot, and violence against police...though those charges had been overturned by a court that determined the event to be a *police* riot. When he went underground, he was fleeing conviction for entrapment by cops on a cocaine bust. Like Ms. Power, he turned himself in to try and escape depression."

The boys were listening intently. Robert said, "He had never killed his former self, even though his new self was flourishing."

Scottie concluded his speech. "What's the moral of these historical examples? You can't fake your own death. It has to be real, or it will kill your new chance at life.

"Remember this: dead people don't run and hide from the law...because they're dead. And a totally new and different person doesn't run and hide from the law, either...because they haven't done anything wrong.

"You boys are lonely and depressed over missing your old selves. But your new self is just that. New. And it's about to reach adulthood. Every positive possibility is waiting for you."

They all cleaned up supper in contemplative silence.

2.23 A CODE THAT YOU CAN LIVE BY

All the plans were in place. All the preparations were complete. Columbus Day was to be the last full day the three outlaws would spend together. Scottie knew he could not treat it like any other day.

For one thing, Scottie wanted to supervise their packing. As he kept a close eye on making sure all their things were in order, he used the time to keep doing what he'd always done, day in and day out, for the past two years. He talked.

There had been a method to the madness of his incessant talking. He knew that the brain mimicked everything it was exposed to, including accent and inflection, as well as the vocabulary and grammar of the spoken word. His great unknown was, and would be, whether or not it will have worked once the boys left his presence.

While engaged in all their final 'wrapping up' activities, Scottie didn't want to leave a stone unturned. "The morning 'shake it up and shake it out' routine that you both have mastered is useful beyond this house. It's meant to be a challenge to yourself. It's a statement of your will to survive. 'Bring on the challenges and the obstacles,' type of thing. It's meant to show your enemy that you're not scared…and who is your enemy?"

Both boys answered in tired unison, "Our greatest enemy is self-doubt."

Later in the morning, Scottie brought up another topic. "Last night, we finished reading *Mutiny On The Bounty*. Captain Bligh was so hyper-humanly skilled as a navigator that he could row a rowboat full of seventeen sailors for over 1700 miles across the open Pacific Ocean and return them all safely to England. Yet, when he sailed back to the South Pacific to bring the Mutineers to justice, he couldn't find them. How did that happen?"

Robert spoke up. "Because Pitcairn Island had been wrongly plotted on the sea charts by the previous great explorer, Captain Cook."

Scottie said, "Right. It was only wrong on the maps by how much?"

Michael answered begrudgingly, "Twenty miles."

Scottie continued. "Right. So if the most skilled sea captain in the history of the world couldn't find an island that was only off by twenty miles, then what does that tell us?"

Robert said, "The cops just need to be thrown off by a little bit in order to be thrown off by a lot."

At one point before lunch, Michael asked, "Why is it so important that Robert and I never have contact again?"

"Michael...what would happen if all the branches on a tree grew out of one side of the trunk?"

Michael and Robert looked at each other. Robert answered for Michael. "The tree would fall over."

Over lunch, Scottie talked more than he ate. "Be aware of the judgments of others. The more harshly you're judged, the more deeply you'll be remembered. And the goal is to *not* be remembered.

"Take advantage of people's hard-wired biases. Remember the bias that makes people think that people who speak with a British accent are smart? And the bias that makes people think that people who speak with a Southern accent are stupid? Don't be fooled, yourself...but know that the way you speak alters people's judgments about you.

"Be cautious of early acceptance. Trust people who have gotten to know you little by little over time before you accept them fully opening the door for you. And you do the same toward others.

"The obvious ways people will make instant judgments about you are your hygiene and your clothing. But an equal, if not more subtle, source of judgement is your teeth and the quality of your footwear. So, to deflect judgment, shave and shower, keep a rotation of new clothes on hand, brush your teeth, and get to know your dentist on a first-name basis. And don't be afraid to spend money on footwear. The double-bonus of the footwear thing is that your feet carry your body, which carries your soul. Make your feet happy, and you'll make your soul happy."

Robert couldn't resist. "So...what you're saying is...if I'm hearing you right...is that if I have a good sole, then I'll have a good soul?"

Michael laughing out loud made him lean back. He pointed at Scottie from the lean-back position. "He got you there, man," and continued his laugh.

Scottie was satisfyingly impressed with their ability to create a homonym pun and to recognize a homonym pun, respectively. To Scottie, it was another confirmation as to the boys' readiness.

While they were cleaning up after lunch, Scottie asked, "Can you respect a person when you don't respect their choices?"

Michael showed great depth of insight in his response. "A person *is* their choices. So if you can't respect a person's choices, you can't respect the person."

Scottie was gentle in his counterpoint. "A person's choices are just a snapshot of a moment in time. With new information, people often change their choices. What if they change their choices, but you've already alienated yourself from them forever?"

After the lunch cleanup was complete, Scottie recited a poem from memory:

> "If you can keep your head when all about you
>   Are losing theirs and blaming it on you,
> If you can trust yourself when all men doubt you,
>   But make allowance for their doubting too;
> If you can wait and not be tired by waiting,
>   Or being lied about, don't deal in lies,
> Or being hated, don't give way to hating,
>   And yet don't look too good, nor talk too wise:
> "If you can dream—and not make dreams your master;
>   If you can think—and not make thoughts your aim;
> If you can meet with Triumph and Disaster
>   And treat those two impostors just the same;
> If you can bear to hear the truth you've spoken
>   Twisted by knaves to make a trap for fools,
> Or watch the things you gave your life to, broken,
>   And stoop and build 'em up with worn-out tools:

"If you can make one heap of all your winnings
    And risk it on one turn of pitch-and-toss,
And lose, and start again at your beginnings
    And never breathe a word about your loss;
If you can force your heart and nerve and sinew
    To serve your turn long after they are gone,
And so hold on when there is nothing in you
    Except the Will which says to them: 'Hold on!'
"If you can talk with crowds and keep your virtue,
    Or walk with Kings—nor lose the common touch,
If neither foes nor loving friends can hurt you,
    If all men count with you, but none too much;
If you can fill the unforgiving minute
    With sixty seconds' worth of distance run,
Yours is the Earth and everything that's in it,
    And—which is more—you'll be a Man, my son!"

Robert said, "Rudyard Kipling. *If.*"

That bolstered Scottie's confidence some more.

Robert brought up his concern about not having worked out a defined story about his life. A hard narrative.

Scottie said, "Keep your narrative soft and flexible. You never know when something will happen that requires it to be modified.

"If people ask you where you came from, have some vague, yet crisp, answers ready. 'I've just returned from an extended life-enrichment quest to the mountains of Peru.' Or, 'I grew up on Machu Picchu.' Anything that gives you leeway to dodge and dance, and confuses your questioner's questioning.

"And use your new accent all the time. I remember seeing a well-known actress in the movie *Loopers* who I knew well from a bunch of her other work. When I saw her in *Loopers*, I knew I'd seen her before...I knew that I knew her from somewhere...but I couldn't identify her. So I watched for the credits at the end of the movie. It was an actress who had a legendarily strong British accent...but in the movie she had a New York accent. The change in accent made her physically unidentifiable to me. Remember that.

"Now, tell me the strategies for people asking for your backstory."

Michael and Robert said in unison, "Ignore, deflect, confuse, or be confused."

Then Michael added, "And talk like a gddmnd Yankee."

Scottie was satisfied, but he continued. "I know I don't need to say this, but give me confidence about how you're going to reference me when people ask you questions about your erudite ways."

Both boys said together, "Mother."

By the middle of the afternoon, Scottie had a summary thought to share in response to his knowledge that the boys were not, and would never be...if they knew what was good for them...*fully* ready.

"You'll know you'll make it if the knee-jerk responses that come from you are acts of kindness and thoughtfulness toward others, and if you demonstrate a positive passion in all that you do." He watched both boys until he believed that they got it. Then he added, "And remember the old farmer's sarcastic saying,

There's never enough time to do it right, but there's always enough time to do it twice.' Sometimes lessons come by remembering what *not* to do."

Over supper, Scottie wanted to remove any stumbling blocks that might trip them up along the way.

"For two years I have exposed you to anything and everything I could think of that were things you might not have been exposed to in the past. And did I do that so that you could be a scientist or a mathematician or a computer technician?...an astro-physicist or a national park tour guide?...a teacher of the English language, or of the great works of literature and poetry written therein?...or so you could be a DJ in a nightclub?"

The boys said together, between mouthfuls of food, "No."

Scottie prodded them further. "Then why did I expose you to all those things?"

Robert gave the rote answer, "So we could know what was possible." Michael was nodding his head as he chewed.

Scottie said, "That's right. To know what's possible...Not to *know*...but to know what's *possible*. Do you get it?"

Both boys were looking at him as if to say, 'Get to your point.'

"If you try to make people think that you know things that you only know *about*, then you put yourselves in two dangers.

"The first danger is to expose yourself, outwardly, as a fraud. The consequence of that would probably be limited to your audience not believing or trusting anything else you say.

"The second danger is that you will find the limits of your pretend knowledge internally, which will break down your confidence.

"So this is my final instruction about everything you've been exposed to: forget it all. If you think it was to make you smart, then it will sink you. If you know that it was just to light your path to keep you from stumbling or tripping...and to keep you on the path...then that's all it was meant to do."

The boys were nodding in agreement, but Scottie wanted a greater assurance that his efforts would help them and not hinder them.

"Forget it all. Say it after me. 'Forget it all.'"

The boys said together, "Forget it all."

Scottie wanted some further assurance. "Why are you going to forget it all?"

Robert said, "We got exposed to things so it would be a guiding light...not a blinding light." Michael nodded his head.

Scottie then wanted a final read of their states of mind. He ferreted it out with this charge: "It's time for you to evaluate me. If you are anything less than purely honest, I'll know it...and it will mean another two years of training."

Both boys groaned. Robert spoke first. "You're a puzzle piece that got put into the wrong box. I'm commenting on my summary of you as a person...not as a teacher or a drill-sergeant...or whatever this was."

Michael threw his coin into the pot. "You're a Sophomore. If you were a Graduate, we'd be more ready."

Scottie was pleased. "I'm satisfied that each of your answers show that it's time. The stars have aligned. All the pieces are now in place."

While they were cleaning up after supper, Scottie was ready to give the Commencement Address.

"Feeling that you're 'not ready' will keep you sharp to accomplish things you've never dreamed of accomplishing. Never forget the lessons we learned from Beethoven. Michael?"

Michael loved the Beethoven story. "The greatest symphony choir music...*ever written in the history of mankind*..." Micheal laughed with Robert about his imitation of Scottie, "was written by a man who was one-hundred percent deaf. A man who had to lay his head on the piano as he wrote, just so he could feel the vibrations against his skull. If a deaf man can write great music, we can do anything we set our minds to."

Scottie was pleased. "And never forget the lessons we learned from Django Reinhardt. Robert?"

Robert summarized a story he still had trouble believing. "The greatest acoustic guitar player...*ever in the history of the world*..." Robert got a return laugh from Michael because of his Scottie impersonation, "was born with only three functioning fingers on his chord-making hand."

Scottie didn't hear enough. "Was only having three fingers his only obstacle?"

Robert finished what he left out of the story. "No. He was hated by the Nazi's because he was a Gypsy, even though they made him perform for them."

Scottie kept prodding him. "And what did he do about the Nazi's?"

Robert finished the story. "He walked over mountains in the dead of night, in the middle of winter, and at the risk of being killed for trying to escape to his freedom."

Scottie looked at both boys with a solemn stare. "Just as the two of you are about to do." He continued looking at both boys until he was convinced that they knew the precipice on which they were standing.

"I once heard the best commencement speech of my life. Let me share what I remember of it.

"The word 'commencement' means the start of something, not the end of something. But in this choice we've all made, the 'start,' the 'beginning,' the 'new,' is defined by an act that usually defines a hard 'end.' A hard 'it's over.'

"That thing that represents your new beginning is the lowering of the casket into the ground, and the throwing of dirt on it...to symbolize that the casket and its contents will never be seen again.

"Now that it's a *living* person that will walk the earth, keep your eyes open for the thing that will bring the most meaningful meaning to your lives. It will be something that doesn't allow you to be satisfied to just hum the tune. It will be something that makes you want to learn all the words, get all the meanings, know how all the melodies and harmonies and rhythms work together. That kind of deep interest will help you to know that you've found your *Raison d'être*. It will be your passion."

After that, the trumpets sounded, the organ blasted out its recessional march, and the capped and gowned graduates moved their tassels to the opposite side of their mortarboards. Then the boys, trying not to trip over their royal blue polyester gowns, marched in lock-step down the stairs to shower and put their finishing touches on packing for the coming launch into their brave new world.

2.24 KUM BA YAH

The night of the boys' last bedtime had arrived. The plan was for Scottie to wake Michael for a pre-dawn exit, and that Robert was to have his bags packed and be ready for his exit before lunchtime.

Scottie gave the boy's time to settle into their beds before he walked down the stairs with three bookmarked books in his hand. When he got there, the boys were sitting on he edge of their beds with books of their own choosing. Robert said, "It's our turn, Scottie."

Michael added. "Yeah, man. Its time for us to read, and for you to listen."

The boys opened their books while Scottie just stood there, partially stunned, partially proud.

Michael went first. "O Captain! my Captain! Our fearful trip is done. The ship has weather'd every rack, the prize we sought is won."

Robert continued from there. "The port is near, the bells I hear, the people all exulting. While follow eyes the steady keel, the vessel grim and daring."

Michael read the chorus. "But O heart! heart! heart! O the bleeding drops of red, Where on the deck my Captain lies, Fallen cold and dead."

Robert started the next verse. "O Captain! my Captain! rise up and hear the bells; Rise up—for you the flag is flung—for you the bugle trills."

Michael continued. "For you bouquets and ribbon'd wreaths—for you the shores a-crowding. For you they call, the swaying mass, their eager faces turning."

This time, Robert read the chorus. "Here Captain! dear father! This arm beneath your head! It is some dream that on the deck, You've fallen cold and dead."

Michael picked up the next verse. "My Captain does not answer, his lips are pale and still, My father does not feel my arm, he has no pulse nor will.

Robert went on from there. "The ship is anchor'd safe and sound, its voyage closed and done. From fearful trip the victor ship comes in with object won."

Then both boys read the final chorus together. "Exult O shores, and ring O bells! But I with mournful tread, Walk the deck my Captain lies, Fallen cold and dead."

Scottie tried to keep the tear that had welled up in his eye from falling onto his cheek. "I tried to teach you to be dead to your old selves. That is how our journey together began. And here we are at the end, and it is me who is dead to you." Scottie was fully humbled by their insight.

Michael said, "We're not finished."

Robert added, "Yeah, Scottie. For every end, there's a new beginning. Isn't that what you've said over and over?"

Michael added, trying to say it under his breath, "And over, and over, and over."

As the boys opened to a bookmarked page, Scottie leaned back against the end of the stairway wall with his arms folded across his chest.

When they each got to their preselected page, Michael and Robert read in unison.

"Out of the night that covers me, Black as the pit from pole to pole, I thank whatever gods may be For my unconquerable soul.

"Beyond this place of wrath and tears Looms but the horror of the shade, And yet the menace of the years Finds and shall find me unafraid.

"It matters not how straight the gate, How charged with punishments the scroll, I am the master of my fate, I am the captain of my soul."

That was all Scottie could take. He turned his back to hide the contortions in his face and walked up the stairs. As he was walking, he said loudly enough to be heard, "Be ready before the break of dawn, Michael. We have an early start."

After Scottie had departed from their joint reading performance, the boys pulled the covers over their heads for their final night of sleep together.

When breathing was the only sound remaining, Michael spoke into the darkness from under his blanket. "When the rooster crows at the break of dawn, look out your window and I'll be gone."

Robert absorbed the imagery for a moment. Then he answered from under his own blanket. "Don't think twice. It's alright."

3

PYGMALIA IN BLOOM

3.1 WILL YOU REMEMBER ME

Scottie and Michael had a pre-dawn breakfast. Robert had said his goodbyes and didn't want to watch Michael drive away.

Scottie and Michael, bags in hand, made their way out to the garage. The cocks from the woods across the river were crowing. Scottie removed the dust cover and the GPS tracker from the Batmobile.

Michael loaded two large duffel bags into the trunk and threw his shoulder bag in the back seat. They left the property as the sun was making it dawn.

During the two hour trip, Scottie shared all the things he didn't want Robert to know.

He handed Michael a piece of computer-printed paper. "We're driving to the Nashville bus station. This is the list of connections you'll make. See the last destination?"

"Denver, Colorado? Why Denver?"

"Because I've already lined up a place for you to rent."

"Who do you know in Denver?"

"I found an ad on Craigslist for a private rental room with a kitchenette in an all-White suburb called Highlands Ranch. I inquired, pretending to be you, through an email account. Then I spoke with them as your employer on a computer Face Char. You'll need to know all the details of those communications, so here they are:

"You want to relocate to a high altitude because you're a runner, thinking of getting into marathon training.

"You're renting so you can get to know the area before buying a permanent residence.

"You have a background in the service industry, starting out in fast food, then moving up to a menu restaurant where you were promoted from bussing to chef's assistant.

"You're taking a bus from your current residence and employment in Des Moines, Iowa."

Scottie pointed to Michael's bus transfers itinerary. "Des Moines is your last bus transfer before going to Denver.

"After a couple of emails, you emailed to ask if it would cause any problems with their friends and neighbors that you're Black. They're liberals. They replied that it would be wonderful to get some diversity in their neighborhood.

"They asked for an employer reference, so you emailed them back saying your employer would call them as a reference. You asked if a Face Chat computer call from him was OK, and what was the best time to find them home for the call."

"So I, personally, called them back as your employer on a computer with a Face Chat. I was the restaurant owner.

"I said that you're Black, but without the attitude. That all 'my' customers think the world of you, and that I'd never had a complaint. I added that there are no Black customers where we live in Iowa...just to assure them that you know how to behave in an all-White environment.

"They asked if you were financially responsible. I told them that I'd never had an employee who was more financially responsible...that you have no trouble living below your means. That you're a saver. And that I happen to know that you are leaving Iowa with a bankroll that you plan to use as a downpayment on a house once you're established there.

"They said, 'We'll take him.' They added that some neighbors might object, but there are few Blacks in their town. They reiterated that a little more diversity would be good."

Michael was nodding the whole time, trying to absorb it all.

Scottie handed Michael some screen shots he had printed out from the Street View of neighborhoods and parks around the town of Highlands Ranch.

One was a Street View picture of Main Street that had centered in it a picture of a Cafe/Restaurant. The plate glass was painted with the boldly visible name, *The Sunflower Cafe and Restaurant*.

When Scottie arrived near the bus station where there were no cameras, he pulled over to the curb and stopped the car. Scottie pulled a piece of paper from his shirt pocket. He reached over and stuffed it into Michael's shirt pocket.

Michael leaned over and gave Scottie a hug. That was something that had never happened before.

Scottie hugged him back. Then he said, "Be careful. In the game we've chosen, sentimental acts can create chaos."

Michael nodded, wondering if he should not have hugged Scottie.

Michael got out of the car, retrieved his shoulder bag from the back seat, and then went to the trunk for his duffel bags.

Standing on the sidewalk, Michael watched Scottie drive away.

When Scottie was gone from sight, Michael, with his shoulder bag strapped over his shoulder, bent over to lift his two large duffel bags. Then he remembered Scottie stuffing the note in his shirt. He stood back up, pulled it out, and opened it.

"Blackhawk, take these broken wings and learn to fly. You were only waiting for this moment to be free."

Michael refolded it and put it back in his pocket. He looked at the empty space that Scottie had driven off into. He thought, 'Sentimental acts can only create chaos?' Then he thought, 'What a hypocrite.'

Michael went to the ticket window in the bus station and bought a ticket for his first leg to Chicago. Then he sat down with his baggage to wait.

He saw a woman sitting two rows away from him talking on her cell phone. He watched her until she ended the call. Leaving his bags at his seat, he made the long walk over to her.

"My friend just dropped me off. I accidentally left my cell phone in his car. Could I borrow yours for a second to call him and ask him to come back before my bus gets here?"

She looked him over. He was well dressed. He was well groomed. He was well spoken. His teeth were white and straight. His shoes were new and expensive. She unlocked her phone and handed it to him.

Michael punched in the seven digits of a well remembered number and took a few steps away from the young lady.

"Grandma?..."

3.2 LOVES BABIES AND SURPRISES

When Scottie returned from dropping off Michael, Robert was fed and packed and waiting.

"Based on how long you were gone, did you take him to Nashville, or Murfreesboro, or Muscle Shoals?"

"There's no turning back, so have you double-checked that you have everything?"

"It's all here. So, where are you dropping me off?"

"Get in. We'll talk while we drive."

Scottie and Robert got onto the Trace at Jack's Branch and headed South. It was a short jump to Highway 64 where Scottie exited to the West.

Robert said, "Memphis?"

Scottie was silent.

"When are you going to tell me where you're going to drop me off?"

"I can tell you right now, but it's going to be a long drive, so perhaps you'd like to know where we're going *first*."

"Enough of the mystery, Scottie. Just tell me where you're dropping me off."

"At the Pacific Ocean."

Robert thought Scottie was playing with him, and he was getting frustrated. He displayed his frustration by being silent.

When Scottie turned off 64 West and headed South, Robert asked, "New Orleans?"

Scottie was silent.

"What is your problem, Scottie? Did you do this Michael? Did you not let him know where you were taking him until you were already there? And what's the deal with this 'Pacific Ocean' nonsense?"

"We have a long drive ahead of us, Robert. And we're going to make some stops along the way. And you're going to do some of the driving because we want to stop as infrequently as possible."

"OK. Now we're making some progress. So, what is our first 'stop,' as you call it?"

"Big Bend National Park."

"Along the Rio Grand in Southwest Texas?"

"One in the same."

"Why are we going there?"

"For a visit."

"Why?"

"To begin a final rounding off of your exposure to all things different from whence you came."

3.3 ANGEL FROM MONTGOMERY

During the two years since the Mark Johnson murder, the case had wound down to dormant because of a lack of new leads for the investigation.

The audio wiretap on Jacinda Jefferson had been left to expire. However, a search warrant remained in effect for phone-number traffic surveillance. No manpower was assigned to that warrant but, instead, it was carried out by a computer program that sent a notification whenever a 'new' number or a 'flagged' number was dialed or received. A computer generated notification would be sent to an FBI computer in Washington, D.C., which in turned sent a notification to the Agent in Charge. That Agent in Charge in the FBI computer database was still John Watkins.

Watkins' notification came in the form of an email. It listed a number called into Jacinda Jefferson's phone from a number with a Montgomery, Alabama, telephone exchange number. Watkins saw this as more of a chore than a lead. At that point in time, he was doing his own lead investigative work in that he no longer had any agents assigned to the Mark Johnson murder case.

Watkins used an access node granted to the FBI by all the telephone service companies in America. It returned the name of the cell-phone-in-question being owned by one 'Treytina Parker,' along with her street address in Montgomery, Alabama.

In his investigative interview call, Watkins was told by the phone's owner that she had never heard of Jacinda Jefferson. But then, after checking her call record, she remembered that she had loaned her phone to a man in the Nashville Bus Terminal on the day in question.

All of a sudden Watkins was interested. The very first thing he did was order an activity report on the GPS trackers on McNally's vehicles to see if McNally had made a trip to Nashville.

3.4 NEEDLE IN A HAYSTACK

By the time Watkins got to the Nashville bus station, the day shift had ended, and there was only a skeleton night crew.

Watkins had three cameras' videos to review, but he knew the time of the call. That made quick work of finding the event.

Just as the Montgomery woman had said, two of the videos got different angles of her sitting a couple of rows from a man who got out of his seat and approached her for the use of her phone.

Watkins went in for a closeup on the caller. 'He's well disguised. The ball cap obscures his face.' But the surprise was the man's clothing. 'This guy looks like he just walked into the bus terminal from a country club.' It created a sliver of doubt in Watkins' mind.

Watkins ran the videos backward to find the time when the man made his ticket purchase. Then he went backward some more to find out how the man arrived.

The curb video only showed the man entering the terminal from the sidewalk, having come into the frame from outside the camera's viewing range.

Watkins watched his person-of-interest approach the ticket window. From the ticket purchase time stamp on the video, Watkins found out that his suspect had bought a ticket to Chicago with cash. He then ran the video way forward to confirm that his suspect had actually gotten on the Chicago bus.

Watkins, with a downloaded copy of the Nashville videos, and with all his notes in hand, got into his car after midnight to make the seven hour drive to Chicago.

Watkins arrived at the Chicago Bus Terminal at nine in the morning. The traffic leading into Chicago had been a nightmare.

The office manager in Chicago played a video for Watkins that showed the Nashville bus arrival. Watkins watched each person step off the bus. When the bus driver closed the doors on the empty bus, his guy in the baseball hat and the country club clothes was nowhere to be seen. Watkins thought, 'He got off in transit.'

The office manager placed a call to the bus driver. Watkins spoke to him.

The bus driver reported that there were no stops between Nashville and Chicago, and that there was a toilet on board the bus for the passengers' comfort. "…yes, Sir. We inspect the entire interior of the bus, including the toilet, before we allow the next-run passengers to board." He added, "We check the luggage compartment as well."

The bell went 'Ding!' in Watkins' head. 'My guy had to get his two duffel bags out of the luggage compartment when he de-boarded.'

Watkins went back to the tapes. When he saw a man removing the two large duffel bags from the luggage bay, he freeze-framed the guy and went in for a close-up.

'Son-uv-a-bitch! Would ya look at that! He changed clothes during the bus ride. No more ball cap. Now he's wearing what has to be a wig of braids. He's in an athletic suit. He's wearing a pair of eyeglasses. And the nice shoes are gone for a pair of very expensive-looking sneakers.'

Then Watkins noticed the guy had something under his arm. He went in for a closer look. It was the shoulder bag that was now rolled up under his arm like a bedroll. The shoulder bag was a different color than the first shoulder bag. 'He turned it inside-out before he rolled it and the contents up.'

Watkins had a moment of respect for the planning and the effort that went into this attempted Houdini act. The profile workup on the boys made Watkins believe that neither one of them could have planned all this on their own.

'McNally.'

Then Watkins got back on the case.

'Unless Jamal has beefed up since his disappearance, this has to be Muhammad.'

Watkins asked for another video so he could track who he now believed to be Muhammad.

Watkins tracked him around the terminal until he finally went to the ticket window. Watkins wrote down the time stamp in hour : minute : second format, just like it was on the screen. He passed the time stamp to the office manager and asked for ticket information.

"Des Moines, Iowa."

In Chicago, it wasn't yet noon. Watkins calculated he could be in Des Moines by five o'clock. He collected downloads from the Chicago videos and, along with his notes, got into his car, heading to Des Moines. But for the adrenaline, the trip to Des Moines would have represented a hazard to other motorists on the Interstate.

Watkins had called ahead, but when he pulled into the Des Moines bus station, it wasn't much more than an office attached to a gas station. Watkins didn't care about that. What he cared about was that it was all closed up.

Watkins called his contact number. As he stood outside the locked office, he could hear the phone ringing inside the office.

Watkins saw a motel down the street. That was what he really needed, anyway.

The only video camera in the Des Moines bus stop was the security video inside the office. The office manager had queued it up according to Watkins request from the day before, but it was a waste of time.

Watkins had the one-terabyte USB disk containing the Nashville and Chicago videos in his pocket. "If I show you the guy on these videos, do you think you might be able to I.D. him?" Watkins found the best spot in the Chicago video.

"Nobody who looked like that guy off the Chicago bus here."

Watkins thought of the clothing change. Then he thought, 'Reverse elimination.'

"If I show you the line of people who got onto this bus in Chicago, do you think you might remember the one person who is *not* one of those people that de-boarded here in Des Moines?"

The office worker didn't understand the question, so he just shrugged his shoulders.

The office worker watched the line of people board the bus from Chicago to Des Moines. He pointed at people whom he remembered by their clothing. It was a good sign to Watkins when he pointed at Muhammad and said, "That guy wasn't on the bus when it got to here, in Des Moines."

When they had watched all the people board, Watkins asked, "Do you remember anyone you saw get off here, but who was *not* in that line in the Chicago video?"

The office worker said, "Do you mean the Black guy with the braids in the athletic suit?"

Watkins nodded.

"Now I know what you want." Watkins was nodding at him in anticipation. "The only person that got off the bus here who didn't get on the bus in Chicago was the guy in the athletic suit with the braided hair."

Watkins was about to give up hope. "Do you remember what he looked like when he got off the bus...here."

"Of course I do. He stood out like a sore thumb. He was a bald Black guy. His head was shaved. When he went to get his bags, I expected him to pull a golf bag out from underneath."

"Do you remember if he had gold teeth?"

"Gold teeth? No way. He wasn't *that* kind of Black guy. I just told you. He looked like he just finished eighteen holes."

"Do you remem…"

Before Watkins could finish his sentence, the office worker said, "He bought a ticket to Denver and, when the Denver bus showed up, he went to Denver."

With no more Agents at his disposal, it had taken two days for an administrative clerk to get back to him with the McNally GPS tracking data. The clerk reported, "No trips to Nashville. In fact, no trips that day at all. In fact, his truck going to his mailbox is the only activity on either one of the vehicles over the past week. That covers before and after the bus station alert."

Watkins wondered if McNally had found and removed them. 'No. They both show activity from time to time. The truck goes to get his mail. Even the little car goes out every once in a while for grocery trips, confirmed by coincident receipts tracked from his bank account.' Nevertheless, Watkins was undeterred about his suspicions…no, his con*clu*sions…about McNally.

Back to the pressing matter at hand, Watkins resolved he wasn't going to make the nine or ten hour drive to Denver, so he called his Assistant Director Boss for a referral to the Denver Field Office Assistant Director.

The Denver Assistant Director assigned Watkins to a Special Agent in Charge. Watkins relayed his information and his request that a Denver Agent download video from the Denver Bus Terminal before and after the Des Moines bus.

Then Watkins made the nine-plus hour drive back to his home in Memphis where he arrived in the wee hours of that Saturday morning. There was no more adrenaline left, so he had been a danger to fellow travelers the whole way home from Des Moines.

3.5 ROOM WITH A VIEW

Michael Dean had set his bags down on the sidewalk to review the street map of Denver and Highlands Ranch and, specifically, the house that had been rented in advance for him.

While he was studying the map, a car stopped at the curb next to him. The passenger side window was electrically lowered by the driver. A Black teenager was in the driver's seat of his parents' Volvo station wagon. Micheal leaned down to see what he wanted. The driver leaned over to see Michael's face.

"Where you going, Sir?"

Michael suddenly felt old. "Highlands Ranch."

"Put your bags in the rear. I'll drive you there. That's where I live."

Michael thought he should look to the sky to see if he could see an angel.

"You new in town? Or are you just returning?"

"I'm new, but I already have a place to stay."

"Oh, really? We're a pretty small town. Where are you staying?"

Michael was thankful that he had rehearsed the names throughout his cross-country trip. "Judy and Devin Beshires?"

"Sure. I know who they are. They have a son that was a Senior in High School when I was a Freshman. He must be a Junior at college now because I'm a Senior at Highlands Ranch High. I don't know if I ever heard where their son went to college. Do you know them through their son?"

"Ah...no."

"Oh...that's cool. Where you coming from?"

"Ah...Des Moines, Iowa."

"What brought you here? We don't have a lot of Blacks in town."

"Ah...the thin air. I'm a runner and I thought this would be a great place to train for my dream of running marathons."

"Oh, cool. Well, here we are. This is the Beshires' house."

"Wow, that was quick."

"Yeah. We're close to everything. Hey, good luck, man. I can't wait to tell my parents that the Black population of our town just increased by double-digit percentage points."

"Ha! That's funny. And thanks for the ride."

The Beshires knew the estimated time of Michael Dean's bus arrival from Des Moines. Michael chocked another one up to Scottie taking care of everything. They had left their front door open as a sign of 'Welcome.'

When they heard the car doors opening and closing, the couple came to their open front door and stood behind the glass of their storm door to watch Michael finish up his interaction with Stan Woodruff.

As Michael and his bags walked up their front steps, Judy and Devin Beshires opened the storm door for him. "It was so nice of Stan Woodruff to give you a ride here. How do you know him?"

"I don't, M'am. He was passing by the bus station when I arrived, and I guess I looked like I was heading to Highlands Ranch."

Devin Beshires took Michael's two large duffel bags, and Judy led them both through the house and up the stairs to the back apartment.

They gave him a tour of the small space. The kitchenette, the refrigerator, the cabinets, the bedroom, the living room, the full bathroom, the mirrored medicine chest for storage, the rear door to his private entrance steps. Michael felt well taken care of. By more than just the Beshires.

To the Beshires, Michael looked weary from his journey. If only they knew. So the Beshires excused themselves, offering "anything we can do to help you get settled," as they left him alone.

Michael unpacked his duffel bags into the closet and dresser in his bedroom, he wolfed down his last snack from his shoulder bag, and then he took a long hot shower. He knew he was paying for the hot water because Scottie's dossier on the place included the fact that the electricity had already been established in Michael's name, along with the deposit money. 'No more of those cold and tepid showers like at Scottie's place.'

Michael used his last waking moments before his first night's sleep in his new digs to scan the Cable TV channels on the widescreen High Definition TV in his living room area. As he flipped from channel to channel to channel, he couldn't help thinking how different this world was from the one he had come from. From the *ones* he had come from.

When Michael woke up, he made it his first order of business to make a list of his tasks for the day:

Find a Mack Donald's for breakfast.
Find a clothing store.
Register to vote.
Sign up at Denver YMCA for swimming laps.
Find a job.

Scottie's encouragement had been to get a bank account established, as well as a driver's license and a cellphone, as a first order of business. Michael didn't feel good about doing any of those chores. Becoming discovered was dominating his brain. 'Paranoia is a disease. Awareness is a virtue,' he remembered Scottie saying. Michael convinced himself that he was just being aware.

He knew the most important thing on his list was to find a job. But he also knew it would be the forth thing he would do that day.

He laid out all of Scottie's computer printed maps and pictures on the kitchenette table. He reviewed them. He found the retail district in town and used his finger to plan his walk there.

Michael had to walk down Main Street to get to the mall-type retail district, so that gave him a chance to check out all the Mom and Pop boutique-type stores. He was quickly getting acclimated to what 'up-scale suburb' meant.

As he strolled down the sidewalk checking out all the store fronts, he came upon one that was familiar. It was the restaurant with the plate glass window that was in the Street View screenshot that Scottie had included in his information package. Michael decided to forego Mack Donald's and have breakfast there.

A young woman whose name tag said 'Marie' greeted him as he entered. "One for breakfast?"

"Yes. Thank you."

"Can I get you a coffee while you decide what you want?"

"Oh...no thank you. But is your orange juice fresh-squeezed?"

"We don't squeeze it ourselves, but it's the Simply Orange brand...with lots of pulp. I'll bet you won't be able to tell the difference. Is that what you'd like?"

Michael nodded his head as he picked up the menu. "Thank you."

He had just decided on the Chef's Breakfast Special when his waitress arrived with his orange juice. Michael was shocked that she was Black. 'Has everyone been lying to me about this being an all-White community?'

"Good morning. My name is Shauna. Are you ready to order?"

"Yes. The Chef's Breakfast Special, please."

"Whole wheat or regular pancakes?"...

"Real maple syrup or Aunt Jemima?"...

"Eggs over light, over easy, over medium, or hard yokes?"...

"Fried in butter, or fried in margarine?"...

"Bacon, sausage patties, or sausage links?"...

"Sausage patties mild, medium, or extra-spicy?"...

"Would you like some sprigs of peppermint, spearmint, or parsley to adorn your Chef's Special?"...

"May I interest you in a cup of tea and a shortbread biscuit with your morning paper while you wait?"...

Michael thought, 'Damn! It ain't easy being 'upscale.'

Shauna returned with the morning newspaper.

Michael opened it and leaned back in his chair to feign a morning review of the previous day's events. Two minutes later, Shauna returned with an apology.

"I'm sorry, Sir. Our dishwasher quit this morning, and our Chef is doing double duty with the dishwashing and the cooking. It will only be a few minutes longer than usual."

Michael folded his newspaper and set it down on the table. "Hey...Yeah...That's alright...I'm not in a hurry." He had to pause to find his words. "I just got into town yesterday, and my first order of business is to find a job. As a new person to a new town, I've been told that, to succeed, I have to be willing to start at the bottom. What are you doing about filling that position of dishwasher?"

A minute later the hostess with the name tag 'Marie' came to his table. "Shauna told me you might be interested in the dishwashing job?"..."Where did you work before?"..."Where do you live in this area?"..."Oh, yes. We all know the Beshires. They're regular customers here. The job is really designed for a kid who lives at home with his parents. It doesn't pay much."..."Oh, then you must have done well at your last job in Des Moines. Can you start today?"..."Great. Breakfast is on the house. You can report back to the kitchen when you've finished eating."

Michael enjoyed every bite of his 'free' upscale breakfast. While he got ready to put on the apron, he thought, 'The job might not be much...but the scenery is fine.'

He was looking forward to learning more about that 'fine' waitress, Shauna.

3.6 THE MILE HIGH CLUB

When Watkins entered his office on Monday morning, he was well rested. His first order of business was to get a download from the Denver Bus Terminal. The uploads from the Denver Agent were waiting for Watkins on his office computer.

Watkins saw his presumed Muhammad get off the bus in his braids and athletic gear and sneakers. 'Another costume change.'

Watkins didn't need to track him to his next bus connection. He watched his subject, along with his two big duffel bags and his shoulder bag, march right out of the bus terminal. There was no way Watkins would be lucky enough to watch him get into a cab or an Uber...or any other vehicle. Muhammad just walked out of view.

Watkins called the Denver Special Agent in Charge and told the story of the bus terminal video. Watkins asked that the neighborhood be canvased for any possible security camera videos.

On Tuesday morning, Watkins had the neighborhood uploads from Denver.

Every time Muhammad would appear in a different video, he was still walking. Then, videos from further down his stroll came up blank. He'd disappeared.

Watkins got the approval from his Assistant Director to go to Denver to give and to get a full briefing on this new and promising lead.

In the Metro Denver briefing room, there seemed to be sparse attendance. One familiar face was that of Union Rep, Neal Knopfler. He assumed Knopfler had flown out after Watkins had briefed the Metro Chief about the bus terminal information.

Despite the near-empty briefing room, Watkins was assured by the Metro Denver Chief that Watkins' briefing was being streamed to all

Metro Denver detectives and Patrolmen, as well as being made available to all Denver area local police forces. "As an affiliated group, we call ourselves *The Mile High Club*. But its all virtual...just so there's no misunderstanding about its meaning."

Watkins proceeded with his briefing in the good faith the someone was watching.

The first part of his briefing was on the murder of Officer Mark Johnson. The video of the Walmart parking lot encounter was shared, with Watkins narrating.

An addendum to that video was a morgue photo of Officer Mark Johnson's neck wound. An explanation of its lethality, despite the small size of the puncture laceration, was given. "We don't know if this was a planned method, or if the perps just got lucky."

Watkins explained the effects of a carotid artery slice-and-separation. When he got to the part about the heart pumping all the body's blood out the wound, spurt by spurt, in rhythm with the heartbeat, and sending no more blood to the brain, thus causing the brain to lose all its blood in seconds, a Patrolman monitoring the briefing from his Desk Sergeant duties at a nearby suburb leaned away from his desk and vomited toward his trash can. The trash can was not all-capturing of the Patrolman's disturbance.

Watkins then put up an artist's sketch of Muhammad and explained that it was confirmed as accurate by neighborhood people who knew the perpetrator.

Watkins moved on to his former 'Mona Lisa' profile to his near-empty briefing room, but now supplemented that profile with information gleaned from the bus terminal videos.

"The auxiliary profile of our suspect is that he is a Black man disguised to be unnoticeable in a White world in terms of dress. Therefore, his arrival date might be the most helpful clue you have." After giving the arrival date, Watkins went on to encourage all officers to take note of any new Black arrival to their town or to the neighborhoods they patrol.

In the all White nearby suburb of Highlands Ranch, Patrolman Roger Crest wrote down the arrival date as he was cleaning the puke off his mouth with a napkin.

After the briefing, Watkins saw Neal Knoffler pull a Denver Sergeant aside.

After Knopfler left the room, the Sergeant approached Watkins with some intelligence.

"There's secret money in this for the officer that brings the kid in. $5,000 for the preferable delivery of the kid being dead. $1,000 if he's brought in alive."

3.7 SEE THE USA IN YOUR CHEVROLET

Scottie and Robert would stay in some motels, as well as some National Park cabins, and even a couple of nights in a fancy hotel in Las Vegas. But Vegas was the exception.

They had spent four days in Big Bend. Then they spent a long day driving through the desert Southwest to see the Sand Monuments. That was on the way to the Grand Canyon, where they stayed in a National Park cabin, took a donkey ride down into the Canyon, and made a guided overnight hiking stay in the Canyon, sleeping in tents along the Colorado River. All of which had been pre-arranged over the internet by Scottie well before they had left Tennessee.

When they left the Grand Canyon, they took a couple of days to drive toward Four Corners, adding in lots of stop time so they could converse with Native Americans about their cultures and about their perceptions of America through the eyes of another minority. Most wouldn't share, but they had several meaningful conversations. There was consensus. 'White people feel the need to dominate us, too.'

From Four Corners, they drove North along the Eastern Slope of the

Rocky Mountains until they got to Colorado Springs, at which point they made a day trip driving up Pike's Peak. Then they headed West, deeper into the Rockies, over roads that were more safely traversed in a Jeep or, better yet, a Land Cruiser.

Then they took small roads up toward Salt Lake where Scottie drove to a ski resort where an off-season ski lift to the top of the mountain gave them a panoramic view of most of Salt Lake.

Scottie then drove to the Nevada Salt Flats where he and Robert talked about land speed records and geologic history and UFO's.

From the Salt Flats, Scottie drove to the bright lights of Las Vegas. They spent three days there learning about organized crime and prostitution and casino odds. Odds at the slot machines. Odds at the Poker Tables. Odds at the Black Jack tables. Bright lights and sleep depravation. Alcohol and judgement degradation. Money from and money to. Suckers...and those preying on suckers.

They were both overstimulated when they headed up to Lake Tahoe. There, they enjoyed perches above the Lake's perimeter for viewing and an overnight in a lakeside cabin. From the cabin, they experienced the world famous and world practiced morning polar-bear swim. They both took the cold water plunge, but they knew they weren't getting the full frigid experience of the first ice-out...but still...it took their breaths away.

Then they took the circuitous route through Arizona to enter Southern California from the desert to the beach. Yuma to San Diego.

When they got to San Diego, Scottie parked in a beach parking lot. They got out of the car, took their shoes and socks off, and walked in the sand to the water's edge.

"We're heading into Winter? And we could just dive into the ocean from this warm sand and take a swim? Is this the Wonderland where you're dropping me off? I mean...this is the Pacific Ocean."

"No. I stopped here so I could show you two looks at Mexico."

They registered in The Eldorado Hotel in downtown San Diego, then drove to the Mexican border the next morning.

When they got to Mexican border police booths, Scottie lowered his window and handed the Mexican Officer two passports.

The Mexican Border Guard turned back into his booth and started punching on his computer. A minute later, he handed the two documents back to Scottie and waved their car through.

Scottie handed one of the documents to Robert who was impressed by the heavy blue cover and the gold embossed eagle on the front. When he opened it up, he saw a picture of himself with address and other information from Tennessee.

"How did you get me a passport?"

"The same way I got you your social security card. Hard work and good luck."

"What is the address on here? Looks like yours."

"It's close, but it's not."

Scottie and Robert drove around some of the neighborhoods in Tijuana. If their car had been fancy, they would have garnered more, and possibly more dangerous, attention. But the old, nondescript, shifting colors Toyota-Nissan fit right in. They drove in and out and around the condensed neighborhoods without drawing too much attention.

Robert said, "So this is what poverty looks like?"

"That's one way that it looks. But let's drive to something more positively stimulating to the senses."

Scottie drove out of Tijuana and South to the Baja Peninsula.

Scottie drove along the Mexican Pacific beaches until he turned inland and got within view of the inviting Sound. He then drove North along the Sound until he got to the top of the Sound. Scottie pointed to a wide and flat piece of hard ground. "Care to take a guess what that is?"

"Hard ground, it looks like."

"Picture the two times we touched the Colorado River in the bottom of the Grand Canyon."

"OK."

"This is the mouth of that river. This is where that Colorado River empties into the sea."

"OK. So what's the joke? There's no water here emptying into anything."

"Right. It's been a half-a-century since the Colorado emptied here."

"So where does it empty now?"

"It doesn't empty anywhere."

"How does *that* work?"

"Water is too scarce in this part of America to support the massive population you will get a glimpse of tomorrow, and it is too scarce to supply the farmland in this part of America that feeds most of America. So, to take advantage of all the sunshine for growing and the need for water recreation around here, they have to rob the water from wherever they can get it.

"One of the places they get it is from the Colorado River that flows through the Grand Canyon. And they take so much that the Colorado now runs dry long before it gets here."

Robert was looking at the dry rock and sand around the former mouth.

"I'm going to take you a couple hours North of San Diego for you to get established there. This is just a small introduction to some of the issues you will have to adapt to to make it in this part of the country. Over-population, leading to over-usage of resources, leading to a sermon full of issues that need to be figured out by all the people here."

"So, how does it all get figured out?"

"The few and the brave run for public office. They're the ones who have to eventually motivate the population to solve the problems. They are the Rainmakers. Whether a person is any good at being a Rainmaker...only time will tell."

Scottie and Robert spent their last night together in the El Dorado Hotel in San Diego. The next morning, they had a fancy and filling breakfast in the Hotel Restaurant, then re-packed the car to drive through Los Angeles.

Before doing the 'Five' run up to L.A., Scottie drove along the beach to the next door town of Del Mar. Scottie made some trips around several of the commercial horse stables. "Horse breeding and racing is a lot like what we saw in Las Vegas. People making gambles are in and out of these stables all the time. Some get rich. Some lose everything." Robert was impressed with the obvious money it took to build and maintain the grounds. Then Scottie added, "Some get rich *and* lose everything." Then Scottie got on the 'Five' for the run north.

Before showing Robert downtown L.A., Scottie drove West off the 'Five' toward the beaches. After a visit to the pier at Huntington Beach in Orange County, he got on the Pacific Coast Highway and headed North, their next tourist destination being a drive-through in and around Compton, and then touring various and iconic parts of downtown L.A. A study in contrasts for Robert.

After Los Angeles, Scottie got onto the Coast Highway and headed further north. Finally, a street sign on the PCH announced that they were entering the town of Pacific Palisades. Scottie pulled over so Robert could get a good look at the sign. "This is where I'm dropping you off, Robert."

"Here?...At the beach?...At a town line sign?"

"No. Let's take a tour of your new hometown...however long it may or may not be your hometown."

Scottie drove around the neighborhoods in the town, slowing down around the couple of buildings that were apartment complexes.

Then he drove to the top of the remnant of the rim of a prehistoric volcano that defined Pacific Palisades. There, he got onto Ocean View and pulled the car over at the base of a long uphill driveway so they both could get out and look at the panoramic view of the town, the beach, and the Pacific Ocean.

"So this is what you meant when you said you were going to drop me off at the Pacific Ocean?"

"Yes," as they gazed at the natural and man-made beauty all around them.

When the salt air had cleaned out their lungs, they both got back into the car.

Scottie drove back down into the town and found several commercial/industrial areas. He and Robert were bending their heads down to see the names of the companies that occupied the buildings in this area.

As Scottie drove, he said, "This might be a good place to start looking for a job."

Robert was nodding while he was looking.

Scottie pulled over to the curb. "Gimme a second. I have to take a leak."

Scottie parked the car, got out, and made his way between two buildings where he disappeared from sight.

Robert kept looking around. He looked at the building right next to where Scottie had parked. *The Washington Construction Company.* Robert saw office space, warehouse space, and a fenced-in barbed-wired parking area that enclosed every manner of trucks, plus equipment on equipment trailers. Then he saw Scottie come out from behind the buildings, pulling up his zipper.

"This is it, Robert. I'm going to drop you off at a motel and say goodbye. It would behoove you to find work as soon as possible. The longer you don't work, the harder it will become to get a job. So don't dally. It's time to giddy-up."

Not far from where he had parked to take a leak, Scottie pulled into the parking lot of a motel. He waited in the car while Robert went into the office to see if he could get a room. Scottie watched the transaction take place through the plate glass on the side of the office.

Robert came out with a receipt and a key in hand. "I prepaid for a week. That'll give me time to get a job and find a place to live…close enough to whatever job I can find."

Scottie drove over in front of Robert's room door and helped him load his duffel bags and gear and souvenirs into his room.

When the car was empty, the time had come. Robert looked beyond the area of the motel parking lot. "So, this is it? Random? I would guess that you're going to leave it a mystery how you selected this place?"

Scottie said, "The day I met you, I told you I knew what I was doing."

Robert swung his arm wide for the goodbye handshake. But Scottie didn't return the gesture.

"Handshakes to me have always meant, 'Until I see you again.' That's not our reality, Robert. Barring some wildly unforeseeable circumstance, this is it. This is, 'I will never see you nor have any contact with you ever again.' Mostly for your protection, but a little bit for mine, as well."

Robert's eyes squinted at Scottie. It was part of his continuous, but unfulfilled, effort to try and figure this man out.

Scottie's outlook was not simpatico with Robert's. To Scottie, *everything* didn't need to be figured out.

Robert took a step back from Scottie and looked him in the eye. "If the sky should tumble and fall…Or the mountains should crumble to the sea…And the moon is the only light we see…I won't be afraid…As long as you stand by me."

Scottie's voice broke when he tried to answer, "In spirit."

Scottie knew how to control the lump in his throat and the opening of his sinuses and the blood flow into his eyes and the saltwater wash that wanted to keep his eyelids moving smoothly. But none of the control techniques were fully working at that moment. "In this game we've chosen, sentimental acts are the greatest threat to us overcoming." Robert knew Scottie was masking his emotions.

Scottie pulled a folded piece of paper from his shirt pocket and stuffed it into Robert's shirt pocket. Robert's emotions were about to burst. Scottie saw it coming, so he forcefully said, "Fledge!"

He turned his back, entered his car, and drove out of the motel parking lot without looking back.

Robert watched until Scottie was out of sight. He was really watching to see if Scottie would take a look back. Once Scottie was gone, Robert thought to himself, 'Michael was right, Scottie. He and I both knew it the whole time. There was something bad wrong with you.' He turned back toward his motel room and started walking. 'But I'm glad there was.'

When Scottie was beyond sight, his chest started heaving in stuttered breathing. He inhaled through his nose to try and suppress any further physical reaction.

As he drove out of Pacific Palisades, Scottie contemplated taking the long way home, driving six hundred miles North to see the sun set from a bluff overlooking a beach that was once his home turf...but then he thought, 'This is not a moment for accolades or claiming victory.' So he headed back to rural middle Tennessee as the crow flies.

Once he was back in the privacy of his motel room, Robert's eyes were blood red. He had to catch the tears that he couldn't suppress with a wipe of his sleeve.

He reached into his shirt pocket and pulled out the folded piece of paper that Scottie had stuffed in there. He read it out loud to himself so he could absorb every word.

"I am the master of my fate, I am the Captain of my soul."

3.8 I DID IT MY WAY

Absent the constant voice of Scottie in his ear, Robert modified his plan. He decided to get settled before going to look for a job. 'I am the captain of my soul.'

His first order of business was to walk to the nearest bank and open a bank account. He did so with five thousand dollars in cash. His social security card and passport made that task quick and easy.

His second order of business was to walk to the DMV to get a driver's license. That was more of a hike. Having had no previous driver's license, he was required to make an appointment so he could be given a driving test. That was scheduled for two days out.

On his long walk back toward his motel, he passed one of the apartment buildings Scottie had driven him past. His new bank account checks created some pause, but a confirming phone call to his bank suddenly made him a desirable tenant. First and last months rent, plus an application to Pacific Gas & Electric with a security deposit got his apartment's electricity turned on.

Then Robert contemplated walking his duffel bags and other baggage from the hotel to the his new apartment...but rejected that picture. 'Too exhausting. Too 'homeless' looking.'

So the next day Robert went in search of a used car lot but, while walking, he came across a car in a front yard that had a "For Sale" sign on it. He approached the door of the house. A teenage-looking boy answered.

"Yeah. My parents bought it for me as my High School car. But now I'm heading off to college, and I want something a little nicer."

Robert looked it over and was surprised that there was no rust on a seven-year old car. "Have you had body work and a paint job done to cover up the rust?"

"Rust? You must not be from around here. Cars don't rust in California. There's guys driving cars from the 1950's, and even long before that, around that have never had a rust spot on them. No, what you're looking at is the way it came from the factory. It's never had *any* body work done on it."

Robert said, "I'm waiting on my appointment at the DMV for my driver's license. Would you mind taking me on a test drive?"

"Oh, that's all right. I don't care that you don't have a license. It's insured. You can take it for a spin."

"If you don't mind, I'd rather not. I'm not looking for a formal introduction to California State laws."

Robert said he wanted to put new tires on it and negotiated the price down two hundred dollars. Then he took the signed title with him to his driving test appointment. 'Kill two birds with one stone,' as Scottie used to say. I'll get plates for the car while I'm getting my license.' Both of which happened.

On his way out of the DMV with his car plates and his driver's license in hand, he walked by a wireless telephone store. It took some extra deposit and pre-payment money because of him having no credit record, but he walked out of the store with his most treasured asset...a cell phone. Even though he had no numbers to call.

While walking to pick up his car, Robert saw an insurance office. He went in and bought the minimum liability insurance that California would allow. Then he went and, with the teenager's help, he removed the old plates, installed the new plates, and drove back to his motel. There, he loaded his new means of transportation with his belongings, signed out of the motel, and made what felt to him like his first step of independence in his new hometown.

'*Now* I'm ready.'

3.9 CH CH CH CHANGES

When Scottie returned from the West Coast, he reattached the GPS tracking device underneath the Batmobile. As the garage door was closing behind him, he noticed movement on the woods-line to the right of the driveway. He saw a deer being shy about coming out, so he slowly and quietly walked in her direction. She held perfectly still.

When Scottie got about thirty yards away, the deer cautiously stepped out into full unprotected view, her ears twitchingly keeping track of all activity in the three-hundred-sixty degree circumference around her. As Scottie inched his way closer, he saw her raise her head slightly as her nose started working overtime.

Then her nose stopped, and she did something Scottie had never seen before. She started walking backwards into the tree line. When she was fully enveloped, she made a sudden turn and leap, and disappeared into the brush. Scottie's heart sank. 'Mary.' As he was walking back to the house to begin an aggressive assault on his chores, his saddened heart said, 'She knew who I wasn't.'

The arduous task of cleaning out all remnants of the boys began.

All of the furniture and bedding were taken, trip by trip, to the burn pit, along with all the linens. A fire burned with flames all that day.

Kitchen-stored tableware and pots and pans supplemented his own cabinet-stored supplies upstairs. Where there was no room, they were also brought to the burn pit.

The burn pit left all the metal and the glass and the ceramic remnants to form a good base for the dirt and loam re-covering. Nothing went to the landfill. People manned the landfill. Scottie didn't want to create any reports.

Scottie then donned rubber gloves and a fumes mask...along with rubber boots...to scrub the ceilings, the walls, and the floor of the basement, along with all traces of smells and marks...and DNA. He left the vent fans running for five days.

The former burn pit was back-filled with dirt from the mature compost pile. Then he raked it into a smooth transition with it's surrounding landscape. Winter grass seed was planted and covered in straw, then well watered. Scottie would wait until Spring to rake the straw away. The beginnings of a seamless patch of lawn would be in its tender-shoot stage by then. 'If uncovered by a future landowner, this pit will just be considered a dump spot common to all country properties before the days of county landfills.'

Scottie did a similar cleaning upstairs as he had done downstairs. Then he serviced the Batmobile with a fresh oil change and a thorough interior disinfectant wipe-down.

And on the seventh day...

Once everything was under control again, he used the vacuum of activity to walk around the outside of his house in the cold morning air with a cup of steaming lemon tea cupped in his hands. He inventoried the state of nature for everything he could see, as well as for all the sections of the property he could not see...but could picture in detail in his mind.

'After a couple years of intense labor, this place seems to be in a very manageable state.' A sense of satisfaction started to rise within him.

When he had finished his survey and was returning to his kitchen, he thought, 'Stealing young men to cut sugarcane.'

3.10 THE BEAT GOES ON

The computer music that now filled the house had moved away from historical-timeframe-orientation for the nubile listeners. Now, it had succumbed to the gravitational pull of sounds that made Scottie's body move. But his moves were awkward. He knew he danced like a White guy. After decades of neglect, all his muscle memory for dancing had atrophied.

An internet search revealed that there were dance classes an hour and a half from his house. He contemplated the drive time. He contemplated the gasoline and the wear and tear on his vehicles.

He removed the GPS tracker from his vehicle of choice for the weekly trip up to Franklin. His sensitivity about providing evidence was gone. Now it was just an issue of being embarrassed that anyone tracking him would know that he was taking dancing lessons. Plus, he didn't want to advertise his absence from the property. He wanted to make sure that no nosy government data tracker would come in and steal his book collection. But he still left everything unlocked. A complicated psychology.

Scottie had signed up for Salsa lessons on Thursday nights. After a couple of trips up, he noticed that the class before his was a ballroom class. When he saw some of the soft-shoe moves, he remembered those moves as also having once been among his favorites...so he started coming early. He wasn't about to pay for two classes, but he used his observations to take home with him for soft-shoe practice with his air partner.

It also became obvious to Scottie that many of the people who signed up for the classes were doing it to meet people. When women near his age would approach him with inquiries disguised as conversation, he became skilled at being coldly and blandly and deflectively polite. It was effective.

He practiced at home a lot. When he started to get back into the 'groove,' it brought back warm and meaningful memories.

3.11 HELP! I NEED SOMEBODY

On Robert's first day of having his life in order, he rose with the fire of a purpose. He was going to find a job.

He tried to picture all his possibilities and how to execute finding a job, but every thought he had was drowned out by the memory of seeing Scottie get out of the car and disappear to go the bathroom. Subconsciously, Robert couldn't separate that image from the image of being parked in front of *The Washington Construction Company*.

Subconscious rose to conscious, and Robert selected his work boots and woods-working clothing for the drive to where he remembered *The Washington Construction Company* to be.

Robert saw a car in front of the office door, so he approached and knocked. Nothing. So Robert tried the door handle. He found it to be unlocked. The door opened easily. Robert looked in to see a middle-aged man looking up from behind a counter.

..."I don't need to hire anyone right now."

Robert had a line that came to him with no practice. "I'm not looking for a job as much as I'm looking for a chance...a chance to show my value. If you give me a week to show my worth, you don't even need to pay me. That's how confident I am that you won't be able to live without me." Robert wondered, 'Where did *that* come from?'

The middle-aged man behind the counter looked Robert up and down a few times.

"We're gonna break ground on a new project in a couple weeks. 5450 Maple Street. The lot needs to be cleaned up and prepped before we go in strong. Maybe I can use you over there. But shut up about this 'not paying you' nonsense. I have to pay everybody that works for us so my liability insurance will cover any mistakes that might happen."

Robert said, "Thank you, Sir," and turned and left the office.

When he got outside, he did a jump off the ground and kicked his heels together. 'Wow! That was easy!' Then he realized he had leapt into the air and clicked his heels. 'Some of the Irish musta rubbed off.'

By the time Robert reached his car, a closet door that had been open and blocking a wall of metal shelves closed. A recent college graduate stood there. She was wondering what she just heard.

"Hey, Dad, why did that guy just walk out of here? It sounded to me like you had just told him that you'd hire him."

"I don't know, Christine. It's beyond me to figure you kids out. That's why I have foremen. If he's not smart enough to hang around to do payroll paperwork, then it's just as well that he left."

Mark Mack was looking down at his paperwork while he shuffled it. While shaking his bowed head, he whispered to himself, "Who can figure these kids out."

3.12 DO YOU HEAR WHAT I HEAR

On the third day after Robert had knocked on the door of *The Washington Construction Company*, Robert returned with a file folder under his arm. Even though this was not going to be a day of labor, Robert still thought it best to wear a clean set of work clothes to the office.

When Robert entered the office, the closet door was closed. That allowed him to see a girl moving some papers around on a wall of metal shelves. She was so attractive to Robert that it made him embarrassed. He looked at the owner to purposefully avoid eye contact with the young woman.

"Hey, I remember you. You can just turn around and walk back outta here. We don't need people who think they can just appear and disappear at their own choosing." Mark Mack's finger was pointing toward the door as he spoke.

Robert couldn't read what was going on. "But it took me two days."

Mark Mack wasn't sure if he should even engage the kid. "Two days to what? Decide if you wanted to respond to me? Excuses don't work in this business."

Robert said, "OK, but I'm finished."

"You're right you're finished," as Mark had his finger extended again, pointing toward the door. "Slackers don't make it here."

Robert said, "OK. But I still need to be reimbursed for my expenses."

Mark Mack was about to explode. "What kind of scam is *this*? Get your ass out of here before I call the cops."

Robert got sheepish from the rejection and the threat. "You don't need to call the cops, Sir." He laid his file folder on the counter. "But at your convenience, I will need reimbursement."

With those gentle words, Robert turned and exited the office.

Mark Mack turned the folder around and opened it. "What the..."

His daughter, Christine, walked over after witnessing the exchange and stood next to her father. She joined him in looking at the folder full of receipts.

"Call your mother and tell her we'll be late for supper." Mark picked up the folder of receipts. "Let's take a ride."

3.13 LET THE SUNSHINE IN

As Mark Mack and his daughter, Christine, were locking up *The Washington Construction Company* for a road trip, Robert was already gone.

The father and daughter arrived at the lot address of 5450 Maple Street. Both Mark and Christine jaws dropped.

"I'll...be...damned! Look at that lot! Where are all the trees and the bushes and debris and the big rocks? It's even been leveled...and our equipment never left the yard."

Christine was flipping through receipts in the file folder. She pulled one out and handed it to her Dad.

Mark looked it over. "*Palisades Equipment and Tool Rental*...Let me see that folder."

Mark reviewed every receipt. He pulled one of particular interest out and showed it to Christine. "Look at this one, Christine. He hired some day-laborers...and had them sign their names for receiving their cash payments." He studied the rest of the receipts. "Who *is* this kid?"

Christine said, "You do know what happened, don't you, Dad?"

Mark closed the file folder. "What?"

"That day that he came into the office looking for a job, you told him you had this lot that needed cleaning and preparation for the groundbreaking. He took that to mean that you wanted him to do it." She was watching for the light bulb to go off in her father's head. "He isn't trying to scam you, Dad. It looks to me like just the opposite. That he's a sincere person who was hyper-interested in showing you what he could do." She looked back out her window at the cleared lot. "Your crew couldn't have done this is two days, Dad."

Mark circled the car around in the middle of Maple Street and headed home for supper. "Yeah. I can see how this happened." He thought, 'This kid is good. I wonder what else he can do?'

3.14 IS IT TOO LATE TO SAY I'M SORRY

Robert realized that the business owner had no way to get in touch with him, so he waited two days. Then he returned to *The Washington Construction Company* office.

Mark Mack looked up when Robert walked in. "I apologize for my presumptions when we spoke a couple of days ago..."

Robert thought, 'Sure. Presumptions about the color of my skin.'

"...but when my daughter and I realized that you had left a folder of receipts, we took a ride over to Maple Street and were happily surprised at what we saw."

Robert looked around the office for the beautiful girl that he had not been able to get off his mind since his last visit.

"You looking for my daughter? She's gone to Nashville for a couple weeks with her mother and grandmother. They all have life-long friends there that they visit every so often."

Mark saw that Robert seemed distracted. "When we saw your work, she became a fan...but don't get any ideas."

Robert was too distracted to be thinking about 'ideas' any longer. The only thing on his mind was, 'Nashville, huh?'

Mark had to snap him back into the present. "Hey! Over here! I have an offer for you, and I don't want any miscommunications this time."

Robert re-focused on his new boss. "OK."

"I have three renovations to start at the same time the Maple Street project has to start. My residential foreman can't do it all, so I want to try you out as supervising the three reno projects. If you juggle a crew between all three, you should have them all wrapped within about six months. It's a 'pass or fail' opportunity. I wouldn't want to demote you to being grunt labor if it doesn't work out."

Robert was looking within himself about Nashville as he was nodding his head and listening.

Mark gave him a second. "So? What do you say? Wanna take the risk? Do or die? Sink or swim?"

Robert had decided mid-explanation that he wanted to try it. All he was thinking about now was the daughter. The daughter in Nashville.

"Yes."

3.15 **BOOTSTRAPS**

In Highlands Ranch, Michael bussed tables, washed dishes and pots and pans, and even hustled for the Chef when he got behind. But the waitress, Shauna, didn't work every day, so he spent most of his time looking forward to watching her from a safe distance on the days when she *did* come in.

Michael hadn't been on the job for a month when he arrived to work one Saturday to find there was no Chef. Orders started coming in right away, so he switched aprons and donned a new, stylish Chef's hat, knowing that the dishes would stack up.

Michael knew the whole menu well and had helped the Chef enough to have all the dish preparations in his memory. Shauna was working that day, and he caught her exchanging looks with the hostess, Marie, that were clearly meant to communicate how impressed they both were that the Chef's absence was going unnoticed. The *coup de gras* for the girls was Michael using a lull to walk the tables to inquire about the patrons' satisfaction instead of trying to get the dirty dishes caught up.

Michael never knew he had a public relations personality until that day. But then he second guessed himself. 'It might just be I have a way with old, rich White ladies.' A murmur started to circulate about him. The good kind of murmur.

In between the breakfast crowd and the lunch rush, Michael looked at the pile of dirty dishes and chose to hold off on his attack. Instead, he went to Marie to ask for a phone book. Marie brought Michael into the office and pulled it out for him.

He took the phone book and looked up at the ceiling, trying to remember a name. Finally, he lowered his head back to normal and said, "Oh, yeah. Stan Woodruff."

Michael opened the phonebook and went straight for the 'W's.' He was psyched that someone named Woodruff had a land line.

"Is Stan home?"..."Hi, Stan. This is Michael Dean. You gave me a ride to the Beshires home the day I arrived in town?"..."It's because I'm the Chef at *The Sunflower Cafe and Restaurant* on Main Street, and I have an urgent opportunity for someone. I thought you might be able to hook me up."..."Great, Stan. Thanks."

Michael returned to the kitchen and attacked the stack of dishes and pots and pans. Just after he had started making a dent, Marie came in. "There's a phone call for you in the office."

By the time lunch orders started to come in, Danny Montagne was finishing up the breakfast dishes. As Danny washed away, Michael made conversation.

"So...Stan Woodruff is the Captain of your fencing team?"..."So you're a Freshman this year?"..."Yes. Stan's a great guy."..."Have you ever heard of a fencer named Helen Mayer?"..."Yeah. Nobody would have heard of her. She was an Olympic Medalist back before World War II."... And so it went. Michael wasn't really sure about how to be the boss of somebody.

After the lunch rush, Michael went to the office to take a rest in a real chair. Marie was on the phone, but she didn't mind speaking in front of Michael.

"Yes, Miss Lilly, he made the call himself."..."Yes, Miss Lilly. He's a friend of someone Michael knows from in town."..."No, Miss Lilly. There was no interruption in service. The customers never had a clue."..."Yes, Miss Lilly, I'm sure he'd like to meet you at some point, also."

Marie hung up the phone and said to Michael while he was stretching out his legs in the comfortable office chair, "Word's getting 'round about you." Then she left the room to go back to preparing the restaurant for the Saturday evening supper crowd.

Michael was only concerned about the word about him getting around to one person.

3.16 STILL WATERS RUN DEEP

At *The Sunflower Cafe and Restaurant*, Michael Dean was making everybody's work life run a little more smoothly. He had expanded the menu as well as laying out the new menu format for the printers. Plus, he had a stable of phone numbers of friends of friends of friends of Stan Woodruff that ensured the dishwashing chore was always covered.

And then there was the customer relations. Michael came to know the regulars by name and was always formally polite to them. His reason for mingling with them was to get feedback on their level of satisfaction with his cooking. And then the magic began.

When Michael came to know the tastes and preferences of individual regulars, he began doing custom ingredient modifications to their orders. Then, when the meal was near completion, he would make a round through the restaurant, his goal being to get to that one customer to find out if they liked his modifications. Market research.

When Michael got a tweaked recipe to where he was getting an effusive response, that customer would tell her friends, and she would tell her friends, and she would tell her friends…

There came a day when the owner of the restaurant, a near-mythical creature whom everyone referred to as 'Miss Lilly,' and who was rarely seen, and who only spoke with the hostess/manager, Marie, when she *did* make an appearance, came in, by-passed Marie, and made a direct walk back to the kitchen.

"Michael, I presume?…Word is getting out about your Chef skills. Many of my friends gush over you. I rarely get involved in the affairs of my restaurant…it's really just a thing my husband encouraged me to do after we both had nothing left to do...but I've never had all my lady friends come to me with anything to say about my little restaurant...until you. Now, all I hear about is your tasty treats. And my accountant tells me I'll be paying more taxes this year. So, I came in to tell you I'm giving you a raise."

"Oh...thank you, M'am. But as long as you're here, what I *really* think would help you to pay more taxes..." Miss Lilly laughed, "...is if I could post a new category of menu items under the heading 'Chef Michael's Greatest Hits." For a while, Michael had pictured this idea as a stepping stone to his next career move, perhaps opening his own restaurant someday.

Miss Lilly said, "Do your thing. Far be it from me to stand in the way of a good idea."

As Miss Lilly was leaving her restaurant, the door was held open for her by a uniformed policeman. As she walked past him, she said, "Thank you, Roger." He bowed his head in acknowledgement and entered for a coffee.

Patrolman Roger Crest had heard about this new Chef at *The Sunflower*...and it was mentioned that he was Black. So Patrolman Crest took it upon himself to eliminate this newcomer from the suspicion of being FBI Agent Watkins' fugitive. Crest had folded up a printout of the sketch portrait and had slid it into his pocket.

"Good morning, Marie."

"Well, good morning, Roger. What brings you here? We thought you forgot about us."

"You know how it is, Marie. Busy, busy, busy."

"Do you want to sit?"

"Oh, no thanks. I only have time to get a coffee and run."

"Shauna? Can you get Officer Crest a black coffee with a little cream, no sugar?"

Patrolman Crest watched Shauna disappear into the kitchen. When the door opened, he saw that a Black man in an apron and a Chef's hat was back there. He knew that had to be his person-of-interest.

Patrolman Crest beat feet to the kitchen and swung the door open to see Shauna pouring his coffee into a to-go cup.

"Oh, Shauna. Could you make that without the cream this time? I'm trying to cut down on my fat intake."

"Sure." She set the pot back on its burner, placed the sip-lid on the cup, and handed it to Patrolman right then and there. "It's on the house."

"Thanks, Shauna." He turned his attention to Michael. Stretching out his hand, he said, "Good morning. My name is Roger Crest."

"Michael. Michael Dean."

Crest thought to himself, 'Right height. Right build. But that's not the guy in the sketch.' "It's nice to meet you, Michael. There's a buzz around town about your cooking skills."

While shaking Patrolman Crest's hand, Michael smiled. "Thank you. I appreciate you for mentioning that. I love to get customer feedback. You'll have to come in sometime for a meal."

When Michael smiled, Patrolman Crest got a look at Michael's pearly whites. 'Nope. Definitely not the guy.'

"Well, keep up the good work. And it was nice to meet you."

When Crest got out onto the sidewalk, he pulled the folded up sketch out of his pocket just to make sure. He reviewed all the features in the sketch. 'Nope. Not the guy.'

During the lull before lunch, Shauna approached Michael in the kitchen. "Nice job with Miss Lilly and Officer Crest. Where'd you learn all these tricks that are making you the toast of the town?"

This was the day...this was the moment...Michael had been waiting for. But he was tongue-tied. He choked. "Mother."

Shauna thought, 'Mother? I've never heard a brotha call Mama 'mother.' Even in her thoughts, Shauna pronounced brotha without the 'r.'

Shauna knew how to be bold when it served her. "Why don't you just take a leap and ask me something about myself?"

Michael knew the door was finally being opened. He wanted to rush right in…but girls were not part of his skill set. "Do you dream in color?"

Shauna was gobsmacked. She was not expecting a question with any depth. She was so taken aback that she walked away with her mouth open, caught up in the unexpectedness of that little treat.

Michael wasn't sure about what just happened. All he could do was watch her walk out the kitchen door. And to Michael, the view was splendid.

Shauna's most regular schedule was to do all the prep work for the lunch crowd and then go home. She was a part-timer. When her shift was over, she passed through the kitchen to the office to change her shoes. Michael approached her and said, "I hope I didn't say anything wrong." She was still in wonder about his question. "What I'd really like to say is that I'd like to take a walk in the snow with you tonight after I get off work."

"This is my house address. What time should I expect you?"

Shauna's four-year-old son had been in bed for a couple of hours when Michael knocked on her door.

"I'm sorry, Michael. I should have known this was too late when you asked me. I have a four-year-old, Blake, who I put down a couple of hours ago."

Michael didn't want to invite himself into her house, so he said, "I saw a playground behind your house on my walk here. And the full moon is out, so we don't need a flashlight. Is there any chance you can see his bedroom window from there?"

"Yes. His bedroom window overlooks the playground. But I can't take a chance to leave him alone in the house."

"What if you turned the hall light on outside his bedroom? That way, if he wakes up and opens his door to look for you, you can see the light from the open door through the window to the playground."

Shauna pictured that idea in her mind and was impressed by his planning skills. She said, "OK."

She put on her winter jacket and wool pullover hat and lined gloves. Then she slid her stocking feet into her winter boots. Then they walked a couple houses down to a side street that took them to the fenced playground's entrance. Their footprints were the first footprints in the freshly fallen snow.

Conversation was a bit awkward for both of them. Lots of little fears had invaded both of their psyches. Shauna kept looking up at Blake's bedroom window.

Finally, as they both were silently admiring the magic of the sparkling snow in the moonlight, Michael started the conversation.

"The moonlight on the snow makes a unique and magical color."

Shauna was being hypnotized by its wonder. "Yes. It's beautiful. It really fills my soul with something that feels really good."

Michael asked, "What's the name of that color? The color of moonlight on the snow?"

Shauna thought about it. "I don't know. It is a unique and remarkable color, but I've never heard the name of it. Do you know?"

Michael said, "As far as I know, there is no name for that color. It's the most magical of all colors, and yet there's no name for it. Would it be too assuming if we were to give it a name?"

Shauna had rushing thoughts of all the complications of a romance pass through her brain. "You're a poet, Michael. That's so refreshing. But sometimes, to me, the most beautiful part of a poem is what is left to my imagination...between the words. I think it would be more magical if we remembered the feeling this color gives us and *not* put a name on it."

Michael was deep in the romantic thoughts that Shauna had just brushed aside. "You're the poet, Shauna. And you're right. The feeling is more important than the words."

Shauna looked up at Blake's bedroom window. "I have to go home. I think we've been out long enough."

On the walk back, Shauna's only thoughts were, 'He's a poet. A dreamer. An artist. Not practical as a life partner, but nice to be around.'

When they got back to her front door, she said, "My ex-husband has Blake weekend after next. Maybe we could do this again, then."

Michael said, "That'd be great," as held the front door open for her to retreat back into her house.

It was a positively thoughtful walk home for Michael in the crisp air of a Colorado Winter night. Michael noted that he was perfectly dressed for it.

'Scottie.'

3.17 TELL ME SOMETHING GOOD

Two Sundays after their moonlit walk in the snow, Michael walked to Shauna's house for their appointed second 'date.' At least it was a date in Michael's mind.

Shauna had decided that a driving tour of Denver would be a good orientation for Michael...and a good chance to find out more about him in the private confines of a car.

Their conversations were broadranging. They learned some things about each other's interests. Most importantly to both of them, it was comfortable...easy.

Midway through the tour, Shauna had parked in an underground garage that was part of the Denver Hilton. "They have a restaurant with booths overlooking the sidewalk. We can get a coffee and do some people watching." That answered Micheal's internal question about why she was pulling into a hotel. He knew he had to live with the second best answer.

Three hours after they had left Shauna's home, they were back.

"I didn't drive you home because I thought we could throw a pizza in the oven." That was another encouraging sign for Michael.

They ate the pizza in the living room which allowed their conversation to continue on Shauna's couch. It was all relaxed until the front door opened. Shauna got up from the couch.

"Hi, Wayne. How many times have I asked you to knock?"

Wayne looked at the pizza leftovers on the coffee table. Michael got up from the couch and approached Wayne with an open hand.

"Hey. My name's Michael. I work with Shauna at The Sunflower."

Wayne didn't like it, but he shook Michael's hand. "Wayne."

While the introduction was going on, Blake had run into his mother's arms and got a big kiss on the cheek for being back home.

Michael tried to make conversation with Wayne. "Shauna told me you two met in college and are both software engineers. Is that what you're still doing?"

Michael tried to remember the names of some of the programming languages that Scottie had repeated so often that Michael had tuned them out. Wayne was embarrassed for Michael trying to carry a conversation on a subject he knew nothing about.

"Gimme a kiss, Blake. I gotta go."

When Wayne left, Shauna told Blake to leave his jacket and boots on because they were going to give Michael a ride home.

Michael waved her off. "No, no, Shauna. I enjoy the walk. It's good thinking time for me."

Michael put his jacket and boots on at the front door and, when he was fully dressed for the walk, he called over to Blake who had been watching Michael's exit ritual. "How about a high five before I leave, Blake?"

Blake walked over to Michael with a little bit of hesitancy, but he held his hand up. Michael slapped it gently and said, "Nice to meet you, Big Man," and thence waved goodbye to Shauna. "Thanks for the great day. I'll see you at work this week."

Shauna had just finished cleaning up the pizza leftovers and was about to take Blake up for his bath when her phone sounded with Wayne's ringtone.

"Who the hell was *that* guy."..."I know you want some male friends, but him? Really? You got all that education to hang with some blue-collar thug looking guy?"..."Well, he didn't seem literate to me. He was talking out his ass when he talked to me."..."Seriously? Wanted to be friends with me? He's an example of why Black men get pulled over by the police all the time. If he's scary-looking to me, how do you think a *White* cop sees him."

Shauna had had enough. "Scapegoating a fellow POW is just another way of giving the police permission to continue their misbehavior."

Her statement was incredulous to Wayne. "Misbehavior? You're now referring to racist assaults as misbehavior?"

"Drop it, Wayne. And besides, he was nice to our son, and our son seems to like him."

"That was the wrong thing to tell me. I don't have a good feeling about that. Can't you at least find someone with a degree?"

Shauna didn't want to acknowledge that she'd already had that thought. "We're just friends who happen to work at the same place. Goodnight, Wayne. And stop sticking your nose in where it doesn't belong."

Wayne got his back up a bit. "When it comes to our son, my nose belongs…"

Shauna had hung up on him.

3.18 MOVIN' ON UP

For six months, Robert worked long hours managing the three renovation projects. The crew, the customers, the paperwork, learning the company tool inventory, learning whom to give what paperwork to, learning how to fit in when he had to deal with the company people who were not on his crew…it was a busy climb up another learning curve.

He didn't know that everyone back at the company was aware of what he was doing, and that everyone was waiting in anticipation, hoping he would 'pass' Mark Mack's trial period.

Robert was worried, too. Not about the 'pass or fail.' He knew he'd adapt no matter the outcome. "I am the master of my fate.'

And not about the crew. They had come to appreciate his gentle nudging ways of managing them, and they admired his work ethic.

And not about the customers. He was responsive to their inquiries and change requests, and by the end of the projects he felt like he was treated with a casual familiarity that made him feel almost like he'd be welcomed into their families at any time.

Robert's only point of concern was about the boss' daughter. Robert never had a thought about a possible romantic connection. He had shut that door at the beginning. In his own mind, she was so far out of his league that the thought of being attracted to her stunning beauty and easy manner embarrassed him about himself.

But in the six months from when the reno gig had begun, he never saw her again. That bothered him because he wanted to know more about her Nashville connection. 'Nashville is a pretty small town.'

Little did he know that the girl whom he hadn't seen in six months was constantly in and out of the office, tracking his progress. But she wasn't part of the crowd waiting to find out if he would 'pass.' There was never any doubt in her mind about *that* outcome. No, her interest was in learning more about the *character* of this person.

She had gotten a lot of good insights from hearing the observations of others and confirming the validity of those observations as she monitored his consistency of quality in all the auditable aspects of his day-in and day-out interactions with people. Plus, how he handled bad, antagonistic people in bad, antagonistic situations. She was like a hunter doing homework on her prey before going into the wild for the kill.

And Robert had no clue.

When he turned in his final paperwork, he gave Mark a guided tour through each of the projects, all coordinated with the customers so they could be there to express any concerns to Mark that might be above Robert's pay-grade.

After the third tour, Robert said to Mark, "Pass or fail?"

"Just signed a contract for a residential new construction project at the other end of Maple Street from where you first prepped that lot for us. But, I also have two more renovation projects. I want to try you out on the new home construction. Do any one of your guys on the reno crew have what it takes to run the reno jobs? I want you to be solely focused on the new home construction project."

"The guys on the reno crew seem to be pretty comfortable with Sandy. He knows his way around the fine details that the others are still learning. And he's real comfortable and patient with the customers. But I don't know about his abilities with the paperwork. He didn't seem to catch on so fast to what I was doing on that end of things."

"Sounds good. I'll tell Christine to step in on the paperwork side until we find out about his limits. So, does that mean you accept the new assignment?"

Robert thought, 'So Christine *is* still around. I need to keep my ears open about her Nashville connections.'

Mark allowed Robert a little thinking time. "So, does all that mean that you accept the new assignment?" Mark was concerned that he had to ask twice.

"Yes."

3.19 THERE'S SOMETHING HAPPENING HERE

In the intervening months of no activity on the Officer Mark Johnson case, Agent John Watkins had been busy with more administrative work than field work. But he would use his break time to ponder the possibilities of finding the two fugitives, Muhammad and Jamal Jefferson. And he never let go of McNally being the key. Watkins recognized that his biggest obstacle was his own ability to sell McNally up the line. Watkins recognized that he was short on hard evidence.

Watkins would spend what time he could reviewing the High Definition video from the search warrant that had caused him so much trouble. Watkins spent a lot of time on the details of the bookcase. He reviewed every title for a hint of a new connection between the books and the fugitive boys. Watkins repeated facts in his mind, trying to find pattern or connection. But it just made his brain tired.

'Muhammad left the area out of Nashville after a two year absence. Had he returned to the Nashville area before his trip to Denver?...or had he been in Nashville all along? Was he connected to McNally during those two years?'

'Muhammad was dressed in White country club attire. Where did he get the new wardrobe? Did he have a job while he was in hiding? McNally seems to have some hidden money...but enough so that the fugitives didn't have to work?'

'Muhammad had a rehearsed plan for escape, evasion, and disguise techniques. Did he come up with that plan on his own? Doubtful.'

After way too much contemplation, a thought crept into Watkins' mind...and got bigger with every contemplation. 'The books are training manuals. McNally wasn't training the boys to be fugitives and live underground in a Black environment. If he wasn't training them to be school teachers, he was teaching them to fit into a White environment. And not by just upgrading their wardrobe.'

Once that thought had come into focus for Watkins, a memory that had been planted as a seed in his memory sprang to life. 'Lowe and Werner did a great job reconstructing George Bernard Shaw's *Pygmalion*.'

Watkins knew all the books in the bookcase by heart. '*Pygmalion*. That thin little title squeezed in amongst the throng of training manuals.'

Then the seed that had been planted in Watkins' memory blossomed again. 'If Shaw could convince us that a statue can come to life and be human, then a poor *Black* beggar can be trained to be *White* to fit into high society.'

'A poor *Black* beggar can be trained to be *White* to fit into high society'...

'A poor *Black* beggar can be trained to be *White* to fit into high society'...

'A poor *Black* beggar can be trained to be *White* to fit into high society'...

Watkins finally slapped himself on his forehead. 'That's it! I need to change my profile a full 180 degrees. We need to be looking for the two fugitives in an upscale, White suburb, not a gang- and rat-infested inner-city Black neighborhood! They weren't just trained to fit into a White environment. The boys are fully *White*, gddmn it! The boys are White! They will be found in a place where they are indistinguishable from the White people all around them. And White people *will* be all around them. And *that's* what they were trained for!"

Watkins wanted to sell his totally revamped profile up his chain of command, but he wanted more rehearsal time first. So he set about reviewing all the bookshelf titles. He saw each title as a step toward indoctrinating the fugitive boys on how to be White in a broader, White society.

As Watkins was reviewing the bookshelf titles over and over, he let the video run beyond the titles during one review. As the camera and the videographer were pulling away from the bookcase, Watkins noticed an impossibly brief flash of light that appeared to be coming off the tile floor, so he replayed that section of video over and over to see if he could determine what it was.

He estimated that the flash was less than one-tenth of a second in duration, and that it had the appearance of a geometric arc. After many attempts to freeze the video at the flash, Watkins felt he was distracting himself from his purpose: to sell another search warrant up the line. 'If the boys were there for two years, there has to be some kind of evidence left behind. DNA. Something. Anything. Nobody can live in a place for two years and not leave a trace.'

Before he made the call to his Boss, Watkins reviewed his sales pitch for a second search warrant in his mind.

"Hey, Boss. On the Mark Johnson fugitive case...I have new information that makes me change my profile on where to look for the two fugitives. It's based on the bookcase in McNally's house. All the books were training manuals on how to train the fugitives on how to be White...so they could fit into White society...where they would be unrecognizable and outside the definition of my initial profile. *Pygmalion* is even one of the books in the bookcase."

His Boss sounded tired. "*Pygmalion*? What the hell is that, John? Is it evidence, John? Is it something concrete that can be presented in a court of law to convict, John?"

Watkins protested. "McNally is the anti-profiler. He knows the profile we're looking for, so he changed their profile to be what we're *not* looking for.

"We've been looking for Black inner city kids in Black intercity neighborhoods. This guy has fully turned them into White Black kids, and has turned them out into White America."

Watkins' Boss had impatience in his voice. "White America is more square miles than we can cover. Narrow it down. Then come back. Facts and evidence, John. Facts and evidence.

"You're making a case based on nothing but a hunch, John. You're showing signs of tunnel vision. You're a profiler by your Bureau experience, but you're also a lawyer. We need you to think more like a lawyer, because this new profile idea is way out there. You could take a pic of *my* bookcase and request a search warrant on *me*, John!

"If you can't see it, yourself, then I'm just going to have to tell you. You've become fixated on a person instead of evidence. This country-hermit guy has become your Great White Whale. Wake up, John! Wake up! You need to get smart or get out, John."

Watkins was stunned into silence.

"Look, John. I have to end this phone call right now...before I start saying things that I'll regret. Your retirement is coming up sooner rather than later. If you can't produce sound and presentable evidence...well...John...start thinking more about retirement and less about wild goose-chase hunches."

Then the phone went dead.

3.20 NO-KNOCK WARRANT

Robert's transfer to the single home building contract got him out of the field and into the office. And there she was. Christine *hadn't* fallen off the face of the earth.

Christine took over the administration side of the renovation projects at the same time that Robert had to sit behind a desk and read architectural drawings, line up schedules for the subcontractors, and purchase all the building materials in the order in which they were needed...

Christine came in on a part-time basis. But when she was there, it was common for her to pass by Robert when he was working at his desk. He loved her presence, but when she stood behind his chair, looking over his shoulder at what he was working on, he would glance back at her and immediately turn back to the work in front of him.

He was embarrassed by the possibility that his awareness of her beauty would betray him. And, anyway, his underlying curiosity about her was her Nashville connection. His 'attraction' issues were just a distraction, setting himself up for failure. And he knew it.

After four months, the single home construction project was closed with satisfaction on everybody's part. Robert had gotten to work with a whole new set of people within the company, and he enjoyed the challenge of learning how to deal with subcontractors as opposed to a crew of employees.

Mark pulled Robert aside during the wrap party back at the office. Christine had her eye on the interaction.

"I need more time with the Commercial/Industrial end of things. The only thing holding me back has been my need to keep my eye on the details of the Residential projects. I want you to oversee all the Residential Projects in the company, but hands-on all the way.

"You've shown you can adapt quickly and not sacrifice the end product when you have to climb a learning curve. I don't want to put too much on you, but I think you're ready for the next step...Do you think you're ready to take over Residential?"

Robert had wondered what was coming next. When Mark made him the Residential offer, he instinctively looked away from Mark. He felt he was being watched.

He was right. His glance caught Christine on the far side of the room watching his conversation with her father. He got scared when he realized he had made eye contact with her. He quickly turned his head back to Mark.

"Yes."

A week after Robert had started climbing the learning curve of his new responsibilities, he was ready to take an after-supper rest on his couch in front of the TV. But then the first knock he had ever had on his apartment door happened.

He was more curious than scared when he opened it. Perhaps he should have been more scared. With his hand still on the doorknob, he was frozen with that 'deer in the headlights' freeze.

"Are you going to ask me in?"

It took Robert an extra second, but he opened the door the whole way. Christine walked past him like she was walking into her own house.

She looked around from the entryway. "Did you eat out tonight?"

Robert was fog-brained. "'No. Spaghetti with homemade meatballs in a boiled down fresh tomato sauce, seasoned with a finely tuned balance of herbs after much experimentation. And a fresh garden salad, dressed with an avocado oil garlic and herb dressing. Family recipe. *Somebody's* family."

She was amused by his detailed response, but also impressed by his choice for homemade over store-bought.

"Where are the dirty pots and pans and dishes?"

"Where they belong."

"In the dishwasher?"

"I prefer to hand-wash."

"May I use your bathroom?"

Robert's eyes where partially squinted in an effort to figure out what was going on. He closed the door and swept his arm toward the hall where the bathroom was.

Christine closed the bathroom door behind her. Her first look around was to see if there were any signs of a girlfriend. She opened the mirrored medicine chest. Nothing but guy things. And only one toothbrush.

She then lifted the toilet cover. She was impressed that the cover had been closed.

When everything under the cover looked clean, she lifted up the seat. 'The way men use a toilet, pee splatter is unavoidable.' But it was immaculate.

She pulled back the shower curtain. Shiny clean. No wet washcloths or towels hanging on the curtain rack. And the curtain had no slime build-up on it.

She went to wash her hands, but opened the vanity cabinet under the sink first. 'All the spray bottles to keep the place sparking.'

She washed her hands. She noticed that the towel was dry and straight. If she didn't know better, she would have thought that he knew she was coming.

Robert was still standing near the entrance door when she walked back to him from the bathroom.

"Did you come by here to use the bathroom?"

"No. I came by to see if you're for real."

"I don't know what that means. You're making me uncomfortable."

"I have an interest in getting to know you better...on a personal level. But it's not my nature to dive in until I know how deep the pool is."

"This isn't fair, Christine. You're out of my league. *Way* out of my league."

"Because you think I'm rich?"

"Partly."

"I'm not slumming. I see something in you that more than compensates for rough edges. I see the person. It's the content of your character that I'm attracted to."

She could see that he wasn't buying in. "What's the other part that makes you think I'm out of your league?"

"You're White."

Christine burst out with a loud laugh...which she quickly subdued.

"Excuse me a sec..." while she took her phone out of the back pocket of her jeans. "...Grampi? I have a friend I want you to meet. It's a boy...I'd like you and Grammi to invite us over to your house for supper on Saturday...because I want to know what you think, silly...Anything. He doesn't have any food allergies that I know of. And if he does, we'll find out, right?" She started laughing like she was laughing with the other person on the phone. "Tell Grammi I can't wait."

She slid her phone back into her pocket and looked at Robert. "How's Saturday night?"

Robert felt like was in the vortex of a tornado.

After the dust appeared to have settled, Christine asked if they could sit on the sofa.

"All through High School and four years of college, I never went on a date because I didn't want to reward hounding. But I'm here to find out if I should ask *you* out on a date."

"You just did. We're going on a non-consensual date to your grandparents' this Saturday."

"Yeah, I guess you're right. I'm sorry if I seem forward, but I've gotten an idea of who you are...and if we had to wait for you..."

"I've never had a girlfriend, Christine. And you're out of my league. Seriously."

"What's *in* your league?"

"I don't want to be blinded by your beauty."

"No problem. If things move forward between us, I can get a

crooked nose job, chop my hair up with scissors and stop washing it, and get a double mastectomy. Don't you get it? If you were attracted to my looks, that would disqualify you. It would make me reject you."

"The broken nose, the hair chop, and the mastectomy would help."

"I knew you had a sense of humor buried deep down in there somewhere."

"I'm not being funny." Robert felt he knew how to put it into words. "I'm on a track to build something from scratch. It might dampen my focus if I started having things given to me. I know there's no way I could 'earn' you."

Christine was shaking her head. "There's a reason people get doors opened for them. Part of anybody's building process is to walk through the doors that are opened for them and that are right for them. And if you think anybody gets where they're going all on their own, you have less insight than I've given you credit for. For my part, I don't know enough to close this door...yet. I can't see how you would, either."

Robert had no trouble trying to reason with her. "You're not one of those 'I'll improve the world by lifting a poor, underprivileged, excluded, downtrodden, preyed-upon Black person out of his condition and into my White world' people, are you?"

"Do you mean am I afflicted with a case of 'White guilt?' Have you never met my parents?"

"Of course I have. You know I work with your father all the time."

"And that's all? My mother's never come by the office when you're there?"

"If she has, I've never been introduced to her. I'd probably recognize her if you pointed her out to me."

Christine thought, 'Obviously, you wouldn't.'

Robert walked Christine down to her car, opened the door for her, and closed her safely inside.

As she backed out of her parking space, Robert watched her drive out of apartment building's parking lot.

Nothing was resolved inside himself. All the questions he had posed to Christine remained.

Robert started thinking, 'Maybe I have a little 'due diligence' to do of my own.' But he had no idea where to begin.

3.21 FRIEND ZONE

Michael Dean, the popular Chef at *The Sunflower Cafe and Restaurant* in Highlands Ranch, Colorado, kept up his friendly rapport with his part time waitress friend throughout the Winter. When there came a Winter melt with some rare warm Spring air, he offered a suggestion.

"Things are turning prematurely green. How would you like to spend some time at the playground?"

Shauna laughed. "I think we're both too big to fit into the swings."

Michael chucked with her. "I meant for you, me, and your son, Blake."

On a Sunday morning, Michael got the private time with Shauna that was his goal. As a bonus, he got to meet and play with her four-year-old son, Blake.

Throughout his conversation with Shauna, Michael pushed Blake on the swings while artfully interjecting dialogue with the boy. Plus, he seesawed with Blake, met him at the bottom of the curvy plastic slide, and raced him the width of the playground a couple of times.

When it was time for a rest, all three of the revelers sat down at a picnic table. Shauna had brought some juice packs from her fridge. When Blake had trouble getting the straw to insert, it was Michael who helped him.

When they were finishing up their juice packs, Michael asked Blake if he knew how to play any musical instruments. Blake shook his head 'no.'

Michael reached down next to the leg of the picnic table and broke off a small cluster of broad grass shoots. Michael spread them out on the picnic table and took one for himself. He then held his blade of grass between the knuckles of his thumbs, put the assembly to his lips, and blew. It made a trumpet sound.

Blake was enthralled by the whole process and picked up his own grass sliver from the tabletop. When Blake had trouble making it sound, Michael coached him through all the adjustments until Blake got his first 'honk.'

Shauna was impressed with Michael's interaction with her son. She was cautious about the warm feeling it gave her.

Shauna picked up a blade and tried it herself. She felt the feeling of victory when she got to join in with her two companions' noise-making.

As they were leaving the playground, Michael told Blake that he could now call himself an accomplished musician. Blake smiled at the notion of 'being' something.

When the trio got back to Shauna's house, she put Blake down for some quiet time in front of the TV.

In the kitchen, Michael asked, "What's the story with your ex?"

Shauna gave the history. "We met at the University of Colorado, Boulder. We both majored in Software Engineering, so that's how we met. It was a college romance. For my part, it was nice to have a boyfriend to do things with. Since both of us were studying to have lucrative jobs, we thought we'd be the richest couple on the planet.

"We got married after graduation, and we both got those great paying jobs we knew would come. When I got pregnant, I realized that the call of Motherhood was greater than the call of Coding.

"Wayne appreciated that his son would be given the security of a full time mom. But he also felt that he didn't sign up to be a one-income household. He wanted the toys. The fast cars, the fancy clothes, the exotic vacations. It became obvious pretty quickly that his dream was on hold. He didn't like that. The quiet resentments rose to the surface. We got to a place where we both wanted out.

"There was no acrimony. He agreed to housing, transportation, food. He said they're the expenses he'd have to pay a nanny, anyway. I thought that was pretty insulting, but I let it slide.

"I agreed to cover the 'extras,' hence my part-time waitressing job. I'm happier not living with him, but my first choice would have been him being happy with our reduction in household income."

Michael's summation was, "He sounds like he's good to you. I mean, he didn't abandon you and leave you to support yourself."

Shauna responded, "You do know there are laws, don't you? It's not like it was completely his choice."

Michael countered, "I know there are laws, but not everybody follows them."

Shauna did a little tilted head-shake, as if to say, 'That may or may *not* be true.' "A lot changed after he left that made things more clear to me. He became 'roommates' with a female software engineer from work. He got some semblance of a higher income living back. That was what he really wanted."

Michael asked, "But you get along? No fighting or under-the-surface hostility?"

Shauna was sharing more than she imagined she would. "His quest for his vision of the American dream seemed to turn bitter. I don't think it was all about the divorce or his subsequent reduction in money. I think it had to do with him having a baby boy."

Michael asked, "How's that?"

Shauna explained. "You know that being Black is the reason the cops disproportionately pull you Black males over, right? Wayne has always done the whole servitude and humility act to avoid escalation…"

Michael interjected, "I feel him."

"...but having a Black baby, especially a Black baby *boy*, made him resent the fact that his son would have to grow up in such a system. His anger seems to have risen to the more visible surface now. Please never speak of this to anyone, but I think he's capable of killing a cop if just the wrong confluence of circumstances were to arise. And not for himself. It would be an act to protect his son...as crazy as that sounds."

Michael had a memory rush. Michael was liking Wayne more than he thought he should have been. "Why do you say that?"

"He carries a gun on him all the time. I told him I don't want a gun ever being around our son. He just said that Blake would never know it was there. I'm nervous every weekend that Wayne has Blake."

Michael observed, "You're not big on confrontation. I can tell it makes you nervous...takes your peace away. Most people would put their foot down...make an ultimatum."

Shauna responded to his observation. "I'm stronger than you might think...but a person has to pick their battles."

Shauna moved the conversation forward. "You skipped school, but you're thoughtful and creative. I never saw myself being friends with a blue-collar type, but I think you'll go far...based on what I've seen at the restaurant."

Michael felt a sudden deflation from realizing he'd been exiled to the friend zone. He had been thinking that the conversation was getting deep and personal, but now he wrote it off to her just being good conversationalist...like a good waitress would be.

For just having friend-zoned Michael, Shauna kept the conversation personal. "If you could change something about yourself, what would it be?"

Michael's friend-zone dejection showed up in his voice. "I don't want to be White."

Shauna pulled her head back. "But you're not."

Michael still felt some dejection. "I'm more White than I ever have been...more than you know."

Shauna was puzzled. "You're being cryptic." Then she brushed it off. "It must be the poet in you."

The conversation entered a lull.

Shauna broke the air of silence. "If I knew you from the inside, what would I find out that I don't know?"

Michael just flat-out said, "That I'm Muslim."

"Have you ever practiced? Like, as part of a church?...or whatever they call it?"

Michael chuckled at her. "It sounds like you've reached the envelope of your education."

She just replied, "Ha, ha." But her thoughts went to, 'Envelope? Seriously? Who are you, Michael Dean?'

Michael asked, "Have you ever heard of Muhammad Ali? He was Muslim."

Shauna engaged. "Of course I know Muhammad Ali. Why is his Muslim faith so important to you?"

"He refused to get drafted into the Army to fight in Vietnam. He asked why he should fight and kill a Vietnamese person who's never called him a nggr."

Shauna countered, "He said that because he was Black, not because he was Muslim."

Michael continued. "Nobody would have paid attention to him if he tried to say the same thing while calling himself a Christian. Allah Akbar."

There was a long silence.

Michael broke the silence. "But, no. I haven't practiced for a while."

Shauna asked, "Isn't 'Allah Akbar' what terrorists say before they blow up innocent people...along with themselves?"

"No. The terrorists are reprobates and apostates. 'Allah Akbar' is what Muslims say when something good happens and they want to give praise or thanks to Allah for a good thing."

Shauna noted, "Christians say 'Praise The Lord.' Sounds like the same thing."

Michael was becoming contrary. "It's hard for me to believe that we're both talking about the same God. Muslims are willing to die for Allah. Christians don't want to die at all costs, despite what Jesus said about it."

"What did Jesus say about it?"

Michael felt he was venturing outside his knowledge base, but he'd attended the First Baptist Church as a kid. He'd been a tag-along with neighborhood kids whose mothers made them attend.

"Jesus said that if you love your life you'll lose it. And that if you're willing to give up your life here on earth, you'll save it."

Religious topics were not an area of interest to Shauna. "You sound like you need to connect with the Muslim community here...find a...a Mosque. That's what they're called. It sounds to me like you miss it."

There was another long silence.

Shauna had to satisfy an itch of curiosity. "You used the words 'apostate' and 'reprobate.' Were those words part of your religious indoctrination?"

Michael was still feeling defensive. "No. Why would you ask me that?"

"It's just because I wouldn't have predicted those words to be part of your daily working vocabulary." Shauna was still curious. "If it didn't come from some kind of religious training, where in your life did those words come from?"

She had alerted Michael to pictures of Scottie. Those pictures caused him to do his best impersonation of Scottie, yet.

"It's egalitarian of you to presume that tuition money is the only way to pay the toll for the road to knowledge."

Shauna was blown away by Michael's constructed response. And she knew it wasn't Michael who had constructed it. She decided to let it rest as a pleasing mystery. She wanted to move on.

"Aren't you going to ask me what you might find in me if you knew *me* from the inside?"

Michael never shook the dejection from being friend-zoned. "I already know."

"OK, smart boy. What?"

Michael was still in Scottie mode. "You have a goal inside you that you're so focused on that it causes you to leave no room for good things that might come into your life from outside of that goal. Good things that present themselves in the here and now.

"That end goal will have no value when you get there if the journey to get it excluded fun and interesting side trips. What good is a nutritious meal that's placed before you if you won't put it in your mouth?"

Shauna was liking his ever-surprising use of verbal imagery. "I knew there was a poet in there somewhere. That was beautiful."

Michael meant it to be a wake-up call slap-in-the-face. 'Hey!' Michael thought. 'I was talking about you and me!'

Something about Michael's overtly direct slam must have worked. As he was leaving, Shauna asked him if he'd like to take Blake out for the day in two weeks.

"I'm committed to an afternoon to help my mother that weekend."

3.22 GUESS WHO'S COMING TO DINNER

On Saturday night, Christine drove Robert to dinner at Grampi Eli's and Grammi Nancy's house at the top of the rim on Ocean View. Robert remembered parking on the road below the driveway with Scottie the day he was dropped off in Pacific Palisades.

As Christine drove up the steep slope of the driveway, Robert got distracted by the long view of the Pacific Ocean to his left. Then they passed the seven-bay garage. Then, between the garage building and the house, Robert got a glimpse of the pool, surrounded by a large stone terrace. He saw a pool house on one side and a covered outdoor kitchen on the other.

Then they arrived at the house and its front door Portico where Christine parked.

As they got out of the car, Grampi Eli opened the front door. That was the moment Robert understood why Christine had made the call for a dinner date. 'Grampi Eli is as Black as the Ace of Spades.'

"Before you meet my wife, Nancy, I want to show you something. Look over at the garage building."

Eli stood at the door with Robert and pressed one of eight switches mounted into a custom made wall plate that was made to match the light-switch plates in the entrance hall. Instantly, fourteen garage doors all raised themselves open at the same time. Each bay had a front and a back garage door, and each bay lit up to show a car in each bay. Robert was impressed beyond words.

Eli asked, "Are you impressed? Because I've wasted an untold amount of money if you're not impressed."

Robert was staring at the spectacle. "I'm impressed."

"Good. I'll take you on a tour after supper and show you my seven antique Mercedes. I have seven because I drive one for each day of the week. I have a mechanic come to the house at the first sign of any problems. When we go out there, you'll notice there's not a drop of oil on the floor beneath any of the cars. Maintenance. The key to life.

"Each parking bay has a door on the front *and* the back so I never have to back in or out. Whichever car I happen to be driving, I drive straight out when I leave. And when I come back home, I drive straight in. Now tell me, Robert. Was that *smart* planning...or was that planning to be lazy?"

Christine jumped in. "Stop it, Grampi. Robert doesn't have to answer any of your silly test questions."

The three left the entrance hall to go to the kitchen so Robert could meet Grammi Nancy...and to eat.

On the way to the kitchen, with Christine walking out in front of them, Robert pulled on Grampi Eli's sleeve. When Eli looked at Robert to see what he wanted, Robert strained his neck toward Grampi Eli's ear and quietly said, "*Smart* planning."

Grampi Eli got a twinkle in his eye as he smiled at Robert and nodded his head. Eli thought to himself, 'Yep. Christine's got herself a smart one.'

Grammi Nancy, as White White as Grampi Eli was Black Black, was equally as friendly and welcoming as Grampi Eli.

The supper and the conversation were both delightful and stimulating to Robert. It was a welcome spice to his bland daily living routine. And Christine was as comfortable with her grandparents as she would be if they were her parents. Robert was relieved to see that because he took it as a sign that Christine didn't worry about them being judgmental about him.

After supper, Eli pulled Robert away from the women to his study. He poured himself a snifter of cognac and offered one to Robert. Robert politely declined. "I'm not used to drinking. But thank you for offering."

Grampi Eli sat next to Robert in the Argentine-leather chairs in front of his desk. "I know how to solve the Middle East conflict."

Robert was impressed that Grampi Eli didn't focus on small goals.

"Intermarriage. Arabs and Jews, Israelis and Palestinians...for that matter, Black and White in America. A person has great difficulty hating 'his own blood' as we used to say. 'Hating their own DNA' might be a better way to say it today.

"Nancy's Nashville family was racist and didn't even know it till they met me. But once we had their granddaughter, Charleen...your boss' wife...now they scold anybody who breathes a disparaging racist breath.

"By the way, Nancy insisted on spelling Charleen's name the way she did because she thought it was a 'more Black' spelling. Come to find out, it's the common spelling. All I'm saying is that it was important to her White mother, Nancy, that Charleen identify as Black. I couldn't help but tell her that that was the definition of a racist act."

Robert asked, "What about Christine? We've talked about race. She said no-one has *ever* thought *she* was Black. How does Christine's mother, Charleen, feel about Christine being so White?"

Eli was glad to have an engaging companion for conversation. "Exactly! It *wasn't* important to Charleen that Christine look like or identify as Black...*or* White. Why? Because Charleen is Blackish, so Christine being Black would have been unnoticeable. And Charleen's husband, Mark...your boss over at the construction company...is White. So Charleen doesn't notice Christine's Whiteness because her husband, Mark, is White."

Robert said, "My Blackness has been a concern to me as Christine and I have gotten friendlier."

"In case Christine has never told you this, she never mentioned you being Black to her Grammi Nancy *or* to me. And just so you know, Christine would have never invited you over here unless she thought a lot of you. She's never invited a boyfriend over here. I'm not sure she's ever even *had* a boyfriend."

Robert let out a small laugh. "It's hard to believe a girl like her could go so long, even all the way through college, without someone working hard enough to woo her and nail her down for a commitment."

Eli lifted himself up onto his fake high horse. "Now...just what did you mean by, 'a girl like her?'"

Robert stumbled to explain. "Err…I mean a girl who is so thoughtful and kind and generous with her time and caring."

Eli got out of his chair and put his arm on Robert's shoulder. "I think you and I are gonna get along just fine, young man. Why don't you walk with me out to my garage showcase. I think you're gonna like this."

3.23 MINI ME

When Michael showed up to take Blake around town for the day, he was sure he had blasted the 'friend zone' out of the water. Michael and Blake walked to the playground and got in some good physical activity.

Then they walked to the retail section of town where Michael treated Blake to an unhealthy, but tasty, lunch at *Chuck E. Cheese*.

From there, they walked over to an indoor arcade where they worked off their lunch, playing as many different games as Blake wanted.

The game that Blake liked the most was the shoot-as-many-basket-balls-into-the-hoop-as-you-can game. He loved it because it spit out a line of tickets after each round of balls.

When they first played the game, Michael held Blake up on the edge of the basketball reservoir and handed each ball to Blake for a shot. That method lasted one game. Blake told Michael he wanted to shoot the balls himself. So Michael found a step-stool for Blake to stand on, and Michael shot his own game next to Blake's game. A faux competition. Blake won every game. But in order to keep some competitive pressure on little Blake, Michael started saying 'Allah Akbar' every time Michael got a basket.

Little Blake was competitive enough to stick it right back in Michael's face. Blake started saying 'Allah Akbar' every time *he* got a basket, too.

With more tickets than little Blake could hold in his hands and stuff in his pockets, Michael took him to the prize counter to redeem the tickets. Blake chose a frisbee.

Michael and Blake walked by the Park on their way home, but after they had thrown and chased down the wild throws of the frisbee several times, they both sat down with their backs against a tree. There they honked on a couple blades of wide grass. Then they decided it was time to go home.

Shauna pulled in her driveway as Michael and Blake were approaching her house. "You guys look beat. Who did this you?"

Blake overrode his fatigue and ran into his mother's arms in excitement. "I beat Michael in basketball! I really beat him, Mommy!"

Shauna looked over at a smiling Michael and returned his smile. She set Blake back on the ground, and said, "My two big boys look like they need to come into the house for a cold drink."

Blake was quick to fall over into a nap on the couch with the TV on.

Michael made his next move. "Hey, Shauna. *The Denver Art Museum* is exhibiting of one of your favorite artists, Georgia O'Keeffe, on Saturday, March 14. If you drive, I'll buy."

Shauna said, "Wayne has Blake that weekend. We can make the jump up to Boulder afterwards, and I'll take you on a driving tour of my Alma Mater, the University of Colorado, Bolder Campus, and show you all my old haunts."

Michael's brain did a fist pump, but his voice was more calm. "Yeah. That sounds like a good day."

3.24 WHY CAN'T WE BE FRIENDS

After supper with Grampi Eli and Grammi Nancy, Robert started to get the picture that Christine was really interested in him. The biggest part of him not being able to see her interest was his self-image.

Robert had great confidence that he was well equipped to do the things that had to be done for him to 'make it' on his own terms, but he had developed a picture of attracting a wife *after* he had proven that he could make it. That is, after he had made it. In relation to that movie of his life, Christine was premature in her attraction to him. 'I don't have anything to offer her yet.'

But believing that it was possible that she was interested in him changed his *modus operandi*. He asked her to go to a cafe/confectioner place in town, called *Nothing Fancy*, where they could get a lite sandwich-plus and hide out in a booth for some private conversation while they looked across the Pacific Coast Highway at the beach and its companion ocean.

Robert said, "If we're going to morph into something that resembles a boyfriend/girlfriend relationship, it might help us both if we talked about what that looks like." He was looking for a reaction. "At least I think it would help me."

"No, it would help both of us."

"Look, I'm sorry to keep bringing it up, but the notion that you're 'out of my league' hasn't gone away. It's a source of some insecurities around me getting involved. I'm not interested in the short-term thrill of dating a goddess."

"For four years, I lived on-campus at USC. It was just an extension of High School as far as the boys went. I was constantly being hit on. Some girls *loved* that kind of attention…but I hated it.

"I saw that it wasn't about me. It was about the jerks that were hitting on me. I realized they were all in some kind of competition. While I was trying to focus on my studies and learn something in return for all the money the place was costing my parents, the alpha-males that were hitting on me were trying to get a different kind of return on their investment. When you're a prize in some kind of sick competition, it makes *you* sick. Then, it was like word of the competition spread. The hitters became just the star athlete jocks. I knew all they wanted was to be seen as the victor of their sick competition.

"There were plenty of beautiful girls on campus, but it never stopped. The ones who persisted didn't know me. They just wanted to be the one seen driving around with the car top down and the radio on with their arm around my shoulder. I mean...how shallow can it get? Wanting to be seen with someone doesn't even move the needle on the 'connection' meter. Whatever happened to the good ole 'content of your character' standard?

"The ability to create envy in others is barter-value in that world. And envy is one of the seven deadly sins. And, who am I if I want my so-called 'friends' to be envious of me?...or, even people I don't even *know* being envious of me? It would be like I'm setting up their death to satisfy my need for something that is only a 'need' because I don't have what I *truly* need...a true, meaningful companionship."

Robert had listened attentively. "So, am I the anti-jock in this story? Because I can throw a ball...of some kind...maybe."

"Ha, ha!. Very funny." Christine appreciated that he had heard her. "You're not the jock or the anti-jock. You're someone that I've had a chance to watch. I feel like that's led me to knowing some of the things that make you tick...the content of your character...and I like what I see. At the core. Not your reaction to some event on some random day, but the predicable parts of you that will always show up over the arc of time. That's what I'm talking about. Your core being."

"Thanks. That about neutralizes my 'out of my league' insecurities."

"Great. So...that sounds like I've satisfied you." She had a coy look in her eyes. "Are you going to satisfy me?"

Robert started laughing. "I love the way you talk. You're such a titillating conversationalist." Robert could see that was Christine was enjoying their point/counterpoint...but not to the point of laughing.

"But, seriously, Christine. I'm not blind to who you are. I just never thought I was deserving of it. You take the time...you put in the work...to be thoughtful and kind toward those lesser than you...like me." They both ha-ha'd. "You know that homework matters, so you do it. And the things that matter to you are so far outside of yourself. You go to great lengths to ensure that everyone around you can have a soft landing when they need it."

Christine's face had grown a big grin. "Go on, Cyrano de Bergerac, you have my full attention." Christine was doing everything she could to not laugh out loud at herself for putting Robert up to this.

Robert felt the laughable reflection rising in her which made him so sincere that it would only add to the laughter. "Everything you've said about your struggles to get to this moment reveals core values in you that are incredibly attractive. Like I want to kiss...even *maul*...those parts of you. And if you don't change the subject soon, I'm going to attack you with a ferocity that will leave marks for a very long time. And *then* you'll be sorry you ever started toying with me!"

At that, they both broke out into a shared and bonding laughter. After the laughter, they both took a bite of their sandwiches and a sip of their vegetable blend beverages.

Robert asked Christine about her friends in Nashville. "Your Dad has told me about a couple of times that you'd traveled out to Nashville to see friends."

Christine valued this 'getting to know you' question. "My great-grandmother still lives there, but now has full time nursing care. And I don't want to put a big damper on our evening, but my Grammi Nancy grew up with a girlfriend out there, and that girlfriend and my Grammi both had daughters at the same time, and then those daughters both had daughters at the same time. So I'm one of those daughters' daughters. We're three generations of family friends. And we generally exclude the men.

"The one that's my age…my lifelong friend, Cathy…married a police officer straight out of High School. We went to the wedding the year Cathy and I both, on separate sides of the country, graduated from High School.

"I never really met, in a conversational way, her police officer husband. He was murdered several years ago by two boys that were cousins of a boy that Cathy's husband had shot during a crime."

Robert's jaw hung so far open that it was resting on his chest. And it didn't help that his eyes were bugged out, also.

Christine saw his reaction. "I *know*…that's awful, isn't it?"

Robert became aware of his reaction, so he closed his mouth.

"Anyway, sorry to dampen our evening, but I see her every summer, and some Thanksgivings and Christmases and Easters. It's really sad. But the last time I saw her, she said she was in a relationship that's pretty serious, and that she expects he'll pop the question any time soon."

Robert had to rise above a shock that opened all kinds of doors of horrible possibilities. "That's nice that she found someone."

"Yes. He's a cop, too. He was a friend of her late husband."

Robert was driving Christine home. Their conversation had never subsided.

"So, your grandfather's Black. How do you pass so easily for White? I mean, I know it's obvious that you *look* White. But in a small town like this…where everybody knows your Grampi Eli…and your mother…"

"I don't *pass*. I *am* White. That's all I know, so that's all I've ever been treated like. Grampi is a City Councilman, and I have trouble seeing anyone treat him as anything but White. And if everyone is being treated like they're White…then is there even such as thing as *anyone* being White? Unless, of course, when he's driving in one of his fancy cars out of town. He's been stopped a lot over the years. He has an air about him that has kept him safe from that kind of thing turning into trouble."

"Have you ever thought about having Black children...children that actually *look* Black...and subjecting them to those kinds of burdens in life? I mean, dating is all about finding a good partner match, which, not trying to get ahead of ourselves, but that means kids. Have you considered the ramifications of having Black children?"

"I've seen things in you over the past many months that have kept me watching. I still have things to see, I'm sure. But I'm not attracted you because you're Black...just like you're not attracted to me because I'm rich and beautiful." They both had a short laugh-break.

"Intimacy is always thought of as sex. But I don't think that's true. To me, intimacy is sharing oneself in a totally private way. I have girlfriends. You have friends...at work, at least. Your and my private knowledge of each other will never be any of their business. If I share my personal stuff with you, and you share those things with anyone else, we've lost our intimacy. And its too much work to get it back...in fact, I don't think you ever get it back."

Robert was interested in her view. "So...divorce?"

"OK. New intimacy can be established. But it's so much work. And all the old intimacies that defined you are lost. Gone. But, no. Divorce isn't all that's left. Trying to work things out is probably better. But how much time do people have? And how much time would it take to redefine an old relationship on new intimacies?"

Robert knew where she was coming from. "I think that the things we're talking about underscore the reality that building intimacy is like building a work of art by adding one brush stroke per day. And that violating that intimacy by sharing it with someone else is like taking a big black magic marker and scribbling over the piece of art you've so patiently and diligently made into a thing of beauty."

It was all pretty heavy and pretty serious. It created the first real lull in their conversation all night.

"Before you take me home, take me by your apartment. I want to see your bedroom."

"But you just said that sex too soon gets in the way of intimacy."

"Yes, I did." Then she leaned over and kissed him on the cheek.

When Christine and Robert got inside Robert's apartment, Christine led him by the hand down the hallway to the bedroom. Robert opened the door and switched the light on. He was so nervous that he thought he was about to break into a sweat.

Christine walked to bed, threw the pillow aside, and pulled back the bedspread to reveal the bedsheets and blanket. Christine turned to Robert with a sultry look and a cheshire smile. Then she stepped into him so he could feel her body against his.

Her sultry voice matched her body language. "See? I just learned a private detail about you that will be part of our intimacy forever...if we let it."

Robert didn't know what to do with the physical reaction that was taking over his body. 'Does she want me to act on this?...cuz I will...' But what he said out loud was, "What's the intimate private detail?"

Christine had her arms around him to ensure they both felt everything. "You sleep in clean bed sheets, and someone has taught you the right way to make a bed so that the top sheet folds over the edge of the blanket to reveal its print. You've never been more of a man in my eyes."

Instead of thinking about baseball, Robert pictured Scottie teaching them his bed-making technique and thought, 'Oh, Scottie. You sly dog. How did you know?'

Christine separated her body from Robert's. "See what an intimate moment we just had? I mean, who else knows this about you? Only me?"

She then turned her back to Robert and remade the bed, during which time Robert experienced the full meaning of the word 'lust.'

When the bed was remade, Christine walked up to Robert, stopped, took his face in her hands, and pressed her lips into his. It was a long and deep kiss that caused the reunion of their bodies.

When it became too dangerous for Christine, she broke off the kiss, but stayed holding their bodies together. She looked at Robert, and said, "If we're both lucky, there'll come a day when I can take care of that for you."

This was a new level of patience that Robert was learning about. "If we're *both* lucky, it won't be just you doing the 'taking care of.'"

Christine pulled away from him but had not lost her sultry demeanor. "Now that we've been intimate, you can take me home."

3.25 I GET BY WITH A LITTLE HELP FROM MY FRIENDS

On the Saturday morning of March 14, Shauna honked her horn outside Michael's rented room. He was listening for her and came down to her right away. They made the short trip to *The Denver Art Museum* where Michael paid for their lunch.

As the couple walked through the Art Museum, stopping to absorb Georgia O'Keeffe's masterworks, Michael whispered to Shauna, "Is it my imagination, or are these paintings really sexual? This one of the white flower looks more to me like a vagina than a flower."

Shauna laughed. "She was a feminist, and she celebrated the female body in her flower paintings. Flowers are metaphorical studies of the vulva." She looked at Michael with that continuing amazement...and that mystery about what he was made of. "Good eye," she said.

After a stimulating afternoon at the museum, Shauna made the continuing drive up to Boulder so she could share some of her college memories with Michael.

Michael Dean felt like an alien in a foreign land, though he enjoyed feeling Shauna's nostalgia.

After a driving tour of her old haunts, Shauna parked in the parking lot across the street from a large off-campus bar named *Biederman's Tavern*. It was the most popular watering hole for Bolder students, especially after U-Colorado sporting events.

Michael told Shauna he wasn't a drinker for religious reasons. Shauna told him that was cool, and that she can't drink excessively and drive, so it would not be a wild night.

When Michael and Shauna bellied up to the bar, a bartender shouted, "What'll it be?"

Michael shouted back, "I'll have a cranberry juice, straight up, on the rocks."

A group of drunk frat boys were crowded together at the bar, and the one standing next to Michael shouted at him above the crowd noise, "What? Is it your period?"

Michael had a surge of adrenaline as he looked over the guy to size him up. Shauna pulled him by the arm and spoke close to his ear. "It's a line from a famous movie. Don't be offended. It was said to Leonardo DeCaprio. Maybe he's mistaking you for Leo." She leaned back and smiled at him.

Shauna leaned in close to the bartender in an effort to not be heard by anyone else. "I'll have a *Sex-On-The-Beach*." It was her go-to drink when she was a student at Boulder.

It was clear that the frat boys were acting wild and sloppy, so when their drinks came, Shauna diverted Michael's attention by speaking close to his ear.

"See all those huge guys over there? My girlfriends and I used to call them the 'Big Boys.'"? Michael liked speaking close to her ear. "Yeah, I see them. Football players?"

Shauna kept speaking close to Michael's ear. "Close. Can you see the big one with the massive arms?"

Michael looked back over. "They're *all* big with massive arms!"

Shauna tried to discreetly point to one of the Big Boys in particular. "See the shield tattoo on that one guy's forearm?"

"Yeah."

"That's the emblem of the Rugby Club."

It was all new to Michael. "What's 'the Rugby Club?"

"It's like football, only much rougher...and they play with no pads."

"How do you know so much about it?" Michael wanted to keep this conversation going because his head touched her face every time he leaned into her to say something.

"My boyfriend in college...you know, Wayne, my ex..."

Michael thought, 'Oh, yeah. Your boyfriend in college. That's what I came here to hear about. Your boyfriend in college.'

Michael started to think she was feeling some nostalgia about Wayne from being around campus and at the Pub. He was feeling some jealously rising from within.

"Well, Wayne and I used to go to the Rugby matches. They were free, and we were both saving what little money we had for after school. So, we learned about the game. It became better than football for us."

"Do you mean you knew you were going to get married while you were here at school with him?" Michael knew he shouldn't be asking about it. The jealousy was just getting a little too warm.

Shauna touched him on the shoulder. "Stay right here so I know where to find you when I come back from the ladies room."

Alone, Michael started looking around the bar. He noticed that he didn't see any Black people, so he looked in earnest for one. He was still searching when a preppy looking frat boy, who was sloppy in his walk as well as in his words, bumped into Michael and spilled some of his drink on Michael's shirt. Michael looked down at the wet.

"Oh, sorry. I'll get you another one," at which point the drunk frat boy called out to some of his buddies who were bellied up to the bar. "Hey, Mikey, get me another tequila."

Michael, in a moment of rational clarity, realized the guy was slobbering drunk and decided not to reason with him about who he was ordering the drink for.

The drunk frat boy turned back to Michael and said, "Hey, man, what are you doing here? I think your people are at *The Jungle Room Watermelon Patch Bar and Grill*. They serve bananas over there."

Michael reminded himself, again, that the guy was drunk and, for the sake of his date with Shauna that he was hoping would go somewhere, he just said, "I'm here with my girl. We're just checking out the places she used to come to when she went to school here." Michael could feel his blood rising again, and he knew it wasn't jealousy this time.

The drunk frat boy said, "Hey, fck you man. You can't talk to me like that. Why don't you just get your nggr ass outta here," and pushed him away with his near empty red solo cup that held his former tequila, spilling the remaining swill onto Michael's pants.

Just then, one of the frat brothers swaggered over with a fresh refill. "Hey, what's going on here, Jonesie? Has this house-monkey lost his way?" He turned back to his buddies at the bar, "Hey, Alpha Phi, we got a problem over here."

A line of Alpha Phi boys weaved their way through the crowd until Michael was surrounded. Just then, Shauna was pushing her way into the circle.

"What's going on here, Michael?" as she looked at his wet shirt and the wet spot on his pants.

"Nothing. Let's get outta here. These guys are all drunk."

He turned and grabbed ahold of Shauna's arm and led her out

through the circle, having to lean into some the Alpha Phi to make way.

One the guys he leaned into shouted to his buddies, "Hey, this guy wants to fight! Let's make his wish come true!"

Michael kept parting the sea of people to make way for Shauna and himself.

The Alpha Phi were forming a line in Michael's wake to follow him outside. Shauna was getting nervous. As she passed by the group of Big Boys, she heard one of them shout across to another, "Hey, Stevie! Fight! Fight! Let's go check it out!"

When Michael pushed through the front door onto the sidewalk, he pulled Shauna up next to him. "Which way is your car?"

She pointed, "It's straight ahead." Michael held her arm as he entered the street, looking both ways. Michael was aware that he was about to explode. Then he felt a reminder to choose a different way. He began the slow-count to ten.

The whole group of frat boys had poured out onto the sidewalk by then. One of them shouted, "That's it, little Suzie. Take your little Jungle Bunny home instead of protecting her like a man!"

Michael stopped in the middle of the street and let go of Shuana's arm. He knew this feeling. Worse, he knew where it led. He felt the outside of his pocket for the outline of his boxcutter. It was there.

He visualized a quick reach into his pocket, a quick move to the neck of the closest asshole to him, then the next closest, then the next. He saw them struggling on the ground. He saw the police arrive. He saw a jail cell. He saw a judge. He saw an orange jumpsuit with himself in handcuffs being led out of the courtroom. He interrupted his vision with a conscious thought. 'The blade isn't gonna work.'

He heard an audio memory of being told his fight is against himself, not another person. It brought back the morning routine he had used for two long years to get psyched for the day ahead. He heard an echo in his mind. 'It's a statement of your will to survive. A 'bring on the challenges and the obstacles,' type of thing. It's meant to show your enemy that you're not scared.'

With his back to the frat boys, he spread his legs shoulder width. Then, with a thousand-yard stare in his eyes, he started shaking his hands at his side, making sure he could feel his fingers shaking, also. Then he slowly turned around and faced the gang of Alpha Phi's.

Shauna, unaware that Michael had stopped, kept walking for a few steps until she realized he wasn't with her. She turned to see the back of Michael's head. He had turned to face the drunken crowd...who had stopped when he stopped.

Shauna looked down to see Michael's hands and fingers shaking at his side. 'Oh, gawd, no, he's having a seizure.' She stepped up to his back and put her hand on his shoulder to turn him back around.

Michael was firm in his stance, so she stepped beside him to coax him away. Her eyes got wide and her jaw dropped when she saw his tongue hanging out of his mouth to below his chin. She knew for sure he was having a seizure when he shouted, "Kee-ah ree-tay!" with a look that would scare the ghost out of a sober person.

His eyes were bugged out of his head like he was getting a bolt of shock therapy to his temples, and he shouted, "kee-ah maw!"

Then he started rhythmically slapping his ribs below his breasts, and shouted, "Kee-ah ree-tay!" for a second time.

Shauna was disoriented by this bizarre behavior and put her hand more firmly on his shoulder to try, again, to get him to leave. She heard the frat boys saying to each other, "This ngga's crazy."

Michael immediately dropped into a knee squat, then shouted a second time, "Kee-ah maw!" and started rhythmically slapping the tops of his thighs with both hands.

When Shauna turned her head toward the sidewalk to assess the threat, she saw the two Big Boys turn to each other, all wide-eyed themselves, and do a jumping chest-bump on each other. She heard one of the Big Boys say to the other "This is epic! Go get the rest of the team!"

Meanwhile, Michael was still slapping his thighs loudly, and shouted, "Ringa ringa pah-kee-ah!"

Shauna now feared an act of drunken intimidation was going to turn into something much worse.

Michael, still in a crouch position, his thighs parallel to the ground, started slapping one forearm, then the other, and shouting "Wawh-ay wawh-ay tak-kah!" as he kept alternating slaps to each forearm, his tongue still hanging down his chin, and his eyes still bugged out.

Shauna saw the tops of the bar doors swing open behind the crowd, and then she saw a mass of the Big Boys start making their way to the front of the crowd, interspersed with the Alpha Phi's in the front row. She was disheartened that they had come out to see the slaughter, if not participate in it.

Michael, still squatted with his thighs parallel to the ground, started stomping his feet, one foot and then other, and shouted, "Kee-ah kee-no nay-ee hoe-kee!"

The Big Boys were all nodding back and forth at each with clenched chins, looking angry and stern. Shauna interpreted this as an ominous sign that the Big Boys were about to join the coming beat-down.

Michael kept his squat position and started slapping his ribs again, and shouted, "Ah kah-mah-tay!" while keeping the rhythm of his rib slaps going.

Shauna backed away from Michael when she saw the frat boy, the one who had called for his brothers to fight Michael, step forward with his fists clenched and his jaw set. The Alpha then raised his arm back over his head to strike as he moved toward Michael.

Immediately, the arm of one of the Big Boys reached out from the front line, grabbed the frat boy by the collar, and threw him down to the pavement backwards. The frat boy's head took a bounce off the curb.

Michael, still crouched, crossed his forearms in front of his face, opening them to look between, his tongue still below his chin and his eyes still bugged out. He shouted, while still stomping his feet, "Nah nah-tay nah oh-rah rah oh-rah!"

The frat boy on the ground had hit his head on the curb so hard he was unconscious.

Michael shouted through his crossed forearms, "Ah kah-mah-tay nah nah-tay nah oh-rah rah oh-rah!"

Two of the front row Alpha's moved to get to their unconscious and bleeding-from-the-head brother to drag him back through the crowd and back into the bar.

Michael shouted, "Tay-nay-ee tay tahn-gah-toe poo-hoo-roo-hoo-roo !" and started rotating his hand movements between slapping his thighs, slapping his forearms, slapping his ribs, and crossing his forearms in front of his face, never losing the fearsome and crazed look on his face.

The Big Boys were all mesmerized and squeezed out the remaining frat boys from the front of the crowd.

Michael rotated through his arm movements again, with his tongue hanging out and his eyes popping out, and shouted, "Nah-nah nay-ee ee tee-lee mah-ee!"

The Big Boys, now all shoulder to shoulder, crossed their arms behind each others backs, forming an intimidating line facing Michael.

Michael rotated through his slapping movements again, and shouted, "Whak-kah whee-tee tay rah!"

The arm-locked Big Boys started rocking, side to side, in rhythm with the cadence of Michael's shouts and slaps, and their jaws became more clenched. Shauna thought back to all the pictures she had seen of lynchings. 'I'm as helpless as the families of the all those people strung up for public amusement.'

Michael rotated through his slaps and arm movements once again, and shouted, "Ah oo-payn!" When he shouted that, he used his stomping feet action to take a step forward toward the line of Big Boys. Michael was focusing inwardly until he took that step forward. The only thought that entered his conscious mind was, 'Will I die...or will I live.'

The line of Big Boys didn't move back or forward with Michael's advance, but kept swaying side to side with determined angry looks on their faces.

Michael shouted, "Ah nah oo-payn!" in rhythm with his body slaps, and moved another step forward toward the line of Big Boys, all the while keeping his face in a state of crazed insanity.

The Big Boys just kept swaying and staring, locked as one immovable object.

Michael shouted, "Ah oo-payn ah nah oo-payn!" and took one last step forward, putting him in spitting distance of the line of Big Boys. He was staring at them like a madman.

The Big Boys stared down at him with concentrated meanness.

Michael shouted, "Whee-tee tay rah!" and slowly rose back up to a standing position to be face to face with the biggest of the Big Boys in the center of the line.

The line of Big Boys stopped their swaying and stood staring at Michael, arms still locked behind each other's backs.

Michael dropped his scary look, relaxed his body, and said with a calm voice, "Hee." He then calmly turned his back on the Big Boys and started walking back toward Shauna, who was now shaking in fear.

Suddenly, a roar rose up from the line of Big Boys as they unlinked their arms, started separating, and giving each other high fives and chest bumps.

Michael didn't turn around, but he saw the look on Shauna's face go from fear to confusion. He saw her eyes widen as he felt the breath of three massive beings on his neck.

One of them turned Michael around, embraced Michael's shoulder, and pulled Michael into his chest. Pretending an Australian sounding accent, he said, "You're a beast, mate! Where do you think you're going? You don't think we're gonna let you get out of here without letting us buy you a drink?"

Another one of the Big Boys, also pretending an Australian sounding accent, said to Shauna, "Quite a man you have here, lass. Come in with us and you'll never pay for a drink again." Shauna didn't know the meaning of the Aussie accents combined with the Irish nickname.

Michael was as confused as Shauna, but they had no choice when all three of the Big Boys surrounded them and started walking them back into *Biederman's*.

Once through the doors, a roar went up that drowned out all other noises in the bar, and Shauna and Michael were herded into the center of the gathering of the Big Boys.

"What are you drinking, mate?" the biggest of the group shouted.

Michael thought it would be in his best interest to remain alcohol free. "I'll stay with a cranberry juice, straight up, on the rocks."

"What? Is it your period, mate?" A deafening roar went up from the Big Boys, who were all listening closely.

"And you, lass, what are you drinking?"

Shauna didn't want to say it out loud, but shyly and quietly said, "*Sex-On-The-Beach*?"

The Big Boy taking their orders raised his head above the crowd and shouted for all the bar to hear, "One cranberry juice, straight up, on the rocks for the man..."

The entire crowd of Big Boys shouted, "What? Is it your period?" The laughter was, once again, deafening.

"...and one *Sex-On-The-Beach* for the lady!"

Then all the Big Boys squeezed Michael and Shauna into the center of their tight circle so all the Big Boys could hear.

"You're a rugger, mate? Have come to us from New Zealand?"

Michael, not upset that he was squeezed in tight to Shauna, said, "I don't know what a rugger is."

The entire circled busted out in another uproarious shout of laughter.

"You scrummed for the 'All Blacks' over in New Zealand, did you mate? You look a little small for that, but we see your arms. You're stout as a mule, aren't you mate?" The rest of the Big Boys were listening intently over the hum of their own comments to each other.

Michael was afraid he was being accused of being in a gang called the 'All Blacks,' and it suddenly revived his nervousness.

"I don't know and never heard of the 'All Blacks.'"

Another uproarious shout of laughter went out from the Big Boys.

"He's lying, ruggers! He's lying! Tell us then, who's your team, mate?" Michael was lost. "Did you play in High School *and* college, mate?"

Michael was nervous. "Play what?" Another deafening outbreak of uproarious laughter hurt Michael's ears.

Another Big Boy stepped in. "C'mon, mate. Nobody's supposed to do the 'All Blacks' haka but someone who's played for the 'All Blacks'? When did you play for them, mate?"

"I never played for them."

The Big Boys were getting more curious about Michael. The Big Boy closest to him asked more quietly, "Then who taught you the 'All Blacks' haka?"

Michael had no idea what to say. He looked up at all the faces he could see. He thought of Scottie. He knew nothing in the moment but to be honest. He said, "Mother."

The crowd of Big Boys went back to their shouts of laughter and started tapping their red solo cups to one another. "To Mother!" They all start toasting. "To Mother!"…"To Mother!" Loud laughs, cups toasting, and drinks spilling out was going on all around Shauna and Michael, both.

His examiner bent down to Shauna, "Why does your man hide himself? It's not like a rugger to be quiet about his achievements."

Shauna tried to speak into the Big Boys ear through the noise of the crowd. "I don't know where he learned that stuff, but I can assure you he's never been to, and doesn't know anything about, New Zealand...or World Cup Rugby."

The Big Boy turned to his fellow ruggers, "Have you ever known a rugger that didn't know how to crow? The Lady is keeping his secrets from us! He's committed a crime, and he's on the lam!"

There were big laughs and more toasting all around as the cranberry juice and the *Sex-on-the-Beach* arrived.

The Big Boy turned back to Michael and Shauna. "You'll never buy a drink in this place, again. Not as long as we're here."

Michael and Shauna finally slipped out, their backs, shoulders, and necks sore from being congratulated by every member of the U of Colorado, Boulder, Rugby Club.

When they were in the car and leaving *Biederman's* parking lot, Shauna asked, "Did you play rugby somewhere? How else do you know about all the haka stuff the Big Boys were talking about? They seemed especially impressed about that haka. You just became the toast of the University of Colorado, Boulder, Rugby Club."

"I've never heard of rugby before tonight. How did you know that the 'All Blacks' was a New Zealand Rugby team, and that they played World Cup Rugby?"

Shauna answered, "Wayne and would catch some World Cup Rugby on TV after we left Boulder."

Michael thought, 'Here we go with the 'Wayne' again.'

Michael said, "I'm surprised those guys were so hyped up about a team called the 'All Blacks.' None of those guys were Black."

Shauna explained, "They were hyped up because the 'All Blacks' are the best rugby team in the history of the world, and they obviously knew their haka. 'All Blacks' refers to their team *uniform* color, not the color of their skin."

Michael thought back to Scottie having them practice that routine every morning for two years. 'It's a challenge to yourself to face and engage the day,' he would say. Michael wondered, 'Did he know there would be a day when I would need this? It couldn't be. He taught it to both of us.' Michael wondered what Robert was doing at that moment...if Robert, also, had just escaped peril by using their morning wake-up routine.

Shauna pursued the questions from the bar. "Somebody had to teach you. Who is Mother? They got a big kick out of that."

Michael recalled in his mind how this whole event began with the Alpha Phi's, and he shared his thoughts out loud with Shauna. "White people are as dangerous as I always thought they were."

Shauna countered, "The Big Boys were all Whites, and they embraced you as one of their own."

"That was only after they saw they had something in common with me."

Shauna allowed that thought to settle into Michael.

After a bit, and half-focused on her driving, Shauna mused, "We're all racists. Drunkenness just allows us to lower the curtain of politeness about it."

Michael continued to wonder out loud. "Did I do something to get the ire of those frat boys up? Is there something about me that makes people want to challenge me...assault me? I even felt like they wanted to kill me."

Shauna answered, "Frat boys are too pussy to kill you. But I've seen examples of some evil that lurks, not too far under the skin, that seems to come out of people when they're acting as part of a gang."

Michael jumped in, "Are you talking about Adam-12?"

Shauna appreciated his insight. "People take on gang behavior in any social-fraternal organization, whether it's Adam-12, your local church, the Elks club...anytime humans coalesce into a group...that's a gang. And gang behavior follows. Always. No matter the group.

"The French actually have a name for it. They call it *folie à deux*. It means 'the madness of two.' It refers to an actual psychological condition where two people transmit their psychosis to each other spiritually...or metaphysically...or by a means not explainable. It amplifies the psychosis as it invisibly gets shared back and forth. It's an actual disorder that explains gang behavior. We Americans don't have a name for it. That's why we don't understand it.

"You were asking if they were going to kill you? As a gang, they might have been able to put the hurt on you pretty badly...behavior that would not be characteristic for each of them individually, outside the group."

Something amused Michael. "You talk fancy, putting the 'l' 'y' on the end of bad, making it a adverb."

"...making it *an* adverb." Shauna then smiled inquisitively, "You've got an interesting set of abstract knowledge. Tell me the truth. You dropped out of school in the fifth grade, and you're self-taught after that."

Michael needed to deflect again, as he often did. "Let's just be happy we got out of there alive."

Shauna told Michael on the ride home that World Cup Rugby was on satellite TV from Australia/New Zealand that night. "Don't get any ideas, but if you want to celebrate the survival of your near-death experience, we could swing by your room, you could pick up some comfortable sleeping gear, like sweatpants and a t-shirt, and you could come over to see what all the fuss was about. You can crash on my couch. Wayne won't be bringing Blake back until lunchtime. I can take you back home before that."

Michael was psyched. 'This is all ending up according to plan.'

3.26 LOVE THE WAY YOU LIE

Robert and Christine were well into a phase of needing to be with each other as often as possible. Some form of kissing was always part of it. One night after work, Christine came to Robert's apartment so he could make supper for them.

After supper and clean-up and brushing their teeth…Christine now had a toothbrush in Robert's bathroom…they lounged on the couch in a horizontal and intertwined way.

"Why are you here all alone, and you don't have any family that you're in touch with?"

"It's a tale of dysfunction and lots of moving around from one welfare city to another. I would come to believe that crimes were the motivation for all of our moves. Drug abuse was part of it. One way or another, everybody died. At no time were any of the deaths a loss. They were a relief."

Christine saw some missing pieces to this very generalized tale. "Clearly, you've had some positive influences."

"I had a couple meaningful years with Mother before she relapsed and O.D.'d. I think I stay healthy by not returning to the memories."

Christine wasn't interested in pushing. She was confident in the person she had. She wasn't afraid of what circumstances he had come from.

Robert interrupted their long pause. "Does it matter that I don't have a pedigree?"

"If it mattered, I would have asked about it a long time before now.

I just love learning who you are...what made you you. I love knowing everything about you."

Robert said, "I don't want to know everything about you. The 'I wonder' is a special part of the sparkle that I never want to have go away. So, the only things I want to know about you are the parts of you I'm going to have to deal with in our daily struggle to stay in love."

Christine loved these parts of their conversations. There was always a light humor in it. "Struggle? Don't tell me it's already work for you." She snuggled up until she was eye to eye, mouth to mouth, with him. She breathed into his mouth, "Has another already caught your fancy?"

Robert took advantage of their lips being so close.

Christine got her fix and then added, "OK. Then I'm going to ruin the mystery for you. I used to make my dolls beat up my other dolls...who were any girls that were mean to me."

Robert pressed impression parts of his body in tight to her. "OK. But I refuse to tell you about being held prisoner in a mind-control concentration camp where I was brainwashed into being White."

She rubbed her finger up and down his arm, then looked at the inside of her finger. "It didn't work...but don't you ever go White on me."

"Too late." Robert started instigating some friskiness.

She repositioned herself for comfort. "I'm in love with you. And even if you're too under-spoken to admit it out loud, you're in love with me, too. I have no feelings of judgement about your upbringing. A person's upbringing is out of their control. I just want to get some insight into how the person I think so much of got to be the person I think so much of. And by the way, was it 'Mother' that taught you the word 'pedigree?'...And who calls their mom, 'Mother?'"

If Christine had eyes to see, she would have seen the careful way Robert had been putting on makeup...to match his earrings.

She pulled him in tight to her body and started returning his friskiness.

Robert pulled away for some seriousness. "I want you to answer this question for yourself in your own time…and the question is, are you ready to marry me? Because…you've led me to a place where I can see clearly what I want in a forever friend and companion. And you check all the boxes. You're the one. You're the one for me….but I don't want any pressure on you to agree or disagree. I don't want you to feel that the clock is ticking while I wait for an answer. I'll take either answer as being what I will live with…but I won't hide the fact that I predict that one answer will make me happier than another. Not that my happiness is your burden."

Christine surrounded the back of his head with all her fingers so that it wouldn't move. She got him locked into her eyes. Then she started kissing him deeply and passionately…like she was trying to start something. Then she broke off the passion-kissing, looked him back in the eye, and said, "Stop the clock."

The faux sex was great for both of them. They were climbing a ladder one rung at a time.

Afterwards, they talked about a combined dinner for both her parents and grandparents so everyone would learn the news at the same time.

They were already happy together. They already loved each other. They had already been planning their lives out. The hopes, the fears, the dreams…as well as supporting each other through tragedies. But this agreement added a dimension they both wanted so passionately.

What they both wanted so passionately was never having to say, 'It's time for me to go home, now.'

With their memorable night duly marked in both their mental calendars, they brushed themselves to pretend they were getting all the wrinkles out of their clothes. Then they shook out their bodies to get used to being vertical again. Then Christine said to Robert, "It's time for me to go home, now."

3.27 THE IDES OF MARCH

World Cup Rugby had been on the TV the night before...until Shauna couldn't stay awake anymore. She had said 'goodnight' to Michael and went upstairs to bed.

Michael didn't go to sleep that easily. He still had some adrenaline in his body from the *Biederman's Tavern* experience the night before, plus he added to it with some excitement about the chances of getting closer to Shauna...considering in his mind that she had invited him to spend the night. He found a pen and a pad of paper, then he killed the time composing his thoughts.

Michael's double adrenaline rush not only kept him awake late, but it also awakened him early.

Upon waking, he foraged around Shauna's kitchen to find coffee and a coffee maker and set to brewing. He wanted to see her to get to spend more private time with her so badly that he walked two cups of freshly brewed coffee upstairs on a plate and knocked lightly on her bedroom door.

He heard her say, "Come in," in a soft, asleep voice. He opened her door.

She had just sat up in bed, having been awakened by his footsteps and his way-too-early enthusiasm.

Even though she was wearing a non-sexy flannel nightgown, there was something about the scene and the circumstance that excited Michael. He was only there for coffee, but there was something very appetizing to him about the whole aura...in his mind.

"Oh, that was so sweet. I need it," as she took one of the cups from him. He knew how she liked it from the restaurant.

Michael set the plate with his coffee on it down on her nightstand. He reached into the pocket of his sweatpants for the poem he had written the night before. When he felt for the paper, he rattled his boxcutter.

Shauna perked up a little. "What's that?"

Michael switched hands to reach into his other pocket and pulled out the scrap of paper. "It's something I wrote last night." He handed it to her.

All of a sudden, their Sunday morning moment was distracted by the sound of the front door opening and slamming shut downstairs. Shauna heard the noise, cocked her head to listen for a second, and said, "I think that's Wayne and Blake coming in the front door."

As she peeled the sheets and blanket off her and got out of bed to put on a robe, she said, "Something must be wrong. They're back several hours early."

She walked out of the bedroom and headed down the stairs. Michael thought to himself, 'Son-uv-a-bitch! I'm beginning to not like that mthrfkr.' Then he turned and slowly followed her footsteps.

Wayne saw Shauna coming down the stairs and said, "I was just about to come up those stairs to see you."

To Shauna, he seemed to be angry about something. "What is it, Wayne? I don't appreciate you barging in like this, unannounced." She looked down at Blake and held her arms out for Blake to come to her.

Just then, Wayne saw Michael in his sweatpants and t-shirt at the top of the stairs, just emerging from Shauna's bedroom.

Wayne exploded. "Are you fckng kidding me? What in the *hell* is *he* doing here? He's what I came over to talk to you about!"

From the bottom of the stairs, and with Blake in her arms, Shauna turned her head to see Michael above her. She turned back to Wayne.

"That's none of your business, Wayne. Am I going to have to get a restraining order to keep you from storming into my house like this?"

Wayne seemed to be getting hotter. "It might take more than a restraining order. That son-uv-a-bitch has been teaching some gutter-religion bllsht to our son. Are you in on this, Shauna? Are you on some kind of insane kick about turning our Blake into a Muslim?"

Shauna was shaking off Wayne's gibberish. "Stop saying stupid things in my house, turn yourself around, and go home." Then she put her arm around Blake more tightly. She looked down at Blake, and said, "Everything's OK, honey. You didn't do anything wrong." Shauna got on her knees next to Blake and ran her hands up and down his arms. Blake was sullen and shaken.

Wayne was undeterred. "That wild jack-ass you've been hanging around with…and now more than just hanging around with, obviously…he's been teaching Blake to say Muslim words." Wayne directed his words to Blake. "Tell her, Blake. Tell her what the bad man taught you to say."

Blake turned his head into his mother's chest and mumbled, "Allah Akbar."

Shauna pulled her head back from Blake so she could hear him. "What did you say, Blakey?"

Blake started to cry, and said through his tears, "Allah Akbar."

Shauna asked, "Where did you learn that, Blakey?"

Michael had just reached the bottom of the stairs.

Blake, who was now full-on crying, pointed to Michael.

Shauna turned and looked at Michael. "Is that true, Michael? Did you teach him that?"

Michael was offended that both Shauna and Wayne were taking offense.

"Yeah. We were playing basketball at the arcade, and he heard me say it whenever I got a basket. Then he started saying it. There's no harm. It's an expression of happiness and victory. Wayne-boy, over there, is taking something beautiful, and he's trying to make it ugly."

Wayne broke in. "See, Shauna? See? You're sleeping with some kind of Muslim, Nation of Islam thug. And because of your wickedly bad judgement, our innocent son has been infected by this trash."

Michael was about to rise up in anger, so the first place he went in his mind was the haka...and to slowly count to ten. But he couldn't get either place soon enough. "Change your tone, mthrfkr, or you and I are gonna dance...and you're not gonna like the outcome."

When Shauna heard the swear-language, she scooped up Blake and ran him upstairs to her bedroom.

Wayne pointed his finger at Michael. "Can't you see what you're doing? You're taking this gutter, illegitimate religion of yours, and your gutter, illegitimate Prophet, and you're puking it onto the good and the innocence of my son..."

When Wayne blasphemed the Prophet, there was no turning back for Michael. He reached into his sweatpants pocket and, in one move, pulled out his boxcutter, extended the blade, and lunged at Wayne with his open, free hand.

When Wayne raised his arm to defend himself from Michael's empty hand, Michael made a full-force stab with his other hand into the side of Wayne's neck with the blade. As Michael perpetrated the fatal wound, he thought, 'Why does everyone hate me? Why does everyone want to kill me?' "You think you know who I am, you college boy mthrfkr?" as he watched the blood start to spurt from Wayne's neck. "Well, think again, mthrfck! Allah Akbar!"

Michael immediately had a rush of clarity penetrate his entire being. He let the knife go out of his hand as Wayne clutched his neck wound and dropped to his knees. Michael became aware of the horror of his own rage as he watched Wayne fall prostrate on the carpeted floor.

Just then, Michael heard something behind him. He turned to see Shauna had come out of her bedroom and was standing at the top of the stairs. Michael's bottom lip started shaking as he could come up no words to express his apology and sorrow.

In her own horror, Shauna turned to go back into her bedroom where Blake sat on her bed, protected from the sounds by cartoons on Shauna's bedroom TV.

While Michael was turned to looked at Shauna, Wayne had reached around his own back and felt for a small .22 caliber handgun tucked in his belt, under his shirt.

When Michael turned back to look at Wayne bleeding out quickly on the floor, Wayne aimed the pistol at Michael and squeezed off one, small, firecracker-sounding shot directly into Michael's chest.

Michael felt like someone had just tapped his chest, like a finger-flick. He didn't realize he had been shot through his heart.

He watched Wayne drop his arm and the gun to the floor and close his eyes. An uncontrollable rush of thoughts were flying through Michael's mind...faster than he could hold onto any one of them.

He saw the flow of blood soaking into the carpet and thought he was feeling it, sympathetically, in his t-shirt. He put his hand on his t-shirt only to realize it was his own blood that was making his chest warm. As he felt the blood flowing over his hand, he looked back at his victim on the floor and mumbled out loud, "You, too, Wayne?"

He tried to look back down at his wound, but started coughing. The coughing was spraying the blood out in front of him. After a couple of coughs, he couldn't take in a breath. The blood was choking him. Suffocating him. In wondering what to do, he began to feel panic. But there were no more choices left for him to make. His panic quickly transformed into resignation.

Michael, for lack of air, fell to his own knees, and then immediately face first on the carpet. His head landed only inches from Wayne's head.

Shauna had come back out of her bedroom when she heard the 'pop' of Wayne's pistol only to see from the top of the stairs both men laid out like crime scene chalk lines. The two bodies were lying in two pools of blood that, as they were saturating the carpet, were now combining as one.

Michael's last conscious thought was not of his mother, nor his grandmother, nor either one of his cousins, Jamal or Jimmy, nor even of his mentor and tormentor. Michael's last conscious thought was not of this earth. 'Allah Akbar.'

Shauna was in her bedroom with Blake who was still engaged in the cartoons. She called her girlfriend, the manager of the restaurant, to come pick up Blake until Shauna's mother could get there from Boulder. "Come to the back door. It's an emergency. Take Blake until my mother can get here. I can't explain." She ended the call.

Shauna then called her mother and told her to pick Blake up at Marie's house, and to take Blake home to her house in Boulder...that Shauna would be in touch with her later to explain, and that she would pick up Blake later.

Shauna then picked up the receiver from her land-line phone on her nightstand and dialed 9-1-1. She answered the operator, "My husband and a male friend of mine have killed each other and are on my living room floor." Shauna knew her address was automatically reported.

The operator preceded her next questions with, "Please stay on the line." Shauna just hung up. When the phone started ringing again, she reached down behind the nightstand and unplugged the wire from the wall jack.

After her calls were done, she walked Blake down the back stairs of the second floor and directly out the back entryway off the kitchen.

3.28 BLACKHAWK DOWN

Shauna had handed Blake off to Marie in the back yard just in time for Marie to drive off with Blake before the police...several of the police...screeched to a halt in front of Shauna's house. Police response time in upscale towns was fast.

Shauna stepped around the bodies and the blood and answered the front door. Two officers had their service weapons drawn. Shauna guided them in to the bodies. The officers swept the downstairs for any other people while they got the report from Shauna that there were no other people in the house. Then they holstered their weapons.

When Patrolman Roger Crest holstered his weapon, he looked down at the two bodies stuck to the floor by blood. He held his mouth as he ran toward the front door and vomited off the porch onto Shauna's rose bushes. He wiped his mouth, shook it off, and told arriving officers to tape the yard.

When the detective arrived, Patrolman Crest escorted him in to the scene. The detective interviewed Shauna.

"My husband, which is this one, had our son for the weekend. He brought my son home early this morning because my husband was mad about something my friend, who is this one, had taught my son to say"..."he's with a friend here in town. She took him away from all this before you got here."..."It was about some religious saying my friend had taught my son, and it angered my husband, which is why my husband barged in here without any warning this morning."..."It was a Muslim saying, 'Allah Akbar,' and it set my ex-husband off into a rage."..."No, I'm not, but my religious beliefs have nothing to do with this."..."My friend...I should say, my *former* friend, had something in his pocket. He used it to cut my husband's neck. There it is, right there. It's a boxcutter, if you can see it in the blood."..."Yes, I knew my ex had a handgun and that he usually had it on him, but I didn't know he had it on him this morning."..."Wayne King."... "*Vernon Software Systems.*"..."Michael Dean."..."*The Sunflower Cafe and Restaurant.*"

The whole time Shauna was giving her statement, Patrolman Crest, who had regained his composure, was studying the bodies.

After all the crime scene photos and forensics had been collected, ambulance crews bagged up and removed the bodies to their ambulances for a trip to the Denver morgue. Highlands Ranch didn't have a morgue.

The Highlands Ranch Chief had suited up on a Sunday when he got the call and had arrived late to the scene. The Chief debriefed the detective.

As officers and support personnel and the Chief were leaving the scene, Patrolman Crest approached the Chief.

"Chief? Do you remember that Denver Metro had a briefing last year about a Nashville cop killer that might have come to Denver?"

"What about it?"

"The morgue photo of the Nashville cop had a neck wound in the same place as the neck wound on the ex-husband in this case."

"What's your point, Crest?"

"Is it possible that the cook from *The Sunflower Cafe* could be the Nashville cop killer?"

"That's farfetched, Crest. Based on a similar wound? Way too random. You told me, yourself, that the cook had a different face and no gold grille on his teeth. But just to satisfy your curiosity, I do remember seeing the Nashville perp's artist rendering portrait. Do you remember it, too?"

"Yes, Sir, I do."

"Then let's go take a look before they leave with the bodies."

The first bodybag that was unzipped for them was the ex-husband. "No, Sir. That's the ex-husband. But look at the neck wound." It was now impossible to see detail with all the blood-smear around it from the body being handled.

The second bodybag was unzipped for them. Both men stared at the lifeless face for about thirty seconds.

"I can't see it, Crest. Can you?"

"No, Sir."

The ambulances headed toward Denver.

After the blinding flurry of activity from the day before, Shauna had had Blake, he being unaware of the carnage that had happened, go with her mother to Boulder. Later that day, Shauna had followed.

She returned home from Boulder the next day, early in the afternoon, without him. She didn't want him to see or smell the cake on their living room carpet. She went up to her bedroom to sit for a rest on her bed and to call her mother to tell her she had gotten home safely.

When Shauna rolled back on the bed after hanging up the phone, she was distracted by the ruffling sound of paper. She lifted her buttcheek and looked to see what it was. It was the paper that Michael had given her before they were interrupted. She read it.

"Something come
Run Dogg run
Light from sun
Not infinitum
Mother son
Not born, spun
But not undone
Are wars won?
Pandemonium
Just a pendulum
Next? Too dumb"

Shauna was too braindead to contemplate it. She put it in the drawer of her nightstand. Then, she re-opened the drawer of her nightstand, retrieved the piece of paper, and tore it into small pieces for the trash basket under the nightstand. 'Some fckng poet you are...you asshole. I wish I had never met you.'

She called The Home Depot to get her living room carpet replaced. She told them to come next week. Then she called her mother back and said she was coming back to Boulder to stay there with Blake for the week.

After his weekend shift, Patrolman Crest had Monday off. He just couldn't let the similar boxcutter wound go.

He drove in his own car in his civvies to the station. There he searched the computer for the BOLO (Be-On-The-Lookout) for the Nashville suspect. The artist sketch of the suspect was included in the BOLO.

When Crest saw the sketch, he shook his head. 'Nope. That's not the guy.' But he *still* couldn't let it go.

He went into the computer to retrieve and replay the Profile Briefing given to Metro Denver by Special Agent in Charge John Watkins. Crest took notes. The note that stuck out to him as meaningful was the known arrival date of the suspect to Denver.

Crest left the station and drove to *The Sunflower Cafe and Restaurant*. The place was abuzz, and they were short-handed. Marie, the manager, was filling in for the cook, Michael, who had not shown up for work, and for the waitress, Shauna, who had quit.

Crest showed his badge to Marie. "This is official business, Marie. I'm sorry. Can you tell me what the date of hire was for Michael Dean?"

Marie led Officer Crest back to the office and pulled Michael Dean's file.

Crest said, "Thank you," and left to go to the house in which Michael Dean had rented a room.

"M'am, can you tell me the date that Michael Dean moved into his rented apartment?"

Crest returned to the station in his civvies. The Highlands Ranch Chief was present but tired.

Before the end of the day, Agent Watkins got the call from the Metro Denver Chief.

3.29 GOT TO BE GOOD LOOKING CUZ HE'S SO HARD TO SEE

After his flight landed at Denver International, Agent Watkins was picked up by an unmarked Metro Denver car and driven straight to the morgue. It was lunchtime. Watkins hadn't even eaten breakfast, but hunger was the last thing on his mind.

He was met at the Morgue by the Metro Denver Chief and several officers, but he was only introduced to one of the Uniforms. "Agent Watkins, this is Highlands Ranch Patrolman Roger Crest. He's the one who put the pieces together that brought you here."

Watkins shook his hand and said, "Nice work. Let's go inside and see what we've got."

The bodies of both Wayne King and Michael Dean were removed from their respective refrigerated lockers and transferred to rolling exam tables. Watkins approached the body of Wayne King. A gloved Watkins pushed around the cleaned neck flesh-wound of the ex-husband. He nodded his head. "Yep. Same wound on the same side as our Nashville officer."

Then he moved to the body of Michael Dean. "Height?"

The coroner answered. "Five-eight, plus a little if he were still standing."

Watkins nodded. "Right height."

Watkins bent over Michael Dean's face to get a straight-on view. Then he backed off and opened Michael's lips with his fingers. Watkins inspected Michael's teeth and gums.

"Sorry, boys. No physical resemblance, plus the perp we're hunting has gold teeth. This guy is all ivory."

Patrolman Crest's heart sank. "But what about the arrival date, Agent Watkins? It matches the exact day you said the suspect arrived in Denver when you gave your briefing. And we could find no prior history on this guy."

Watkins wanted more from Patrolman Crest. "I was told your detectives searched the studio apartment this guy rented, and that you interviewed the landlords?"

Crest was anxious to contribute. "Yes, Sir."

Watkins probed. "Where did the landlords say he came from?"

Crest. "Des Moines. And in your briefing, Agent Watkins, you said your perp traveled from Nashville to Chicago to Des Moines to Denver. So, Des Moines fits."

"How did the landlords find out this guy existed?"

"They were contacted by email, so they asked for an employer reference. They then had a Face Chat interview with the employer from Des Moines."

"What was the employer's story?"

"That he owned a restaurant in Des Moines where Michael Dean had worked for years. That he was an outstanding employee, always on time, and never missed a day of work. Plus, that the clientele loved his cooking and his interactions."

"Any description of the employer?"

"Just that he was an old White guy."

At that point, the Coroner inserted herself into the questioning. "You're looking for gold teeth, Agent Watkins? All his teeth are porcelain capped and adhered with white dental epoxy. Expensive. Plus, he only had one personal effect on his person." She held up a Zip-lok baggie with a gold ring enclosed. Watkins took the bag and inspected the content.

Watkins then opened the baggie and removed the gold ring to inspect it in the light. It had the initials "MD" stamped onto the outer surface. Then he started rolling and twisting the ring in the light. That's when he noticed scratches on the inside of the ring. Watkins asked the Coroner, "Do you have a magnifying glass?"

She produced a handheld magnifier, about six inches in diameter. Watkins inspected the scratches off the reflection of the overhead examination lights. He said out loud, "These handmade scratches look like they were made with the diagonal edge of a mini-file. There are two letters that look like cave wall scratchings. But they're discernible. 'M' and 'J.' Muhammad Jefferson. This guy could not let his old self go!" Then he began circling around the body.

On his second circle around, he stopped dead in his tracks...an assaultive epiphany had just slapped him in the back of his head.

Watkins got directly in front of Michael's face, again. This time, he placed the butt of his palm on the tip of Michael's nose, leaving his fingers to cover up the nose. When he did that, his eyes started to widen. Everyone in the room heard him whisper to himself, 'That's him!'

Watkins yanked his hand away from Michael's face. "Plastic surgery." Watkins stepped back from the body. "Welcome home, Muhammad Dogg Jefferson."

Watkins was pumped. All the other officers in the room waited for an explanation.

Watkins turned to the coroner. "Has a DNA sample been sent to Quantico? We have family DNA there from Nashville we can match it to."

Then Watkins turned to the other officers, his feet feeling like they were three feet off the floor. "Plastic surgery on the nose. I want each one of you to cover his nose, and then tell me he doesn't match the sketch portrait...And the dental work. The gold was extracted and the teeth were re-capped. I'll bet a steak dinner that the gold from his teeth was used to make the ring."

It wasn't premature for the morgue full of cops to start celebrating and congratulating each other for this monumental victory.

Watkins stepped outside the room and pulled his phone from his inside jacket pocket. He called his Assistant Director in Charge.

"Boss?...We got him!"

Watkins drove to Metro Denver headquarters where he was received as the returning conquering hero. Someone had managed to come up with some bottles of Champagne, and it wasn't long before the Chief's office resembled the locker room after a World Series Pennant win.

Watkins wasn't about to actually drink any of the Champagne, but he allowed himself to be showered. It was all exhilarating while it was happening, but shortly afterwards Watkins had to find the showers in the HQ and make a full clothing change.

He then found Patrolman Crest. "Drive me back to Highlands Ranch."

Crest gave Watkins the tour of the town, including the boarding house, Shauna's house, and lastly, *The Sunflower Cafe and Restaurant*. Then Watkins asked to be taken to the evidence room at the Highlands Ranch Police Department.

Watkins poured through the evidence. Clothing that matched bus station video was another confirmation. Watkins then asked about the money. "How much cash was found in the apartment?"

"Twelve-thousand three-hundred twenty-seven dollars, and some coinage. Over nine-thousand dollars of it was older bills."

Watkins started doing some addition. 'The dental work...the big money plastic surgery...money...money...money. Over twelve-thousand in cash? Somebody was bankrolling this operation.' Then Watkins remembered the mystery of how McNally was living on no income. 'Could his inheritance have been converted to cash and be sustaining him?...as well as funding the two fugitives?' It was a question Watkins had asked himself, before. Many times. The answer had always come up, 'No. There is no evidence in the McNally lifestyle or data that supports the existence of meaningful cash reserves.'

Watkins was now trying to make room for the possibility that the answer was, 'Yes,' but he couldn't imagine a motive for why McNally would spend down his own money for these two fugitives. Without a motive, Watkins couldn't feel confident about concluding that McNally would have spent whatever cash-money he had.

Watkins then suspected that Muhammad had embezzled the little cafe/restaurant that he had worked at. "We'll check that out at *The Sunflower Cafe and Restaurant.*"

Patrolman Crest parked at the front door entrance steps to the Beshire home. He and Agent Watkins were welcomed in.

"Thank you, Mr. and Mrs. Beshires, for your continuing help.

"Patrolman Crest, here, tells me that you had received an email introducing you to Michael Dean, and that his employer gave Michael Dean a reference via a computer Face Chat. May I see your computer? If I can retrieve the email address and the Face Chat username used to contact you, it would help us in our investigation."

Crest then drove Watkins back to Shauna's house. A knock on the door and a walk around the house made them conclude nobody was home. Watkins asked if Crest had Shauna's phone number. Crest made a call to the station to get it.

"My name is Agent Watkins. I'm at your house with Officer Crest. We're doing some digging into the man who died in your house...Michael Dean? I was told you worked with him, and that you spent some personal time with him. Can you give me an overview of who this man was?"

Shauna was forthcoming about everything she knew. She was no ally to Michael Dean. She covered topics that were big surprises to Watkins, such as his interests in art and literature. She told Watkins that Michael Dean quoted a lot of poetry...and then she remembered the poem she had thrown away after the deaths. She told Watkins about that, though she couldn't recall what it said.

Watkins was flummoxed. 'These things are the polar opposite of who Muhammad Jefferson was. At least who I *projected* him to be in my profile.' Then the echo come back. 'A poor *Black* beggar can be trained to be *White* to fit into high society.' Watkins mind went to the possible ways that Muhammad could receive that kind of training. But he had tunnel vision. He tried to see other possibilities, but the book of possibilities had already been closed because of his obsessive study of the bookshelf.

'McNally.'

At the restaurant, Watkins asked Marie, "Your chef was found to have an inexplicable amount of cash at the time of his death. Is it possible that he was siphoning money from here? The restaurant?"

Marie was quick to answer. "I give Miss Lilly, the owner, a weekly report on the money in, as well as the money out that pays the bills. The ratios are the same, now, as they were before Michael came to work for us. The only difference is that the raw numbers are bigger. Michael was responsible for bringing in a lot more business than we had before he came to work here."

Watkins couldn't reconcile that with the profile he had generated on Muhammad Jefferson. Watkins then had an investigative light bulb turn on. "May I see Michael Dean's employment file?"

Marie walked Watkins and Crest back to the office. When she gave the personnel file to Watkins, he opened it on the office desk and took a picture of the employment application.

Watkins got a night flight from Denver International to Nashville International. The late night flight wasn't going to bother Watkins. *Nothing* was going to bother Watkins that night. There was too much adrenaline coursing through his veins for him to sleep. On the plane ride, he outlined the next action steps.

'FBI team to Denver; sift and sort evidence for clues about contacts…and hints about any contacts with Jamal Ali Jefferson; interviews with the girlfriend; interviews with the landlords; pass off computer email and Face Chat username to foot soldiers to investigate where those contacts originated from; interviews with employer staff and any significant customer relationships for documentation to support a court trial. Not Muhammad's trial. He's already been sentenced. But the trial of Jamal Jefferson. That's where all energy gets focused now.

'And the plastic surgery…Where'd the money come from? What plastic surgeon could have been found to do it? Same with the dental work. Money? What dentist? And who would have thought to have a personalized gold ring made from the teeth? An artist. A poet. A romantic.

'Scott McNally? Doesn't fit my profile of him…but I know he's the one. And I know there's more to him than he shows.

'If McNally…where did he house them? Not at his property. The woods were searched.

'And after plastic surgery and extensive dental work, the boys would have needed convalescent care. Where were they convalesced? A hospital? A nursing home? Impossible.

'How did he pay for all these procedures? We track McNally's movements and his bank statements. Those things align. McNally only buys for himself. Cash infusions to his debit card account are just enough to cover his monthly documented cost of living.

'Scott McNally. That little bastard has a secret. I need to figure out how to find it.'

Another celebration briefing lay ahead for Watkins that next day in Nashville.

When Agent Watkins arrived at Nashville International in the early morning, he was met by one of his agents and was driven to the hotel where the FBI had a block of rooms permanently reserved. He sent a morgue photo from his phone to another assisting agent and asked him to have a poster printed and brought to Metro Nashville HQ as soon as the printer opened his doors that morning.

The Metro Nashville briefing auditorium was filled when Agent Watkins arrived at about 11AM. He walked in to a standing ovation amplified by cheers and whoops and hollers.

When the crowd settled down, Watkins reminded the Task Force that all of the evidence from this capture was going to be processed for the purpose of finding the second perp, Jamal Ali Jefferson. And that Watkins' profile summation still included the likelihood that the two perps would be found together. "That means a new scrutiny on the Denver area suburbs."

He put morgue photos on the screen to explain the plastic surgery, along with changes to the Jamal photo that replicated the plastic surgery found on Muhammad.

He showed morgue dental photos to show teeth capping. "We've rescinded the gold grille from our previous profile. We're now looking to find the second perp with white, shiny ivory."

"And, lastly, I've had a poster printed of Muhammad Jefferson's morgue photo as a gift to your Chief. I hope he chooses to proudly display it in the Task Force work area."

Suddenly, a familiar voice shouted above the din. "I have my own surprise, Agent Watkins." It was the Union Rep, Officer Neal Knopfler.

"When I found out about the morgue photo, I took it upon myself to have one hundred poster copies made from our Union funds." Officers started passing copies down the rows of seating. "These posters are meant to by used at the shooting range for target practice. Right between the eyes is considered a bulls-eye."

A wave of laughter and comments filled the auditorium as all the Metro officers took several copies each.

As the Task Force was dispersing, Agent Watkins approached Chief Rand. "Chief, I'm not anywhere close to being comfortable with this stunt that Officer Knoplfer has pulled." The Chief was listening and nodding.

Watkins continued. "Knopfler has been a weak link in this investigation from the start. He clearly has a racist agenda that he's infusing into an already racially charged situation. This stunt with the target-practice posters is going to make the Black community in your jurisdiction explode when word gets out...and you know it will."

Chief Rand said, "Knopfler is one of a very few bad apples we have in this department..."

Watkins interrupted with, "...and we all know it only takes one bad apple to spoil the whole barrel."

Chief Rand said, "Affirmative. But my hands are tied. He's the Union Rep, and the rank and file see the Union as their only protection from over-zealous, politically motivated prosecutors who might want to serve loud voices from the 'Public' rather than the work-a-day cop on the beat.

"My entire force goes to work every day looking over their shoulders about whether or not this is the day something will happen that will get them fired, or put a mark on their record, or worse yet, get them locked up in jail...not to mention the daily risk of being killed.

"Knopfler, or anyone else in his position, is seen as their protector."

Watkins pleaded, "He's *not* their protector, Chief, and I think you know that. His racist views border on…no, I'm just going to say it…*are* White Supremacist at their core. And he uses his position to spread those views to any eager ear that will listen."

Rand replied, "C'mon, John, you know the way it is. We all have to work with the tools we're given. Knopfler is just one of those tools."

Agent Watkins phone sounded with the first four ominous notes from Beethoven's Fifth Symphony.

"Excuse me, Chief. I have to take this."

"John, I'm getting some ripple echoes coming all the way from D.C. You're the man of the hour. There's talk about moving you up to Assistant Director, and that you should start thinking about which of the open Districts you'll take."

"Thanks, Boss. But I have to give credit to a Patrolman who was paying attention out in a Denver suburb."

"Got it. Your humility is admirable." There was a moment of humble silence. "So, John, this would be the right moment for a politically aware Agent to cash in on any favors he's been waiting to ask for."

"Well, Boss, as long as you bring it up…This Nashville Task Force has a bad apple that will take some extraordinary political influence to get him removed from the Task Force. It's not a personality conflict. There's a deficiency in the guy's person that is interfering with the outcome of our efforts."

Watkins had always included in his profile, 'Find one, and you find the other.' He felt the end was near for Jamal Ali Jefferson. Then Watkins remembered his biggest prize that he brought home from his Denver trip. He wondered what he would learn from it as he was returning to his Memphis Office. Michael Dean's Social Security number from the employment application at *The Sunflower Cafe and Restaurant* would be his next focus of attention.

3.30 ARE YOU SAD BECAUSE YOU'RE ON YOUR OWN

Christine was going to meet Robert at his apartment at seven o'clock for supper. Robert got a phone call from her as he was getting out of the shower.

"Come to my parents' house as quickly as you can get here, Baby. I'll explain when you get here."

"There was news from Nashville this afternoon. One of the kids who murdered Cathy's husband was caught."

Robert had to cover his mouth with his hand...because he couldn't close it.

"He was found dead in Denver, Colorado. But they've identified his body. My mother and my Grammi Nancy and I are getting on a plane tonight to fly to Nashville to be with them."

Robert's hand was still over his mouth.

"Baby? Are you alright?"

Robert let his hand drop from his mouth, but he still couldn't close it.

"Baby? Are you listening to me? I don't know how long we'll be out there, but I'll keep you aware of our plans."

Robert knew he had to go into emergency recovery mode if he didn't want to have to start answering questions.

"Yeah, Babe. Yeah. I get it. That's horrible."

"Well, it's not *horrible*, Baby. It's more like a macabre sort of celebration for Cathy. But we know it will bring up sad and disturbing memories for her. So, we'll all be there to support her for as long as it takes."

Robert had the wherewithal to throw his arms around Christine. After a long hug, he said, "You're a good friend to Cathy. You're gonna make sure she has a soft landing. Just let me know about your return plans. And call me for anything that you need."

"Thanks, Baby. You're the best."
They kissed.
Robert left.
He couldn't get out of there fast enough.

Robert was able to stay semi-focused on his work during the following days. But at night, when he was usually spending time with Christine, Robert would find himself stuck in a rabbit hole, wondering about what Muhammad's life and death must have been. He watched every news report he could get on it, but the story got moved out of the news cycle as quickly as it had come in.

Robert spent a couple of evenings doing internet searches. All of the information on the internet fit like puzzle pieces to Robert. He either saw Muhammad or Scottie in everything.

Highlands Ranch. A White, upscale suburb. Scottie.

Restaurant Chef. Scottie and his constant cooking and experimenting.

A knife fight with a girlfriend's ex-husband. Muhammad.

The matching box-knife neck wound. All Muhammad.

Robert was concerned about the details about the plastic surgery and the dental work being known. But he was glad for the luck of his own Dennis Rodman growth spurt.

By the end of Christine being gone for a week, Robert had processed everything he needed to process. He finally got back to where he needed to be. 'I am the master of my fate. I am the captain of my soul.'

3.31 THE PARENT TRAP

It was a rare night that Scottie got a stable enough picture on his TV to leave it on. But call it fate. Call it luck. Call it coincidence. Scottie got the news of Michael's identification and death over the six o'clock evening news from Nashville. Despite the good reception, Scottie turned the TV off.

He walked out of the inner sanctum to stare out the front hall picture window. Every individual thing he saw out his window created a visual memory of Michael touching it or pruning it or digging it or hauling it away.

The next day was a fog. Scottie wandered around the inner sanctum. He saw Michael sitting at the dining room table, looking through books on the couch, preparing and eating and cleaning up meals.

The morning after that, Scottie opened the bookcase and walked downstairs to the immaculate basement. He saw the beds and the other furniture all set up, and all the different positions he had ever seen Michael using them. He stood, fully clothed, in the shower to feel the faint echo of Michael's former physical presence.

The next day, Scottie returned to the basement. He listened for Michael's voice. He could hear it. The complaints, the arguments, the revelations, the unveiling and maturity of his logical mind...his understated, even if misguided, protection of and love for Robert.

Scottie spent the next day deep inside his own head. It was a self-inspection.

His mind went down a long hallway with many rooms off the corridor. As Scottie walked down this path of memories, he opened each door to see and hear himself giving Michael an instruction. Each door opened a different speech of guidance, a nudge toward understanding, a reinforcement of knowledge gained. It seemed like hours before Scottie could find no more doors to open. 'All my words come back to me in shades of mediocrity.'

Scottie involuntarily bowed his head. 'Could I have done more?...What instruction or guidance did I miss?'

By the next day, Scottie's thoughts shifted more toward Robert. Scottie was sure the news had made its way to Robert. Scottie paced back and forth, trying to picture how Robert was handling it. He tried to reassemble all his knowledge of Robert so he could know how to affect a new stream of guidance to him.

By the day after that, Scottie wanted to teleport the modifications of his guidance he'd wished he could have re-spoken to Michael.

He pictured Robert standing in front of him. In his mind, Robert and he were connected through their eyes. He wanted to upgrade everything he had ever said to Robert. It was important. It was urgent. He needed another chance. He needed a do-over to compensate for his inadequacies that had caused Michael's death. He had to spare Robert a similar fate.

By the end of the day, Scottie was becoming aware that he was grasping at wishes for which there was no genie.

The next day, Scottie had corralled himself back into the straightjacket of sanity. He revisited what he had known before the news of Michael's death. Scottie teleported the only message he knew to be true. He mutely spoke directly into Robert's eyes.

'You are the master of your fate. You are the captain of your soul.

'Peace.

'Out.'

3.32 WHAT'S THE BUZZ? TELL ME WHAT'S A HAPPENIN'

Christine and her mother and her grandmother had been in Nashville for that week that Robert was processing the cataclysmic event. Christine went straight to Robert when she got home.

Christine reported a bit of a celebratory atmosphere, and that Cathy didn't really need much comforting or other support. That she had a new boyfriend whom she had quietly married. That all the Pacific Palisades girls were astonished that they had not been kept in the loop about Cathy's remarriage, but that Cathy's reason for keeping it quiet was that, to some, she would always be 'the merry widow' for ever having remarried. "She just found out she's pregnant." And that the pregnancy was a bit of a surprise.

"She's pretty excited about that. So, it was more like being there for a baby shower than a *Ding Dong The Witch Is Dead* party. Grief counseling never seemed to enter into the picture.

"Cathy's new husband is also a cop. He was some kind of inside guy on trying to find the two killer kids. He said it was some kind of random luck that this one kid showed up dead."

"What'd he say about the other kid?"

"He said their only lead had been some old White farmer guy who lived somewhere out in the middle of nowhere...but that it never panned out. And that it was a stupid lead, anyway. He said, 'What would an old White retired farmer dude have to do with a couple of inner city thugs?' He said it was some FBI guy's dumb idea, and that the old guy lived out in the middle of KKK country, anyway.

"So...he said the case has been cold for a long time. He said the second guy would probably have to randomly die, too, if he's ever going to be caught. 'Thin air,' he said. 'Those murderous gangsters,' he called them, 'just disappeared into thin air.'

"It doesn't really matter anymore. Cathy has a new life now.

"How did things go here, Baby?"

3.33 IT'S AN ILL WIND THAT DON'T BLOW SOMEBODY SOME GOOD

"Thanks for your help in getting the toxic Union Rep, Knopfler, off the case, Boss. And there is one more thing on my mind right now...if I still have any juice left?"

"Strike while the iron's hot. What is it, John?"

"I only have the second perp on my radar now. And...I could use a little boost from your position to help expedite the bureaucracy of getting some SSA data I need about the first dead perp. I feel 'pronto' would help me move forward."

"Always available to be your secretary, Watkins."

"Thanks, Boss. I know Muhammad Jefferson was using a stolen Social Security number so he could work. I need to have the number researched at SSA for the birth certificate used to issue the number. Plus, I need all records related to the true owner of that number. If I can find out whose number he stole...or was using...that person and his connection to Muhammad might be the key to the whole case. That connection might even lead us to the second perp...our primary focus and our solitary goal."

3.34 WHAT IT IS AIN'T EXACTLY CLEAR

Watkins reviewed the report from field agents assigned to backtracking the computer contact between Michael Dean, his Des Moines employer, and the Beshire landlords in Highlands Ranch, Colorado.

The report stated that both the email contact from Michael Dean and the Face Chat contact from his Des Moines employer had come from the same computer IP address, and that both accounts had been deleted, one with the email host, as well as the one from the Face Chat application provider.

The computer IP address was tracked to a computer owned by a young married woman in Saginaw, Michigan. A pre-interview background investigation revealed that she was married to a city sanitation worker and that she was a stay-at-home mom for a three-year-old daughter.

A door-knock interview revealed that the computer the woman had in her home was not the IP address of the computer they were looking for, and that her computer was the only computer she had ever purchased. The agents' report from interview included, "The couple we interviewed are too mentally simple to orchestrate a technology-based scheme." Later in the report it was stated, "This couple has no African-American friends. This appears consistent with some observed racial animosity cues."

Watkins pondered, 'Either Michael Dean had become a tech guru, or someone helping him is a tech guru.' Watkins thoughts immediately went to Scott McNally. 'McNally's computer use and history were infrequent and plain vanilla. There was nothing to indicate that McNally knew his way around a computer.'

Watkins was shaking his head. He was growing tired from the number of leads that were turning into dead ends.

Even with help from his connected Boss, it still took a week to get the Social Security birth certificate data on Michael Dean back to Agent Watkins.

'Hmpf. Michael Dean: Address at Applicaton: Columbia, Tennessee. Birth Certificate: Father, Roland Patrick Dean, born Columbia, Tennessee; Mother, Centilla Bennett Dean, born Columbia, Tennessee.'

Watkins thought, 'Columbia, Tennessee. That's within a cannon shot of McNally. The only employment history is *The Sunflower Cafe and Restaurant*. Time for a door-knock to meet the 'real' Michael Dean.'

A Black man, older than himself, in a clearly Black neighborhood of smaller houses and smaller yards, answered the door for Roland Dean's address. Showing his I.D., Watkins introduced himself, asking, "Michael Dean?"

..."Oh, Michael Dean is your son? Is he home?"..."Oh, I'm so sorry. When did he pass?"..."Oh, my. As a child?"..."I'm so sorry. Do you know, or have you ever heard of a man named Scott McNally?"..."OK.

Can you tell me where your son, Michael, was buried?"…"It's an investigation into a murder suspect who was using your son's Social Security number."…"Oh, a Denver TV investigative reporter already called you about it?"…"Yes. Clearly, it was a mistaken identity. Where did you say you buried Michael?"

Agent Watkins' heart was pounding. He had finally figured it out. 'McNally surveyed a Black graveyard for a Black child that had a White sounding name. A list of other Black children from that graveyard will give me my list for possible new identities for Jamal Ali Jefferson.'

Watkins made a list of all the children who were born within ten years of Jamal and Mohammad and who had died as children before the age of twenty-one. He stopped for a moment of respect when he came across the headstone for Michael Dean.

For all his time in the graveyard, his list only had three names on it. His hopes were low because all three of the names were identifiably Black sounding names. But he left room for McNally straying off-course to use of them. Watkins resolved to do an SSA search on all three of the names to see if there was any post-mortem employment records for any of them. Then he got frustrated, remembering how slowly the SSA was able to produce computer search requests.

He relieved his frustration by estimating the number of minutes he was from a manicured wilderness in that part of Middle Tennessee. His frustration and his eagerness for an answer were blinding his better judgment. A rookie mistake.

McNally was cleaning up a few bushes of underbrush from the hollow next to his house when he heard, then saw, a car coming down his driveway. He walked up out of the hollow to see who it could possibly be. 'I always think it's someone who's lost…but I've never had a lost person pull in here. I have some work left to do on the way I think.'

"Mr. McNally. I'm Agent Watkins..."

McNally interrupted him. "I know who you are. Did you think we became friends since your last visit? Or do you have another search warrant on you?"

"No, Mr. McNally. I was in the area and thought I'd swing by for a friendly visit."

"Well...I admire your nerve. And why are you trying to bllsht me with the 'friendly visit' lie. I heard you got demoted over your last adventure into these parts."

"Yes...well...I still have some lower level investigative responsibilities."

"What are you investigating now? Why the air is invisible? Or why the sky is blue?"

"OK. I can see that this is not going to be friendly, so let me just come out with it. Surely, you know that we got one of the Nashville murderers, Muhammad Jefferson?"

"I *did* hear that. I still get an occasional TV picture."

"Well, I was monitoring the investigation of that find, and I came across a record of Muhammad Jefferson's new name, Michael Dean, being a dead boy from Columbia. It caught my attention that the graveyard was only forty-five minutes from your home, here."

Scottie knew this was meant to fluster or inflame him, and all of a sudden he *did* feel flustered and inflamed. So he called on his practiced technique of finding peaceful calm. "Congratulations. Sounds like your parents' investment in detective school finally paid off for them."

"Mr. McNally, I've come from Michael Dean's graveyard...where I've also found the name you stole for Jamal Ali Jefferson..."

Scottie let out a psychological breath of air. He remembered, 'Robert's name came from a separate graveyard.'

369

"...At this point, your criminal charges might find room for being lessened if you're prepared to fully cooperate."

Scottie replied, "You're exhibiting all the behavior of a person who is *assaulting* the public, versus protecting and *serving* the public. Give it up, Mr. Watkins. You're continuing to bark up a tree where there ain't no coon. You've become old and tired, like me. The difference is that your decline has afflicted you fifteen to twenty years too soon. If you were demoted before, you're going to be fired this time. Now, get off my property. I have to go in and make a phone call to my Congressman about you and your rights-violating organization. And this time...I won't settle for you being demoted."

Watkins felt McNally had successfully called his bluff. He was embarrassed to himself about his premature visit. 'Never ask a question to which you don't already know the answer.' He liked to convert his sayings into their correct grammatical format.

Watkins was mumbling to himself as he was getting into his car. 'That lying sun-uv-a-btch doesn't even have a working telephone in his house.'

When he rolled down his window on the way out past McNally, Watkins feared the words of McNally about Watkins being in decline might be true. "You *do* know I'm not quitting until they're both accounted for, right, Mr. McNally?"

3.35 FIND THE COST OF FREEDOM

After John Watkins had returned from his victory tour in Denver and Nashville, as well as from his ill-advised trip to the McNally property, he came home from the office to find MaryLou and her Law School fiancé, Brandon, sitting at his dining room table with his wife, Jackie. They all looked pensively serious.

John walked over to the group and asked, "If this a meeting of official business, why wasn't *I* invited? Or has everyone just been lonely without me?"

Jackie looked at MaryLou for permission to speak. "MaryLou wanted to tell us, in person, that she wants to go on to Graduate School...to get her Master's Degree in Applied Nursing after this Senior year."

Without looking at his daughter, John spoke directly to Jackie. "Does she realize that I would have to extend my retirement date out into an unknown, and possibly dangerous, future in order to accommodate her aspirations? We did make a deal as a pre-condition to us getting married all those years ago. But I don't remember the words 'Graduate School' being in the pre-nup."

Jackie wanted to lessen the weight of that conversation by being a little playful. "And just how many years ago was that, Mr. Watkins?"

John replied, "Let's just get to the bottom line. How much additional is this going to cost us?"

Jackie said, "I've taken a close look at our finances, and it won't leave us hungry or in fear of no place to live."

John said, "But what about those extravagant winter vacations to warm islands in the stream?"

"Honey, how many of those extravagant winter vacations have we ever taken?"

"Exactly! I have a better plan. Why don't MaryLou and Brandon move up their wedding date to now, and then *he* can be financially responsible for her."

Brandon was keeping his mouth shut.

"Daddy, without an advanced degree, I'll just be another blue-collar worker working for blue-collar wages. Is that what you want for your little girl?"

Everyone seemed to know that the decision had already been made, so John said, "This is a scam. You've never planned to work. You want to be a stay-at-home mom."

"Yes, but with an enriched education...which can only have a directly positive affect on my mothering qualities."

Jackie closed the sale for MaryLou. "John, if your hesitancy is about your retirement date, we can put MaryLou through her Master's Degree and not have to extend your retirement date."

John knew the FBI was getting unpredictable in their certainty to continue employing him. Jackie's financial analysis sealed the deal for him. "OK. We're onboard, Master MaryLou."

The body of Muhammad Dogg Jefferson lay on a roll-out tray inside a near-freezing refrigerated locker at the morgue in Denver, Colorado. It was unknown how long it would remain there. There were no signals from any direction regarding who would claim the body. If not claimed soon, the body would be moved to deep-freeze.

By keeping updated on the news through a pixel dance of in-and-out picture delivered through a roof-mounted TV antenna, it was clear to a certain person-of-interest that Muhammad Jefferson's dead body was still lying in a morgue a half-continent away.

A clandestine trip was made, with the GPS tracker removed, to Nashville, under the cover of early evening darkness.

A pedestrian wearing blue nitrile gloves passed by Loquisha Davis' car that was parked in her driveway. The pedestrian checked the car door. It was locked. House lights that were filtered through closed curtains showed the pedestrian that somebody was home.

The doorbell was rung, and the passing pedestrian withdrew to a secluded vantage point.

The homeowner turned on her porch light before looking around. Then she saw and retrieved a small gym bag from her stoop. She retreated back into her house, then the porch light went back to dark.

Loquisha Davis opened the small gym bag on her dining room table and removed three mustard-colored bank bands of $100 bills. Then she found a note written on flash paper that said, 'Muhammad Jefferson.'

The morgue in Denver coordinated arrangements through a Nashville funeral home to have the body of Muhammad Jefferson air-freighted to Nashville. All payments for all delivery charges were covered by the funeral home.

A large, new, shiny black Cadillac hearse delivered Muhammad's body to the North Nashville Northside Cemetery. There, a large crowd of community faces were waiting at the ninety-six inch excavated hole in the ground for the funeral service to begin. Outside the cemetery grounds was a cordon of Metro police squad cars.
Inside the cemetery, and spread out all around the graveside funeral gathering, were an army of plain-clothed police from multiple agencies and jurisdictions.
any had high definition video cameras attached to their faces.
The casket was rolled out of the hearse and transferred to the geared roller straps over the grave.
The mother of Muhammad Dogg Jefferson, along with her two sisters and their mother, all of whom had also suffered irreversible life losses, were dressed in finery rarely seen in North Nashville.
All four women had hairdos that had taken a full day of labor at the salon. All four women had various design patterns of braids in their hair, interlaced with gold wire within the braids. Twenty-four carat gold wire.
A preacher said something short. The ornate casket was lowered into its hole. Then the speeches began. They were all words of thanksgiving and praise for the life of Mr. Jefferson.

A Christian hymn was sung by the attendees, *a cappella*. '*Amazing Grace*.' Four verses.

The headstone monument had been set back from the hole, ready to be placed after the grave had been back-filled. It was the largest and most ornate memorial in the whole of the cemetery. At the bottom of all the descriptive information were the words, 'Family Hero.'

It would have been an understatement to say that there was outrage throughout the ranks of law enforcement, including the FBI.

Agent Watkins and the Metro Chief had waited in the lobby with other gala attendees for the elevator to take them to the top floor of what used to be Nashville's highest high rise, The Wyatt Regal Hotel.

When they stepped out of the elevator together, they were greeted by an old Black man in a tuxedo behind a podium that was placed at the card-access-only elevator doors.

The *maitre di* greeted them both by name. "Good evening Chief Rand and Agent Watkins. My name is Charles. We're pleased to have you join us this evening." Charles didn't make eye contact as he leaned his old shoulders forward in his elderly version of a bow.

Agent Watkins was not surprised that the *maitre di* knew the name of Chief Rand, but it caught his attention to hear his own name. 'Fortune and fame is a curious game. Perfect strangers call you buy name.' Watkins was surprised he didn't hear the words, 'Yessah, massah,' from one of the blackest Black men he'd even seen. Agent Watkins expected to see the film credits start rolling for *Gone With The Wind*.

Agent Watkins and Chief Rand found their way to their seats of honor at the head table. There, they engaged in chit-chat and introductions in front of a packed room...a full house.

The buzz of the crowd was deafening. Waiters were busy delivering flutes of Champagne and mixed drinks, made-to-order, to all the patrons. Then the buzz died down as people, as if on cue, began to take their seats. Watkins thought, 'That's the beautiful thing about being a part of a herd. All you have to do is whatever the person next to you is doing.'

The Club President, seated to left of Chief Rand and Agent Watkins, headed to the mic'd lectern.

"Good evening, friends. What a night for celebration." Wild applause, shouts, and whistles.

"If you don't know that I'm your President, then you shouldn't be here." Laughter.

"And if you don't know my name is Doctor Joel Higginbotham...then you should follow the other people who are already leaving." More gentle laughter.

"And that's my lovely and charming wife, Angela, seated to my left at the head table." Gentle applause.

"Please be nice to her. It will make all the difference in how my day goes, tomorrow." A murmur of laughter.

"We are gathered here tonight to pay special tribute to our Metro Police Chief, Chief Harold Rand, whom we all know as being highly respected and dutiful. If the person who stole your diamond bracelet is in jail, it is Chief Rand that you have to thank." Murmur mixed with light laughter.

"If the person who stole your diamond bracelet *isn't* in jail...then speak to the Mayor...who could not be with us tonight." Silent pause. "Because he's a socialist!" Laughter and the clinking sound of silverware tapping on glasses.

"I'll quit talking shortly..." Applause and laughter.

"...You'll pay for that. Dues will double next month for all who applauded...and we have the video recording of all this for evidence." Groans and light laughter.

"But before I turn the dais over to our esteemed guests that we're here to celebrate, let me kick things off by summarizing their work.

"We, the movers and the shakers in Metro Nashville, are fully invested in insuring that our law enforcement personnel have all the tools and resources they need to get their job done. And what is that job? To keep us safe. Safe from the forces of evil who would work to take away our sense of security, not to mention the statements of position we have all earned to get us into this room.

"Chief Rand was challenged a few years ago by some young thugs who thought they could take justice into their own hands by murdering one of our employees...one of our finest. But Chief Rand has proven to us that he is up to the challenge.

"In close association with his FBI counterpart, Special Agent in Charge John Watkins, seated to the right of our Chief, they tracked down the ruthless killer and instigator of anarchy who had gone to great lengths to disguise himself.

"But evil is plain for all of us, here, to see, and there was no disguise that could cover up the evil in that person. It is my understanding that the junkyard dog of whom I speak was buried tonight in the Northside Cemetery.

"That was too fine an ending for such a person as he. May he never rest in peace." Thunderous applause.

"I now give you the man of the hour, our own Chief, Mr. Harold Rand." Standing ovation and three minutes of applause.

"That was way too generous an introduction, Doctor Higginbotham. And you gave me way too much credit for the finding and identification of the perpetrator of this heinous crime that all of us remember all too well.

"One thing you said that resonated with me...it was that our sense of security was at stake as long as that animal was out there." Watkins shifted uncomfortably in his seat at those words. "And now that he is, and will always be in custody, I, as well as all of you, will sleep better from here on out. One more bad guy erased from the planet. Score one for the good guys!" Standing ovation and one minute applause.

"Now, it is my honor to introduce a man that none of you knew before tonight, but who was the leader of the out-of-state effort to bring the evildoer back here...for all of us to know that that savage won't be lurking outside any of our walls or windows tonight...nor *any* night in the future. I give you FBI Special Agent in Charge, Mr. John Watkins." Chief Rand made a sweeping hand gesture to direct Watkins to the dais as Watkins walked toward the Chief. Mild applause.

"Good evening, good citizens of Nashville. My remarks will be much shorter than the brief remarks of my partner, Chief Rand.

"All I want to tell you is that my participation in the investigation...and the eventual discovery of the perpetrator of Officer Johnson's murder...was solely for the purpose of supporting your own Chief, Chief Rand. Our ability to provide such support is a continuing example of your Federal Tax dollars at work..."

A voice from the crowd shouted out for all to hear clearly, "But we don't *pay* taxes!" Widespread laughter, then applause, to a din of light-hearted chatter.

"Nonetheless, the FBI is at the disposal of crime fighters, like Chief Rand, whenever we're called upon." Agent Watkins returned to his seat in the midst of polite applause.

The mingling and the smalltalk after supper was awkward for John Watkins. At his first opportunity, he said goodnight to Chief Rand, and then to the staggeringly well inebriated Dr. Higginbotham, who threw his arm around Watkins and slurringly said, "You're welcome in my house anytime, Mr. Watkins." And then he laughed at himself before he even said what made him laugh. But then it came out. "As long as you can make it past my security guards."

Instantly aware of his *faux pas*, Higginbotham made it worse by trying to explain. "No, no, Mr. Watkins. I'm only joking. We don't screen people who come to our front gate based on skin color."

Dr. Higginbotham usually compensated for the depth of his contempt for Black people by being friendly, often to the point of being effusive. But there was something about reaching just a certain tipping point in his consumption that made the alcohol better than a finely tuned dose of sodium pentathol.

Watkins thought, 'I'll help you to stop digging your hole any deeper...by politely leaving.'

While the speeches and friendly banter were going on at *The Nashville Club*, sledge hammers and chisels were hard at work in the North Nashville Northside Cemetery.

The lynchings that had made America great had happened in broad daylight because the sheriffs and the mayors and all the clerks and other public officials were in on it. To show how far America had come as a people, lynchings by authorities now had to happen under cover of darkness.

The lynchers no longer had their pictures taken next to the tortured and mutilated bodies of their entertainment. Now, they wore the metaphorical mask of Guy Fawkes, the legendary symbol of the anarchist group, *Anonymous*. But just like in centuries past, the anarchists were the people hired to protect and serve the 'Public' from the anarchists.

Anonymity in lynchings was a sign that humans actually *could* evolve.

The day after *The Nashville Club* gala and the cemetery vandalism, Agent Watkins and Chief Rand coordinated an investigation into how all the fancy funeral and related costs for Muhammad Jefferson were paid for. The interview at the funeral home came back, "Loquisha Davis provided the funds...in cash."

The interview with Loquisha Davis came back, "The money was

raised by the community. You boys know how it's done...like the way you do fundraisers when one of your own goes down. Or, maybe you don't have to do fundraisers. Maybe 'We The People' pay for your funerals."

There were no interviews to try and determine where the wealth of *The Nashville Club* members came from.

That same night after the money investigations were conducted, a clandestine trip had been made to Columbia in a car with its GPS tracker removed.

Under cover of early evening darkness, a pedestrian wearing blue nitrile gloves placed a gym bag, large enough for sneakers and workout clothes and a large towel, on a doorstep. Then he rang the bell. Then the pedestrian made a quick exit to across and up the street where his own car was parked in darkness. He stood on the back side of his car. He was watching the doorstep through the car's windows.

After turning on the porch light, a Black man opened the door. He looked around. A Black woman came and stood behind him to see who was visiting. They both looked around in vain. Then the woman saw the gym bag on the stoop.

The husband opened the screen door while still looking around for a visitor.

The husband and wife looked at each other, and the wife appeared to nod at her husband to bring the gym bag into the house.

It took a long time for them to come to rest over what they found in the bag. It was tightly packed with one-hundred mustard colored bank bands of money. Each bank band contained one-hundred one-hundred dollar bills.

When they had put all the banded money on their dining room table, they found a note in the bottom of the bag. 'Losing a child is never forgotten. This money is gifted to you in memory of your late son, Michael.'

3.36 MIEN KAMPF

Agent John Watkins was aware that the 'bounty' money and the target practice posters offered by Union Rep Knopfler would compromise the integrity of the investigation. So, after he had asked his Boss for a favor to support the removal of Knopfler from the Task Force, it was without hesitancy nor concern about repercussions that Watkins summarized the removal of Knopfler to Metro Chief Rand...in writing. 'In writing' was always used to communicate that the issue was unapologetically being documented for any future reference, as needed.

When he was notified that he was pulled from his Liaison duties, Knopfler was neither fearful nor shy about approaching Watkins.

"You people...you don't work, you make children that you don't support, you live off the welfare system...which means you're supported by White people. You can't get educated. You can only do menial jobs. You live like rats..."

Nothing was new to Watkins in anything Knopfler was unloading on him. But Watkins wasn't going to take the role of play-the-passive-whipping-boy for him.

Watkins took a step up to Knopfler's chest and was close enough for Knopfler to get a good taste of Watkins' spit. "How...do...you...fix...stupid?"

Like any bully, Knopfler didn't know what to do with Watkins' boldly standing up to him. He looked around the room to see if anyone was watching.

Watkins took a step back and said, "I think it's time we settle this with some hand-to-hand combat. *Mano-a-mano*. You choose the ground." Knopfler didn't know what to make of this challenge.

Watkins gave him a minute and then said, "Your place. Tomorrow night. Eight o'clock."

Knopfler just nodded his head with a look on his face that said, 'Game on.' Then Knopfler went home...because he had been instructed by his Chief to not be present at any more Task Force meetings.

After the electricity had dissipated, Metro Chief Rand made his way to Watkins. He asked Watkins, "Do you know the two ways to know you're being lied to?"

Watkins wasn't in the mood for a quiz. "How?"

The Chief answered his own riddle. "A preacher who tells you he's pure and holy, and a police chief who tells you he ain't got no bad apples."

Watkins nodded his head with a half smile. "True. Both true."

The Chief continued. "Sadly, in all the expertise we've fine-tuned over the decades, one of the things we've gotten best at is covering up for our own. What do you do? Get rid of the Union? Tribal behaviors will remain...and in our line of work, tribal means covering up for your brother officers when you're asked to. The famous 'Blue Wall.'

"You guys in the FBI have fostered a pretty good reputation for being straight arrows. But in big city police forces like mine, we don't have the will to use the full force of the political system to clean things up. The Attorney General's office, which is responsible for bringing charges, are reluctant to do it because my officers are their investigators. The AG needs my officers to do his job.

"Everyone up the political chain is afraid of the police Union because the Union knows how to rally a block vote. And the biggest thing that scares politicians is voters."

Watkins felt he could level with the wise Chief. "Since 1908, when the FBI was 'founded,' we have accumulated 91 cases of deadly use of force against a person in our custody. To date, all 91 cases have been deemed 'Justifiable Homicides.' That's one hundred percent. That means we've never made a mistake."

The Chief raised his eyebrows in surprise. "That's an amazingly outstanding record."

Watkins told the Chief a dirty little secret. "You're right, Chief. That is amazing. And it's because there's nobody to investigate us but ourselves. Who was it that said the FBI has never made a mistake? The FBI, itself."

All the Chief could say was, "Wow. That sounds a lot like us."

Watkins offered the Chief a nugget from his psychology bag of knowledge. "A person who is incapable of saying, 'I'm wrong,' is known to be psychologically impaired...it's a red flag for psychosis and psychopathy."

The Chief responded, "I get it. That goes for organizations as well as individuals."

Watkins appreciated being on the same page with the Chief.

Watkins reported the encounter and the challenge he had with Knopfler to his Assistant Director. His Boss asked him if he wanted backup. Watkins answered, "It's not that kind of challenge." At least it wasn't in the mind of Agent Watkins.

Watkins arrived at Officer Neal Knopfler's home at 8:00PM with a file folder under his arm. He had trouble parking because of three or four additional cars that filled up all the available space in Knopfler's driveway. Expecting a brawl, Knopfler had sent his pregnant wife to her mother's house for the night.

Watkins parked in the street. Then he rang Knopfler's doorbell. Knopfler came to the door in a white wife-beater t-shirt. It was in stark contrast to Watkins' suit and tie and polished shoes. Knopfler looked at Watkins with some surprise. Behind Knopfler was a team of a half-dozen t-shirt clad cops who had obviously spent a lot of time at the Police gym.

Watkins said, "Well...are you going to ask me in?"

A path was cleared for Watkins as he found his own way to the dining room table. There, Watkins pulled out a chair for himself, sat down, and opened his file folder.

Knopfler stood over him. "What are you doing?"

Watkins replied, "I'm here to lay down a challenge to you. Please take a seat."

Knopfler looked around at his buddies like he didn't know what was going on. That's because Knopfler *didn't* know what was going on. He remained standing.

Watkins pulled the top sheet of paper out of his folder.

"This is a photograph of a boy named Emmitt Till." Watkins showed the photo around to Knopfler and all his companions.

"Emmitt was renditioned from his Uncle's home one evening. He was taken to a White man's barn where his hands were tied and strung up above his head. He was suspended from the floorboards in the hay loft of the barn.

"With the young White wife of one of the kidnapers watching, Emmitt was slowly beaten, one kick and one punch at a time, while being made to apologize to the young White wife. Which he did. Until he couldn't any more. His genitals were also mutilated, though his mother didn't have those photographs released to the public.

"But the point of this torture was not an apology. The point was domination. And not domination over a young Black boy held in place by a rope from above his head. It was about the unquestionable domination of a young White girl and her young White husband over every Black person in America. You see, the young White wife had told her young White husband that the Black boy had whistled at her in a store. Which, by the way, she would later say never happened...decades later.

"The beating went on all night. The young White wife watched her young White husband keep the Black boy alive all night so the lesson would not be shortened.

"The next morning, Emmitt's dead and mutilated body was driven back to the Uncle's house which was full of Black children. Emmitt's dead and mutilated body was thrown out of the back of their pickup truck so the Uncle and all the little Black children in that home could see the price of forgetting to be subservient to all Whites in any way, shape, or form.

"And did those White kidnappers disguise themselves by wearing masks when they picked Emmitt up? Or when they returned his dead and mutilated body back to the Uncle and young cousins? Of course not. They knew they had immunity for any and all crimes committed against a Black."

Watkins pulled the next piece of paper out of his file folder.

"Who do you think these two happy and smiling White young men are in this picture? If you think it's the young White husband and his White companion, who had beat and tortured Emmitt for his young White wife's amusement, then you would be right. And why are they happy? Is it because they were just acquitted by the Court for their actions?

"No. This laughing and joking picture was taken *before* the trial began. They knew in advance that the trial was just serving to bring publicity to the rights of a White person to perform any heinous and unspeakable act on a Black person they chose. They knew they were going to get off scot free because they knew they were heroes in their White community...and all the jurors were their White neighbors."

Watkins pulled out the next picture from his file folder.

"These two bodies that you see hanging from a tree in their tattered clothing, and with their hands tied in front of them, are Thomas Shipp and Abram Smith. But I'm not showing you these pictures to show you the two young Black men hanging from a tree. I wanted you to see the spectators. All the good and decent White folk who had come out for the celebration.

"See these two young White girls in the corner? See how happy they are to be having their picture taken in front of the hanging corpses? And do you see all the other White citizens in their stylish hats and clothing? And do you see this White guy pointing to the hanging bodies, as if to say for the camera, 'See what happens when they're not subservient?' Can any of you Metro friends-of-Knopfler see yourself in this picture?"

A bunch of 'Hey, fck you, man' mumbles came from the circle of officers standing around Watkins. Watkins pulled out his next picture.

"Do you see this burned body that is tied to a wooden cross? His name is Will Brown. He was lit on fire, and then his burning body was driven up and down Main Street for all the good White citizens to watch a human body burn to death. It was a show. It was a celebration. It was entertainment.

"What do you notice about the three dozen or so men in this picture? That they're all well dressed in suits and ties? Which one of them do you think is the Mayor? Or can you find the Sheriff among them? What do you think about a picture like this showing the Sheriffs, the dutiful churchgoing citizens, the Mayor, the community leaders...? Ask yourself what ignorance caused these people to behave like this? All under the guise of Law and Order. All under the guise of being good Christians.

"Do you get that these actions cannot take place without the sanctioning and the participation of the political structure of the town? Do you get that it happens because the political structure of the town is the people who are the ones *doing* it?

"Do you get that that's you? Every one of you?

"All of us are part of a law enforcement community that we need. We as a people need us. We as a people need to look up to us. But you have chosen to use the political power of your Union to protect...even glorify...the bad apples among you.

"The goodness in you should be wanting to get rid of the bad apples. But instead, you make them heroes. One bad apple spoils the whole bunch. So the goodness and purity and the respect that is rightfully due to those of us who choose to serve as Law Enforcement Officers is erased in the eyes of many...because we fail to cull the bad apples from within our own ranks...hence, spoiling all of us with their rottenness."

With that, two of the t-shirt clad officers slapped each other on the arm and said, "Let's go. We're outta here. I've heard enough of this bll-sht."

Watkins was unfazed. He pulled the next photograph from his folder.

"This charred body with the bottom of his legs burned off, hanging by this rope, face-first into the tree, is Jesse Washington. But I'm not showing you this to show you a burnt, hanging body. I brought it show you all the happy and laughing White faces that are getting their picture taken with the charred hanging corpse." With that, the other three officers all mumbled to each other that they were heading out, also.

With only Knopfler left, Watkins pulled out his remaining pile of photos, about an inch thick in his hand.

"I'm sorry that all your friends have deserted you because this is the most important part. In my hand are all pictures of police murders of Black men, many with the officer smiling for the camera with his slain victim below him, sometimes actually under the polished jackboot of the policeman's domination...like in this picture."

Watkins pulled out several examples. "Look at this one, Knopfler. Can you tell by the smirk on his face that he's saying, 'I got me one.'

"Some of these pictures are from a hundred years ago. Some are from fifty years ago. Some are from ten years ago." Watkins shuffled through the pile, "Here are two from last year.

"You use the police Union as a shield against justice. In so doing, you rob yourself of the dignity of 'doing the right thing.' And you strip all those around you of their dignity...a dignity they *should* wear proudly for choosing to protect and serve...but a dignity that you have taken from them.

"Weed out the bad apples, Knopfler. You make the good cops think you're looking out for *their* jobs, but what you're doing in infecting the good cops with the bad apples."

Knopfler decided to put up a defense. "Hey, Watkins. What your little dog-and-pony show failed to show is that Black people are mostly killed by Black people. The most recent national statistic says that 88% of violence on Black people in America is committed by Black people. Black-on-Black violence. They're animals, and you know it."

Watkins was well armed. "You must have told me that out your willful ignorance, Knopfler, because those same national statistics tell us that, of all the violence committed on White people, *90%* of that violence comes from White people. So if your intention was to say that only Blacks are violent on their own people, you have revealed the base problem of why we're even having this discussion...Your Ignorance!

"And it's your *willful* ignorance. This information is available to you, but you *choose* to ignore it. That's the definition of willful ignorance. And that's the definition of you."

Watkins looked at Knopfler with fire in his eyes. "Is this what you're working toward, Knopfler? To get your picture taken with a dead nggr? So you can be a hero to your tribe? Or to make heroes out of your protégés on the Force?"

Knopfler offered, "This is the way we were raised. There's plenty about you, too, that isn't about right and wrong. If it's the way you were raised...it's right."

Watkins conceded, and countered, "Life has lots of grey areas. But the ultimate test of morally distinct right and wrong is this: Would you like to see these things happen to *your* child?"

Knopfler answered, "That's why I'm not going to have any Black children." Knopfler pushed the papers back toward Watkins. "It's time for you to get out of my house."

Watkins reorganized all the pictures to return them to his file folder. "You're making America weak, Knopfler. You're not protecting your community of scared White people. You're making them *more* scared by constantly presenting justifications for your anarchist actions, and those of your worst Union members, while making the White people believe they're immune from your anarchy reaching them.

"You're not doing anyone any favors by helping a bad apple keep his job. You're only emboldening the other officers by communicating to them that they can kill with impunity."

Knopfler mounted his last defense. "These are the facts, Watkins: You live in an ivory tower with your FBI buddies. They don't live on the street view, and that's why they'll never understand it. And that goes double for you, Watkins...because you're Black.

"You have no idea about the threat level to a person's person that is heightened when a Black man gives you an attitude that is disrespectful...that is scornful...that is meant to be aggressively intimidating...and has an underlying threat of imminent violence. And then to be the officer who is chastised for that being the environment he has to respond to. That's the reality of being a cop on the street in a Black neighborhood.

"Maybe Jimmy Jefferson wasn't doing anything wrong when Mark Johnson approached him. But whether Jimmy Jefferson was or wasn't doing anything wrong is a side issue compared to having to be constantly dealing with non-compliant Black men.

"That event that happened between Jimmy Jefferson and Mark Johnson might have been the hundredth time that Mark Johnson had dealt with a non-compliant Black man. And Mark Johnson would have correlated the non-compliance as a threat to his personal wellbeing. And, when he shot Jimmy Jefferson for fleeing, deep down in his psyche, he was probably saving himself in the way that he had wanted to the hundred times before that. It was a way of taking some of the accumulated pressures off of himself. Self preservation. 'Here's a nggr that will never threaten me in the future.'

"Can we be a little too aggressive sometimes? Yes, we can. But it's a response to all the other times we have to sit back and take the disrespect and the outright aggression from Black men...and the women, too."

Watkins had listened patiently. "So, when White boys treat you with aggressive disrespect...and you and I both know they do...does that make you approach all White boys with the fear and trepidation that you say is why cops are justified...or a least why it's understandable...to kill a Black man? Really, Knopfler? According to your logic, White boy slayings by cops should be proportionate to Black men slayings. Your argument just reveals your deep-seated racism. Which is the root danger of you having the job you have."

Knopfler was incensed. "The Whites don't give us the problems that the Blacks do."

Watkins replied, "Or, is it the other way around, Knopfler? You don't give the *Whites* the problems that you give the Blacks."

Knopfler moved to open his front door. Holding the door open with one arm while pointing out the door with his other, Knopfler angrily said, "Get the fck out!"

As Watkins walked toward the open door, he said, "Remember Marie Antoinette...and how the guillotine was used on government officials across France? It's a lesson about what happens when those in authority don't serve the needs of the people whose interests they're supposed to represent."

When Watkins got resettled in his hotel room, he called his Assistant Director.

"How'd it go?"

"I thought it went quite well. He told me to 'Get the fck out.'"

"That doesn't sound like it went all that well."

"He could have told me, 'Get the fck out, nggr.'"

3.37 EVIDENCE

Agent Watkins had remained deeply disturbed by his own decision to make a surprise visit to Scott McNally, a visit that continued to haunt him for its unprofessional nature. However, Agent Watkins made a conscious decision to *use* his angst as a motivation-lever on himself.

In his heightened state of motivation, he mapped out a plan to review every event and every piece of evidence that tied, or possibly tied, Scott McNally to aiding and abetting the two murderous North Nashville youths. One remaining.

Watkins would spend hours closed in his office sifting through all the details. The expense of his energy was him trying to mentally juggle all the information into a form that would allow him to make cohesive, communicable decisions on how to proceed.

By the end of the week, he found himself helplessly and hopelessly playing and rewinding the high definition videos taken from the original search warrant raid that had gotten him into so much hot water...because of finding no evidence.

Over and over again, he would freeze-frame, movement by movement, all of the camera shots, looking for any new detail that he had overlooked before.

McNally's bookshelf was revisited. He would often use a large magnifying glass up against his high-definition video monitor.

By Friday afternoon, a couple of hours after everyone else in the building had gone home, his efforts had left him blurry-eyed and lazy-eyed. He had lost control of his eyes being in muscular sync with each other. And, even though he could not stop seeing everything he looked at as two separate and distinct images, he learned to let his brain review each eye's image separately.

Finally, there came a point when, letting the video advance slightly forward, both of the images that his brain was collecting saw the same thing. He remembered seeing it before. Right before he had been slam-dunked by his Boss. It was only in the video for a fraction of a second...a *fraction* of a fraction of a second...but he knew it was real because he could still see the momentary flash each time he rewound, and then forwarded, click by click.

Watkins made several attempts to freeze-frame the flash, but he couldn't do it. He would freeze-frame right before or right after. When his inability to do what he was trying to do brought him to the edge of a breakdown, he had enough sense to shut all the equipment off and go home for the weekend...for some restorative rest.

By Monday morning, Watkins' double vision had healed, and he was re-charged. He was still curious about the momentary flash of light he had seen, so he decided to pick up where he had left off on Friday night.

When he started turning all the equipment back on, his phone played the ominous sounding first four notes of Beethoven's Fifth Symphony.

"Yeah, Boss."

"John, there's some pressure from above to wind down the last of your support staff budgeted for the Officer Johnson case. And I'm having trouble defining meaningful outcomes from the remaining payroll on the case. That would be you, John."

"Boss, it's too soon to let go. I've spent the whole past week re-formatting an action plan for forward progress."

"Is it all around that farmer guy out in the middle of nowhere, John?"

"Come on, Boss. You know my history. You know my successes

around profiling. I'm still focused on this guy because nothing has been able to fully disprove his involvement."

"You're starting to worry me, John. We don't make cases based on people not being able to prove their innocence. We make cases based on evidence that proves their guilt."

"OK, Boss. I hear you. I'm on the final leg of a full evidence review on the guy. Just let me finish that before we start re-defining our assignments."

When his equipment was all up and running, Watkins went back to the place in the video where he had seen the flash. He found it again. But despite all his rest over the weekend, he couldn't get a freeze frame on the flash.

It was just before lunchtime that he was going to quit. That's when he made a random stab at the pause icon. And there it was. The source of that momentary flash of light…frozen on the screen.

John looked at it to define what it was. It was on the floor, away from the bookshelf. It was in the shape of a geometric arc segment. A variation, a wear-line, on the surface finish of the tile was capturing a reflection of light.

For fear of losing the image, John didn't dare touch the video controls. He tried to figure out what it was long into when he should have been eating his sandwich.

To preserve the image, Watkins pulled out his phone and took a picture of the video screen. As he looked at the phone picture, his memory of the room came back to him. 'There were mirrored canisters in the ceiling to bring daylight into the 'inner-sanctum,' as McNally called it. I must be seeing sunlight from those ceiling canisters of daylight reflecting off the floor. But what would make such a perfect geometric arc segment?'

His phone rang. It was his wife, Jackie.

"Honey, did you eat, yet? Because I forgot to put pickles on your sandwich this morning. I was just wondering if you noticed."

The distraction from his focused thinking was all it took for the whole picture to come together. He said out loud, "Oh...my...God!"

Then he heard Jackie, still on the phone. "Well, honey, it wasn't *that* big a deal. I was only calling to ask if you noticed."

"Boss? I need a second search warrant on the McNally property."

"John...you've completely lost it. You almost lost your career over the *last* search warrant you requested for that guy. We had to wiggle out of a lawsuit to keep it from going to court. I have budget pressure looming. And now this? Unless you have a photograph of this guy standing with his arms around Butch Cassidy and The Sundance Kid...then I'm officially closing the door on you and your involvement in the whole case."

3.38 RAIDERS OF THE LOST ARK

The second search warrant request for the McNally property took the eyeball confirmation of the evidence from every lawyer and every bureaucrat in Watkins' FBI chain of command and beyond. Agent Watkins' reputation from the first search warrant warranted that kind of attention. It turned out that Watkins had done a smart thing by taking a phone-photo of the screen freeze-frame.

Watkins pitched it up the line that it was a mark left by a wheel hidden behind the floor molding on the bookcase...which meant the bookcase could be pulled away from the wall.

"That's where the boys lived before they took off. Assuming both of them took off. One possibility is that the second one is still there. If he's gone also, we'll still have the evidence of McNally aiding and abetting murder...from right below his house."

Watkins was challenged all along the way about plastic surgery money and dental money, food and clothing for the boys, and no confirmation from arial surveillance, among a list of non-supporting corroborative evidence.

Watkins pitched the proximity of the Columbia graveyard to McNally, and the Highlands Ranch find of Muhammad Jefferson which confirmed the 'White' Pygmalion theory. And that McNally records couldn't show any means of support for himself?... "That means he has invisible money. That would be how he financed the boys."

But Watkins made the final sale based on the phone-pic of that momentary flash.

This time, posts from local law enforcement and State Police were used to monitor all three of the egress roads out of the McNally property. They wanted him away when they swooped in. This was a large manpower stakeout.

McNally drove out in his pickup truck for his weekly supply of fresh food. His bank debit card was on hand, and he had left the GPS tracker in place.

He drove past an unmarked car that was pulled into a pullout that hunters used during hunting season. He said to himself, 'That's a cop. They're about to spring something on me.' But he didn't care.

When Scottie returned home from his out-of-town shopping trip, he found a copy of the search warrant taped to his front door. Inside the house, he found the bookcase open. He could tell that books had been removed from several of the shelves on the latch end of the bookcase, but they had been returned to their out-of-position positions.

Nothing had been torn up or thrown around. In fact, if they had closed the bookcase, the car tire marks outside his house and the out-of-position books would have been the only indication that anybody had been there.

Nobody wanted to talk to Watkins on the phone. All they wanted was a written report.

It was a week later that Watkins had his prioritized lab reports in, and that he finalized his written assessment.

"hidden staircase found"..."ample room to house two adult males"..."no furniture or personal affects of any kind. Bare concrete throughout."..."touch DNA tests revealed no evidence of any human presence, concluding that the space had been wiped clean. Although there was no smell of bleach or other cleaning agents, an air circulation system could have removed that odor evidence"..."the conclusion from the search warrant request is that this hidden space provided sanctuary for the fugitive murderers, and thus, that Mr. McNally was the principle aider and abetter of their crime of murder. The discovery of the 'hideout space' justifies the continuing investigation into Mr. McNally for the purpose of finding Jamal Ali Jefferson."

Watkins had been informed that a large roomful of lawyers and higher-ups were waiting for the written report, and that they were all wound tightly to spring for a pound of Watkins' flesh. After Watkins pressed the 'Send' button on his computer...all he heard was crickets.

3.39 SEE YOU ONE, RAISE YOU ONE

The lawsuit filed by Mr. McNally's small-town attorney had lots of Harvard-Law and Yale-Law language and structure in it. The DOJ lawyers were baffled, once again, at the legal prowess of such a small-town counselor.

The small-town lawyer got a call from a DOJ lawyer, supposedly to acknowledge receipt of the court filing, but actually to see if the small-town guy knew anything about the complaint details...or if he was just a straw-man.

The small-town lawyer was on guard for the inquiry in advance. He wouldn't engage in any talk about the filing, but suggested, "I think your burden is going to be explaining what is 'probable cause' about a person having a storm shelter under his house...in tornado country."

Some small-town lawyers, when given the chance, just can't resist poking the bear.

The second lawsuit didn't name the FBI as the primary defendant, but rather the whole of the Department of Justice.

Addenda to the court action were requests to the House and Senate Judiciary Committees to launch an investigation by the Department of Justice Inspector General into the systematic violations of Mr. McNally's civil rights, based on, and especially in light of, the disregard of former contractual agreements on violations of Mr. McNally's civil rights.

The spanking arena had grown considerably.

Furthermore, an addendum petitioned that the conclusions of that report be 'not sealed.'

Ahh...the disinfecting power of sunlight.

Agent Watkins was, one more time, on the defensive.

"Boss, we found the Ark. There was just nothing in it."

"C'mon, John. Nothing in it? The place was as clean as the Pompeii ruins...buried and sealed by ash for centuries. How long did that basement have to be empty to be that clean?"

John protested. "The fact that the Ark even *exists* is an indication of involvement."

"Seriously, John? You're going to use a movie analogy to try and bolster your case? Do you remember that in the movie, all they found was dust? You didn't even find *dust*!"

Watkins had enough self-restraint to keep from explaining that his boss was using a metaphor and not an analogy. "Come on, Boss. In the movie, the dust was the evidence that the Ten Commandments were once in there."

"John...were you not listening to your own contrived argument? You didn't...even...find...any...*dust*!"

3.40 LOST IN SPACE

After his bosses had time to digest and discuss Watkins' report on the McNally search warrant number two, the ominous sound of the first four notes of Beethoven's Fifth Symphony sounded from Watkins' phone. John frowned to himself.

"Yeah, Boss?"

"John, I've just come out of a war meeting with the higher-ups. They had their bean counters with them. You and I need a private meeting tomorrow. Ten o'clock. My office."

"OK, Boss. Should I bring anything?"

The Assistant Director had hung up before John could finish his sentence.

At 10AM, Special Agent John Watkins sat down for his appointed meeting with his Assistant Director.

"Congrats on finding the first perp, John. You should know, if you don't already, that your little victory sent a wave of celebration throughout the Agency. You'll go down in FBI history for exposing the most hidden perp ever to get dragged out from under a bushel and into the light of day.

"So...I *should* be hosting a celebration party for you. But, I had a less-than-friendly meeting via the computer, including with one of the Assistant Chiefs of Staff in D.C. They were grilling me about my budget. They were armed for bear. The most highlighted case they had in hand was your Mark Johnson case."

Watkins questioned, "Armed for bear? I thought you said 'waves of celebration?' They should have been calling to ask what kind of Champagne we like. Wasn't their ire really about the lack of supporting evidence from the second McNally search warrant...and not budgets?"

"They're one in the same, John." The Assistant Director took a breath. "John, look. We all get slower with age. If anything actionable pops up on the case, we can put some younger eyes on it. If nothing actionable comes after younger eyes look at it, then I'll move it to the back of the rack."

Watkins was too close to retirement to scream about 'ageism.' Plus, he had too much respect for his Boss to do that. "Tell me how you can praise the fruit of my profile theories...while telling me there's nowhere else to go on this case. This is about the Brass, isn't it? The higher-ups? They want to punish me for two unfruitful search warrants...right?"

His Assistant Director answered, "Not a chance. This is about a budget concern...and the decision is for my level of management. But, I will admit that the Brass are all about 'what have you done for me lately,' the word 'lately' seemingly to mean...'today.'

"They have to submit a reduced budget to Congress this year, and they grilled me on your case. Specifically, they wanted to know what active leads the case was producing at this moment. You and I know both know we're spitting into the wind, now. Because of you, we found one of them. The other kid will turn up someday, probably dead, like the first one."

"That's not true, Boss. I have a list of potential discoverables. Give me an agent, and I can move it all forward, faster."

"Like?"

"Highlands Ranch. The other perp might be in that area, same as the first perp."

"Evidence brought you to that area for the one perp, and him only. This is a big country, John. You want to pursue a no-evidence lead? At a time when there's pressure to defund this thing? It's time for me to back-shelf this case."

Watkins couldn't let it go. "Predictive human behavior is not evidence, but it is the basis for an investigative lead. And the guy who knows where the second kid is is our target.

"Predictive human behavior says we need to look at that guy's behavior *pattern*. We'll investigate the Highlands Ranch/Denver area. Beyond that, we have an ancient military record to explore for connections. Oh...and by the way...I could use your authority for another round of info on the first perp's social security number."

"John..." The Assistant Director was getting exasperated. "I didn't ask you in here so you could *not* listen to me."

"Boss...The guy we need to unleash more resources on knows where the other kid is. And he was a Silver Medal recipient, for heaven's sake. Those aren't the kinds of guys who cut all ties. Brothers-in-arms, and all that. We still have paths to follow."

"Without imminent, hard leads, the Director's office wants this case's budget to be zero'd out. And I need it out of my budget, as well. I have other, more promising directions from other cases. Without active leads, or a promising action strategy..."

John was getting indignant. "Cold file? No. This case is unfolding at its own pace. I can't control that. But it is *still* unfolding. Can I appeal, with you at my side, to the higher-ups to make the case for seeking a new round of evidence?"

"We both need to be careful with the higher-ups, John. When their judgement is challenged, they take it as a threat to their egos. These guys have moved on. They're not sitting around waiting to hear if we have a better idea than they. I'm not going to push them. If there's anything they won't tolerate, it's a subordinate that gives a hint that the higher-ups are anything but gods.

"Look, John. You have a retirement coming up, in what? A couple months? A few weeks? Predictive human behavior tells me you should be acting like a short-timer, not like a young rookie on steroids."

"This is my last case, Boss. And it's not closed, yet. Do you think I've built my career reputation up to this point in order to go out with a whimper?"

"John, you know I respect you and the results you've been able to produce. But there are shortcomings in your recent record, as well. Upstairs wanted to demote you over the first search warrant lawsuit. They don't even want to talk to you about the second one. They don't like the tarnish you're putting on them. On the Bureau.

"I successfully argued that you should be allowed to retire with your 'Special Agent In Charge' title and pay-grade…that a demotion was not consistent with your contributions over the span of your career. But I have immediate pressure on me to submit a greatly reduced budget. And you are one of their specific targets. Are you willing to retire a little early with your title and pay-grade in tact?"

"Boss, you're not seeing where we are on this case."

"John, you're turning this investigation into a profile hunt instead of an evidence hunt. And you have to be able to read the room. You know how to profile people. So profile the legion of suits above our pay-grade. Do you think their egos will allow them to position a person to become a superman that they have collectively decided has gone past his expiration date? Do you know what an uphill battle is, John? I wanted to handle this as cordially as possible…but you're starting to piss me off. And don't take my words wrong. Nobody's forcing you out. You know that if it were anybody else, they'd just get an email from personnel informing them of their 'done' date. We're treating you with kid gloves because…"

Watkins waited for him to say, 'because you're Black.'

"…because you've earned better than that. Everybody knows about the esteemed parts of your record. But you have to give me a compelling reason to keep you on the case…keep you on my payroll…a reason that can be sold up the line. Otherwise, I have to pull the plug.

"Look, John, nobody's going to be calling you in for meetings. Sit out your last month or so at home. There's nothing for you to do here."

"Could you have insulted my integrity any deeper? What if I could find a way to be removed from your budget altogether...and stay on the case as the sole investigator? No agents. No administrative support. I'm telling you, Boss, there's more to see in this case. We're closer than I can prove, but I can smell it. We're close to new evidence being revealed."

"First of all, you're talking nonsense about budget loopholes. And secondly...not to downplay the value of a hunch...but you want to put more money into a case based on a hunch? Have you lost your way, John? Have you lost your ability to conclude when it's time to cut bait? Have you lost your ability to hear a single word I've said?"

"What if I could be put on the Director's budget? My costs would be unnoticeable there...and you know as well as I that they won't touch their *own* budget. And it would be for such a short time. And that would allow you to submit the budget they want from you. And it would allow me to crack open what might be the final nut that leads us to the second killer."

"There is no way I could sell that, John. I would be making recommendations...budget games...that are way above my pay-grade. Moves like that don't happen unless you have a "P.I." stamped on the outside of your personnel file. And if you *did* have your job because of Political Influence, you wouldn't still be a Special Agent In Charge at the end of your career."

Instead of blowing a gasket, John Watkins left the meeting with a 'last resort' plan.

"This is FBI Special Agent In Charge John Watkins calling for Congressman Hemmings."

"The Congressman is in a meeting. May I take a message?"

"Please tell him I have an urgent request of him."

Congressman Samuel R. Hemmings had hired John Watkins for the summers while John was in Law School. The Congressman had been shown an Op/Ed piece in The Boston Globe about how the Congressman's plan to tie environmental cleanup money to oil-and-gas industry subsidies and profits from the business they do with the government was good government for all Americans.

The Op/Ed had made the Congressman call the article's author with a job offer to do some speech writing and for writing publicity pieces. The author of that Op/Ed was a very young Harvard Law student named John Watkins.

Congressman Hemmings was in his last term before retirement and had ascended to occupy the Chairmanship of the House Committee on the Judiciary. That committee oversaw the Department of Justice and, thereby, the FBI…and its budget.

"Agent Watkins? Please wait for Chairman Hemmings."

"John, old boy! Did you think I forgot about you? After all these years, you're still the best speech writer I ever had. I remember submitting a recommendation for you to the FBI. My secretary told me 'Special Agent In Charge John Watkins' had called. So it looks like it turned into a career, eh? Has it gone well?"

"Yes, Sir. Very well. It has been everything I'd hoped it would be, and I always think of you with feelings of gratitude for how it's all worked out."

"Now *that's* some nice ass-kissing there, John. I'm surprised you're not the Director, yourself."

John gave a polite chuckle.

"I'm calling with a small but special request."

"Anything, John. Spell it out for me."

"I *am* near the end of my career, and I have one case left to close out. But for budget reasons, they want to put me out to pasture early and move this active case to the cold files. It's a case involving the murder of a police officer by two young perps. We got one of them, and we're closer than anybody knows to the second one."

"Sounds like you should be calling *Dateline NBC*, not me."

"I called you, Sir, because it's a simple and insignificant line-item budget issue that involves no real money, and nobody seems to have the wherewithal to figure out how to make happen."

"So, I'm a line-item bean counter now? This is what my Congressional career has brought me to?"

"No, Sir. My solution to the whole SNAFU is to have me put under the Director's budget where I can finish this case without ruffling anybody's budget feathers. But my Boss doesn't have the juice to make that request. And I know you do."

"I love it when people talk about my juice, John. So, you're calling me to have me put you on the Director's budget instead of your Field Office's budget?"

"It sounds so easy, Mr. Chairman..."

"I love the sound of *that*."

"But nobody seems to be able to do it."

"Betsy? Are you on the line?"

"Yes, Sir."

"Do you know what Agent Watkins is asking for?"

"It sounds like a ten-minute administrative chore, Sir."

"Can you see to it that it gets done?"

"Yes, Sir. I'll do it as soon as we hang up."

"That good enough, John?"

"Yes, Sir."

"Normally, at a time like this, I'd say, 'Remember me on election day.' But there are no more election days for me, John. However, it still makes me feel good to do a constituent a favor. You're still registered to vote in Lexington, aren't you?"

"You have a great memory, Congressman. I'll make you proud."

With that phone call, Special Agent John Watkins disappeared into the bureaucracy of the FBI Director's office. His title and pay-grade remained in tact, along with his physical office staying in Memphis...but with no agents nor administrative staff to work his investigations, and with his only boss being a nameless, faceless, inspector general staffer, whose office randomly conducted case audits. Watkins felt free.

Any administrative support or expense report paperwork would go through a low-level clerk who worked for a clerk to one of the Assistant Chiefs of Staff, to the Chief of Staff, to the Director, himself.

John knew he wouldn't get away this forever. But then again, his remaining time was being measured in weeks, not years.

Watkins reviewed his top two agenda items.

First, was to order the address history on the Michael Dean social security card number to find evidence that Scott McNally was the person who had effectuated the fake I.D.

Second, was to dig deep into McNally's military history for possible connections that could have been used to hide the two murder suspects. McNally seemed to have no local friends. The military history was a long shot, but Watkins had to eliminate all possibilities...and there were no other places to turn.

Both agenda items would require Watkins learning how to work his new chain of command...a chain of command that didn't seem to actually exist.

3.41 DUCKS IN A ROW

Agent John Watkins called the FBI Director's office in D.C. and was directed to a clerk that would send him to the 'right' clerk about his administrative inquiry into why his authorization number did not allow him to make a records request to the Social Security Administration.

Watkins told the appropriate clerk about his new designation, and that he needed an authorization to request an SSA address history on a card number. While he was speaking with the clerk, the clerk entered Watkins' info into a personnel records search. The record came up with the letters 'P.I.' following his name.

"Yes, Agent Watkins. We can submit your request for an address history on that name and number directly from here. That should avoid any administrative delays."

Watkins then called the switchboard at the Pentagon and asked for the Office of the Secretary of the Air Force. A secretary to The Secretary answered.

"This is Special Agent John Watkins calling from the staff of the FBI Director. My Director has requested that I expedite an information request for a DoD record on an active and urgent case. To whom should I detail my Director's request?"..."Terrific. Then this is the request..."

Two weeks after his request, a physical, grainy photocopy of Scott McNally's DoD 214 arrived in Watkins' physical mail.
Date of Service: April 21, 1971
Date of Discharge: April 20, 1975
Station of Discharge: Lackland AFB, San Antonia, Texas
MOS (Military Occupational Specialty): Para Rescue
Decorations: National Defense; Outstanding Unit x 2; Vietnam Service x 2; Purple Heart; Silver Star.

His Fred Flintstone return was the same DoD 214 that he had received via email at the beginning of the investigation. And it did *not* include the additional information he had requested: The names of McNally's fellow Unit members.

Watkins was frustrated by the time it took to *not* get the information he had requested, so Watkins did what every other American would have done. He turned to Google.

'Scott McNally Silver Star'
Watkins had never seen a blank Google return.
Then he typed in, 'Silver Star, Vietnam, Para Rescue'
The Google return was over six million web pages found in .9 seconds. When Watkins started reviewing them, none of them had all three search parameters.

Watkins got back on the phone to the Pentagon, Department of the Air Force. "Special Agent in Charge John Watkins calling from the FBI Director's office. The Director has ordered some data collection for an active case. He needs records on Air Force E-5 Scott McNally's Para-Jumper Search and Rescue Unit and Vietnam PJ Unit. The Director is seeking a list of personnel in that Unit...as well as the citation details on the Silver Star medal award for that same E-5 McNally. Is there any way this request can be hand-carried to all appropriate administrative destinations? The Director has marked his 'need-to-know' as 'urgent.'"

Watkins was told, politely, that nobody 'hand-carries' that type of request because the records are 'off-site' physical records that have not been digitized. Watkins was left to hurry up and wait.

Three days later, Agent Watkins' email received the Silver Star citation with and a note that said, 'a record of the members of this Unit does not exist.'

Agent Watkins read the general summary citation for relevant information. '29 June 1973...conspicuous acts...gallantry...against the enemy while engaged in military operations.'

John called his Pentagon contact back. 'The Director thanks you for your timely response. So, if you ever need a favor from us...you have my contact information.

"In reviewing the citation...is there any way to find out what happened on 29 June 1973...a document of the specific acts regarding the Silver Star?"

Crickets.

Watkins entered his new search parameters into Google. '29 June 1973, Silver Star, Vietnam, Scott McNally.'

There were no hits that included all four criteria. But on page 3, Watkins knew he had hit pay-dirt with a web-site reference that included two of the search parameters. It was a one page, amateur-looking web-site that had hotel room reservation dates at the Denver Hilton along with room blocking information. A quote at the bottom of the page said, 'Lilly and I look forward to seeing all of you that can come for our ninth quinquennial reunion of my Vietnam Rescue on June 29th, 1973.' The name below the quote was 'Christopher 'Ernie' Mineau.'

A further Google search showed that Christopher Mineau had retired at the rank of Lieutenant Colonel after 26 years of service.

Another amateur website was a blog that included a narrative about the blogger's Vietnam experience. It said that Colonel Mineau had been shot down in Vietnam as an F4 Phantom pilot, that his navigator had been killed from the ejection, and that Mineau's F4 had the distinction of being the last F4 ever shot down in Vietnam. And that the date of the shoot-down was June 29, 1973.

Agent Watkins went back to Google for contact information. His mind was shorted out when he saw the search results.

Christopher 'Ernie' Mineau, Lt. Colonel, USAF, Ret., had a current residence address in Highlands Ranch, Colorado.

John Watkins reached up to grab onto his own hair. If he'd had any, he'd have pulled it.

'Are you serious? The very town that domiciled the now-deceased Muhammad Jefferson?'

Agent Watkins was, once again, reminded that the rule of thumb in investigative work is…'there's no such thing as a coincidence.'

'Am I smelling a connection between McNally and this Colonel Mineau guy? Could this be the connection I've been praying for? Could Highlands Ranch be the landing place of Jamal Ali Jefferson, also? Just like I have suggested many times?' Watkins thought he was onto the final leg of his quest.

"Colonel Mineau? My name is John Watkins. I came across your story of being downed in Vietnam and am thinking of writing an historical account of it as a retirement research project. May I schedule a time to come talk to you about it?"…"Yes, Sir. I know a lot of F4's were downed during the war, but I think your case is unique because yours was the *last* F4 ever downed…and there was a Silver Star awarded in connection with your rescue."…"Oh? *Two* Silver Stars?"…"Yes, Sir. Homework is what it's all about."…"Thank you, Sir. I look forward to meeting you."

3.42 THE IMPORTANCE OF BEING EARNEST

Agent John Watkins rang the doorbell of a stately looking four-bedroom Colonial at the end of a Cul-de-Sac in the upscale suburb of Highlands Ranch, Colorado…a town with which Agent Watkins was already familiar.

"Colonel Mineau, I'm glad to meet you."

"Welcome. Please, call me 'Ernie.' I come from a family where the middle name is the name all your friends call you. It's what separates your friends from those who don't really know you."

"Thank you, Ernie. My friends call me 'John.'"

"I've hosted a reunion every five years for the team that saved my life. It's become a multi-generational family event. I started out to have been fortunate enough to pay for it out of gratitude, but it's grown so big over the decades that now I just pay for the rooms of the original principles. Even still, their families attend en masse at every meeting. Some of the finest people and families you'll ever find on the planet."

Agent Watkins felt he was on the path to pay-dirt. "That's a great story, in and of itself, right there. What size rescue squad are you talking?"

"The S&R ground crew was twelve...plus the Huey pilots and co-pilots, and all four of their gunners...and the O-2 pilot who was scouting out and marking the LZ. Altogether, there are *twenty-one* individuals who were directly responsible for saving my life that day. Nineteen of them have shown up for a celebration that I host every five years."

Agent Watkins asked, "That's a wonderful thing that you do. And the nineteen all still attend?"

"No. Sadly, some have died. And two of the original twenty-one *never* showed up. Captain Gary Baxter, the O-2 pilot, and an E-5 PJ named Scott McNally. We talked about them on that first reunion. I had even hired a private investigator to find the ones I couldn't. That was long before the days of Google.

"My investigator's report came back that the two names I gave him had disappeared off the face of the earth. We all knew what that meant. CIA deep undercover recruitment of field operator specialists was rampant back then. Probably still is today. We all agreed that they both had the right stuff. The CIA knew what they were doing when it came to recruitment."

Watkins rusingly asked, "My research showed that a Silver Star was awarded from that mission. Was that one of the CIA recruits?"

Colonel Mineau answered, "Actually, there were *two* Silver Stars awarded from that mission. Remember the importance of homework? One went to E-5 McNally, one of those missing from our quinquennial reunion. The other was awarded to E-5 Elijah Washington from the same PJ S&R Unit as E-5 McNally. I see E-5 Washington...'Eli,' we call him...and his family at every reunion. He has a wonderful family. It's a beautiful thing to see these families grow over the decades."

Watkins asked, "May I contact some of the people on your list? And may I tell them that my project has your blessing?"

Colonel Mineau was humble and proud. "No, that's fine. A 'good' history is worth the telling. And the people who performed so bravely that day deserve to have their story told."

Colonel Mineau turned on his computer. "I know them all like they're family. In fact, they've become quite a large family over the decades.

"Give me your email, and I'll send the names and contact information to you...

"...An FBI email address? Is that where you're retiring from? The FBI?"

Watkins offered, "My wife and I made a commitment to each other before we got married that I would retire only after our children were graduated from college. We had one daughter..." John pulled out his phone and brought up a picture of his MaryLou. "She graduates from Notre Dame this Spring."

Colonel Mineau was always happy to see a family picture. "She's a beautiful girl. My wife and I have two daughters and a son, ourselves. Does your wife work?"

Watkins answered, "Yes. The deal was a two-way street. We both would work until our daughter graduates. Jackie, my wife, is an administrator in our local school district, outside Memphis." John pulled up a picture of Jackie on his phone.

Colonel Mineau looked with interest. "It looks like you have a great family. My wife and I didn't have any kind of agreement about it, but once the kids were gone and I retired, she decided she needed a project, so she opened a little cafe/restaurant right here in Highlands Ranch. You should stop by for coffee or a meal...if you have time before you leave Denver. It's called *The Sunflower Cafe and Restaurant*, and it's on Main Street in town."

Agent Watkins almost gasped out loud. 'OMG! His wife was Muhammad Jefferson's employer? This is some kind of a setup...McNally sent Muhammad here because of his connection to Colonel Mineau...but if it's a setup, why would Mineau expose his connection to Muhammad Jefferson?...And Mineau said nobody ever saw McNally again...Something's going on. I don't just stumble over needles in a haystack every day...'there's no such thing as a coincidence.'

Colonel Mineau leaned in a little close to Agent Watkins as though he was about to tell a secret. "There's a little known fact about my wife and her restaurant."

Watkins waited.

"There was a young man who worked at my wife's restaurant who was *wanted* by the FBI."

Watkins interest intensified.

"When he got into a scuffle with the ex-husband of one of the waitresses..." Colonel Mineau started to show a little sadness. "...both of the men died."

Agent Watkins let out an inaudible, 'Whew.' "That must have been very upsetting to your wife?"

"My wife doesn't really get involved in all the day-to-day operations of the restaurant, but she got great reports about the young man. He was hired on as a dishwasher, and it turned out he could cook...and all the regular patrons of the restaurant loved his cooking.

"My wife said she was told he had great potential...that he was a real self-starter...and creative...that he had become a real crowd favorite. When her business started growing, she went in to meet him one day. She said she was afraid she would lose him because he was talented and personable enough to start his own restaurant."

Agent Watkins was nodding. His first thought was, 'That doesn't sound like the kid that murdered Officer Johnson.' Then he thought, 'Scott McNally did one heck of a job.'

Watkins' next thought was about the Colonel. 'This guy can't act. This is all sincere. And yet...there's no such thing as a coincidence. How could McNally set all this up without anybody knowing?'

Colonel Mineau finished up about the cook by saying, "Anyway, what brought that to mind was that the FBI was involved in finding the young man...and sadly, in finding out his real identity. I don't know how someone can have a fake identity in today's world.

"So, did you know any of the FBI people who worked on that case?"

Watkins got a little more cagey than what made him comfortable. "It seems like, even though we're a huge organization, everybody knows everybody else one way or another. But the FBI does a pretty good job of compartmentalizing all of our jobs. It's hard to know who's doing what. We have over 15,000 agents."

Colonel Mineau then asked, "Are you sure it's OK for me to send my list to your FBI email? I mean, you're not going to get in trouble for using your FBI account for personal business, are you? I'd hate to see a good career man go down over something so small and insignificant."

Watkins needed to seal the ruse. "My bosses do it all the time, so I guess I've become numb to it. Plus, I'll be retired in a flash. That should put me out of reach for them to give me a slap on the wrist."

It was time for Agent Watkins to wrap up. "May I sit with you again after I've talked to everyone? I would never publish anything without a contributor signing off on it."

Colonel Mineau was pleased and nodding. "If we're all dead before you finish, call around to get it distributed to our surviving families."

"Mr. Washington? My name is John Watkins. Lieutenant Colonel 'Ernie' Mineau gave me your name in reference to a piece I'm writing about the history of the rescue mission on the last Phantom ever downed in Vietnam. I'm calling to see if you'd be willing to share your memories with me for my history writing project?"

3.43 RUSES ARE RED

John Watkins followed the map on his iPhone to an uphill, winding driveway in Pacific Palisades, California. When the house came into view, Agent Watkins looked to his left to see the most sweeping view of the Pacific Ocean he had ever seen.

When he got to the very top of the driveway, he drove alongside a long narrow building to his right that had seven individual garage doors. Then the house came into immediate view.

The house was situated to maximize the view of the ocean, and the driveway led to a covered parking area at the front door.

"Thank you for seeing me, Mr. Washington."

"Captain Mineau, 'Ernie' is what he prefers that we call him, called me and told me what a fine fellow you are, and that it would be great if I could add my perspective to your historical writing project about the rescue mission. But he didn't say anything about you being *Black*. And, please, call me Eli. That's what all my friends call me."

"Thank you, Eli. Please call me John. That's what my wife calls me, and she's my best and only friend." They both chuckled.

John Watkins continued. "Why do you call him '*Captain* Mineau?' He retired as a Lieutenant Colonel."

"I guess he'll always be 'Captain' Mineau to those of us who were part of the rescue mission. Even seeing him on such informal and friendly terms over the decades, he never became 'Ernie' or 'Colonel' Mineau to us. But my wife and daughter and granddaughter call him 'Ernie.' They've always gone with me to the reunions, every five years."

"May I get some of the details of the rescue event from you?"

"I'm sorry. Please come in. We can go to my study to get some privacy and some comfortable seating."

"When Captain Mineau called, he said your regular gig is with the FBI. That's a red flag for me. I hope you're not going to be doing any sniffing around about my off-the-grid farming days?" Eli had a sly but inviting smile on his face.

John didn't know what he was talking about but tried to calm Eli's concerns...and took it as a possible note of humor in that Eli had brought it up on his own. "I have no interest in any off-grid farming you may...or may *not*...have been involved in." Agent Watkins chuckled. "I'm not here as an FBI agent. I'm here on my own dime and my own time to get a post-retirement project jump-started. And in case you need further assurance, the FBI is way too busy to chase down Statute of Limitations, un-prosecutable crimes...in case you meant to imply there *was* a crime involved in your 'farming.'"

Eli was smiling and softly chuckling while he thought, 'Statute of Limitations, eh?' "I can tell you that the downing of Captain Mineau's jet fighter was the only hot Search and Rescue mission that our team was ever called on to perform during our team's two tours-of-duty over there. The War was winding down.

"The rescue mission could have been routine...if *any* Search and Rescue calls are routine...but this one got nasty. And to beat it all, his was the last F4 Phantom ever shot down in Vietnam.

"Nobody from our unit died that day...but can you imagine if someone had? Our one and only hot mission? The last F4 ever shot down? *That* would've been the definition of God being out to *get* someone."

John probed. "Colonel Mineau...should I call him 'Ernie?'..."
Eli nodded. "Ernie."
"Ernie told me there were two Silver Star Medals awarded that day. And that you were one of them."
"Ah, yes. The hardware. Get up and step right this way."
Eli directed John to the bookcase that made up one of the walls in his study.

John stood before a beautifully woodworked case with a glass front that had, enclosed, the medal hanging on its ribbon above the citation.

John was looking at it with respect, even awe, when Eli said, "It's on display to fizzle-down the inner-racist of all my White visitors. Takes a little edge off me being Black, and all. I'm the City Councilman for my district, here in Pacific Palisades, you know."

John pulled his iPhone out of his golf-shirt breast pocket and took a picture.

> Know all persons by this citation
> that the
> United States Department of the Air Force
> does hereby grant and award
> with all honors and privileges associated with
>
> The Silver Star
>
> to E-5 Technical Sergeant Elijah G. Washington
> who on the day of 29 June 1973
> did perform conspicuous acts of gallantry
> displayed against the enemy
> while engaged in military operations.

John was overcome with pride for his fellow countryman. "Consider me fizzled-down." He had to hold back a tear. "Ernie said there were *two*

Silver Stars awarded that day." Agent Watkins played dumb. "Who was the other recipient?"

The two men returned to their seats.

"The other went to a PJ named Scott McNally. He and I had formed a bond in Superman School because we were both targets...for different reasons. But at the first reunion, Captain Mineau said nobody could find him. In today's world, what with Google and the internet, you can find just about anybody. So I guess the question came down to...how hard was anybody going to try."

Agent Watkins took that to mean that Eli didn't have any after-Air-Force contact with Scott McNally, but didn't take that assessment as conclusive. Watkins always had his antenna up for deception...as well as the possibility of his own misinterpretation.

Agent Watkins kept sprinkling in the names of other participants to keep Eli's eye off the ball. But whenever John would drop the name of Scott McNally, he'd keep a close eye on Eli. Agent Watkins thought he noticed an ever-so-slight flinch in Eli's facial muscles whenever John said the name.

Agent Watkins finally said, "So the two Silver Stars were awarded as part of the same action. I mean, if you and Sergeant McNally were in combat that closely together...usually, that creates a life-long bond...for better or for worse."

Eli leaned forward over his desk, almost like he was about to assume the position of prayer. "I remember him. He fell off the radar a long, long time ago. Reunion efforts could never find him in the early years. Assumed dead or left the country. Or was a CIA recruit.

"Captain Gary Baxter was another. The reunion guys assumed CIA had recruited them for undercover work. I, personally, would say CIA would not have been interested in Sergeant McNally. He was a broken man. 'Post Vietnam Syndrome,' they called it back then. Reunion efforts didn't continue beyond those first couple of meetings. We figured we were public enough that if Sergeant McNally or Captain Baxter wanted to find us, they would find us if they were interested."

Agent Watkins moved on so as to not seem overly interested in Sergeant McNally. "Isn't there a document detailing the specific acts of gallantry for your Silver Star?"

Eli began lightly shaking his head. "I've long discarded that bllsht about specific acts. It's like the man behind the curtain in the Wizard of Oz. They hand out papers to justify themselves. I know what happened that day. It doesn't matter if they detailed it in their own 'official' words or not."

Agent Watkins moved on. "Ernie said you also received a Purple Heart. Where's that?"

Eli chuckled. "Let's not over do it. Did you not hear anything I said earlier? How much fizzlin'-down does a person need to do? Is the Silver Star not enough?

"Sergeant McNally understood the nonsense of it all. He hid out at the time of the awards ceremony. He had gotten pretty damaged over the whole rescue mission."

Agent Watkins asked, "Purple Heart damaged?"

"There were Purple Hearts all around. It wasn't a peaceful rescue. But when I say 'damaged,' I'm talking damaged in the head. When he took a life, it made him think that his own life didn't matter, either. A whole, 'What's good for the goose is good for the gander' type of thinking. Everybody handles it differently.

"We were all kids. By the time the blood flowed, some of us were barely twenty. When Sergeant McNally would withdraw...disappear into himself...I asked him one time if he should have done the Nuclear Weapons gig...he was initially recruited into the Air Force to be a Nuclear Weapons Specialist...brainy kid. He asked me if I meant, did he prefer a hole in his psyche, or a hole in his lymph nodes and vital organs. He then said, 'I feel like you're asking me if I rode my bike to school or did I *carry* my lunch. One didn't have to do with the other.

"Besides..." Eli leaned in toward John like he was about to tell a secret, "and if you ever quote me on this, I'll deny I said it..."

Agent Watkins said, "OK."

"The Purple Heart is for someone who bled for their country. In Vietnam, *nobody* bled for their country, even if they *convinced* themselves that they did.

"All the blood spilled over there was for the stockholders of the Industrial Military Complex. We fought a war that meant *nothing* to our national security. Its only purpose was to enrich an elite few that made bombs and aircraft...guns and armored fast-boats. The capitalists of war. And if there's any dispute over those facts, let's not forget that our Country's misadventure into Vietnam caused the downfall of two Presidents.

"And if we have to put a bow on it, Muhammad Ali was right. Why should I have been killing people who never called me 'nggr?' I came home and, even to this day, with all my trappings of wealth, with all my visible proof that the American Dream is possible...even with my local high political office...hell, John, people *still* call me 'nggr.' Only now, it's more behind my back.

"When I leave my hometown, here in Pacific Palisades, I'm still Black. I still get pulled over by the cops for the most made-up bllsht you can imagine. I'm always, like, 'you dumb mthrfckr! You musta had to *practice* that line of bllsht over and over in the mirror for you to get it right.'

"The Vietnamese are a peaceful people...when you're not killing 'em for no reason. Much like Black folk, wouldn't you say, John?"

Agent Watkins didn't want to get political with Elijah. But he was still curious about McNally and the 'specific acts of gallantry.'

3.44 THE RIDE OF THE VALKYRIES

"Mayday! Mayday! This is Captain Rankin, flight 6634. We've been hit. Triple-A."

The voice of the pilot, Captain Christopher 'Ernie' Mineau broke in. "Eject, J.J.! Eject!"

The rear cockpit ejection explosions could be heard over the open radio mic of Captain Mineau. "Here I go. Find us near The Trail. I can see people! I can see people!" Radio transmission went dead at the ejection of F4 Phantom pilot 'Ernie' Mineau.

Radio traffic from the air controller in Thailand made a general call for any O-2's in the area. "This is 432nd control calling all Oscar-Deuces thirty to fifty clicks north of Da Nang, in the area over Vinh, over Ho Trail. Come in, any Oscar-Deuces. Come in, any Oscar-Deuces."

While that call went out, a second radio from the control tower at the 432nd Tactical Reconnaissance Wing went out. "Da Nang. Da Nang. Do you copy? Da Nang. This is 432nd TRW. Do you copy?"

"Da Nang, here."

"F4 Recon over Vinh down by Triple-A. Pilot and navigator eject. Need a pick-up. Repeat. Need a pick-up."

"Copy that, Four-Three-Two. On it."

"F4. Pilot and navigator eject. Vinh area over Ho Trail. S&R emergency evac. Repeat. S&R emergency evac. Two airmen. Potential hostiles at Landing Zone. Repeat. Potential hot LZ."

The 'this is not a drill' alarms sounded inside the area of hooches occupied by the newly arrived squadron of maroon berets in the Da Nang Forward Operating Base.

Boots and head gear were attached to bodies in the constant motion of grabbing packs and weapons as two dozen men ran to a staging area where the cold engines of four Huey UH-1N's were experiencing the start of rotor blades trying to warm up into their momentum. Sergeant Washington and Sergeant McNally boarded one of the choppers with a jump and a slide into the depths of the helo's belly.

Lieutenant George Crow was in the pilot seat. He was engaged in radio traffic to the inside and the outside of his flying machine. The doors had been removed from his chopper by the door gunners so that their M60 machine guns, with their attached M13 disintegrating belts of 750 .308 caliber bullets, each, would have maximum swivel. Huey door gunners had the highest mortality rate of any MOS (Military Occupational Specialty) in Vietnam.

Sergeant Washington saw one of the door gunners giving Lieutenant Crow a thumbs up, then all the PJ's were pressed into the floor as the chopper did a fast lift.

Back in Thailand, radio traffic came back.

"This is Oscar-Deuce, Captain Gary Baxter. Eyeballs on fireball. Heading in that direction, now."

The Cessna O-2 was the slowest moving aircraft in the battlefield inventory. It had a pull propeller in the nose and a push propeller in the rear, both geared off the same small engine. There were a couple of minutes of tense waiting back in Thailand.

"Four-Three-Two Recon, this is Oscar-Deuce, Captain Baxter. Located one ejection site. Will mark for Rescue."

With that, Captain Baxter flew in a slow downward spiral over the ejected flyer and dropped a 50-lb. sack of flour out his window. Then he let a second bag of flour go.

"Four-Three-Two Recon, sign of life. Hand wave." Then he saw four bullets fly past his windshield.

"Four-Three-Two, hostile fire near site. Repeat, hostile fire near site. Moving to find second e-ject site."

Captain Baxter started a slow climb in ever widening circles from the first ejection site. He kept his tiny O-2 in as tight a bank as he could to maximize his visual scan. Ten long agonizing minutes later, he was back on the radio.

"Four-Three-Two Recon. This is Oscar-Deuce, Captain Baxter. Second ejection site acquired. Repeat. Second ejection site acquired. Approximately seven clicks West of e-ject site one. Repeat. Seven clicks West of e-ject site one. Will mark now. Repeat. Will mark now."

Two more bags of flour were pushed out the window of Captain Baxter's O-2.

"Four-Three-Two Recon. This is Oscar-Deuce Baxter. No sign of life at ejection site two. Repeat. No sign of life at ejection site two."

Baxter lifted his little plane away from the marked site and headed back to the first site.

By the time Baxter got to site one, he could see two Huey's at treetop level heading toward the first ejection site. "Huey, Huey, this is Oscar-Deuce. I see your approach. You are on line."

"Gary?"

"Hey, George! You got the short straw today?"

"Ha! Yeah. Got two boatloads of eager PJ's. Other two helo's en route to site two. Guide us in, Gary."

"Four clicks...three clicks...two clicks...one click."

"Got it, Gary. Nice job with the baking goods."

"Always here to help. I'll monitor from above. Your boys get the message about hostile fire?"

"Roger that, Gary. Heads up all around."

Lieutenant Crow and his sister ship raised their noses up and came to a hover, their landing skids kept about two feet off the ground. Crow could feel his chopper rise up when his six PJ's jumped out.

Two of the PJ's sprinted to the downed pilot still strapped into his seat. They all gave hand signals to each other over the chopper noise. The pilot indicated he couldn't release the harness.

Both attending PJ's unsheathed their knives, and each sliced through a side of the harness.

The other ten PJ's had positioned themselves in a circle around the downed pilot, M16's at the high-ready position against their shoulders, hunting for targets.

As the two attending PJ's were helping Captain Mineau out of his seat, one of the attending PJ's felt his shoulder shoved back like someone had punched him. Then he felt some warmth. Without looking at his wound, he shouted to the second PJ, "I'm hit," and then tried to shout over the sound of the chopper blades, still spinning at the ready, "I'm hit, boys! I'm hit!"

They couldn't hear him, but they were aware of the incoming fire. The side of the circle from which the fire had come started expanding. They were marching forward into the tall grass and brush to find the source.

Sergeants Washington and McNally were on the back side of the chopper perimeter but, with no action from their side, they had turned to monitor what was going on with their team.

They saw the pilot being dragged back to the Huey by two teammates. They could see the bloody shoulder of one of their fellow PJ's. Based on the aid being given to the downed pilot, they presumed he had suffered some bone breaks or back trauma from the ejection.

The team in the forward semi-circle was disappearing from view into the tall grass and brush as they sought out the source of enemy fire.

As the Washington and McNally side of the perimeter was observing, Sergeant Washington saw some of the tall grass move beyond his team. He put the sights of his M16 up to level with his eyes. When he saw the grass move again, he sent a rapid burst of bullets into the blind.

His teammates turned around to make sure it was friendly fire, gave Washington the thumbs up, and started retreating, walking backwards, back toward their respective Huey's.

The rear perimeter PJ's moved forward to cover the return of their brothers.

The second Huey was fully loaded with six of the PJ team and lifted off to do a visual report and cover for Lieutenant Crow.

All of a sudden, the M60 on one side of the second Huey let loose with a non-stop fire power that could level a forest in seconds. The force of the gunfire moved the Huey off its flight path.

The second Huey pilot radioed, "Hey, George! My gunner spotted enemy squadron in brush. With arms. Get your cargo outta here. We'll cover you."

"Not loaded, Skippy. Cargo secure, but two PJ's still out." The door gunner on that side of Lieutenant Crow's Huey was hand-waving Washington and McNally back into the chopper, but their backs were turned as they scouted the brush for enemy combatants.

A hale of gunfire erupted from the brush. That caused Washington and McNally to unload their M16's in return fire.

Lieutenant Crow called to his fellow chopper pilot over the radio, "Hey, Skippy! You know you're hit, don't you?"

"Yeah, George. Just saw a bullet pass in front of my face. New glass when we get back." Skippy's door gunner was unloading another belt into the brush.

"Hey, Skippy! You got bigger problems than broken glass. There's smoke coming out of your engine. Get outta here before you're in the weeds for good. Call for a rescue in case you don't make it far. I'll cover you till my boys jump back in."

Skippy strained his engine to turn and lift away from the site. He was too high and moving too fast before his PJ's realized what was going on. They couldn't jump out to join the fight.

Washington and McNally were still advancing on the unseen enemy, sporadically releasing gunfire whenever they saw tall grass movement. McNally had turned around to check on the status of their lift. That's when he saw the door gunner waving him back to the chopper. McNally waved his free arm at Washington and pointed back to the Huey.

Washington acknowledged with a head nod as both men started walking backwards toward their ride home. When the two PJ's were about ten yards from the helo bay…that's when all hell broke loose.

About a dozen North Vietnamese 'farmers' ran out of the grass toward the men and the chopper, weapons drawn and firing. Washington and McNally dropped to the ground and permanently stopped three of the assaulters with gunfire. Then the door gunner laid down a chain of fire to scorch the earth, turning the remaining attackers into mincemeat.

The four PJ's in the belly, with the other door gunner behind them, were waving for Washington and McNally to climb back on board so they could get out of there. That's when a line of gunfire came from the behind the grass, again, and mowed through all the bodies staring out the bay opening of the Huey. All six bodies twisted from the force of the bullets hitting their bodies. The PJ's, holding their wounds, climbed over and laid on top of the injured Captain Mineau in the center of the floor.

The door gunner used his one good arm to recover control of his M60, while the other door gunner was working to unhinge his opposite-side M60. One of the PJ's on top of Captain Mineau kicked the weak-side gunner in the ankle to get his attention and passed his M16 to him.

With one wounded door gunner laying down fire from his M60, and the other wounded door gunner adding to the fire with the PJ's M16, the other PJ's were waving to Washington and McNally to get back onboard while providing a human shield to Captain Mineau.

McNally and Washington turned their backs to the enemy fire, ran back to the Huey, jumped about three feet off the ground onto the landing skid, and started to climb into the bay with assistance.

Lieutenant Crow performed a maximum lift maneuver to effect their escape. That caused Sergeant McNally's foot to slip off the skid, causing him to lose his balance and fall away from the bay opening.

As he was falling, he grabbed the skid with his free hand and dangled below the helicopter that was still making a maximum ascent.

McNally's hand on the skid wasn't strong enough to stay gripped against the maximum lift g-forces. His fingers were slipping off the skid. That's when the engine blew.

The Huey dropped out of the sky in a winding circular fall because the blades had not fully stopped turning. Just before impact, McNally let go of the skid and rolled as far and as fast as he could with his M16 held tight, vertically, along his chest and stomach.

On impact, there was only the sound of crunching metal and groaning people.

While all the passengers were shaking it off, Washington turned to his fellow PJ's. "Protect the cargo. McNally and I will end this."

The four PJ's inside, all wounded, lay with their backs against Captain Mineau and their M16's at the ready. Both the door gunners' wounds were made worse by the hard landing. They were temporarily incapacitated. The co-pilot was unconscious in his chair, and Lieutenant Crow was trying to get the radio to work. The impact had severed the battery cables.

Washington and McNally had their M16's at low-ready and were walking toward the source of their consternation. That's when a single gun shot came from the grass. It knocked Washington back with a bullet to his left shoulder. Washington got back up and resumed marching into the madness.

With the Huey now silenced, McNally could hear shouts. "Hey, PJ, come back for this!" McNally turned around and saw one of the gunners had managed himself into the doorway and was standing over a shoulder held flamethrower and fuel pack.

McNally shouted to Washington and pointed back to the chopper. Washington looked back and signaled for McNally to go.

Under cover from Washington, McNally ran back to the dead chopper and took the weapon from the gunner. "Careful. It's loaded with Napalm B." McNally knew that meant a Napalm that would burn for ten minutes...as opposed to the 15-30 second burn of regular Napalm.

He carried it until he was back alongside Washington. There, he strapped the fuel pack over his neck and mounted the flamethrower on his shoulder. He pointed it at the tall grass. He and Washington continued to march toward the unseen enemy.

There was a movement in the grass, and another single shot rang out and grazed Washington's helmet. That was all it took. McNally pointed the Flame Assault Shoulder Weapon in the direction from which the bullet had come and initiated hell on earth.

The flaming gel stuck to everything and burned the tall grass away in seconds. McNally kept the flow of fuel coming.

As the grass burned away, McNally and Washington finally got a glimpse of their target. It was a young woman who was on fire and convulsing from asphyxiation. As her skin melted, muscles and bones became visible. It was a nightmare scene, interrupted by the movement of more grass to the other side of them.

McNally redirected his weapon of horror to the new target and didn't let go of the trigger until everything between himself and his targets was disappearing from the flames. By the time he stopped the weapon's effluence, there were six more individuals on fire, none of them able to scream, all of them using their last moments on earth to flail.

McNally and Washington continued their march forward until they were satisfied that all threats had been neutralized.

McNally set the flamethrower down and pulled the fuel pack strap off over his head. Having set the savior of their lives onto the ground, he pulled his M16 back up to sight and fire mode.

Washington turned back to the Huey and gave the thumbs up to indicate both he and McNally were alright. One of the wounded door gunners returned the thumbs up.

Washington and McNally circled around the burning mounds of flesh and bone while pointing their weapons at each body...just to make sure the burning bones didn't rise up and re-attack.

When McNally made his way over to the lump of fire that used to be a young woman, he saw on the ground, about five yards away from the girl, a much smaller lump of fire. McNally walked over to inspect it. There was nothing left to recognize except the knowledge that it had been a baby. 'This is war? Killing children?' was the only thought he had.

After their inspection was complete, Washington and McNally walked back to the dead chopper, their backs to the final action.

Washington walked up to the hole where the pilot's side window used to be. "Help coming?" He looked over and saw the co-pilot was now conscious.

"No radio. The O-2 followed our sister Huey outta here. Someone's figured it out by now. Rescue should be here shortly."

Washington was keeping pressure on his shoulder wound. He grinned. "Rescue coming for the rescuers?"

Lieutenant Crow smiled. "Yeah. Your helmet looks like it's a good thing you weren't leaning a little more to the right."

Washington removed his helmet and looked at the graze mark. Before he could speak, he saw McNally fall to the ground next to him, then his own leg caused him to buckle to the ground. Then the sound of two rifle reports.

Washington reached over for his helmet and put it back on. Then he reached over to McNally. "You alright?"

McNally was not known for his swearing, but he shouted, either in pain or frustration, "Son uv a fckng bitch! Mthrfckr!" He stood up, but he had to catch his balance as his wounded leg threw him off.

McNally snapped his M16 to the low-ready position and started running...hobbling, really, dragging his wounded leg behind him...back in the direction from which they had come.

Washington shouted, "Get down, Scottie!" as he, himself, rose up and started impaired-chasing after McNally, his own M16 at the ready.

Fire started coming from the grass. Then McNally saw a body emerge and run for the flamethrower he had left behind.

McNally, still hobble-running, shouted a long and constant, "Nooooooo," as he emptied his clip into the wannabe Napalm usurper. The boy's body fell backwards with a shake and shimmy from each bullet.

Another body emerged from the line of grass never touched by the first flame assault. McNally needed to insert a new clip in his M16. As he fumbled for it from his ammo belt, a burst of bullet fire came from Washington's M16 and dropped the second assailant.

McNally never stopped running toward the grass. He snapped the new clip into his rifle and, at the next movement in the grass, he pulled the trigger while still running forward.

Click!

'Son uv a fckng btch!' McNally screamed out loud. 'A mthrfckng jamb!' His running toward the line of grass never stopped as he threw off his assault rifle and pulled his slaughter knife from its sheathe.

When another rifle-wielding body emerged from the grass, McNally let out the most loud banshee cry he could muster and, holding his knife in the hack position, ran toward the boy.

Before he could get there, a burst of fire from Washington's M16 dropped the kid dead. McNally didn't slow the pace of his hobble-running attack.

When two more young boys emerged with rifles at the ready, McNally changed the grip on his knife in mid-air and sliced one boy's neck so deep so as to leave his head hanging by some spine and cartilage. Then he changed his grip back to 'hack' and started repeatedly stabbing the second boy, the whole while screaming at top of his lungs, "No! No! No!" with every stab.

Washington caught up to him and shot at some movement still in the grass. It was an even younger boy...and a little girl.

Washington, still in lookout mode, stood with a foot on the body of the boy next to the dead little girl. He was still scouting for more ambushers with the tip of his rifle.

When McNally was too exhausted to stab his enemy's corpse any more, he got up and dragged his lame leg toward the dead body that Washington was holding down with one foot. McNally dropped to his knees and started stabbing the body repeatedly as he knelt next to it. He was continuing to try and shout, 'No,' but he had neither the energy nor the breath.

After his last meaningless stab into the boy, and with Washington still on the lookout for more comers, McNally turned and walked on his knees to the dead little girl. With both hands, he raised the knife over his head...but he couldn't do it.

The slope of the land kept the crew on the chopper from seeing the last round of kills.

Washington helped McNally stand up and tried to put an arm under him to support him. McNally pulled away and looked at Washington's leg. "Cinch your belt on that thing. After all that, you don't need to be bleeding out on us."

Washington looked at the worse wound on McNally's leg. "Cinch your own sht, asshole."

The two men temporarily cinched their bleeding wounds with their belts. Then they hobbled back to the chopper...to the applause and shouts from everyone on board. Even Captain Mineau, from his position of lying on his back, was clapping with his hands up high.

Everyone in the belly of the Huey, except Captain Mineau, had a bullet wound. All wounds had been tended to, and none seemed lethal, though every move from every person tended to provoke a self-inflicted moan.

McNally and Washington, if they ever had any, had no modesty left. They took off their boots and pants and let one their fellow wounded PJ's exercise his medical training. Everyone else on board kept weapons at the ready.

It seemed like a lifetime, but in reality it was only about ten minutes after the last firefight that the sounds of a squadron of choppers could be heard in the distance. Washington and McNally grabbed their discarded pants and hobbled to opposite ends of their wounded chopper.

They shouted back and forth to each other as the sound neared. "Five clicks out..." "Four clicks out..." "Three clicks out..." "Two..." "One." Then they started waiving their pants in the air.

Four Huey's landed at the four cardinal points around their downed sister. A swarm of the most combat-hardened army soldiers they'd ever seen jumped out and formed an impenetrable perimeter. Door gunners stood a vigilant watch, M60's swinging back and forth in search of a target.

Medic teams ran from under the whirling blades of the angels of the battlefield to find their patients. They were shocked that every person with a gun had been wounded. Even the co-pilot was diagnosed as having been concussed.

Assessments were made. Bandages were added or replaced. Those deemed as needing level-one surgical attention were flown out first, along with Captain Mineau. Everybody else randomly crowded onto one of the three remaining functioning Huey's on the ground. Washington and McNally got split up for the ride back to Da Nang.

Washington sat with his bare legs hanging out of the bay and his bare feet resting on the skids. He replayed the events in his mind. 'I wonder how many times we're gonna have to do *that* before we go home?' He watched the tree tops and the landscape pass below his blood-stained feet. 'God, what a beautiful country...what are we doing here?'

McNally sat on the floor of his chopper with his back against the pilot's seat. His eyes were closed. The screen was blank. There was nothing but white noise.

After McNally had been cleaned up and released from medical treatment, he returned to his hooch. There, the Base Chaplain paid him a visit.

The Chaplain handed him a telegram. McNally read it.

The Chaplain offered, "If you want to talk, my door is always open."

The next day, McNally found his way to the Base Radio Room. He asked if a call could be patched through to Lexington, Massachusetts.

A chain of shortwave radio contacts made its way to the greater Boston area. A local phone call was made with the shortwave radio mic pinched 'open' so the Lexington phone could be overheard.

The phone rang and rang. There was no answer.

It wouldn't be until after his unit had returned to the States that McNally would remember the telegram. His mother's breast cancer had become aggressive and had claimed her life.

Some follow-up calls from Stateside would inform him that his father had committed suicide shortly after his mother's death. Whether the notification had been lost or forgotten didn't matter to McNally. Actually, *nothing* mattered to McNally.

White noise.

3.45 YOU CAN'T PICK YOUR RELATIVES

After choosing to not engage with Eli's political rant, Agent Watkins asked Eli, "What's the 'G' in Elijah G. Washington stand for?" He assumed the answer before he asked, but he wanted to more fully explore Elijah's racial sensitivities.

Eli responded, "It's a little before your time, but surely you know who Lou Alcindor was?...or Cassius Clay?"

Agent Watkins said, "Yes. Kareem Abdul-Jabbar and Muhammad Ali."

Eli nodded, "That's right. They gave up their slave names in an effort to distance themselves from the White Supremacy that was suffocating all of us Black-skin folk...all of us who would be deprived of the same opportunities as White Americans...only because of the built-in system of White Supremacy. And for that same sensibility that made Lou and Cassius change their names, I will not say *that* part of my slave name out loud."

Agent Watkins asked, "Do you really think your parents were giving you a slave name when they named you?"

"No. I think they were hoping I would grow up to be White...so I would have a chance of making it in America."

"But you *did* make it in America."

Eli was shaking his head. "The *exception* is always used by the White Supremacy crowd to hide the *rule*."

Agent Watkins started to leave. "I have to wrap it for today, Eli, but I'm going to stay another day on FBI business in our LA office. I've enjoyed our visit beyond collecting the facts I'm here to assemble. Maybe we could continue this tomorrow?"

Eli was smiling. "It's not like I have a busy schedule. It's not like I have *any* schedule. I've enjoyed meeting you and talking to you. As long as you don't charge me for being my therapist, I'd love to spend more time jawboning with you. We've both made it in a White man's world. *There's* something right there. Not quite like being brothers in arms...but, smelling something like that."

Agent Watkins knew he tended to overthink things, but he had a complex thought about Eli that he had to play out in his mind. 'Was Eli onto my ruse, knowing that I'm here to find out about McNally? Did Eli introduce all this talk about race to see where my loyalties lay?...Whether I am more loyal to my race than to the FBI?'

Watkins had to talk himself down. 'Unless he's heard about me from McNally, himself...how would he know my mission?'

Watkins reviewed their conversation in his mind. 'Eli would have to be a master of deception to talk about McNally so freely...exclusively in the past tense.'

Watkins had to talk himself down again. 'He *did* invite me back. If he knew I was hunting for info about McNally, would he have done that?'

'I'm still in. The slow burn to smoking out McNally connections is still on the stove.'

There was a knock on the door to the study. "My wife, Nancy. She always knocks if I'm in a meeting in here." Elijah walked over to open the door. He turned back to Watkins and whispered, "Don't say anything about her appearance. She spends her days on Skid Row."

"Mr. John Watkins, please allow me to introduce my wife, Mrs. Nancy Washington."

Agent Watkins greeted her politely and noticed that she *was* 'dressed down,' which was consistent with her missing makeup and her tied-back hair. Then he thought to himself, 'She's as White as the driven snow. I wonder how *that* happened.'

3.46 I MET A GIRL WHO SANG THE BLUES

Eli left Mattole Beach with a truckload of tools, cash, and memories. He wasn't sure where he would end up, but he knew what he was going to do. He was going to give it a go in the constriction business.

After he'd driven about six hundred miles, he was exhausted. He needed to get a room for a serious shower and a serious meal and a serious rest. When he could smell the Pacific Ocean again, he turned off the Interstate and drove in the direction of the salt air.

He came to an overlook that gave him a view of landscape that looked like it was once the inner rim of a massive volcano, the western half having been swallowed into the sea millennia ago. From his perch, he could barely make out the Pacific Coast Highway, way down below, along the beach. Once his nostrils had been filled with the salt air, he nodded his head and thought, 'This is the place.'

He drove down into the community. There, it became clear that this was where people with money set up shop. Sure, there were the older modest homes from the 1940's and the 1950's. But they were being bulldozed and replaced with houses and landscaped features that were more fit for movie moguls than for middle managers.

Eli pulled into a motel that was very clean. It had a nice swimming pool.

The office, the rooms, and the pool surrounded the parking lot, forming a protected enclave. The combination of the upscale town and the protected enclave made Eli confident that his treasures would be safe in the open bed of his truck. He parked and entered the office with a friendly smile and hand full of cash.

The clerk looked him over and then looked out in the parking lot at his tool-filled truck. "I'm sorry, but we're all full up."

Eli knew what he was up against. "My construction crew is starting on a house up on the rim, day after tomorrow. They're all going to need rooms for three months. The owner of the house we're building, Mister William McClever, of Paramount Pictures fame, assured me that this would be a safe place for all of his craftsmen to stay while we finish up his dream home for him. His architect said the same thing about your fine establishment. Perhaps you're filled up because they've already contacted you and asked you to hold the rooms for us. Well, I'm the one you're holding all those rooms for."

The clerk felt embarrassed and feared unleashing a flurry of calls from important people who would be chewing out her boss. She turned the guest book around to Elijah and handed him a pen. "You're right, Sir. You're the one we've been waiting for."

Sure that nobody in this neighborhood and in this protected parking lot was going to dig through an open truck-bed full of tools for a boatload of cash that they didn't know was there, Eli got his long and warm shower. Then he walked until he came across a suitable restaurant, nodding to the hostess as he walked by to ensure that she would serve him, and got that big and hot meal he was needing. He went back to his room and slept for two days.

When he finally decided to rise from his rest, he was ready. He started driving all around the town. He was looking for a house that was under construction to see if he could add his labor to the crew.

Up on the rim, he came across a recently cleared lot that had no construction activity, but had two men standing on it, both in business suits, talking and making sweeping gestures with their arms. He pulled his truck over behind two of the nicest cars he had ever been close enough to to actually touch...in his life.

"Gentlemen, my name is Elijah Washington and I'm wondering if you're planning to build on this site?"

The more aggressive of the two said, "Why are you asking?"

"I'm asking because I'm looking for a house to build." Elijah had remembered the cliché, 'Fortune favors the bold.'

"We've already hired Mark Cisco as the general contractor." The man looked over at Eli's truck. "If Cisco drove around with his tools in his truck, we'd have never hired him."

Eli bowed his head and tipped his fake hat at the two men. "Thank you, Sirs. And...good day to you both."

Elijah found the Pacific Palisades police department, walked in, and said to the Desk Sergeant, "Sir, I'm supposed to meet the contractor, Mark Cisco, today, and I can't find where his office is located."

The sergeant pulled out a piece of paper and drew a map. "He's usually only in the office at the beginning and at the end of the day. What time are you supposed to meet him?"

"Oh...not until about five o'clock this afternoon. I'm just early...in case I couldn't find his office."

"Mr. Cisco, my name is Elijah Washington. The architect and the homeowner of the house you're going to build for them up off of Ocean View gave me your name as the person to see about contract labor."

"We don't hire Blacks...but what's your trade?"

"My friends call me Jack. Jack-Of-All-Trades."

"Get the fck outta here, you fckng nggr," and he turned back to his paperwork.

Elijah politely turned and walked out the door.

Elijah found an apartment building to rent that was tucked away from public view...as were *all* of the very few apartment buildings in Pacific Palisades. He made all the necessary payments to get in, then he unloaded his truck into the second bedroom of his rental. He then drove back toward his hometown of Compton, but turned toward downtown L.A., instead.

In downtown L.A., he found what he was looking for. A nice, upscale used car lot.

There, he saw just the car he was looking for. A 1983 Mercedes-Benz

380 SL convertible with a removable hard-top and, most importantly, an impeccable midnight-blue paint job. Plus, it had no wear on the seats. He paid cash.

Then he paid a lot attendant to follow him in his truck back to Pacific Palisades from whence Eli drove the kid back to L.A. in his shiny Mercedes-Benz.

For over a week, Elijah made multiple trips per day to the lot on Ocean View, and then multiple trips to the offices of Contractor Mark Cisco.

From outside the offices of Mark Cisco, Elijah would copy down the names on all the subcontractors' vans and trucks that he saw pull into the Cisco parking lot.

Finally, after about ten days of scouting the Ocean View property, Eli's patience was rewarded. The homeowner guy, and the guy whom he presumed to be the architect, were standing on the lot. The architect was holding a set of plans.

Elijah pulled his Benz in behind their Benz's.

At first, the two men didn't recognize Elijah. They were distracted by looking at his shiny car. Then, when Elijah spoke, the homeowner said, "You're the guy who pulled up here a couple of weeks ago in a pickup truck full of tools." The guy looked over, again, at Eli's car. "What do you want?"

"I want to be the contractor to build your house."

The homeowner had a short fuse. "I told you last time, Mark Cisco already has the contract to build it."

Elijah spoke softly but plainly. "You will have a big problem with Mr. Cisco."

The architect broke in. "I've used Cisco on more houses than I can count. I've never had a problem with him."

Elijah said, "I'm only giving you fair warning. Something big's about to happen, and I expect the timing of things blowing up for Mr. Cisco to be right in the middle of this project of yours."

The architect was starting to show signs of impatience. "What? What's going to blow up for Cisco?"

Elijah said, "Mr. Cisco is about to be sued in Federal Court for a violation of Title Seven of the Civil Rights Act of 1964. Apparently, he had never heard that it's illegal to discriminate in hiring based on race. Did you know that he doesn't, in his own words, 'hire nggrs' to do any of his work?"

The homeowner spoke up. "I'm a lawyer. What's the proof?"

Elijah said, "I don't know your field of practice, Sir, but Federal Court allows tape recordings of conversations to be admitted as evidence."

The homeowner said, "Tape recordings don't mean a conviction."

Elijah said, "The verdict is irrelevant. The *point* is that every dollar and minute he has to put into his defense is just time and money that will take his eye off the ball of his projects."

The homeowner said, "So, I presume you're here to offer to step in and save the day?"

"No, Sir. I'm going to build a house for myself, here in Pacific Palisades, and since we're going to be neighbors...well...I always like to do a favor for a neighbor whenever I can. Friends are better than fences...if you know what I mean."

The architect said, "You were in a pickup filled with tools the last time we saw you. Are you a contractor?...or aren't you?"

"I am."

The homeowner said, "So cut the sht. What do you want? The contract?"

"No, Sir. Just an appreciation for the favor I've done you for delivering this 'heads up.' If what I've shared ends up saving you cash and headaches...well, that should be worth something in our future friendship as neighbors...wouldn't you say?"

The homeowner said, "Well, then, here it is. 'Thanks for the heads up.'"

Eli bowed his head and tipped his fake hat as he retreated to his shiny Benz.

Elijah then drove his shiny Benz to the office of Cisco Contracting.

"Mr Cisco, I just thought I'd give you a heads up that I recorded our conversation a couple of weeks ago..." Elijah flashed his jacket pocket open, "just as I'm recording you right now...that my lawyer has filed a lawsuit in Federal Court against you and your company for violation of Title Seven of the Civil Rights Act of 1964. Rest assured we're going to take you for everything you've got." Elijah leaned into Cisco and said quietly, "And you should know I make a living doing this..." as he swept his hand toward the window so Cisco could see his shiny Benz.

"Get the fck outta here, you..." Cisco remembered he was being recorded and held his tongue.

Elijah was barely out of Cisco's parking lot when both the homeowner and the architect from the Ocean View lot pulled in in their separate shiny Benz's. They walked into Cisco's office together. Cisco was out of sorts when they walked in.

The architect asked, "You look all bent out of shape, Mark. What's going on?"

"It's nothing. I just got informed that a Federal lawsuit's been filed against me for not hiring nggrs. If it's not one thing, it's another."

The architect and the homeowner looked at each other.

"So...what can I do for you gentlemen, today? Another change order? Should I get my accountant in here?"

The architect said, "No, Mark. We just wanted to check to see if we're still on track to break ground next week?"

"Yes, Sirs."

Two days later, the architect called Mark Cisco.

"Mark? The homeowner has changed his mind about starting next week. Things are up in the air for him. He needs to cancel the contract...and he wants his deposit back."

"Are you sure? That'll cost him to cancel so close to the start date."

"Yeah, Mark. About the deposit. This is an important client for me. And you're my go-to contractor. I don't want to look bad to either one of you. If you waive the cancellation fee, I'll feel better about continuing to line you up with other clients."

Eli had a steep learning curve to climb in the contracting business, but he had a good starting point. A list of all of Mark Cisco's sub-contractors.

His first call was to the excavation sub for the Ocean View lot. That provided him the opportunity to meet all the city inspectors, including water, gas, electrical, sewage, and general building codes.

As Black as he was, Eli proved to be a very friendly person to many, including all those subs and all those City inspectors. Elijah would later say, 'The more money people make from you...the lighter and lighter your skin becomes.'

The Ocean View project was spectacular in every way. And it was an education in and of itself about the kind of money people were willing to pay for 'spectacular.' But then came the hitch.

The architect showed up at the job site one day to inform Elijah that Peter Berlesconi was divorcing his wife, and that the project had to stop until the court issued its ruling on a final divorce settlement.

"And there's another hitch," the architect told him. "There won't be any more money until the court finalizes its ruling...and even after that, everything's unknown."

Eli was concerned for his subs. "This is a problem. There are subs who have finished their work and are waiting for payment. You know how it is for these guys. They can't go without pay. Family. Kids. They work just to keep it all together."

"I know, Elijah. Sht happens."

Elijah informed all the subs who had not yet done their work that there was a hold on the job. Then he had the hard job of calling the subs who were waiting to be paid. The blowback was fierce.

"Hey...c'mon, Elijah. We don't deal with those people. That's all up to you. We do the work, and we expect to be paid. Should we just show up in the middle of the night and tear our work out of the walls?"

Elijah asked all the subs whose work was complete, but who had not been paid yet, to meet him at the site after work the next day.

"Listen up, guys. We're all in bind, here. They pay me, and I pay you. It's a system of trust. Somebody breaks the chain of trust...and we're all screwed. And that's what's happened, here.

"I've made a little extra money on this job so far. But I give more of a sht about you guys than I do about the money. It's not enough money to pay all of you all that you're owed, so this is my plan...but it only works if *all* of you agree.

"I take what money I've made, and everybody gets a part of it according to how much you're owed. That can happen tomorrow.

"I sell my fancy car, and all *that* money gets proportionally split between you...according to how much you're owed. That could take a week, or so.

"Meanwhile, I go to the bank with my contract, and I take out a loan against the contract being finished. If that goes through, I pay the rest of everything you're owed. That could take two or three weeks.

"If all that works, you're all paid. But then I've got nothing. So, I need something in return."

All the subs seemed pretty upbeat at that point.

"I need a personal pledge from each and every one of you that you will stick by me...and put my projects at the top of your list in the future. We all know I can't enforce it, so it's an honor pledge. I'm showing you how much I appreciate you being on my team. I just need to know that you're onboard with me, as well."

'Here, here's,' went up all around. Chants began. "Eli...Eli...Eli..." Elijah knew it meant nothing until he needed one of them, but Elijah was always looking toward an unknown future. A good one, he expected. And he knew he had a back-up that meant he wouldn't really have to go the bank for a loan.

Elijah used the time away from his Ocean View contract learning curve to get three more contracts for houses. He had started all three by the time he got the call from the former Mrs. Berlesconi.

"Mr. Washington? My name is Nancy Grant. I was recently granted a divorce from Peter Berlesconi. In the divorce settlement, I got the house we were building on Ocean View. Can we meet to discuss that?"

Elijah said, "I'm sorry to hear about your divorce. Would the job site be a good place for you to meet me?"

"I don't know how else to say this, Mr. Washington, except to say it plainly. My ex-husband is a lawyer, and he out-lawyered my lawyer. I got screwed. Our marriage lasted a year and a half, and the only thing I got was this unfinished mess...and no cash to finish it. Before I talk to a realtor, I wanted to speak with you about what I should expect to get for it. I feel like a fish in a pool of sharks."

Elijah knew how to speak plainly. "You're right to think you're a fish surrounded by sharks. If you put this project on the market in it's unfinished state, you'll get a small portion of the money already put into it. I'll finish it for somebody else...if they hire me...which they would, since I know the whole plan by now. I'll get paid the same as if you and your husband finished it. So it makes no difference to me how it moves forward. But before I counsel you on real estate swindlers, I have some burdensome news to add to your dilemma.

"When payments stopped coming on this contract, I had to pay subs that had already done their work. I paid them out of my own pocket. I need that much from you, at least. If you don't have it, I need to put a lien on the deed so I can get paid before the place is sold."

Nancy Grant just felt the feather weight of the straw that broke the camel's back. She was so embarrassed, but she couldn't hold back the tears. She bowed her head into her hands and started sobbing. Elijah excused himself to go out to the Porta-Potty so as to not add to her embarrassment.

He gave her a good long while to finish her tears and to wipe up her face. When he came back in, she seemed recovered. She was walking around the unfinished floor plan.

"If anybody would give me credit, I could finish the place and *then* sell it. You said you would finish the work as long as you were getting paid?"

Elijah was glad she had sense. "That's sounds like your best plan, even though construction loans are unnecessarily high. What's your credit situation?"

Nancy said, "I've never borrowed money for anything. And I have no extra income. But would that matter if the bank has this place for collateral?"

"If you have no income...and you got no cash in your divorce...please forgive me for asking...but...are you staying with friends?...do you have a place to live?"

Nancy Grant turned her head away in modesty. Elijah thought she was turning her head away in embarrassment. "I'm sorry I asked." Elijah kept looking at her to make sure she was OK. "But there was a reason I asked."

Elijah wasn't always comfortable when his head started spinning...because he was never sure what number on the spinning wheel he would land on. But his head was spinning, so he threw the marble.

"Construction loans only make *bankers* rich. I might know a different way for you to get the money...but I have some more questions, first."

Nancy was curious. "Yes?"

"I worked on this site for five straight months until we had to quit. I saw and met with your architect and your husband many times. All the time, really. But I never saw you. Were you disinterested? Did you not care about this project? I mean, it's a spectacular house on a spectacular property. A home 'fit for a queen,' as some might say. Where were you...and why weren't you here, helping?"

Nancy collected her thoughts for a moment. "I don't feel like I know you well enough to tell you this...but I appreciate your direct question.

"The answer, if I don't sound too 'victimy' in saying it, is that my husband excluded me from every facet of his life. That's why we got divorced. I remember the day he said he bought this property. I was thrilled. But he told me he couldn't get me into the meeting with the architect, and that he would tell me how it all worked out. That was my life with him. He would tell me how it all worked out...afterwards."

Elijah knew everybody had their own problems. He'd heard worse. But he also wanted to see this showpiece in his own portfolio in the end.

"At the risk of sounding anything like your ex-husband, I can tell you how this can all work out. The difference will be that I will want your involvement at the same level that your architect and your husband had."

She didn't really like the sound of open ended proposals. "What do you have in mind?"

"I have access to a funding source that could finish this project. But you would have to sign off on all the money being put in so that I get it back when the house sells…plus my contractor fees. Your involvement in the day-to-day will familiarize you with the finish details. That will be crucial when it comes time to sell because you will be a more effective salesperson than any realtor…everything will be 'lovely' because everything will have been finished to your specs. In other words, if somebody is going to buy the Queen's estate, wouldn't they want to buy it from the Queen, herself?"

"You're quite the salesman, Mr. Washington. Were you perceiving that I was needing to be the Queen in my own story? Pull me up out of the gutter, if you will? Is there a con somewhere in this plan of yours?"

Elijah had no idea what she was talking about. "This place is a palace. Palaces go for short money because they only get sold out of desperation. I mean, who would move out of a palace unless they *had* to?

"I can tell by the way you dress and carry yourself, and by how articulate you are that, even amongst whatever temporary insecurities you're feeling, you have an innate sense about what will work in a project like this. Design-wise. This will take a time commitment. That's why I asked earlier about your living situation."

"The truth is, Mr. Washington, I took a waitress job near where I live and work. That's how I keep my head above water."

"You took a waitress job near where you live and *work*? Isn't the waitress job the place where you work?"

"The waitress job and the room I rent are in the only affordable neighborhood in L.A. And, honestly, I wouldn't have it any other way."

"Do you mind me asking where there's an affordable neighborhood in L.A.?"

"Skid Row, Mr. Washington. Skid Row." She was staring at him for a reaction. "Do you still think I'm the Queen in my own movie, Mr. Washington?"

Elijah felt he had been pulled off track from his idea. "I sense an excitable personality inside you. Excitement is contagious. I'm only saying that I can see you infecting a buyer...in all the best ways. In other words, so that the outcome is what works out best for you."

Nancy said, "I'm not used to being thought of as a contributor. Thank you for *that*. If I owe you a therapist's fee, you'll have to add it to my bill at the end."

Eli said, "I don't know what you're talking about, but if you're saying I should line up the financing, and that you're in as a partner to make design decisions...then please say, 'I'm in."

In Nancy's eyes, this was all too easy. It was outside of anything she had anticipated coming from this meeting.

Elijah didn't understand the pause. "Is this all too easy for you? Is it too far outside anything you expected to come from this meeting?"

Nancy was stunned into a state of 'frozen' when she realized he was reading her very thoughts. So she gave up. She quit.

"I'm in."

Over the course of the following months, Nancy discovered her true calling. Interior design. She was excited to wake up every morning and do her work on Skid Row and her waitress job. Those jobs were now augmented by buying trips to some of the finest interior design boutiques from downtown L.A. to Beverly Hills. Then by five o'clock, she'd show up at the job site for her daily meeting with Elijah. There, she would drop off what she had bought and make a list of all the buying she had to do for the Ocean View property. When her buying list was complete for that day, she would get the money she needed to make the purchases. The money was always in cash. Green cash.

She and Elijah worked themselves into a relationship of trust. He trusted her to make design decisions that would sell. She trusted him to trust her. The money never seemed to be an issue.

Near the end of the Ocean View project, Nancy confided in Eli. "I was raised with all these subtle cues to think of Black people as 'less than.' I didn't realize the extent of the effect that had on me until I started working with you. Whenever I would see these wonderful characteristics you have, I would hear a voice in my head saying, '...but he's Black.' I had no idea how to undo that. But I think I've figured it out, now.

"The more time I've spent with you, the more quiet that voice has become...to the point that it's gone. It's even affected the way I see all my Black friends that I work with. That feeling of, 'is that Black man going to kill me?' has gone. When I see a Black person on the street, I get a warm and tingly feeling, because...well...thoughts of you remind me that 'Black' doesn't mean 'scary.'"

Eli was impressed by her self-awareness. "I've felt our friendship for quite a while, now, also."

Nancy said, 'Well...what are we going to do about it?"

Eli fumbled and punted. "We'll just have to see, I guess."

The after-hours meetings at the job site had long since transitioned from Elijah approving Nancy's design ideas to Eli getting a list of what she needed money for...and handing over the cash for the next round of purchases.

"Why do you convert all your bank loan money into cash? An auditable record is going to be necessary to write off all these expenses against the eventual sale price of the house. Is the business side of your business even something you know much about?"

Eli awkwardly confessed, "I've been unsure for some time now about whether I want to see this project on the open market. It's too nice to let go of. I want to talk to you about not selling it."

Nancy was alarmed. "But, Elijah, how will you get paid for all your work...and how will *I* get paid?"

Eli, once again, didn't have the right answer. He didn't have any answer. "Following a gut feeling is the downfall of every gambler in the world...so you're right. I shouldn't think like that."

Nancy asked, "What is your gut telling you, Mr. Gambler?"

Eli just blurted it out. "That you should marry me."

Nancy's face turned bright red...but she didn't step back. "Can I get back to you on that?"

At their next meeting, Nancy had a cassette tape in her hand. Eli saw it and said, "Brought your favorite music to a business meeting?"

Nancy walked over to the ever-present battery powered boombox that was older and more beat-up than it needed to be. She put the cassette tape in. She pressed where the missing 'Play' button used to be. Then she walked over to Elijah.

Aretha Franklin started filling the nearly-finished house with her angelic voice. "Looking out on the morning rain, I used to feel so uninspired..."

Nancy put her arms around Elijah and started slow dancing with him. He welcomed this new addition to their business meetings.

At just the right point in the song, Nancy pulled her head away from Elijah's chest to look him in the eye. She mouthed the words as Aretha belted them out, "Cause you make me feel, You make me feel, You make me feel like a natural woman."

When the song ended, Elijah wouldn't let go of her.

Ever, it turned out.

3.47 NIGHTS IN WHITE SATIN

Elijah had become a favorite in the City offices of Pacific Palisades. Everyone seemed happy to see him walk in whenever he had business to do there.

One day, he went to his friend who was the City Clerk and asked for an unusual favor. Marissa was so happy to do it.

One evening after work, when the Ocean View property was nearing completion, Marissa drove up to interrupt the design meeting between two lovebirds. She walked in with papers in her hand. Nancy was taken aback about why the City Clerk was there.

Elijah, holding Nancy's hand, walked the two women down below the swimming pool and terrace, and over the newly laid lawn, until they were under the sprawling canopy of the Chestnut Tree that had been saved throughout the construction.

Elijah knelt down on one knee and looked up to Nancy. "I needed a witness to make it official...will you marry me?"

Marissa's paperwork made it official.

Elijah and Nancy spent their first night together in their nearing-completion house. The master bed had been hand selected for what Nancy would have wanted for herself. Right down to pillows and the linens.

Having watched Elijah work over the previous months had caused Nancy to have a constant question somewhere in the back of her mind. Nancy wondered...and would always wonder...if Elijah was a genius, or was he just the luckiest man alive. She couldn't believe how everything just seemed to work out for him.

For his part, Elijah felt he was the luckiest man alive.

3.48 MEMORIES LIGHT THE CORNERS OF MY MIND

The next day, Agent John Watkins asked, "You said at one point that you and McNally had a bond that went back to 'Superman School' because both of you were targets...but for different reasons. How were you each targets?"

Eli explained. "Superman School is the first round of weeding out the wannabes from the committed and the able. It's where you go right after Basic Military Training in San Antonio. And it's right there, in plain view for all the new recruits in Basic Training to see. Guys in red berets running around the Base in groups, chanting and singing. Climbing ropes and kinking ass. To the uninitiated, that was Superman School.

"The training 'pipeline,' as we called it, is two years long...*if* you don't get sent back for re-training in one of the disciplines.

"The dropout rates vary by each training nodule, but overall, eighty percent to ninety percent of volunteers wash out. It's intense. And it all starts with Superman School in San Antonio.

"McNally had been recruited into the Air Force as a Nuclear Weapons Specialist. We were in the same Basic Training Squadron.

"Nuclear Weapons recruitment earns the recruiters all kinds of bonuses...and, yes. I'm talking cash money. It's because of how high a person has to score on their pre-enlistment exams to qualify for Nuclear Weapons.

"So, as Basic Trainees, we see these guys in constant motion doing the most amazing feats of physical fitness all around the base. The Maroon Berets. Both McNally and I said we wanted to do *that*. To *be* that.

"There's a day in Basic Training called 'Career Day' when all the Trainees speak to a personnel officer to either choose or to confirm their career training path.

"I said I wanted to go to Superman School, and so it was. But when Scottie said *he* wanted to go to Superman School, the Lieutenant Personnel Officer said, 'Your career training has already been assigned. You'll be going to Wyoming for Nuclear Weapons training.'

"McNally said that he changed his mind. That he wanted Superman School. The Personnel Officer closed her file and called for the next Trainee to come forward.

"McNally put his hand on his closed personnel file and told her he wasn't told by the recruiter that he couldn't change his mind. The Personnel Officer was unmoved and signaled for the next Trainee.

"McNally pointed to the telephone on her desk and asked her to slide it over to him, that he was going to call his Congressman to file a complaint about false recruitment, and to be let out of the Air Force altogether. I should have known at that moment that he was going to be trouble.

"The Personnel Officer picked up the phone, herself, and called the Superman School. When she hung up, she gave McNally a disgusted look and told him he was in the next Superman School class. Then she said what you should never say to a determined person. She told him that when he washed out of the PJ pipeline, Wyoming would still be waiting for him."

"Sounds like McNally was pretty strong-willed?"

"We all were. Those of us that made it through the pipeline."

Watkins asked, "You said you were both targets?"

"Yeah. Neither the drill sergeants nor the other candidates liked having a Black man around. There was a hostility toward the idea that Blacks wanted to 'break into' White-owned property."

Watkins said, "I'm familiar with that attitude."

"So, what it translated to was me getting special attention. Not the positive kind."

"Why was McNally targeted?"

"His size. He was the smallest candidate that they allowed in Superman School. Every day, first thing, the drill sergeants would line us all up to watch them put McNally on the scales to measure his height. Then they would curse when the reading was always the same. Five foot, eight inches. The other candidates took their cue from the drill sergeants. Made me wonder if the drill sergeants weren't putting the other candidates up to it."

"How was McNally harassed?"

"Like me, it was a lot of extra attention. More push ups. More trips around the track. More reps climbing up the ropes. Couple of extra trips through the mud belly-ditches under the barbed wire. More 'face time,' if you can picture what that means in the context of a drill sergeant."

Watkins asked, "That all? Sounds like all those things would actually make you *stronger* candidates."

"It went beyond that. Our fellow candidates would conspire to give McNally blanket parties at least once a week."

"What's a 'blanket party?'"

"That's when a group of candidates would throw a blanket over a sleeping fellow candidate and...well, I don't how else to put it...beat the sht out of him. The blanket was for anonymity and to keep the fist lacerations and bruising to a minimum. Plus, the blanket muffled the noise."

"What about *you*, Eli? Blanket parties, too?"

"That was what ended up bonding my relationship with McNally. Word had spread that they were going to give me a 'see-ya-later' blanket party. That was one designed to be the end of a candidate's candidacy. Create some permanent damage. McNally came to me and gave me a heads up. It kept me vigilant...right up to the moment of the 'surprise' attack.

"But what really sealed the relationship between me and McNally was, when the party began, McNally sprang from his bunk and started tearing my attackers off the pile and throwing some pretty nasty punches...that didn't have the cushioning of a blanket.

"The next morning I was unscathed. But several of the guys that McNally had gotten ahold of had some 'splaining to do about their cuts and bruises to the drill sergeants. Everyone kept their mouths shut...but that was the end of the blanket parties."

Watkins asked, "So, you both graduated from Superman School?"

"We both entered the 'pipeline' together."

"What all was involved in the 'pipeline?'"

"Two years of the most grueling training in the most broad-ranging skill sets you can imagine...all designed around saving people's lives.

"We did line jumping with the Army Airborne in Georgia. We did free-fall parachuting with pilots in New Mexico. We did dive training with Navy Seals in the Florida panhandle. We did moutaineering training with the Green Berets. Sniper training outside Quantico with FBI Hostage Rescue Team candidates. We did survival training in the wilderness of Washington State, the deserts of Nevada, the jungles of Panama. We did medic training with Army corpsmen in Texas. Nobody in any branch of the military is as trained as a ParaJumper...a PJ."

"So, you and McNally both made it through the 'pipeline' together?"

"Yes. He developed a reputation for his interest in all things green, and I acquired the nickname 'The Chocolate Rifleman' for being the number one shooter and the only ghillie-suit maker that none of the instructors could find in Sniper School."

"Sounds like half your enlistment commitment was training."

"That's *exactly* right. Two years out of a four year commitment. Add two tours in Vietnam to that...and that's it. Time's up. All of a sudden...it's career choice time."

"You and McNally both chose to get out?"

"McNally went his own way, but Doctor Green from our PJ squad and I got out and hit the road together. And Doctor Green's intimate knowledge of all things green would be a boon to our existence."

Watkins remembered that Elijah had just said that McNally had an interest in all things green.

Elijah leaned forward and jokingly snapped at Watkins, "Hey! You're not a *cop*, are you? You know you have to tell me if you are."

Watkins burst out in a rare laugh. "Yes," while he continued laughing. "I *am* a cop!" Watkins toned down his laugh a bit. "But, why do you care? I'm here on my own. *Not* as an FBI agent. You know that."

Eli was still half joking...but only half. "I have a wonderful tale to tell that I've never told a living soul. Not even my wife. But maybe it's time to get it off my chest."

Watkins asked, "Does it pertain to the rescue mission of Captain Mineau? Because that's why I'm here."

Elijah said in somber seriousness, "I feel I can confide in you. And I've always felt that I had to tell someone. Mostly because it's a great story. But my concern about it being shared is...well...there's a concern for my family...they're the foundation of my reputation as an upstanding member of my affluent, all-White community. Plus, I'm an office holder. If word ever got out about my 'farming' days, it would only confirm their worst fears...that they've had a criminal nggr in their midst this whole time...just as they always suspected."

The laughing and the joking had disappeared. Neither one of them could chuckle at that uncomfortable truth about being Black in America.

Watkins asked, "So...you and this 'Doctor Green' got out? Headed out together?"

"We were discharged in San Antonio where it all began. We bought an old jalopy and some camping gear. Our first big stop was Big Bend National Park.

"You know, John, Vietnam has to be one the most beautiful countries on this earth. But when you get a chance to see the natural wonders here...within our own borders...words can't describe."

Watkins asked, 'Does that mean you went through the Grand Canyon, too?"

"We did the Southwest desert with all the Native American culture, plus the Sand Monuments. We did the Grand Canyon. We detoured out of the Four Corners area to see the Eastern spine of the Rockies...cut west from Pike's Peak via some unimproved roads that were really meant for a Jeep. Then we started our trip up the coast from San Diego."

Watkins pivoted. "I'd love to hear about your adventures after you got out...as long as you're telling it to me as journalizer of your Vietnam experience...and not as 'cop.'"

Watkins thought to himself, 'The hardest part of deceiving someone...is that it requires deception.'

3.49 IT WAS THE BEST OF TIMES

At their next meeting, Elijah picked up where he'd left off.

"Doctor Green and I were discharged at Lackland Air Force Base in San Antonio...where it all began.

"We decided to buy an old jalopy and go camping in the woods for an open-ended amount of time. We had taken the slow route through Big Bend National Park, then throughout the desert Southwest.

"Our trip took us to the Pacific Coast Highway, from San Diego to SanFran, then heading toward Oregon and Washington.

"Above SanFran, we stopped to camp on a beach for a while at a place called Mattole Beach. It was long and wide and had dense gray sand. It was backed up by a small wooded bluff. We stayed there for a couple weeks, and then we decided to go inland to check out the scrub hills of the Emerald Triangle.

"A side road led us to a dirt road that led us to a tractor path that had a pull-off. We parked and hiked up into the rolling hills.

"We kept coming across patches of disturbed ground. And Doctor Green, having that botanical curiosity, was wondering if an animal was pulling up bushes in the area. Then we came across a marijuana plant that was dripping with resin. It was under the leaves and branches of a small shade tree.

"Doctor Green said, 'These don't grow in the wild. Somebody cultivated this.' Then you could see the lightbulb go off in his head. 'Hey, wait! All those patches of disturbed ground? Those were all pot plants. Cultivators would snip the buds off these plants, not pull them out of the ground.' You could see the picture coming into focus in his brain as he talked.

"It was law enforcement! They raided this place,' Doctor Green said.

"I asked, 'Why didn't they get this one?'

"Doctor Green said, 'Let's widen our hike in a spiral from here. I bet we find more undisturbed plants under shade trees. If we do, that means the 'destroyers of worlds' were being directed from a helicopter.' By God, if he wasn't right.

"We figured the farmers who planted and cultivated these plants were all in jail or had fled for their freedom. There was nobody around.

"We set up camp that night and made a plan to find and harvest all the buds…with a harebrained plan to take them somewhere and sell them…and that's how we became criminal pot privateers."

Watkins said, "If you step in horse manure everywhere you turn, it might be a sign from God that you should be in the fertilizer business."

Eli laughed. "That's exactly what happened to us."

Eli continued, "After our harvest, we had so many buds that the trunk of our jalopy wouldn't hold them all. We ended filling up the back seat with the rest of the harvest. Then we covered that load with a large plastic bag.

"We drove down the 'Five' with our windows open to find a buyer. I swear that every car we passed got a contact high just from the smell of the buds.

"We knew that if we got pulled over, we'd be in jail for the rest of our lives. But there was an adrenaline rush to it that was more positive than the adrenaline rush from face-to-face combat. Plus, we liked being criminals…as long as nobody knew. Should I be telling an FBI agent all this?"

Watkins laughed. "Proceed at your own risk." Watkins' laugh covered up the fact that he wasn't sure if he was joking.

Eli continued. "We randomly picked San Diego as a first stop because it was always warm there. We went to a random surfboard shop and asked the owner if he was a cop. He said, 'Fck, no. Why would you say that?' We told him we had harvested some pot buds and were looking for a buyer. He told us we were not too subtle…that we smelled like we'd been bathing in buds. Then he added that the 'bathing in buds' thing was a good idea. 'Marijuana soap. Dermal absorption.' He asked if we had a sample.

"Doctor Green brought in one bud from the back seat. The guy looked at it and his eyes got wide. He said he wasn't going to touch it because of all the resin on it. He asked how much we had to sell. We asked, 'Cash or credit?' He said, 'Cash.' We said we have a trunk and a backseat full.' He said, 'Let me see it.'

"We walked out to the car and pulled the plastic bag off the load in the rear seat area. His eyes got wide, again. He said, 'Credit.' We said, 'Fifty, fifty.' He said, 'OK. Come back in two weeks for the second fifty.'

"We thought we were selling the whole load for fifty-thousand and that we wanted fifty percent in cash…and that we'd take the other fifty percent later. It appeared we had under-priced it, and that our buyer had convoluted the fifty percent now, fifty percent later, into fifty thousand dollars now, and fifty thousand dollars later."

Watkins said, "Stepped in another pile of horse manure?"

Eli laughed, nodding his head. "He met us with a pickup truck at a very private location. He was alone. We took that as a sign of trust. The whole deal was not what we expected as newbies in the drug trade. But life is all about reading people, isn't it? He read something in us, and we had no idea how or what to read in him. We were just winging it."

Watkins was laughing under his breath. "More horse manure?"

Eli laughed. "Better to be lucky than good."

Watkins nodded.

Eli went on. "He had a horse stable muck shovel and two empty fifty-five gallon drums that had stickers for dry horse feed pellets on them, along with two locking lids.

"We emptied our car and loaded the two barrels into the bed of his truck. He brought us a woman's handbag that had five sets of ten thousand dollars wrapped in bank bands. He emptied the money into our hands. He kept the handbag. We agreed on a day and time, two weeks out, to meet him for the balance of the money.

He said, 'The balance payment is based on you re-supplying next year.' We hadn't thought about doing it again, but we said 'yes' just to be agreeable.

"We sold our jalopy to a junk yard because of the smell. They recognized the smell and laughed. We agreed to later replace the jalopy with two nondescript sedans of four to seven years old…just to not draw attention.

"We paid for a cab ride to a nice motel inland, in El Cajon, that had a nice swimming pool. Not too fancy. Separate rooms. Hot showers. Televisions. We ate at diners and middle-class restaurants. And we talked.

"We made some pacts about doing this again.

"No sampling the product. If we were going to do this as a business, we'd better have clear heads at all times.

"No spending money beyond subsistence. That was part of a whole list of things in order to not draw attention to us.

"A fifty-fifty money split, no matter what.

"And, that we would have an end date. Criminals that spend their whole lives doing crime end up spending their whole lives in jail. For my part, having some undefined future end date allowed me to spend all my free time thinking about what I was going to do next.

"We also agreed that, when we do it again, we would return to the farm country separately, and that neither of us would go back directly.

Stops along the way to look for a tail. By the end, we'd worked out a system of staggered stops and leaving so each of us could say what we were seeing for any signs of a tail. We thought it was all scientific. Diligent.

"So, we drove one of our new old cars to collect the second payment, then worked our way back north, staying in town-to-town motels for the winter. Come Spring, we were back in those Emerald hills of northern California.

"Doctor Green went to work cross-breeding and pruning for maximum THC production and the largest buds. He used one of our camouflaged tents as a green house to start new plants. He would put them out when they were ready. Everything we did was so nothing could be seen from the air.

"I bought a brand new Remington Model 700 bolt action rifle, and I stocked up on .308 caliber bullets. I also bought a re-load kit so I could re-load my own bullets to 165 grains each…for maximum knock-down power.

"I spent my days walking the perimeter, finding lookout locations, looking for signs of people traffic. My trusty Model 700 was always on my shoulder…along with enough ammunition so that I could, if need-be, stand my ground for a good long while against a good-sized army.

"I had outfitted the rifle with a 3x9, 40mm Redfield scope called 'The Illuminator.' It did a real good job in the early evening or the early morning when the light wasn't full."

Watkins thought, 'That sounds a lot like the rifle McNally had in his closet. Must have been what they were trained on in sniper school.'

"All the crews that would come in the fall every year to harvest and pack the product called me 'The Rifleman.' It was better than the nickname the PJ team had for me, 'The Chocolate Rifleman.' Those racist bastards. But it was an acknowledgement that I was the best sniper shot on the team.

"It became obvious in summer that our harvest was *not* going to fit in a car. We made plans for packaging and transportation that, in retrospect, were pretty funny.

"That first real harvest, we bought 5-gallon plastic buckets with lids from a paint supply store. We bought a used van from a painting company. We had to buy more buckets. And we went back to the paint company to buy a second van that they really weren't going to sell...but money talks.

"At the end of that harvest, we got a female roommate from the hippies who had come out from San Francisco to barter-work. She was a child, really, when she first stayed on with us. She ended up staying with us the rest of our years of farming. She was special." Elijah took a moment for a reflective pause.

"That first winter in the hills, we built a hidden cabin. We became dug in at that point, an indication that we were going to stay for a while. It was hidden and camouflaged because we had no interest in being entered onto the tax roles for a residence...or kicked off the land, had we been discovered...especially since we were pretty sure we were on public property. Nor did we want to solicit any visits from the Sheriff's helicopter crews.

"The helicopter patrols were from back in the day when Richard Nixon wanted to buy the votes of law enforcement from all over the country. Then Reagan super-charged Nixon's 'War On Drugs' that was just a way to funnel Federal bribe money to a constituency that could be counted on to vote. What a system, America. Wouldn't you say, John?"

John responded. "Hey! Don't knock it. I'm a big fan of Federal money being pumped into law enforcement."

Eli smiled to acknowledge where John was coming from.

"Every year, I would make a trip down to my old stomping grounds in Compton to spend a couple of days catching up with my ever-dwindling family. I would always go in August to get a couple kids for the fall harvest...kids who would benefit from getting out of the city. Sometimes gang problems. Sometimes family problems. Sometimes problems with the law. It was like taking them to summer camp, only it lasted all the way through the Fall...and I was the camp counselor.

"I taught them how to surveil the produce as it ripened for harvest, where all the plants were, how to spot signs of intruders...trained them how to use a radio. I never allowed any of them to carry a gun, even though I had one strapped over my shoulder during all surveillance tours. Nor did I allow them to sample the product.

"The two kids I brought up that last year...it turned out to be our last year as farmers...were younger and meaner than any I'd brought up before. They couldn't let go of that street thing of trying to make everybody afraid of you by your muscular swagger. 'The cock in the henhouse' syndrome.

"I figured that several months camping in the country air would relax those last two...but it didn't. The defense mechanism they couldn't shake was to never be friendly to anyone. It should have been a warning sign that neither one of them could open up. They stuck to themselves for the months they were in the hills with us.

"Delivery changed up every year. Painter's vans with product in 5-gallon paint buckets was insufficient for that third harvest.

"We bought two dually pickup trucks, along with open-caged towing trailers, so as to not make any CHiP's think we were hiding something. We had signs made for the trailers and the trucks with the name of a horse stable on it. It helped, also, that we were delivering to a horse stable in Del Mar, just up the coast from San Diego.

"We went to the 55-gallon horse pellet drums for packaging. And we never drove down the 'Five' together, always trying to never stand out or draw attention.

"That worked for two more seasons, then we needed a bigger truck.

"We had been doing some trading with the local farmer's coop. We noticed that bailed hay would come in or go out in hook-and-drop trailers with heavy locks on the doors. Fill a trailer, lock it up, pay a trucker to drop the trailer at a horse barn down South.

"We'd hire a hay-hauler to drive our packed and locked trailer down to Del Mar. Our distributor would hook on at the Del Mar horse stables and haul it away to wherever his local place was.

"We'd drive down separately to oversee the drop and to work out money with our distributor. Like us, those guys were in it as a business...so there was no using of the product going on.

"Our guy told us that the name for our product...his product...on the Street was 'Emerald City.' So, if you heard any of your FBI buddies talk about 'Emerald City' pot in the late 1970's or the early 1980's...that was our product."

John chuckled, "The only thing the FBI was talking about back then was cocaine from Colombia."

Eli acknowledged. "Yeah. Even with our secluded lives, we heard about that, too. But that seemed to us like more of a gangster business than what we were doing.

"We and our distributor understood the value of trust. He trusted us to deliver the quality and weight that we told him...we were meticulous about accuracy in both...and we trusted him to have the money on hand to pay us when they picked up the drop. There was no gangster nonsense going on.

"Young Bonnie, our roommate, became quite the hippie over the years. From the beginning, she took an interest in food prep. Plus, she helped us build the cabin.

"We built our outhouses for indoor access from the cabin, keeping large supplies of lime on hand. Pit vents to the outside, and an open eve roof over it for ventilation. The coldness in the winter made it a place where nobody dallied.

"We had no pressurized water, but I engineered some ram pumps that force-fed water from some springs, uphill, into a 2100 gallon cistern above the cabin. That fed our bathtub room in the cabin, plus our kitchen sink. All the waste water went into a grey-well we had dug and lined with brick.

"The indoor water was heated from an outdoor propane water heater that ran off 20-pound propane tanks. We had to rig a D-cell battery set-up to ignite the propane when it turned on. We also used that hot water to circulate through indoor radiators that were thermostatically controlled.

"Pretty good living for off-the-grid, wouldn't you say, John?"

John was nodding. "Who needs the utility companies when you have the know-how?"

"Yeah. Utility companies were just another way for 'the man' to find you.

"The 2100 gallon cistern also fed Bonnie's annual vegetable garden. Plus, I had run drip lines, lightly buried, to all the hidden pot plants. It was quite a system.

"We all did our own laundry on a washboard and used clotheslines for drying. A propane cook stove in the cabin was run off of twenty pound propane tanks, just like the water heater. We kept a good inventory of propane on hand. And we used alcohol lanterns when we needed night light in the cabin. The alcohol lamps were a fire hazard, so we were always careful with those."

John and Elijah both needed a bathroom break. There was a half-bath whose door was right there in the study.

John asked, "You keep mentioning the girl you said was a child. Bonnie. What was *that* all about?"

"Bonnie never said how old she was. Based on a later story she told, we figured out she was twelve years old when she stayed on to live with us. And we never knew her real name. She introduced herself as, 'You can call me Bonnie Lass.'

"We never asked about things like that because she would say that 'the new me can't live unless the old me is dead. Really dead. Can't-come-back-from-the-grave dead.' We felt there was something ominous there, so we never asked."

Eli's mind went to a memory of Bonnie. "There was a song we had on cassette tape that she would play in our battery powered boombox. The song was tragic and melancholy. It was called, *At Seventeen*. She said the world that was described in that song was a world she never wanted to experience...which was why she said that she never wanted to leave our cabin in the wilderness." Just to talk about Bonnie made Eli re-live more memories of her.

"She said it was important for people to feel comfortable with the people they interacted with. She said she could see when people were wearing protective body armor, or more casual clothing, or even if they were totally naked.

"She said that during conversations with people, she could see them putting on or taking off more clothes. She said she knew when people were lying because she could see them putting on make-up and jewelry. She was a kick. She could also be pretty intense, sometimes. She turned out to be the best part of that outlaw lifestyle we had made for ourselves."

John asked, "How long was she with you?"

"To the end. Eight?..nine years? Time was hard to keep track of back then."

"You said she became a hippie. Free love?...and all that?"

"O.K. I see where this is going." Eli leaned back in his chair.

"There was a day, well into our communal living arrangement, when Doctor Green and I were cleaning up after a meal. Bonnie was taking her nightly bath.

"When she came out from her bath, she asked us both to sit down. That she wanted to have a serious talk with us.

"She said that her relationship with Doctor Green made her feel safe for him to be the father of her children, and that she wanted to have a baby, and that she was ready because she felt she could raise a child to grow in the wonder of innocence...grow to be a well-balanced adult who was happy to live a life of contentment."

John was doing some age number crunching in his head. "How long was it into your living arrangement that she had this talk with you and Doctor Green?"

"Calendars were nonexistent when we were in the farming business, but there were usually one or two times a year, usually around product delivery time, when one of us would say, 'Hey, can you believe it? It's 1979! Where does time go?' Or, 'It's 1980, a new decade!' But we didn't match things that happened with time. My guess is that Bonnie had been with us seven years or so when she made this decision. Maybe it was her eighth year with us."

John asked, "So, she chose to have children with Doctor Green? Had she been sexually active with both of you?"

"Hey, c'mon, man. We weren't child molesters. She was a virgin to both of us when she sat us down for that little 'family' chat.

"She said she wanted me to hear it to find out if I had any objections, given that we all lived together. She didn't want this decision to make me feel like I was the odd man out, the third wheel."

John was nodding his head. "Oh, I see now."

"I told her that I'd seen, over the years, how she and Doctor Green learned and grew from and with each other, and that I thought it was a match made in heaven...but that I'd appreciate it if they held the sounds of their joyous unions to a minimum whenever I was around. Which they did, seemingly without effort, as far as I could tell.

"She said she wanted Doctor Green to start sleeping in her room...starting that night...*if* he agreed to the relationship.

"He said he was already in the relationship, and that he was ready and desiring a family, also. He wasn't as flat about it as I make him sound. He was visibly overjoyed by this surprise...which I considered more of an ambush.

"I don't know, and didn't want to know, why she didn't come up pregnant for a year or two. But when she did, they both seemed to take it like it was the way it was all planned."

John and Eli were both starting to shift around in their seats from sitting too long.

"By the way, here's another remarkable thing about those two. It was like they became one. I don't necessarily mean like in a marital way. I mean...it was like they became the same person.

"I didn't think about it much at the time, but it got to where, if I had a question for Doctor Green and Bonnie was standing nearby, I'd just ask her. And visa-versa. No matter what the question.

"Nancy and I have the best possible relationship I can ever imagine two people having. But it's not like *that*."

John was chuckling. "I, too, have what I would consider 'the ideal marriage'. But you're right. It's not like *that*."

Just then, the door to the study opened. It was Eli's granddaughter, Christine, and Christine's boyfriend, Robert Smith.

"Hi, Grampi!" she announced cheerfully. Christine reminded John of a White version of his own daughter. Beautiful and self-confident.

"Grammi asked us to come and tell you that you've been in here too long and to get you for supper. She wants to know if your friend wants to stay to eat with us."

Elijah and John were both standing by then.

Eli said, "John, I'd like you to meet my granddaughter, Christine, and her fiancé, Robert Smith. Robert runs a couple of the divisions for my son-in-law over at the construction company."

John looked up at the tall and confident Robert, and thought, 'I'll bet he was a star basketball player in High School, and even played in college, but when he realized he was not big enough to play in the NBA, he got into the construction business.' Watkins noticed Robert's neatly trimmed, squared-off Afro that reminded Watkins of Muhammad Ali. Watkins shook the hand of Robert Smith with a friendly, "Nice to meet you."

If Watkins' eye contact with Robert had not caused such an upward strain in his neck, Watkins might not have let the gold band with the stamped initials 'RS' on Robert's finger go unnoticed. If Christine had not been so bubbly, he might have noticed something familiar about Robert's nose and teeth. Maybe.

"We *have* been in here too long...and I have a plane to catch. But I'll tell your Grammi Nancy on the way out that I appreciate her invitation."

Christine asked her Grampi Eli, "What have you two been talking about for so long?"

Eli said, "John is writing a piece about the rescue mission on Captain Mineau's downed airplane." Eli turned to John Watkins. "Christine and her mother come with Nancy and me to the reunions every five years."

John was nodding, still looking into the eyes of the handsome mixed-race couple. "That's wonderful. I've met Lt. Col. Mineau and his lovely wife, Lilly. From what the former Captain Mineau tells me, your grandfather is a big reason why Captain Mineau is even alive."

Chrisitine loved it when other people spoke well of her grandfather. "I agree with Captain Mineau. Grampi is one of the good guys."

Robert piped in, "Grampi Eli wouldn't even have been there to save Captain Mineau if it weren't for tokenism. Grampi Eli was only allowed into his unit as a Helen Mayer. But he fooled them. He was still Black when he got out."

A mental bell dinged in John Watkins' mind. 'That's the *second* time in my life that I've heard someone say the name of Helen Mayer.'

While driving back to LAX, John Watkins was thinking about the adventure of Eli being in the pot business for all those years.

John had chosen the FBI out of Harvard Law because he had wanted to live a life with some excitement in it. But after that meeting with Eli, John Watkins realized that Eli, in addition to his military experiences and his high risk business adventure, had taken excitement to a whole other level in this life. And John admired him for that.

At supper, Grampi Eli turned to Robert. "Who is Helen Mayer?"

3.50 HEY LITTLE GIRL IS YOUR DADDY HOME

Agent John Watkins flew back to L.A. about a week after his previous meeting.

He opened this meeting with Elijah by asking, "You told me about you and Doctor Green taking in a twelve year old Bonnie, and how she grew into an intimate relationship with Doctor Green. But how was it that she showed up at your place with the San Francisco hippies to begin with? Did she have a family member that was part of the counterculture commune?"

Eli liked remembering Bonnie. "For years, Bonnie was private about things that happened before we met her. But from the first day she stayed with us, she was very open about 'herself.' In the present.

"I told you that Doctor Green had been affected by his combat experience? In World War One they called it 'Shell Shock.' In World War Two they called it 'Battle Fatigue.' In Vietnam they called it 'Post Vietnam Syndrome.' Today we know it as 'PTSD.' Post Traumatic Stress Disorder. They all refer to the same thing. A Ghost Soldier.

"Doctor Green had become a Ghost Soldier, a prime candidate for hard drugs. Heroin was the drug of choice in Vietnam…imported to us soldiers from right here in the U.S. of A. Did you know that, John?

"But when he would disappear into that 'thousand yard stare,' that 'deer in the headlights' vacancy, his medicine became his obsession with learning new things. In particular, his previous interest in botany. That's how he got the name, 'Doctor Green.' He would disappear into his work to the point where everyone in the unit would call out things to him to see if he could even hear us. He would be gone...somewhere else."

John Watkins kept up with his mental notes. 'Doctor Green was a member of the PJ Search and Rescue unit. And Eli has said before that Scott McNally was damaged in the head...Humpf. Pretty sure Doctor Green and Scott McNally are one in the same.' Watkins' confidence in uncovering the truth about McNally and Elijah's relationship was bolstered by the growing knowledge that Elijah was not a competent deceiver.

"Well, then along came our 12-year-old little sister...and guess what? She would do the same thing. Blank out. Disappear into herself. But immediately upon staying with us, she started doing things that were clearly designed to fix whatever was going on inside her.

"When we would travel for supplies, she would go to hippie stores and buy books on foods, and herbs, and meditation practices, including Sanskrit writings. Plus, movement disciplines like Yoga and Tai Chi. She was never self-conscious around us about immersing herself in those things, and we just let her do her own thing without comment.

"She was a great roommate because we didn't have to take care of her. She had open access to our little cash box, and if she needed new clothes as she grew, she bought them. If she needed sanitary napkins, she would buy sanitary napkins. She was really in charge of herself in every way.

"It took her no time to be the meal planner, making ingredient lists and buying what she didn't pull from her garden. Did I tell you she was also a gardener? That was another overlapping area of interest with

Doctor Green. He told me that he actually learned things about plants from *her*. She thrived from learning all those things...and doing them. That was another thing she and Doctor Green had in common.

"I'm sure you know, John, that when a child grows up in a parent's house, it's hard to notice their day by day growth. That's why parents put pencil marks on the door jambs, right? For the kids, of course, but also for us.

"That's what Bonnie's growth was like. We saw her and interacted with her every day, so we didn't really notice how different she had become in those first three or four years. But then one day, Doctor Green and I both commented to each other, 'Do you remember how Bonnie was when she first got here? How she would disappear into herself a lot?' It's like we woke up one day and she wasn't doing that anymore.

"Doctor Green said to her at supper one evening, right after she first joined us, 'Bonnie, I see some of your Yoga and Tai Chi and other body movement stuff you're learning. May I do it with you?' She said, 'Of course.'

"She was a little instructive with Doctor Green at first. But after a short time, they just became in sync with each other. And then, like it had happened with Bonnie, a couple years or so went by, and all of a sudden I noticed that Doctor Green wasn't disappearing into himself anymore.

"The Yoga and all that body movement stuff morphed into dance. We had the battery operated boombox blaring out music whenever any of us were in the house. She started getting Doctor Green into the whole dance moves thing. She took it so far as to buy books with dance steps printed in them.

"That led to new types of music I had never heard before. A lot of Latin type stuff.

"When I would see them doing it, their bodies were like watching a snake sliver around, only vertically. I could see that it was great exercise...plus, it didn't take long for me to figure out that it was part of their healing therapy. But I never got into it. Despite what people say about Black people being able to dance...maybe my DNA isn't pure."

John was chuckling. "I know. Dancing never worked for me, either."

Elijah nodded with a shared chuckle. "Then came the time that Bonnie made her announcement to us that she wanted to start a family, and that she wanted Doctor Green to be the father of her children."

John asked, "What about the San Francisco hippies? How did she get in with them? I mean, they're the ones who brought her to your place, right?"

Eli girded himself for the long story.

"It took a bunch of years for her to talk about that, and I'm glad it did. We say these days that you 'can't unsee' something. I'm glad she was stable within herself, and with us, before she ever brought it up. And *she* brought it up. We didn't ask.

"From things she said, both Doctor Green and I believed she grew up as a young child somewhere in the Central Valley, up north from here. But she never named the town.

"Her mother didn't work and, although Bonnie didn't remember anything about her father, her father was not in the picture when she was about three years old. She knew about being three years old because that's when her stepfather moved in with her mother...she would say 'my stepfather,' but she also said the guy, Chuck, and her mother were never married.

"She remembered the first time he came into her bed at night...because of the searing pain he caused. She would later have a saying, 'trauma enhances memory.' But I'm here to tell you one thing about Bonnie. She never wallowed in *anything*.

"She said that she knew her mother was on the other side of the wall in their bedroom, so she assumed her mother was part of it.

"She remembered it happened almost every night for a long

time...because she considered it a part of her bedtime routine. Her mother would bathe her, slip her into a short nighty with no panties on, and tell her to go on into bed and wait for Chuck. She said it was like waiting for a spanking with a belt. A nightly punishment.

"She said that once he was fully penetrating her, he stopped coming in every night. But she said that was worse...because she would have to lie there and wait to find out if he was coming in. She said it was a recurring nightmare when she would go to sleep, thinking he wasn't coming in, and then he would wake her up, do his thing, and then go back to her mother's bed."

John was horrified...and not comfortable hearing this story.

"By the time she was in school, she said she would look at the other girls and feel bad for them for having to go through this, too. She believed it was part of being a girl, and that what Chuck was doing was part of being a boy. She remembered thinking that girls are born to do what the boys want.

"She said that he would take her whenever he wanted, but always at night when she was in bed. That is until right around when she turned twelve. That's when she got her first period. She said she was so glad to have had sex education in school so she knew what it was when it happened...that her mother had never talked to her about it.

"The night of her first period, he didn't come into her room. She had used a washcloth to try and keep the sheets clean. She said she didn't know what she would say to Chuck if he *had* come in.

"Chuck was always gone to work when she had breakfast before school, so that next morning she told her mother that she was bleeding. Her mother told her she would buy her some Tampax.

"She said she told her mother that's not why she was telling her. She was telling her because she knew that she could get pregnant now, and that Chuck would have to stop coming into her bed at night.

"She said her mother reached back and slapped her hard across the face and told her to watch what she said...that Chuck was the reason they had a roof over their heads...and that if she didn't watch her mouth, she was going to tell Chuck what she said. Bonnie said that she knew that would not be good for her newly minted twelve year old self.

"She said that she told her mother that she was not willing to get pregnant and have a baby. Her mother told her that if Chuck wanted her to have his child, then that's what she would do.

"Bonnie said that she couldn't believe what she was hearing, but that it was a moment of revelation and clarity for her. She saw that her mother was a weak or soulless human being who had no understanding of the sovereignty of a person over their own self.

"She said that the second revelation she had was even worse. It was that she saw herself as that same person that she saw in her mother, and that's why she had let this man do this to her all her life, back to her first memory. And that she would hate herself the rest of her life if she didn't do something about it that day. A 'now or never' kind of thing, she said. It was so sad to both me and Doctor Green to hear her blame herself, but we didn't burden her with that. We figured that by then, she'd figured all that out.

"Bonnie went to school that day after her first period, but the fuming rose up inside her to the point where she knew she would have to do something high risk, with a high potential for negative consequences, in order to get out of her hell.

"She said that Chuck took his pants off every day after work and hung them on the back of his kitchen chair. Then he would go into his bedroom for a short nap...and that he always left his wallet in the back pocket of his pants, hanging on the chair.

"That afternoon when she got home from school, she changed into playground clothes and went outside until Chuck came home. She gave him ten or fifteen minutes to take his pants off and go lie down. Then she came into the house, quiet as she was always required to be.

"She got a drink of water from the kitchen sink and waited for her mother to not be looking. Then she lifted Chuck's wallet out of his pants, opened it up, and withdrew the cash. Then she folded the wallet back over and replaced it into his pocket.

"She stuffed the cash in her own pants pocket and went back out to play until supper. Only she didn't go back out to play.

"Her school bus went by the bus station every day, so she knew where it was. She immediately started walking in that direction.

"Standing outside the bus terminal, she pulled the money out of her pocket and counted it. It was one-hundred dollars. Five twenty dollar bills.

"She went into the bus terminal and asked the attendant when the bus to Redding was coming. He told her, so she went back outside and took a seat to wait. Only she wasn't going to Redding. Nor was she waiting for the Redding bus. She was going to wait for the San Francisco bus, but she wanted the attendant to tell anybody who came asking that, yes, he saw the young girl, and that she went to Redding.

"The San Francisco bus pulled up. She looked around for the attendant and didn't see him, so she boarded the bus.

"She gave the bus driver a twenty dollar bill, and he gave her eight dollars change. And that's how she got to San Francisco.

"She said it was about eight o'clock at night when she de-boarded at the Golden Gate terminal in downtown. It was dusk out, and the impending darkness had woken all the hippies out of their beds. They were beginning to fill the streets for their nightly ritual of tuning in, turning on, and dropping out.

"A hippie guy was wandering down the street in the company of four or five girls when he spotted her. She said she could see him point at her while he was talking to the girls he was with.

"They approached her and asked her whom she was with. She said she was alone. She saw the guy's eyes light up when she said that, and that all the girls said she should come with them.

"Doctor Green and I asked her if she was aware of her 'look.' She had that glossy magazine model look that could easily be interpreted as her being sexual." Eli paused in remembrance. "She was what *all* the White boys on the Lake wanted."

Eli came back to the present. "Anyway, she laughed about us asking about if she knew how she looked, and she said, 'No.' That the only thing that was remarkable about her appearance was the large bulge in the crotch of her pants. She said she was wearing one of her mother's maxi-pads, and that it needed changing.

"She said they were over-sized for her, and that her play pants, though not tight in the crotch, were *very* tight with that swollen maxi-pad stuffed in there. She said if the hippie leader guy was attracted to her sexually, it would have been because he thought she had a giant vagina.

"Bonnie rarely got funny, but she had us both laughing at that one. She seemed oblivious to the fact that she had a face that would let her get away...get whatever she wanted in this world.

"Anyway, the hippies invited her to hang with them, and that she could crash at their place in the morning.

"She followed them around the Haight-Ashbury district while they smoked pot and got into themselves all night. Then she crashed at their pad with about forty other people.

"She said that later that day, the leader guy, who had a look in his eye like Chuck would get before he raped her, said they were going out to the country for a couple weeks or so to harvest and package some pot, and that the payment was a pound of pot for each helper to take home when they left. That they would leave that afternoon.

"That's how she ended up at our place for the better part of a decade. It all started with her harvesting and packaging pot with the hippies."

John was awestruck about this girl's journey. "How did she separate from the hippie group? It sounds like the leader guy was hot for her."

Eli continued. "The cult leader guy...names were never used...was grooming her for his bed, and she knew it. She said he was constantly coming around her, checking on her, putting his hand on her shoulder, teasing her by tugging on her hair. She said she told him at one point that she was twelve, but it had no affect on his behavior.

"At the end of the harvest, when the hippies had been paid their pound of pot and were getting things together to make their way out of the hills to ride the hippie bus back to San Francisco, Bonnie separated from the group and made her way to where Doctor Green's and my tents were. Doctor Green and I were there, making the final plans for delivering the goods to our distributor.

"Doctor Green and I were all done with the hippies, so we looked over at her to wonder, out loud, if we could help her with anything. Before we could speak, the cult leader guy came walking out of the woods, toward her, with a purpose in his step. He told her they were leaving and to come on. She told him she was staying with us.

"We knew something was happening, so neither one of us looked at each other questioningly. We just stood there like we knew all about it, and we let it play out. We passively let the cult leader guy think we were involved in whatever the little girl was saying. So, the guy looked up at us. Neither one of us changed our expression or anything. We just stood there...like statues.

"So then the guy said, 'Come on, Bonnie. We're all leaving now,' and he looked back up at us again.

"Bonnie said, 'Go on without me. I'm staying with these guys for the Winter.'

"That was news to us, but we didn't show a thing.

"The guy looked back up at us, then back at her. 'No, you're not. These guys aren't going to be bothered to be looking after you.' Then he reached his hand toward her like he was going to grab her arm. While he was doing that, he looked back up at us. Still, neither one of us moved a muscle.

"Bonnie turned her shoulder away from him and said, 'If you touch me, I will cut your balls off.' We both said later that we were amazed at this little girl, and that we wanted to laugh so badly when she said that...but still, not a muscle on either one of our faces moved.

"One more time, the guy said with a little more agitation, 'Let's go, Bonnie. You know you'll be warm all Winter with us. Here, there's nothing but tents.' Then he took a step toward her and grabbed her arm and started to pull her.

"You have to know, John, that our ParaJumper training taught us to lay back until all else failed. And the reason for that is because...once we jump in, all we know how to do is to be lethal.

"Well, when he tugged Bonnie toward him, she gave him a sharp kick in the shin with her right foot's sneaker.

"When he reached down to rub his hurt shin with his free hand...he still had her by the arm...she used that same right foot to kick him in the balls. And she clearly landed it perfectly because he bent over in two and squeezed his legs together. And he had a pretty distorted look on his face. And he was making a very painful groaning sound.

"Bonnie yanked her arm out of his grip and stood back. Without turning around toward us, and while watching him bent over in pain, she yelled out, 'Get me the knife, guys. I'm gonna take his balls.'

"He looked up at us from his bent over position of pain. We still didn't flinch.

"He turned and hobbled back into the woods.

"We didn't feel the need to tell him we would not be needing his group's services in the future. Of all the other groups that came in over the years, we never saw him, nor heard about him, again."

John was gobsmacked over Bonnie's will. "So, when did you finally flinch?"

"Bonnie watched that guy disappear into the woods. Then she

turned to us, we still being statue-like, and said, 'And if either one of you thinks you're gonna touch me, I have the same message for you as I had for him.'

"So I relaxed my pose and raised my eyebrows and said, 'Castration?'

"She nodded her head up and down and said, 'No...balls.'

"That was it for me and Doctor Green. We'd held our pose for so long that, when she said that, it broke us. And we broke big.

"We both doubled over backwards and forwards with uncontrollable laughter until the tears blinded our eyes. We were high-five-ing each other while we were laughing and making our way down to our hero.

"She didn't fully understand our reaction, but when we offered her our hands for high-fives, she knew exactly what to do.

"By the time we finished several rounds of high-five-ing her, we were so exhausted from laughing that we both just sat on the ground next to her while we let the last of our laughs peter themselves out.

"Once we were totally laughed out, we helped each other up off the ground and said to our new co-conspirator, 'Let's go get one of the crew tents and bring it up here for you. We have extra bedding, so you'll be fine until we come up with a plan for the Winter."

John had another question. "So the hippie guy? He was hot for her? That's why she wanted to get away from them?"

Eli thought about it for a second. "That was likely a part of it. But over time, I think I saw that what she needed was a place to heal. For reasons I cannot explain, she saw something in us or our situation that would allow her that."

John asked, "So, over time, did she accomplish that? Her healing?"

Eli said with contentment, "She was faithful to her purpose. You know, John, Doctor Green and I had been shaped by a system in our PJ training that required an extreme level of discipline. But it was forced on us. 'Git it done or git out.' But Bonnie didn't need...I'd even say, 'didn't want'...anybody forcing her to be disciplined. It was just something she had a special gift for. Summoning up her own discipline. Making her own way."

John was shaking his head in wonder. "Remarkable."

"Anyway, we all got Bonnie set up in her tent and put together some cozy blankets and pillows for her. That's when Doctor Green asked me, 'Do you think we can build that cabin we've been planning by Winter?' I said, 'No,' but that if we were diligent, we could be in it by plant maintenance time in the Spring.

"Then Doctor Green asked me, 'One more bedroom?'

"I replied, 'One more bedroom.'"

3.51 IT WAS THE WORST OF TIMES

On his next visit, John Watkins asked Eli, "Did Bonnie and Doctor Green raise their family and live happily ever after?"

Eli's mood was suddenly and visibly changed. "Bonnie had a tragic end that had a life-altering affect on both Doctor Green and me...not to mention, on her."

John asked, "What happened to her?"

One of Eli's memorable acronyms from the military was K.I.S.S. He felt that an application of that acronym was that, 'if a person has no choice but to lie, then Keep It Simple Stupid.' "I wasn't there. Doctor Green found her."

John asked, "What happened?"

"Bonnie was several months pregnant, but it didn't seem to affect her energy. All the things she did before becoming pregnant were still the things she did up until the end."

"What was 'the end?"

"I was out walking the grounds as I often did after a meal. Doctor Green was also out inspecting his plants.

"When I got back to the cabin, I heard our battery operated boombox playing a cassette from inside the cabin. It was Joe Cocker singing *What Would You Do If I Sang Out Of Tune.*"

The song thing wasn't true, but Eli's guilt about telling a lie made him want to give John a clue that he was lying. His clue was way too obscure for John to pick up on.

"There was nobody inside, so I walked out the back to the deck. I found Doctor Green holding a lifeless Bonnie at the bottom of the deck stairs."

"Oh, my!" John gasped. "What happened?"

"Apparently, she fell." A silent pause of remembrance came over Eli.

"On that day, we lost Bonnie, their baby, and…I was sure that all the psyche problems from our Vietnam 'heroism days' that Doctor Green had overcome returned to him in that experience of 'finding her'…so I was sure we lost him, too."

To John Watkins, *there* was another piece of evidence that Doctor Green was Scott McNally. 'From our Vietnam heroism days.' Watkins continued to feel good about Elijah not being a good deceiver. But he was saddened by Bonnie's end. And he wondered about the multiple traumas to McNally…whether or not those traumas fit into the puzzle Watkins was trying to solve.

John said, "And after all that that girl had gone through to heal herself, and then chose to start a family…all that work gone…in an instant."

Eli continued to remember his sadness. "Yes." He finished with, "That was the day the music died…that was the day we walked away from the farming business.

"We buried Doctor Green's pregnant Bonnie. We had no idea whom to notify. To add to the grief of that day, we parted company with the agreement that, because of the criminal nature of our farming business, and acknowledging the reality that the implication of one of us would probably find the other of us, we would never have contact again for the rest of our lives."

John commiserated with Eli. "You lost Bonnie *and* Doctor Green on the same day? It's odd how pivotal, meaningful people drop out of our lives. Poof. Gone...sad. In your case with Doctor Green...we tend to rationalize those losses at the time as what's best. But as time weeds out the unimportant people in our lives from the important, it makes me wonder," Watkins pondered, "Couldn't you have re-connected after the Statute of Limitations on pot farming expired?"

Eli said, "There are some things in life to which Statutes of Limitations don't apply." Elijah instantly recognized what he was saying and redirected his commentary. "Based on Captain Mineau and his reunion coordinators never being able to track him down, I always imagined Doctor Green ended up in some anonymous mental ward where he died from the medications or treatment methods he received."

Watkins thought, 'Does he realize he just put the final nail in the coffin of identifying Doctor Green as Scott McNally?' Then he thought, 'This is all either one elaborate lie concocted to hide their contact...or something else. Either these guys are uniquely disciplined in their lying skills...or they never *did* have contact again.' John left room in his mind for the 'lie' part, but something else from John's training and experience told him things about Elijah that made him believe it was all true.

John said, "I'm heartbroken about Bonnie's end. But my heartbreak can't compare at all to what I'm sure was Doctor Green's broken heart."

Eli added, "Both of our hearts. She was truly family. The little sister I never had."

Agent Watkins had a question. "You know, Elijah, I don't know if this comes from my law enforcement training...or just because I'm a parent. But did it ever occur to you that if she had ever been discovered living with you and Doctor Green, that you both could have been charged with kidnapping, or false imprisonment, or child endangerment? You do know, don't you, that a twelve year old doesn't have the legal right to make their own decisions about who their caretakers are?"

Eli pondered this new thought. "It's getting on toward fifty years since those events...and I can honestly say that we never had a single one of those thoughts enter our minds. If Doctor Green had thought about it, he would have shared it with me. And he never did."

Watkins continued. "Well, we both know that prosecutors can be very creative in their means and methods of coercing a confession, especially from children. And it's difficult for anyone to answer a charge of lewd and lascivious behavior. Just by saying, 'No, we didn't do that' associates you with the words. If referring her to child protective services never entered your minds, then I'm thinking about how society and the legal system would have seen your good intentions."

Eli's memories made his current position immovable. "I'm well aware that the legal system...and people in general...make a sport out of taking something good and making it out to be something bad...but I was there. And I remember. There's nothing I or Doctor Green would have done differently in taking her in. I know in my soul that she died a happy and contented person. What I don't know is if she could have gotten there any other way than the way she did."

Elijah wanted to wrap up this line of questioning. "And, as long as you're thinking like a cop or a social worker...you've mentioned before a thing called 'The Statute of Limitations.' I have to believe it would apply."

Watkins hadn't wanted to place those kinds of pictures in Elijah's head. "The Statute of Limitations is of no consideration unless there's a provable crime. And provable crimes are like a tree that falls in the forest. If nobody knows about it, did it actually happen? For my part...I certainly don't know about it."

Watkins stood up to say goodbye to Eli. "I'm retiring soon, and then I plan to compile all my interviews for the Vietnam rescue history. So, this will likely be our last meeting," and shook Eli's hand. With a bit of honest and true sadness, John added, "I feel like I've made a friend out of an interview subject."

Eli, while shaking John's hand, said, "My granddaughter, Christine...you met her and her fiancé here, before. Their wedding date is soon. Please come. I'll see to it that you and your wife get an invitation."

Watkins answered, "Thank you, Eli, that's wonderful. I'd love that. And I've been hoping to get a chance to introduce my wife, Jackie, to you and Nancy."

Watkins had never mentioned Eli, nor any other of his FBI work, to Jackie throughout his entire career. Plus, he felt Jackie's presence at the wedding would be too much overlap with his duties, despite what he now considered to be a personal friendship with Elijah Washington. "I'm glad I'll get to see you one last time." Watkins thought he could have rephrased that in a way that didn't sound so terminal.

Agent John Watkins left with the conclusion that, investigatively, and despite his clear knowledge that McNally and Eli had had a long-term personal relationship decades ago, there was 'nothing to see here.'

He resolved to re-double his efforts in other investigative pursuits to nail down, once and for all, the deceptively deceptive Scott McNally...in order to find the second of Officer Mark Johnson's killers...the illusive Jamal Ali Jefferson.

In his entire FBI career, there had never been any goal greater to Agent John Watkins than 'Mission Accomplished.'

3.52 LET YE WHO IS WITHOUT SIN...

Agent Watkins returned to his Memphis office after having spent the last week in Pacific Palisades finishing his 'debriefing' of Elijah Washington. He spent his first couple of days back preparing a report for the Mark Johnson case computer file.

When he hit 'Send' on the final edited version of the report, he included the military background of Scott McNally, the '27 hours of interviews and the review of 119 documents, attached, summarized as follows:

'The primary goal of this node of investigation was to determine whether or not a connection existed between Mr. McNally and any of his former military associates. This report concludes that there is not, nor has there been, any contact between Mr. McNally and any of his former military associates.

'Mr. McNally was awarded the Air Force Silver Star, the second highest medal awarded by the Air Force, for his actions against a hostile enemy during the recovery a downed F4 Phantom pilot in June of 1973. Mr. McNally and an O-2 pilot are the only persons who participated in that successful Search and Rescue mission, and who do NOT attend, nor have EVER attended, a quinquennial reunion of all the members of his ParaJumper squadron.

'NOTE: The downed-rescued pilot resides in the same town outside Denver in which one of the two suspected perpetrators of the murder of Officer Mark Johnson, Mr. Muhammad D. Jefferson, was recovered as deceased. After exhaustive investigative inquiries and interviews, there is no discovered connection between those two incidences.'

Agent Watkins purposefully left all details about Elijah Washington out of the report, including the SSA record that showed a blackout period of no earnings for Elijah Washington coincident with his 'farming venture.' Agent Watkins became the judge and the jury regarding what facts were relevant to the case and what facts were not relevant.

Agent Watkins was aware that this omission was a compromise of his investigative duties, but his rationale was that he didn't have a boss anymore, so why muddy the waters for the next person who looks at this case. 'Peace be unto you, Elijah G. Washington.'

After his report was filed into the ether...with a high likelihood that no other human being would ever read it...Agent Watkins put his combined profiler/lawyer hat on to make some determinations about his inability to let go of his own perception that Scott McNally was the enabler of the two murder suspects. In an odd twist of logic, Watkins had confirmed a distant connection between Washington and McNally, yet the accumulated information gave Watkins new doubt about McNally being the mastermind of the fugitives' escapes. Watkins had come to know Elijah Washington as an 'innocent,' and knowing the once close connection between Elijah and McNally caused some of Elijah's innocence to rub off on McNally in Watkins' mind. Then the rationalizations began.

'The only thing that matters is what is prosecutable. If a successful prosecution cannot be affected, then let it go.

'McNally is a lonely, heartbroken man who never recovered from the loss of the love of his life. He likely has bouts of depression and self-doubt from PTSD after-affects that re-visit him. Heartbreak, depression, and self-doubt are not motives for accessory to murder. So drop those issues from the evidence file.

'McNally's own testimony, corroborated by Ms. Loquisha Davis, is that he was motivated to avenge the tears of his mother over childhood exposure to racial injustices. That *is* a motive for committing accessory to murder; however, it may not add to a successful prosecution because of jurors' proclivity toward empathy on that motive...'we all love our mothers, and want to do right by them.' So 'avenging mother's tears' should not go in the evidence file.

'Could McNally have some kind of death wish on himself that would motivate him to expose himself to high-risk situations? Suicide by association with dangerous people? Maybe true as a result of war carnage, but not sellable to a jury. Jurors would sympathize with a decorated combat veteran. Exclude from evidence file.

'A savior complex? Never having had children, could this accessory-to-murder behavior been a twisted resolution of his need to parent? To save a lost soul that he never got to do in real life? Likely, but not sellable to a jury, especially because of disbelief that a person would sacrifice himself for an other-race stranger. Do not include in evidence folder as possible motive.'

Watkins was beginning to understand why he was almost fired twice for pushing the McNally theory.

On the other hand, Watkins had no boss, nor any associates, to challenge his rationales exclusions.

Agent Watkins was wearing himself out. And his retirement date was in sight. Had it become a countdown of days?

Watkins could feel the weight of his own fatigue. He logic-ed that he had to let McNally go. Refocus on facts that could lead him to Jamal Ali Jefferson. Facts that seemed elusive. Facts that might not exist.

Watkins was suffering from the weight of time running out.

3.53 FAR FROM THE SHALLOW NOW

Agent Watkins had reasoned that he had to push the McNally connection to the cop-killers to the back shelf. He refocused his efforts on the three names he had recorded from his pre-Elijah trip to Michael Dean's graveyard in Columbia…the trip which had led to his regrettable visit to McNally's house.

When he finally found those names in a file in his desk, it made him remember that he was waiting for an address history on the Michael Dean Social Security Number…on a hunch that McNally might have had it sent to his own residence. 'Damn. And I had just thought of distancing the investigation from the McNally connection.'

Watkins then thought to himself, 'I *am* slowing down. Either that, or I'm just not used to having to do everything myself.' He bookmarked those thoughts as a point of concern.

Agent Watkins called FBI Headquarters in D.C. and reconnected with the clerk who had told him she would order the Michael Dean SSA address history.

"Yes, Agent Watkins. Your request was held up by an inquiry communicated to my boss from our Inspector General's office about chain of command authorization. Your Request For Information was not considered inappropriate. There were just some administrative concerns about who should be on record for ordering your information. I was chastised for circumventing the system in my desire to help you."

"O.K. Where does the RFI stand right now?"..."OK. How do I get a new authorization number?"

"Agent Watkins? Thank you for your patience. I had to re-research your request. This is the guidance offered by the Office of the Inspector General: Personnel may not have an insubordinate RFI authorization code. In order for you to be issued an authorization code, your code must be subordinate to your boss' code. Therein lies the glitch. You don't seem to have a boss."

"Can you give me a code subordinate to the Director, himself? What I mean is, I obviously have a boss. It's the Director, himself."

The silence from the other end of the telephone call was a response in-and-of itself.

"Special Agent Watkins? I am a clerk in the Inspector General's Office. I have researched your situation. There are no regulations that can allow an employee with no ordination to receive an authorization code. In fact, technically, there is no such thing as an employee with no ordination. To put it plainly, Agent Watkins...everybody needs a boss."

"Sir..." Watkins tried to muster up some patience. "My unique circumstance was set up so that I could close a priority case before I retire. I have an urgent request for a Social Security Card Number address history to be generated by the SSA. The most simple way that I can ask this question is this: How do I get that address history that I need for this case?"

"Special Agent Watkins? This is Amanda Shureborne from the Director's Office Administrative Assistants Pool. Mr. Hankins, from the Inspector General's Office, informed me that you are in need of a Social Security records request, but that you cannot be issued an authorization code because of an administrative glitch in your employment chain of command?"

"Yes, M'am. That is correct."

"I will use my personal authorization code for you this one time, and this one time only, based on the urgency of your need and the previous delay. However, it is incumbent upon you to straighten out the paperwork on your chain of command. Do you understand that this is a one-time exception?"

"Yes, M'am. Thank you for doing it, and I will get right-onto getting my employment status straightened out with the Personnel Office. Here is the Social Security Number"..."The name is Michael Dean"..."The report I need is an address history for that social security number."

Watkins hung up. He began shaking and bowing his head in exhaustion and frustration. He thought, 'If this *weren't* a bureaucracy, why would we have the name 'Bureau' in our name.'

He hoped he wouldn't need another interagency report ever again.

3.54 YOU DON'T ALWAYS GET WHAT YOU WANT

The day after Watkins' bureaucratic fiasco that had ended up with him receiving a one-time favor from an administrative assistant in the Director's Office, he was enjoying an after-supper glass of wine with his wife, Jackie.

Jackie was a little out of character for herself in that she was a bit whiney with her husband.

"A wedding, John? Really? As part of a case? Really? The weekend before you sign your retirement papers? Really? It sounds personal to me."

"It was a case in which I put great time demands on the grandfather of the bride. We both developed a personal connection and, as a parting gift to our friendship, he asked me to attend. He wanted you to attend, also, so he could meet you and so you could meet his wife. But you know that's not the way it works, Jackie. You've known for my entire career that there is great danger in you knowing anything about any of my cases. It's for your own safety."

Jackie just thought it was weird. She didn't like the timing in relation to his retirement, nor did she like the non-business nature of the event. She knew the only way to break any tension about it was for her to propose the preposterous. "You're not really going out there to have a secret affair with another woman, are you?"

John laughed out loud. Something he almost never did. It was the laugh that Jackie wanted to hear so she could stop her whining.

At work the next day, late in the workday on Wednesday, Agent Watkins got the email he had been waiting for. It was the address history report from SSA on Michael Dean's social security number.

Watkins almost tipped his chair over backwards. There is was, right in the middle of the only three addresses ever used for that card number: 149 Little Buffalo River Road.

'Got him!' Agent Watkins exclaimed in his own mind. He had no-one with whom to share his victory.

'This is my redemption! I'm going to fill out an arrest warrant. That will trigger the assembly of an arrest team. We're going to bring that little bastard in! Ha, ha! I was right all along!'

Watkins reviewed his calendar in his mind. 'I'm flying out of Memphis Friday afternoon for Elijah's granddaughter's wedding on Saturday. If we schedule the arrest for first thing tomorrow, Thursday morning, I could be done with all the paperwork by tomorrow night, which is Thursday, while McNally sits in a jail cell. There should be no interference in me catching my flight to California.'

Agent Watkins pulled up the previous search warrant so he could transfer the static data from that document to the data fields on the arrest warrant.

When he started copying the static data, field by field, he got to the mailing street address filed from the previous search warrant. Then he went to press the 'Copy' keys to insert it in the arrest warrant. It was then that he realized the McNally address he was copying was number *147* Little Buffalo River Road, and the address of the Michael Dean Social Security card was *149* Little Buffalo River Road.

Agent Watkins was about to go ballistic over a typo SNAFU when he remembered that there were two mail boxes, side by side, up the road from Scott McNally's driveway. They were the only mailboxes he saw on Little Buffalo River Road the day he had been driven out there by the Sheriff.

3.55 SNAP!

On Thursday morning at 11:30AM, Scott McNally brought Miss Dolly's mail to her as he did nearly every day. But when he walked into her house, he could see that she was in a tither.

"I had a Poe-leece man in here this morning. It was a nggr, and he weren't wearing no badge, and he weren't dressed in no uniform."

Scottie became laser focused.

"Dat nggr was askin' about you and dat dare Face Chat machine."

Scottie refocused on his breathing.

"He sed he wuz a needin' da be a lookin' at it, and he showed me his FBI picture card. So then that nggr walked right over ta dat machine an bigun pressin' buttons...liken you do when yur settin' me up fir a call with my babies."

Scottie immediately knew it was Watkins, and that he was getting the IP address to get a warrant for the history on the IP account. Scottie knew it would tell all. That made Scottie think he had at least a couple of days before they could get the incriminating history.

Then Miss Dolly said, "Den dat nggr cop assed me whether I ever heered a name, or if I ever got any social security cards fir dat name. Now don't chew go thinkin' I was a sayin' 'ngggr' whin he was here, in my house. I was raised *better* den dat."

In that instant, Scottie realized Watkins had found Miss Dolly through an SSA address search on Michael Dean's card. Scottie knew they would then do a reverse database search on Dolly's address...which would reveal that the Robert Smith Social Security Card was also mailed to Miss Dolly.

They would then do a search on the Robert Smith card which would reveal his Pacific Palisades address...and his employment at *The Washington Construction Company.*

They would then assemble an assault team to effect the arrest of Robert Smith in California. Scottie knew that John Watkins wouldn't miss that event for the world.

What Scottie couldn't predict was how long it would take to get the SSA database searches done, nor how long it would take to assemble the assault team for the arrest in California.

Scottie told Miss Dolly he was going on a trip and that he wouldn't be back to get her mail for a week or so.

She protested that she couldn't go that long without getting her mail.

As he spirited himself out her door, Scottie didn't hear anything else she was saying.

3.56 RIDERS ON THE STORM

Scottie rushed home, uncovered the Batmobile, and threw a duffle bag of clothing changes into the trunk...along with his sniper rifle case.

He removed the GPS tracking device and, knowing the route to Pacific Palisades in his head, and it being over 2,000 miles, he calculated that it would take 40-plus hours of speed-limit drive time...he couldn't afford to be pulled over and identified...plus back-seat rest stops as needed, meals, and bathroom breaks. He'd be there by Saturday morning.

He hoped he would beat the bureaucracy of the FBI...'Agent Watkins will want to be there to get his glory. That might slow the team assembly. I have a chance to get there first and create all the necessary chaos to disaffect the arrest. If I get there ahead of them, I can locate Robert and swift him away.'

Scottie had sad thoughts that, if he were successful in getting to Robert first...that Robert would have to go underground once again. 'At least he knows how to do it, now.' Scottie left his cell phone behind so his travel couldn't be traced.

After he started the car, he doubled back into the house to get the metal, army-green ammo box from 1973-75 Vietnam that had his name in large marker, all caps, 'McNALLY,' printed on the top.

The ammo box was full of enough .308 bullets to take out a small army...as long he didn't get taken out first. He had a flashback memory of Eli hand-loading all the bullets to 165 grains. 'Maximum knock-down power.'

As he kicked up a chert dust-cloud driving out his driveway, Scottie thought to himself, 'I'll do the best I can. After that, whatever will be will be.'

Scottie's long drive allowed him some free thinking time.

Scottie anticipated a minimum of twenty agents *supporting* the Hostage Rescue Team, the FBI's own version of S.W.A.T. Plus fifteen or so agents from the Hostage Rescue Team, itself. Plus an untold number of uniformed and plain-clothed perimeter support. Although it was never part of his initial plan, he was now ready to go down in a blaze of bullets. 'At this point, my investment has been reduced by half. I'm not willing to watch the surviving half go downstream.'

He remembered an old General Patton quote from World War II that was part of his Superman School training. 'The object of war is not to die for your country, but to make the other poor bastard die for his.'

He remembered knowing when he said, 'I will help you,' that it would have many unforeseeable dimensions to it. He had an ancient but familiar sadness come over him. This time it was because he was thinking of some of his fellow Americans as the enemy...as they would, him.

He had never feared this day. Buried somewhere deep in that 'knowing' of his, Scottie was always aware that this was one...no matter how remotely possible...possible consequence that had always existed.

3.57 NO GUTS NO GLORY

Agent Watkins got back to his office that Thursday as everyone at his Memphis office was going home. He knew he was nowhere on discovering Jamal Ali Jefferson's new identity without the SSA running the 149 Little Buffalo River Road address report...to see what Jamal's new name was...and where he could be found.

Finding out the new name and location of Jamal Jefferson was the end of his involvement in the case. 'And affecting that arrest means I can retire with peace and dignity...and honor.'

"This is Special Agent John Watkins. I'm calling from the Director's office to make an urgent request for a couple of database reports."

"OK, Sir. Give me the search parameters."…"OK, Sir. Give me your authorization number."…"Sir, you must know I can't run this without an authorization number."

Agent Watkins helplessly pleaded his case. "…Is there anything that can be done to make this happen?"

"Sir, you'd have to figure that out on your end. It's after hours here on the East Coast. I'm just the night-shift guy. But even if all the regular staff were on duty, they'd just tell you the same thing. 'You have to figure it out on your end.' All we do is punch in the database search parameters."

John knew he was just talking to himself, but hanging up was the equivalent of never getting this done. He wondered how he could be so close…yet so far away.

"I got an administrative re-assignment so I could close this case before I retired. I'm retiring this coming Monday. Something went wrong in the administration of my re-assignment. I don't have a boss, so I can't get an authorization code. The report I had you guys run on Monday was done as a favor by a secretary to the Director, but she was a bit nasty about it, making sure I understood that it was a one-time-only thing.

"The guy I'm looking for is a cop killer. I got his partner recently. And that led me to where I am today. If I could get this search done, that's it. It's over. I've got the second guy. And nobody believed in me. Yet, here I am. I'm this close."

"Please. Stop right there. You know, don't you, that I'm a computer clerk? I'd get fired for making the decision you want me to make. I'm sympathetic to your plea, but there's nothing in my training or my job description that guides me on what to do with 'sympathy.'"

Watkins thought, 'It's *empathy* I need from you.' "OK. I get it. I'm way out of bounds for pressing you on this."

The clerk continued. "Even if I *could* get the data you want, there's no way I'm going to create a computer audit trail showing that the information was sent to you without authorization."

"I said, 'OK.' I get it. I'm out of bounds. I apologize."

The clerk said nothing. The pause kept getting longer.

Watkins was ready to hang up.

"What's your personal phone number, Agent Watkins?"..."If I can get the reports sent to me on my own authorization code, I could call you and tell you what the reports say. Then there would be no audit trail for the information leaving here. But the search request has to wait in line. If I put it at the top of the queue, it'll draw instant attention."

3.58 THE WEDDING CRASHER

Jackie had left work early on Friday. That gave John Watkins a chance to talk with her before he left the house for Memphis International.

Jackie said, "MaryLou and Brandon are coming over tonight, and they're staying for the weekend. We're all going to a flea market on Saturday."

John said, "Don't say 'we're *all* going' to a flea market on Saturday. I won't be going with you."

Jackie said, "Ha, ha. Your choice. But don't worry about it. You'll come home Sunday night at some gawd awful hour, and then you'll be retired by the time you come home from your office on Monday. Then you'll have all the time in the world to spend with your family."

John was feeling a little melancholy about making the trip out West. "You know what, Jackie. There is a certain amount of positive energy connected to my imminent 'change-of-status' with the FBI. But it doesn't compare to the positive energy I feel for what we've built. I feel like we've done a good job. The proof of it is that there is no place that I'd rather be, and nobody I'd rather be with, than my family. You and

MaryLou...and, of course, Brandon, now."

Jackie said, "Don't go getting all mushy on me. Are you all packed and ready?"

John kissed his wife goodbye. "The biggest thing about me going to that wedding...is knowing that I'm coming home to you."

Jackie kissed him. Then she slapped him on his backside. "Get out of here before I make you miss your plane."

McNally had spent his whole adult life falling back on so many of the things he had learned in Superman School and through the 'pipeline.' One of them was techniques to re-invigorate during extreme fatigue. McNally would put those skills to work on the Saturday morning he arrived in Pacific Palisades.

McNally drove to the apartment address he had gotten from the internet for his own Robert Smith. There was no answer.

McNally then drove to *The Washington Construction Company* on the short hope that someone was working on a Saturday, and that they could tell McNally where to find Robert Smith...or that perhaps Robert, himself, was working that Saturday.

The Washington Constriction Company was locked up tighter than a drum.

McNally thought he could do a random drive-around, but he quickly dissuaded himself because it was the highest probability of a waste of time.

He had the address for Mark and Charleen Mack because Mark was the owner of the construction company. When he drove by their house, McNally saw that it, too, was closed up tighter than a drum.

McNally then found the Pacific Palisades Police building. He wanted to see if there were any signs of an assault raid being assembled. It was as dead as a liquor store parking lot on a Sunday morning in the Bible Belt.

McNally had Eli's home address with him 'just in case,' but he didn't want to have a chance sighting with Elijah because of their ancient agreement to have no contact. But, he thought, short of doing a stake-out at Robert's apartment, he was at a loss for his next search effort for Robert.

That's when McNally passed a car in which he swore he saw FBI Special Agent In Charge, John Watkins, driving. His first reaction was that he was having a fatigue hallucination. Even as he told himself that the sighting was nearly impossible, he banged a u-turn and followed the car from a couple positions back.

After a drive to up above the town, McNally found himself in a line of cars that were waiting their turn to get into a long, uphill driveway. He actually had the thought, 'Is this how they disguise a police action in this upscale town?' But when he got to the base of the driveway, he saw the street name and number on a yard sign, looked around, and realized, 'Hey...this is Elijah's house.'

McNally felt like he was already lost in the herd, and his curiosity was off the charts. So, he allowed himself to stay in line up the driveway.

The line had been inching forward near the top. That's where McNally could see the reason for the backup. There were valets taking people's cars from them to be parked along the outside edges of the house and garage property and along the upper driveway. Car owners, when they got out to turn their cars over to the valets, were dressed in fine suits and dresses, and almost all of them got out of their cars with boxes wrapped in wedding paper and wedding bows. McNally realized he was at a wedding at Elijah's house.

As McNally sat in line, his previous sighting was confirmed. It was Agent Watkins getting out of his car, dressed in a fine-looking suit, and he had a wrapped wedding present in his hand.

McNally was used to adapting to new information and making the necessary adjustments. But what he was seeing put his brain into a temporary snowstorm.

When McNally got to the valets, he could see 'lesser' cars circled around the front portico. He lowered his window to speak to the valet. "I'm with the caterers," and was waved toward the main house.

McNally squeezed his car in-between some of the other lesser cars and waltzed into the house in his 2,000 mile old clothing. He was aware that he had two days' growth on his face, that his hair was unkempt, and that he was less than floral smelling. He made a bee-line through the house to the center of the catering activity toward the back door. He looked around and suddenly didn't feel so out of place. Many of the caterers looked as scruffy as he did.

As he was entering the kitchen, he noticed a bedroom door opening to his left. There was a line of young men in black tuxedos walking out while talking and laughing with each other. McNally waited for a second.

The last person out of the bedroom was a tall skinny Black kid in a white tuxedo. McNally got a clear picture. 'There's Robert...and this is *his* wedding.'

McNally ducked his head and disappeared into the traffic of catering people.

'Robert's wedding? Agent Watkins here? Disguised as a guest?'

McNally reformed his plan.

He saw the pool house off the terrace surrounding the swimming pool. Caterers were setting things up outside the pool house, but there was no traffic in and out of it. A large arbor had been set up outside the sliding glass entry doors of the pool house. McNally knew that was where the wait staff would stand at the ready when the food-action began. McNally looked at the pool house building. He immediately spotted a gable end vent at the peak of the roof. It was overlooking the entire back of the property.

McNally turned back to see if Robert and his crew had passed through...and they had.

McNally walked back through the house, dodging people who were carrying warming trays and food baskets and serving dishes and silverware and glasses and pitchers, to his car and, on his way, picked up a folded table cloth that was in a stack on the kitchen island counter.

When he got to his car, he popped the trunk lid and circled around to it.

He spread the tablecloth open and let it drape over the rifle case. He then lifted the covered rifle case out of the trunk, made a grunting lift of the ammunition box that had 'McNALLY' printed across the top of the lid, and set both items on the ground.

Then he closed the trunk and picked up both items. He was counting on nobody knowing what an ammunition box looked like…and being too busy to notice anyone else, anyway. Then he bee-lined it back through the house to the pool house.

Nobody paid attention to him slipping through the sliding doors of the pool house. When he got inside, he brought his contraband to the back kitchenette. He looked for a hatch or a pull-down set of stairs to the attic. Nothing.

He knew the sound panels in the ceiling were part of a dropped-ceiling system, so he climbed up on the kitchenette countertop and removed a panel.

He saw the subfloor to the attic area was nailed-down rough lumber, so he scouted the whole floor area from underneath…only to see there were no built-in openings.

He jumped off the countertop to grab his rifle case.

He got back on the countertop with the case and raised it to the attic subfloor through the ceiling panel opening. Then he started banging.

It was the fifth bang when he saw that he had loosened an attic floorboard. He then slid the case under the partially raised board. He then used the case as a lever to pry the attic floorboard loose from its nails.

He then repeated that process on three more floorboards. Then he could see he had enough room to climb in.

He slid the rifle case through the opening, then lifted the heavy ammunition box up until it was resting on the attic floor. Then he picked up the piece of ceiling tile he had previously removed. He slid it into the cavity between the false ceiling and the attic floorboards. Then he lifted himself up and in.

Once on the attic floor, he reached back down to put the ceiling tile back into place.

Then he went to the gable end vent. The triangular vent was custom made. He saw that it had been nailed into place from the outside.

Scottie took one of the removed floorboards and used it to pry three of the vent slats off their nails. The bent nails that had been holding the slats stayed in place. Scottie thought, 'Perfect. They'll be easy to re-install by hand...if need-be.'

McNally would normally have had to crouch if he wanted to stand up inside the attic space, but it made the height of the gable end vent just perfect for him being able to crouch back from the vent hole so as to not be seen. Then he could sight down to pretty near ground, as well as out across the yard to the whole wedding ceremony area.

McNally removed his rifle from the case, checked the chamber for a live load, checked the number of loads in the clip, pushed the clip up into its lock position, and opened the lid of his ammunition box. It was full to the brim. He then began scouting the crowd.

The first person he was looking for was Agent Watkins. He spotted him. Scottie thought, 'How heartless can a person be to wait for a *wedding* to take down the groom in front of all these guests.'

In all his activity, Scottie had not given thought to whom it was that Robert was there to marry. 'By God, this is *Elijah's* house. Robert must be marrying a granddaughter of Eli's.' Scottie didn't have time or thought-energy to consider the surreality of it all.

Scottie did a scan of the whole crowd. He was looking for signs of undercover cops or FBI...'detective' sunglasses, earpieces, under-clothing bulges for weapons and gear. Nothing.

McNally had a fleeting thought. 'Are they *all* undercover? Force of numbers?' He let it go. He was still young enough to know insanity when he saw it, even when it was his own.

People were moving to their wooden, gloss-white painted folding chairs that had been set up on the lawn under a sprawling Chestnut tree. A raised platform with stairs leading up to it had been built for an alter. It was all down below the expansive pool terrace over which the large party tent had been set up.

From his perch, McNally was keeping his eye on Watkins.

McNally had a minute to think. He couldn't figure out why Watkins was there without apparent backup, and why he wasn't moving on Robert. 'What kind of sadist would choose a wedding for a takedown? Get it over with, you jackass. What? Are you going to wait until they're legally married? What kind of a sick person are you?'

McNally picked up his rifle and sighted the crosshairs to find the center spot between Agent Watkins' shoulder blades...for a through-shot to the heart.

John Watkins was offered a paper cupcake mold from a silver platter. It was full of water-soluble fake rice. He thought it was a nice touch. As he took it, he was asked, "Bride or Groom?"

Watkins was lost in thought, trying to absorb all the details so he could share them with his wife and daughter, and thoughtlessly said, "Groom."

Watkins was escorted to a seat on the Groom's side. He noticed he was sitting on the grossly lightly weighted side of the aisle, and that the other guests that shared seats with him were clearly construction-type workers, some with their girlfriends or wives.

Christine's childhood playmate from Nashville, Cathy, daughter of slain police officer Mark Johnson, was on Bride's side. She kept turning her head to look at Watkins.

Finally, she pulled on her husband's jacket sleeve and pointed. "I know that man. Wasn't he involved in investigating Mark's murder? I think I remember seeing him at Metro Headquarters right after Mark's death."

Knopfler turned and looked. His jaw dropped. "Yeah, I'm sure he was there...because I know him. He was my primary contact at the FBI for keeping you and the Union informed about case progress. Before we speak to him...do you know why he's here?"

Cathy said, "No."

As Cathy and Neal Knopfler turned away from looking at him, Watkins felt his phone vibrate in his inside jacket pocket. He discreetly pulled it out to see who was calling.

'Alexandria, Virginia? No name attached?' Watkins was about to put it back in his jacket pocket when it dawned on him, 'I bet this is the SSA computer clerk calling on his personal cell phone. The night clerk doing weekend duty.'

Watkins slid toward the outside of his row of chairs as he pressed the green 'answer call' graphic.

When he was outside the seating area, he said, "Agent Watkins, here."

"Agent Watkins. I'm calling with the report information you requested."

"Oh, yes. Thanks for calling back. Give me a second so I can get to where we can talk."

The Bride and Groom were about to walk down the aisle, so Watkins made his way back up the hill to the edge of the reception tent. There, he picked up a folded linen napkin from a place-setting on a big round table-clothed table on the perimeter of the tent. Watkins pulled a pen from his jacket pocket to write on the linen napkin. "Sorry about that. Go ahead."

The SSA computer clerk read off his information. "The address search on all cards mailed to the 149 address came up with the one I think you're looking for. In addition to the Michael Dean card, there was a card sent to a 'Robert Smith' at that same address, at that same time."

Watkins had to physically shake his head. "You're pranking me, right? Did somebody put you up to this?"

"What?"

Watkins backed off when he realized that the clerk didn't know enough to devise the prank. "Did you get the followup reports on the Robert Smith card?"

"The Robert Smith card shows a current mailing address in Pacific Palisades, California, and his current earnings are at *The Washington Construction Company*, also in Pacific Palisades."

Watkins wasn't writing anything down.

"Hello?...Agent Watkins?...Are you still there, Sir?"

"Ah...yes...ah...thanks for the call."

McNally was watching the whole thing. He knew something significant had happened. McNally ran through some scenarios. 'Hostage Rescue Team coming in. Arrest package assembled. Support personnel establishing their perimeter.' It went on and on in his mind. But then McNally wondered why he could see no signs of weapons or gear on Watkins. McNally thought, 'Watch and wait. Watch and wait.'

Agent Watkins moved down to stand outside the guest seating area, laser-focused, now, on the Bride and Groom about to say their vows. That's when he focused on the Groom.

McNally, from his perch inside the pool house attic, also focused his scope toward the Groom. As he did, he noticed that the front row of seats on the Groom's side of the seating was empty. McNally thought, 'No parents or relatives.' He felt pain for Robert.

Then McNally moved his scope over to the Bride's side. It was McNally's first sight of Elijah. McNally only had a side view of Eli's head, but that partial look at his face, along with all the grey hair that had replaced the black, made McNally wonder, 'How did he get so old?'

Watkins, for his part, felt a shortness of breath. He didn't know if it was from adrenaline or anxiety...or adrenaline *from* anxiety.

Watkins' thoughts of Robert Smith, aka Jamal Ali Jefferson, coursed through his brain. Meeting the kid in Eli's study. The tallness. The inexplicable tallness. 'How did McNally pull *that* off? And Eli. How did McNally put this kid together with Eli? And is it truly possible that Eli didn't know?'

Then he felt an anger rise within himself, at himself. 'How did it get past me that the only two people on earth that I ever heard the name Helen Mayer from...were McNally and Robert Smith?' As he came to the realization of how much off his game he had become, he pictured himself putting the cuffs on Jamal Ali Jefferson. His thoughts went to the perp-walk and the accolades. 'The Lone Ranger gets his man.'

The wedding vows were mirrors of each other, each line spoken by each, to each other.

Watkins heard Jamal say. "I will protect and defend you." Then he heard Christine answer him, "I will protect and defend you."

Watkins contemplated breaking in, now, before their nuptials were complete. 'Save them the pain of undoing it all.'

He heard Jamal say, "I will comfort you." Then he heard Christine's answer. "I will comfort you."

Watkins looked for a path to the alter. He gauged any and all obstructions.

McNally could read Watkins' nervousness, and he adjusted the tension in his finger, accordingly.

Watkins heard Jamal say, "I will celebrate you." Watkins saw pictures of celebration. Champagne. Backslaps. Plaques marking his triumphant moment. Then he heard Christine say. "I will celebrate you."

Watkins practiced his approach in his mind while he heard Jamal say, "I will put you before me." Watkins thought, 'It is *I* who will put *you* before *me*.' Then he heard Christine's response. "I will put you before me."

Then Watkins realized…'I don't have my cuffs on me!' Then he rationalized, 'I will traumatize every person in here if I act now.'

McNally picked up the agitation in Watkins' body language. It made him more focused on his own breathing to ensure a clean kill…when necessary.

Watkins continued his worry. 'And how will I do it without cuffs? I must wait until I can whisk him away without creating a disturbing scene.'

He heard Jamal say, "I will be by your side until the end." Watkins thought, 'The end is sooner than you think, young man.' And he heard Christine finish their vows with, "I will be by your side until the end."

Watkins was affected when he heard Christine say those words, 'I will be by your side until the end.' Watkins knew that for Christine to live by that vow, she would be visiting Jamal in prison until one of them died. The end. Then he had a picture enter his mind of his own Mary-Lou making that same vow in her soul to Brandon.

Watkins snapped out of it when the organ broke in to accompany Robert and Christine's walk back out the aisle through their crowd of witnesses.

As the newly wed couple passed each row of seating, the guests showered them with water-soluble fake rice from the cupcake molds they had been given.

McNally had a close-up view of Watkins during the recessional. He watched Watkins dump his cup of rice onto the ground. McNally thought, 'Uh, oh. The trouble's about to begin.'

Everyone found Waterford crystal Champagne flutes, adorned with white bows on the stems, at their name-carded places at each table under the reception tent on the expansive pool terrace. On the back of each name card was a printed message, 'Please take your toast flute home with you to remember this day every time you use it. Love, Christine & Robert."

Watkins had resolved to wait until he could get Jamal into a private setting to give him the bad news and to physically subdue him into an arrest. Watkins contemplated making a call for support...but him constantly seeing Nancy and Elijah joyously intermingling with their guests convinced him that he could handle this himself. 'The element of surprise will make this go down smoothly.'

Watkins convinced himself that he would be less conspicuous in the crowd, so he searched for his name card. He felt a minor tremor move through his body when he saw the name card labeled, 'Jackie Watkins.' His mind had been so distracted from his real life that Jackie had been forgotten in the moment. John recognized some guilt within himself over that.

When he put her name card in his jacket pocket and sat down, what he saw transported him into what he thought was a psychedelic bad trip. There, sitting next to him at his table, was his nemesis, Nashville Officer and Union Rep, Neal Knopfler.

Knopfler made a hand gesture toward his wife. "Agent Watkins, this is my wife, Cathy."

Watkins, not wanting to reach in front of Knopfler, bowed his head. "Pleasure to meet you, M'am. I'm sorry about your husband."

Cathy was puzzled for a moment, then said, "Oh, you mean my *first* husband, Mark? Thank you. I remember you from the early investigation. Then, I just saw you down at the nuptials. I knew there had to be a mistake when you were seated on the Groom's side. Do you know the Washingtons, or the Macks?...or do you actually know Robert?"

Watkins thought, 'Yes. I know Robert.' "Elijah Washington, the patriarch of the family, is a close personal friend of mine."

Knopfler said, "It's a small world."

Watkins answered him under his breath, 'Smaller than you think.'

Knopfler turned from Watkins, back to his wife, and commented, "What's with the all the servers? They all look like they're homeless people who've been hosed down to clean them up for this thing."

Cathy slapped him on the leg under the table and leaned in to him with a snarl in her voice. She thought she was whispering, but Watkins could hear her. "Now you just need to hush, Neal. These are all the people that Grammi Nancy works with."

Cathy pulled back away from Neal and leaned in front of him to speak directly to Watkins. "Grampi Eli's wife, Nancy, and my grandmother grew up together in Nashville. Our families have been close ever since." She looked at Neal and then back at Watkins. "So, I understand you know my husband, Neal, from the investigation?"

"Yes. We were on the same team. We worked tirelessly to find Mark's killers."

Cathy said with less emotion than Watkins would have anticipated, "They got one of them. One down...one to go."

Watkins wanted to change the subject. "Congratulations on your pregnancy. When are you due?"

"In two months. I can't wait for Christine and Robert to start having children. My baby's gonna need a playmate. They'd be the fourth generation of playmates." Cathy looked behind her for her mother and grandmother.

"Please excuse me, Mr. Watkins. It was nice to finally meet you."

An army of wait staff had started delivering meals to all the tables all at one time. Knopfler kept his back to Watkins during conversations of everyone getting to know each other at the table.

Watkins had picked through his meal while he tried to mutually avoid conversation with Knopler, who was busily engaged in other conversations at the table, along with his wife, Cathy. When Watkins saw things were stirring for the toasts at the head table, Watkins excused himself and moved to the edge of the tent without a Champagne flute. There was no way he was going to join in any toast from this Groom.

When McNally got Watkins back into his sights, he began slowing moving the crosshairs of his sniper rifle all around Watkins' head and shoulders in the event that he had to choose a kill spot. He was careful to plan bullet trajectory so as to not endanger nearby innocents.

Robert stood in front of the tented crowd from the raised head table platform and began tapping his Waterford Champagne flute with his knife until everyone was quiet. Robert was quiet, himself, but the microphone allowed everyone to hear. Robert said his short toast while looking at his Bride seated next to him.

"There are truths in this life that never change. They are *eternal* truths.

"A truth that I knew when I first laid eyes on Christine was that she was out of my league...*way* out of my league." Robert never took his eyes off her while he was speaking.

"By the time I got to know her as a person...know what made her tick...see her interactions with other people...by the time I could correctly anticipate how she would respond to any given situation...that's when I realized that my first observation was not just a truth, but it was an *eternal* truth.

"You are out of my league, Christine. *Way* out of my league. And you always will be. I know it...and I accept it." They both felt a wave of emotion building up within them. "Christine, I embrace our eternal truth."

Robert held his hand out to her and guided her to stand up. He was deeply locked into her eyes, and her, his. He tapped his flute to hers and said, "Here's to our eternity together."

The crowd stood up and amplified the clinking sound of crystal by three hundred while murmurs of 'that was beautiful' and 'oh, how nice' were the undercurrent of everyone sipping their toast.

Watkins moved around the edge of the tent to get a little closer to the head table. He was subconsciously positioning himself to block Jamal's escape.

As Watkins walked, he thought, 'If I didn't have the evidence, I would never believe that this is Jamal Ali Jefferson.'

Unlike Robert, Christine was a natural at public speaking. She held her Champagne flute in her hand as she spoke with a conversional easiness into the microphone.

"I knew I'd found my person when I saw him make his freshly laundered bed linens with the top sheet on the right way."

A woman in the crowd shouted out, "Does that mean he makes his own bed?" There was some light laughter.

Christine answered, "Oh, yes. When somebody's good at something, we let them do it. Am I right, ladies?" Chuckles and a light murmur of conversation followed that response.

Christine continued. "And if knowing how to make a bed isn't enough for us, ladies...what is our number one pet peeve about living with a man?" She waited, then she answered her own question. "How about the toilet seat?" There was a loud laughter from the women, followed by clapping and some whooping.

"That's right, ladies. Toilet seat etiquette. Please don't raise your hand...but how many of us have ever sat down on the rim of the toilet and almost fallen in?" Another wave of laughter filled the tent.

Christine looked around the room for Grampi Eli. When she spotted him, she raised her flute and said, "Thank you, Grampi Eli, for giving me *that* experience in life." The crowd laughed again.

"And if knowing that the seat will always be down...well, that's enough toilet talk. But let's just say I've never had to use a brush or a wipe since I've become close with Robert."

Robert was bowing his head and shaking it in embarrassment. The crowd loved it.

"Now, ladies, let's get serious for a moment. How important is it that our man communicates openly and honestly with us?" There was lots of head-nodding in the audience.

"Well, my Robert is a Rock-n-Roll poet. That means he uses Rock-n-Roll lyrics to communicate. He has the best lines for every situation, many of which are too private to share here."

There was another din of light laughter.

"When I say he comes up with the best lines, I mean, he knows how to always make me feel good...to reassure me...to lift me up. It will embarrass him if I over-share, but let me give you just one example.

"In a moment of my own insecurity, he once held my face to look at him, and said, 'I'll be there.'" The women in the crowd let out a group 'Ohhhh.'

"And that makes me remember the time I was having doubts about something serious. He threw his arm over my shoulder and held me tight. Then he said, 'Stand by me. Just stand by me.'" The 'Ohhhh' got a little louder.

McNally had had the crosshairs of his rifle trained on Watkins at the beginning of Christine's speech, but when he heard that, he lowered his weapon and took a momentary knee. McNally knew exactly where all that had come from.

Christine finished by saying, "The most important thing I've learned from Robert is something I can't really say much about." She turned to look at Robert sitting in his chair, flute in hand, and looking up at her.

"It came from a very personal conversation we had before we were committed to each other. In that talk, we shared our thoughts and feelings about what the word 'intimacy' meant. And, no, girls. Our sharing had nothing to do with physical intimacy.

"But it woke me up to two things. The first was that I knew we had defined intimacy in a way that will stay with me the rest of my life." There was a silence of anticipation in the crowd for the second half.

"And, secondly, that this was the man that I wanted to be intimate with for the rest of my life."

With that, Christine held her Champagne flute to Robert, who stood to kiss her on the lips…for a little longer than was necessary…as the clinking sound of crystal and the hum of satisfying comments filled the tent.

John Watkins had been momentarily mesmerized. Christine's toast had made John think if his own daughter's upcoming marriage, and he pined, 'Oh, that my MaryLou has found what Christine has found.' Then he had to physically shake his head to come out of his spell.

McNally had his eye on Watkins' reaction through the whole of Christine's speech. And McNally was not at peace with what he saw at the end.

McNally resumed practice-targeting different locations on John Watkins' spine when he spotted a man walking toward Watkins. McNally identified the approaching man as a law-enforcement. McNally scanned the man with his scope, thinking the two men were coordinating.

Watkins started with a snide comment. "You seem out of place, Knopfler, what with all the less-than-white skin that's here."

Knopfler didn't make eye contact with Watkins. "There's plenty of White skin here."

"But what about the nggrs that are here?"

"Nggr ain't a skin color, Watkins. You know that. It's an attitude. And these nggrs don't seem to have that jungle fever attitude."

When McNally remembered that the pregnant woman was on the guy's arm when he scanned the crowd earlier, he downgraded his own assumption that the guy was part of a coordinated assault. But the interaction that McNally was witnessing through his scope confused him because he was sure they were both law enforcement.

Watkins looked directly at Knopfler. "You really going to let your baby play with a dark child?"

"Let it go, Watkins. My baby's gonna play with whoever my baby wants to play with. And it would be better if our history of conflicts over this type of thing didn't get back to my wife."

"Oh...she doesn't know you're a White Supremacist? The Grand Dragon of the Ku Klux Klan? Are you concerned that she wouldn't approve of the burning crosses and the lynchings?"

Knopfler was looking around. "Keep it down, pardner. Who knows? I might be doin' the Kum-Ba-Yah with these people before it's all over."

Knopfler walked away, toward his wife, to make sure she wasn't coming over to join Watkins' and his conversation.

Watkins thought of turning Robert over to the likes of Knopfler. 'That's just the way it is, Jamal. The price you pay for running.' But thinking of the way Knopfler was...it made Watkins review the meaning of 'justice.' 'Is justice the enforcement of laws at the end of the barrel of a gun?...or is there a higher justice?' He warned himself about departing too far from the doctrines of his job.

Knopfler returned. "How *did* you get invited here?"

Watkins returned the challenge. "The more pressing question is, how do *you* get invited here? A triple-Black wedding? The Groom *and* the Bride's mother *and* the Bride's grandfather? Are you here gathering intelligence for the Klan?"

"My wife...the widow...is childhood friends with the Bride, like she told you. And about all that racist stuff...look man, when I started dating the widow, she said she only saw this friend, Christine, alone, because her husband, the deceased Officer Johnson, hated Blacks. She said she was glad she never had a child with Mark because she knew she was going to make sure her children would have the same vacation play with the Bride's future children that she and the Bride had all their lives.

"Before we ever made love, she asked me if I had a problem with any children that came from our union playing with Black children. I told her I had no problem with it...mostly so we could have sex. But it wore on me.

"I came to a place where I knew I was wrong, but that didn't change my feelings. I learned that feelings are bigger than rational thought. At least for me. I met the Bride, Christine, on a visit, and I couldn't even tell she was Black. It made it easier to have promised my wife that I was OK with it. But when Cathy later showed me a picture of Christine's fiancé, Robert, it was a reality gut check.

"Over the couple of years before Cathy got pregnant, it was like a daily rehearsal to tell myself to be OK about it. And here we are.

"I've resolved that our children *would* play together, whether I liked the Groom or not. Then, as I've gotten to know him better, I came to know that he and I would also be part of the wives' and kids' play relationship. Don't tell anybody I said this...but Robert is a great guy. On our last visit, he actually invited me to his shop to introduce me around to all the guys that work for him. Then he drove me out to see a few of his jobs. He introduced me to the foreman on each job and had each foreman give me a tour of what they were doing. Then, at the last job he took me to, the customer came walking in while I was talking to the foreman. Robert introduced me to customer and told her that my wife was Christine's best friend. Then he put his arm on my shoulder and told the customer, 'He's family now.'

"I don't give a sht about trying to pull one over on you about me not seeing skin color. It's still the first thing I see whenever I meet somebody. And I'm not going to lie to you about not using racist language in the privacy of my relationships with some of my brothers on the Force... But in real life, I'm cooler about the Blacks than I have been in the past. Did you notice that I said 'Blacks,' and not 'nggrs?'

"I should also confess to you that a little bit of me toning down my contempt...no, maybe more than a little bit...goes to you and your little show-and-tell lecture at my dining room table that night."

Knopfler finally looked directly at Watkins. "You *do* know your life was literally at risk that night?"

"What I know is that even a *stupid* cop has better sense than to mess with an FBI agent."

"Fair enough. But the question remains. What *are* you doing here?

"The Black grandfather, Elijah, is a war hero that I'm writing a paper on. We've become the closest of friends over a half dozen or so interviews. Eli and I share family values. He wanted me be here to witness this important day in his family."

Watkins didn't want Knopfler...or Knopfler's wife, for that matter...to be around when the news that Robert Smith is Jamal Ali Jefferson broke. Watkins looked across the yard at pregnant Cathy. 'If she saw me walking Jamal out of here in custody, that could negatively affect the health of her pregnancy...her baby. Could it trigger a miscarriage?'

At the moment of that thought, Elijah waltzed over and broke in. "Nancy had mentioned that she seated John and his wife..." Elijah looked at John and raised his eyebrows, as if to say, 'And where is the lovely Jackie Watkins?' "...at Cathy's table because of the Tennessee connection. But you guys are talking like you two know each other? A law enforcement connection? It's a small world after all?" Eli was a little proud of the Disney reference in his light banter.

Knopfler answered. "Yes, Mr. Washington. I *was* liaison to the FBI on Cathy's deceased husband's open murder investigation. We're still working on finding the second guy that murdered my good friend, Mark."

Eli's eyes widened. "John?...you never mentioned that your FBI work involved my wife's second family?"

Watkins answered, "I just learned about it from Officer Knopfler, here. Just now. You were right. It *is* a small world after all."

Eli put his hand on Watkins' shoulder and looked at Knopfler. "John and I have a mutual interest in war stories. I've been helping him on one about a Vietnam rescue team I was on. He's hoping to publish something after he retires."

As Knopfler walked back over to his pregnant wife, Cathy, Watkins decided it was time to expose Robert's identity to Elijah...and to let Elijah know that Watkins was going to take Robert as a volunteer surrender. He had decided that was as humane as he could possibly be.

Watkins knew Robert couldn't run and escape. Watkins had rehearsed in his mind every reaction Jamal would have. The animal trapped in a corner was not who Jamal was. Jamal was a stranger in a strange land. He would have no place to run. No place to hide. It would be the most cooperative arrest in the history of the FBI. And Watkins would retire in a blaze of glory. He had already pictured it.

McNally still had Watkins in his sights, waiting for Watkins to 'go for it.' McNally had been trained to not jump too soon...because once he jumped...all he knew was how to be lethal.

Eli swung out his big arm and hand to John, "You're here alone, brother? I thought you were bringing your wife?"

John looked at Elijah with some of the pain he knew was about to come. "Nice to see you, again, Elijah. Sadly, my wife could not accompany me...because I'm here on business."

Watkins was turned around at that moment by the Bride bouncing with happiness into their conversation. She always seemed to have a note of cheer in her voice. Her new husband was on her arm.

Christine gushed, "Thank you for coming, Mr. Watkins. Grampi told me you have a daughter with a wedding coming up. When is her wedding?"

Watkins didn't want to be distracted from his uncomfortable task. "Oh, well, thank you for asking. She's getting married later this Summer...next month...before she enters grad school."

Christine was still bubbly. "Is she planning on having children?"

Watkins looked next to Christine at his target. 'I'm sorry, but the games up, my friend.' He was rehearsing. "Ah...yes. Children? Yes. In fact, I wondered why she's going to grad school. Her main focus in life is to raise a family."

He looked back at Jamal. 'Let's not make a scene, and I'll just drive you out of sight of everyone...to the local police station for a proper shackling.'

Christine was excited. "I wish her so much happiness. Knowing how much Grampi likes you, I know she was raised to be a great and loving mother."

Watkins looked at Jamal. 'Are you ready for the justice that has eluded you for so long?' Watkins turned to Elijah to spill the beans.

"Elijah," John began, knowing it was going to be tough to do this to Eli. "We developed such a close friendship over the course of our time together...that I thought it would be respectful to you for me to share something that I have to handle myself."

Elijah wasn't paying attention to Watkins because his eyes were squinting into the sun while he was looking at the roof of the pool house.

"Sorry, John, but I just noticed that the gable-end roof vent on the pool house is missing. Must have just happened. I'd have noticed it right away. I'm always looking for those sorts of things."

Watkins turned around and held his hands over his eyes to shield them from the afternoon sun. He could barely make out the missing vent. He shifted his hands and thought he saw a metal rod inside the darkness...and then a brief reflection off a small circle of glass.

Robert said, "Oh, yeah, Grampi. I see it. Don't worry about it. I'll have someone out here to repair it first thing on Monday."

Elijah said to Robert, "Won't you be on your honeymoon, Son?"

Robert chuckled. "I hope I have time for a phone call, even if I'm on my honeymoon, Grampi."

Something in that exchange touched Watkins in a weak spot. 'A grandson taking care of his grandfather's needs.' His lips pursed as he got sucked deep into thought. 'I am become death, the destroyer of worlds.'

Elijah was happy. "I love the sound of that. Don't you, John? The husband of my granddaughter calling me Grampi, and telling me how he's going to take care of me? It's like the ice cream sundae isn't enough. You just have to put a cherry on top."

McNally saw the small group looking up at him. He knew their eyes were in the sun. He knew it was dark in the attic. He assumed someone had noticed the missing vent.

Just then, Watkins' phone dinged with a notification. He turned away from the group and pulled the phone out of his suit jacket inner pocket.

It was a text message from Jackie. "We just got home from the Flea Market. MaryLou and Brandon bought something for you...but you're not here. We're all so sad. Hurry home. We can't exist unless we're a family. Love and kisses."

Watkins slid the phone back in his pocket and turned back to the group.

Elijah asked, "Everything OK, John?"

"Err...yeah...fine. That was a message from my wife. She misses me."

The whole group laughed from being able to relate. Robert slapped

John on the back. "I want to be like *you* when I grow up, Mr. Watkins." And everyone was still laughing in agreement.

"John," Elijah said. "I'm sorry I interrupted you earlier about the gable vent in the pool house. What was it you were saying?"

That's when Nancy wandered into to the group. "Well, hello, Mr. Watkins. Is your wife not with you? I was so looking forward to meeting her and having some girl talk about the way our husbands gossip with each other for hours and hours."

"Ah...no...oh, hello, Nancy. How nice to see you. Ah...no. Jackie couldn't make it."

Nancy turned away from Watkins to try and cough. Watkins thought she was on to him being distracted.

Elijah stepped in and put is arm over Nancy's shoulder for a hug. He spoke with a concern that Watkins noticed. "You alright, Nance?"

Nancy didn't cough, and so she turned her head back to Watkins. "Well, you'd better bring her by here very soon. None of us standing here would be in the best part of our lives without our spouses to help get us here. And I so much need to meet the person responsible for you making it to that special place, also."

Robert spoke up, "Hey, come on Grammi Nancy, we might be new at this, but Christine and I are in a happy place, too."

Nancy smiled. "Our sweet Robert, time has a bad habit of changing things in people. And unless you and Christine have each other to carry each other when you need each other the most...through the darkest moments...in the toughest times...it's easy to get swept away. Those of us that have done this for a lifetime know the value of having a constant and reliable partner. It grows in meaning over time." Nancy turned to Watkins. "Tell 'em, John. Tell these kids that's the way it is. That the long haul is what weeds out the weak."

John couldn't look the newly weds in the eye, so he answered directly to Nancy. "Yes, Nancy. Jackie has always been instrumental in me getting to a better and better place all the time."

Nancy turned to Eli. "Is what I'm saying true, Elijah?"

Eli smiled. "Do you think I'm going to disagree with you on *anything* you say? Take a note, sweet Robert. This is why I'm as happy today as I was the day *we* got married."

As everyone but Watkins was laughing about Elijah saying that, Christine's mother and father stepped into the group. Charleen asked, "What's everybody laughing about? Please don't tell me it was Daddy telling Mommy how much he loves her?"

Everyone but Watkins laughed again, with Nancy adding, "Yes, Char, that's exactly why everyone was laughing."

Mark said to his daughter, "Hey, Christine, your Mom and I came over here because we overheard the groomsmen saying something about looking for you so they could kidnap you."

Elijah jokingly said to Robert, "Are you OK with that, Robert?"

To Watkins, everyone but him seemed to know what was being talked about. That's when Watkins noticed the band of groomsmen surrounding their group. They started cutting into their little circle and surrounding Christine, but with their backs turned toward her. Watkins was edged out of the way with the others, including Robert.

The groomsmen formed a circle around Christine with their backs toward her. Then they locked their arms together. Then they started shuffling her away from their group by forcing her to move in their direction. They were group-shuffling her back down the slope toward where the wedding ceremony had been.

The guests, who were all spread out around the tent and pool terrace and backyard area, started congregating toward positions that gave them a good view of the alter. Watkins kept looking around and wondering if he was the only one present who didn't know what was going on.

Watkins watched the groomsmen herd Christine back down the aisle toward the alter, and then he saw Robert was following the group.

With Christine trapped in their backs-to-her circle, they walked her back up the stairs until they were all on the raised platform of the alter.

Then, suddenly, all the groomsmen unlocked their arms and ran back down to the lawn, below the alter, under the great Chestnut Tree.

Mark, Christine's father, poked Watkins in the ribs with his elbow. "Wait'll you see this. These kids have been practicing this at the shop for weeks after work, with Robert."

The groomsmen formed an arc on the lawn with Robert in the center of the line. Everyone on the property was silent. Watkins looked around because of the eerie silence.

The silence seemed to be broken, though no sound was made, when all the boys started shaking their fingers at their sides.

Watkins looked at the Bride for a reaction. Christine was standing alone at the alter with a more serious look on her face than he could ever imagine a Bride having on her wedding day.

Then Watkins could see the boys faces at either end of the arc. They all had their tongues laid out over their chins...so far that their chins were covered.

Then he heard all the boys chant together, "Kee-ah ree-tay."

Mark leaned into Watkins. "In the Maori language, that means, 'Prepare yourself.'"

Then Watkins saw all the boys bug out their eyes like they were crazed maniacs. They shouted in unison, "Kee-ah maw."

Mark said to Watkins, "That means 'hold fast.'"

Watkins took another look at Christine. She was staring back at the semi-circle of Groomsmen. She was still looking as serious as a heart-attack.

Then the boys started slapping their ribs below their breasts and shouted, "Kee-ah ree-tay."

While doing that, the Groomsmen all dropped to a squat position in unison, moved their hands to their thighs, and shouted, again, "Kee-ah mauw."

Then the semi-circle of young men started slapping their thighs repeatedly, while chanting in unison, "Ringa ringa pah-kee-ah."

Mark leaned over to Watkins again. "You can probably guess that those words mean, 'Slap your thighs repeatedly.'"

Then the Groomsmen started slapping their forearms back and forth repeatedly, and chanted, "Wawh-ay wawh-ay tak-kah."

Then the young men started stomping their feet on the ground, back and forth, as hard as they could, all still in the squat position. They shouted in unison, "Kee-ah kee-no nay-ee hoe-kee."

Then they all went back to slapping their ribs in unison, and said, "Ah kah-mah-tay."

Mark leaned back over to Watkins, "That means, 'Do you know if you will die?'"

Then all the boys crossed their forearms in front of their faces, making a gap in their forearms to look through, and shouted, "Nah nah-tay nah oh-rah rah oh-rah."

Mark told Watkins that that meant, "Do you know if you will live?"

With their forearms still in front of their faces, Watkins could see the boys had gone back to sticking their tongues all the way out, bugging out their eyes, and wiggling their fingers like crazy. They all shouted, "Ah kah-mah-tay nah nah-tay nah oh-rah rah oh-rah."

Mark leaned over to Watkins. "All you have is the present."

Watkins noticed that Christine's stern and serious face was starting to crack, and she was having trouble keeping her arms at her sides.

The squatting groomsmen all shouted, "Tay-nay-ee tay tahn-gah-toe poo-hoo-roo-hoo-roo," while changing into a rotation of rhythmic thigh slapping, forearm slapping, and arms crossing in front of their faces.

Mark leaned over, again. "That last one meant, 'Introduce the power of the Creator."

Watkins could see Christine's chin shaking, but that she was trying to fight it.

The boys kept their cycle going of thigh slaps and forearm slaps and forearms crossing while they chanted the remaining sayings from their squat positions.

"Nah-nah nay-ee ee tee-lee mah-ee."

Mark said to Watkins, "God brings the source of light."

Watkins saw Christine starting to shake.

"Whak-kah whee-tee tay rah."

"And causes it to shine."

Watkins saw Christine start balling out loud, then raising her hands to cover her face.

The boys chanted, "Ah oo-payn."

"Take a step forward."

Watkins could see Christine's body shaking while she sobbed into her hands that were covering her face.

"Ah nah oo-payn."

"Another step forward."

Christine's convulsions caused her to bend slightly forward, with her face still in her hands.

"Ah oo-payn ah nah oo-payn."

"Take a step upward, then another step upward."

"Whee-tee tay rah."

"The source of light shines."

Watkins was aware that Mark seemed unconcerned about his daughter's apparent distress.

Then all the Groomsmen and the Groom stretched their arms straight out, all still in the squat position, and shouted, "Hee!"

As soon as they shouted that, they stood up in a very relaxed way and started shoulder bumping each other.

All the spectators around the property applauded. Some were hooting and hollering their approval.

Robert hurried up the stairs to hold his Bride in his arms.

Elijah and Nancy and Charleen were wet-eyed.

Mark also had a tear in his eye when he leaned into Watkins and said, "That last word means, 'The End!' And it also means, 'So let's do it!'"

Watkins was watching Robert hold his still sobbing wife. He turned to Mark and asked, "What *was* that? Why is Christine so upset?"

Mark said, "She's not upset. She's just overjoyed. In a very humbling kind of way."

Watkins asked, "Why? What *was* that?"

Mark said, "That was a haka that Robert knew…God knows how…and that he taught to his Groomsmen for this part of the wedding."

Watkins had one more question about Scott McNally piled onto his whole stack of other questions about Scott McNally.

Scottie had witnessed the whole thing. He had to take a knee in the attic at the end of it. He was proud. In a very humbling kind of way.

Watkins asked Mark, "What is a 'haka?'"

"Ha, ha! I had to look it up, myself. It's a celebration dance that's used to commemorate a whole range of events by the Maori people of the South Pacific. It originated as a preparation for battle but, in general, it's used to express a commitment or dedication of the group performing it.

"In the context of a wedding, like this, it's used to communicate to the Bride that the Groom has her back for all time, and that the Groomsmen all have the Groom's back…so he can have the Bride's back. It's sort of like someone volunteering to be a God-parent. 'If there's ever any trouble, we'll be there."

Watkins said, "So, by the way she broke down, it's no mystery that

Christine knew about all this?"

"Yeah. Robert had laid out the whole thing to her in advance."

Watkins was transported into some kind of stupor as he watched the Bride, still nestled in the arms of her new husband, her makeup visibly disturbed, visible even from where Watkins stood, descend from the alter to greet each individual groomsman with some words of thanks and a hug.

The haka seemed to be the end of the day. The sun was setting, and all the guests were making their way to the front of the house to find their cars. All the valets had gone home.

Nancy and Charleen and Mark all were walking down to the Chestnut tree to commune with Christine and Robert.

Elijah saddled up next to Watkins. "John…we keep getting interrupted. What is it that you were saying?"

Agent Watkins knew the time had come. 'I am become death, the destroyer of worlds.'

He looked around for Jamal. Jamal had his arm around the waist of his new Bride as his new in-laws approached. 'I am become death, the destroyer of worlds.'

Watkins could see that the afternoon sun was making a reflective glint in Christine's eye. She was rocking her head back in laughter with Robert and the people in their group. 'I am become death, the destroyer of worlds.'

John looked again to see Nancy with her arm over the shoulder of her daughter, Charleen, and saying something into her ear. Charleen was nodding her head up and down with a smile of contentment on her face. 'I am become death, the destroyer of worlds.'

John saw Mark Mack, Robert's new father-in-law and boss, come over to Robert and squeeze him in a hug between himself and his daughter. Christine was admiring her father's love for her new husband.

'I am become death, the destroyer of worlds.'

Elijah pulled John by the arm. "Earth to John. Earth to John." Eli tried one more time to get back to what John was saying.

"I'm sorry for all the commotion, John. But it *is* a wedding! A celebration of the life we have worked so hard to create for ourselves and our children. You and me, both."

John could barely hear Eli over the noise of his own thoughts.

"I think you were trying to say something earlier. What was it you were saying?"

"I...err...when was I saying something?"

"If you think of it, tell me. In the meantime, I have a parting gift for you. If you have a free day tomorrow, there's a twelve hour drive I'm going to recommend to you...as long as your rental car isn't charging you by the mile."

"Err...no..it's a daily charge."

"Good. Then, if you're up to it, I have some directions for you that are like a treasure map. They will lead you to a very special place."

John didn't see any piece of paper with directions, so John asked, "Do you want to record them?"

Eli said, "That would be great. Plus you'll have my voice to listen to, over and over, during your retirement...and while you're working on that writing project of yours."

John opened up the recorder app on his phone and pressed the 'Record' graphic.

"It should scare me that I know these directions by heart. I can't tell you how many decades it's been since I was up there.

"I think it's about 50 or 60 miles south of Eureka. It's also south of Cape Mendicino and north of the Cape Punta Gorda Lighthouse.

"Take the 'Five' up to the 101. Plan on more than 600 miles, total. Twelve hours or so by car.

"Get off the 101 at Humbolt Redwoods State Park. You're going to drive through Bull Creek and Honeydew, heading toward Petrolia.

"But before you get to Petrolia, take a left onto Lighthouse Road. There used to be a sign there saying Mattole Beach. Park in the Trail Head parking lot, then walk down to the beach.

"Stay along the tree line to the south for about 200 feet. You should see a narrow rock seam where no trees grow.

"Climb that seam up into the woods until you see a huge boulder that stands alone and has a view over the treetops to the ocean.

"Now...stop recording."

John shut the recorder off.

Eli finished. "That's the boulder you're looking for. You'll know it when you find it. That boulder kept one of our treasures safe for a decade. And our *other* treasure for the rest of all time."

Elijah put his hand on John's shoulder and leaned in close to John's ear. "If you go, take a piece of my heart up there with you, John. A piece of my heart is buried there, also."

John was being dismissed. He reached out to shake Eli's hand. "It was a beautiful wedding, Eli. You have no idea how happy I am for you."

"Thank you, my brother. It has meant a lot to me to be able to share my life with someone. The private parts. The parts that would have taken this good family life away from us if it were generally known."

John just knowingly nodded his head. He clasped their handshake with his other hand and said, "Sometimes in life, our best choice is to just let it be." John felt those words were not for Elijah.

Elijah sent John on his way with these words. "May the best of times be always in front of you, for you and yours."

John turned and walked toward the driveway to find his rental car. From there, he would head out on his assigned journey. He heard a voice that was not his own echoing off the corners of his mind...'I am the giver of life.'

Scott McNally watched through the scope as John Watkins turned away from Eli and walked toward the driveway to find his car. Scottie thought, 'Ole Eli still touches people with the finger of God…and I'll bet he *still* doesn't know it.'

McNally packed his rifle back into its case. He slid the vent slats back onto their nails. He felt his cleanest exit would be one trip out of the pool house to his car. That meant that the ammo box, filled with enough bullets to take down a small army…and with the evidence of his name in large print…would stay behind.

4

AND

4.1 SUNSET

John Watkins had put Eli's directions into his phone. He knew he was going to Mattole Beach. John was impressed, once again, that Eli knew John would want to pay tribute to where the Boomers' farming days had ended.

It was the middle of the darkness of Sunday morning when John got within a spit of his destination. So, he drove a little bit past until he got to the hamlet of Petrolia. He was hoping to find a motel. All he found was a firehall and a general store, so he continued up the road for the next sign of civilization.

He came to a lone structure that was seemingly in the middle of another nowhere. The plate window had painted on it *The Yellow Rose Cafe*. John parked his car off to the side and climbed into the back seat to catch up on some much needed rest.

He awoke to the sound of a few people gathered outside the windows to his back seat. He could tell by the look on their faces that they were relieved about him looking up. 'They were wondering if I was dead.' It was around noon, apparently the hour in which *The Yellow Rose Cafe* opened for Sunday brunch.

After slapping his face and brushing out the wrinkles in his clothes that wouldn't brush out, he ventured in for a meal. Small town interest made him say he was taking the scenic route to San Francisco to catch a plane…"back to Memphis…if you must know."

He then drove back through Petrolia to the beach Trail Head parking area. There, he noticed a nondescript car of nondescript color with Tennessee plates. He immediately recognized it. He felt some disorientation.

The first thing Watkins did was to get on his hands and knees to inspect for the GPS tracker. He didn't find it. 'Well, that explains a lot.'

John knew the car would be unlocked. He opened the driver's door and popped the trunk. He walked behind and lifted the lid. A duffle bag and the sniper rifle case he knew from the search warrant were the only items in there. He lifted the case to confirm the rifle was inside. 'At least he's not in a ghillie suit targeting me unaware.' He then took a second look for the green metal ammo box with McNally's name printed across the top.

His suspicious mind went to questions about whether Eli had arranged this 'crossing of paths.' But he shook off that thought and let it go. John Watkins maintained the purity of his conclusion that there had been no contact between Scott McNally and Eli, even up to and including the wedding.

John remembered leaving Miss Dolly's with the knowledge that Scott McNally would know that Agent Watkins was on the scent of finding out about Robert Smith that day…and that Mr. McNally would protect his protégé. It was in the moment of that thought that he realized he had been in the crosshairs at the wedding…and that Mr. McNally was on the West Coast solely for that purpose. And then it made sense why McNally was here at the beach of remembrance. 'At least he didn't bring the ammo box. He was going for a clean, singular kill. Me.'

Following Eli's instructions, John walked down the tree line on the back edge of the beach, found the vein of rock, and followed it up. A footpath was well worn. Other beachgoers had found the monument and had been visiting it throughout the intervening decades.

The boulder came into view for John, and with it there was a solitary man leaning with his back against the great rock. The man was staring out over the ocean. John's footsteps made the man turn from his meditation.

John offered an open-hand wave as if to say, 'I come in peace.' He then approached within quiet speaking distance.

He pulled his iPhone out of his shirt pocket and turned to the ocean, pressed a few buttons to take a picture, then started swiping through existing pics.

"My wife and I had a prenuptial agreement that I wouldn't retire until our daughter graduated college." John turned to show MaryLou's Notre Dame graduation pictures to Scottie when he noticed the carved inscription above the back of Scottie's shoulders. In all capital letters, and with one word centered over the other, he read, 'BONNIE'S SUNSET.' John had to swallow the lump in this throat to continue entreating Scottie.

He held a pic of MaryLou in front of Scottie, and Scottie looked down at it.

Scottie contemplated, 'Who *am* I that I can be prepared to end your life on one day and commune with you over your family pictures the next?' He felt he had more work to do on himself.

John continued. "Because of the timing of her graduation being connected to the timing of my retirement, you almost waited me out. I'm signing my retirement papers tomorrow."

Scottie said, "Then you'd better giddy-up." That saying shocked John with a memory of his former FBI boss.

Scottie looked back at the ocean. "What'd she study?"

"Biology. And nursing. We thought she was going to be a doctor at one point, but her true goal was always to be a mom. She starts graduate school in a couple months...after her wedding."

"That's lovely." Scottie was not engaging John Watkins' friendliness. Scottie then added flatly, "When did you know?"

John thought Scottie wanted to know when John knew MaryLou wanted to be a mom, but then immediately realized what Scottie was asking.

"My daughter's Senior year in High School...she was Eliza Doolittle. It finally dawned on me while reviewing the video we took of your bookshelf. George Bernard Shaw. There it was. Right in the middle of all the boys' training manuals."

"Wow. You must have used 'military grade' cameras, as we used to say." Scottie pondered this revelation for a moment. "*Pygmalion*. It took some high resolution to see that on the binding edge of the book cover."

John continued, "I was an English Lit major at Harvard undergrad. Sometimes we would veer off the syllabus to do a deep dive on a High School Honors English classic."

Scottie rusingly said, "Harvard, eh? Pretty impressive. Did you get in because you're Black?"

"You're a horse's ass...but thanks for reminding me that we're still in America."

Scottie appreciated John's sense of humor about it. "At least I'm an ass to your face. And I knew all about your Harvard prize from when I first met you."

John had no context to help him understand the 'from when I first met you' comment, so he continued his explanation of how he discovered Scottie's subterfuge. "When I saw that range of books, I became aware that you were *not* preparing them for another inner city Black neighborhood like the one from which they came, but for the White suburbs. Like Highlands Ranch, Colorado."

Scottie cocked his head to the side. "Why is it *White* to be exposed to the natural sciences, and literature, and language, and the power of mathematics? Now it's *you* who's sounding like a racist."

John answered, "The upscale suburbs are overpopulated with people who have been exposed to those disciplines of learning, almost all at the college level...and, statistically, the upscale suburbs are disproportionately White."

Scottie objected. "I appreciate that that is your opinion, Counselor. But as the person doing the deed, I have a different perspective on it.

"I didn't make them 'White,' nor expose them to 'White.' I offered them a choice to be exposed to things they didn't know so they could fit into a world that was different from the only world they knew...to make them unrecognizable by the likes of people like you."

John was nodding. "OK...but that world is the '*White*' world."

Scottie suddenly realized that Watkins still had no idea who Scottie was. "You don't remember me, do you?"

John looked at Scottie like Scottie had just...instantly...right before his very eyes...lost his mind.

Scottie took him further in. "You didn't investigate me deep enough...did you?"

John was curious. "I investigated you deeply enough to know that you live on a property once owned by one Wiley Roland McNally. Your grandfather, I presumed."

Scottie was nodding his head with a certain satisfaction from knowing something that Watkins didn't. "I, like you, graduated from Lexington High School. My mother's whole career was as a secretary there. I guess it was so she could keep an eye on me."

John pulled his head back as a picture developed in his mind. "At the Principal's Office." John's eyes were getting wider. "And it was you. The guy eating ice cream in your work clothes during my Valedictorian speech." John disappeared into himself for a moment. Scottie heard him mutter 'son...uv...a...bitch.' Watkins was still dazed and confused.

Scottie allowed enough time for the coincidence to sink in. John was thinking, 'There's no such thing as a coincidence?'

Watkins then looked directly at Scottie in wonder and, while slowly shaking his head, said, "I can't do the math."

Scottie had turned back to quietly contemplating the peaceful ocean. "Why did you walk away? I know it was always your plan to take him."

Watkins, still aghast at their chance connection from decades earlier, queried, "And you were there to stop me? At the wedding? I mean, like me, this stop out here above the beach is an adjunct to having been at the wedding...right?"

Scottie, still staring out toward the horizon, had no response.

After a long pause and some introspection, John confessed, "I walked away because of William Shakespeare."

Scottie knowingly looked over at him. "Mercy falls like a gentle rain from above...?"

John finished the end of Shakespeare's verse. "Making the giver share an attribute with the Almighty."

There was a long silence. "My wife and I have done everything humanly possible to ensure our daughter is prepared to define and control her own happiness. But this I now know: there are crossroads in all of our lives where someone will show us mercy...or they won't. And irrespective of everything my wife and I have done for our MaryLou, being granted mercy at that unforeseeable, unpredictable crossroads in time, ironically, is what will have the greater influence on her continued well-being than all our preparations put together."

John used the pause to look at Scottie deeply. "And you? Why did *you* show those boys mercy?"

Both men watched the wavy edge of the sun fall off the peaceful ocean's ledge.

Scottie lifted himself away from the rock and said, "I was just following instructions," as he turned and started walking away from their enclave.

John followed as both men walked the footpath back to the beach. John thought, 'I really misread how much influence Loquisha Davis had over him.'

Side by side, they walked back along the tree line of the beach to the Trail Head parking area. John broke the silence. "You and Eli are the end of an era. The last Boomers. You both made a positive difference."

Those were important words for Scott McNally to hear. But a retiring FBI agent wasn't the person from whom he wanted to hear them.

When they got to their cars, there was no conversation. John Watkins stood beside the door of his rental car until Scott McNally started to drive away, heading north. Watkins thought, 'He is a bit of an odd duck.' Then he added, 'But at least, now, I know why.'

As Scottie disappeared from sight, John pulled out his phone and pressed the button for San Francisco International Airport directions. He noticed there was no cell service, but the map had already been saved in his phone's memory.

He drove out and headed south...not caring how tired he would be the next day.

4.2 VIOLENCE ARE BLUE

A latish model Toyota-Nissan with Tennessee plates toddled north along the same coastal route taken out of Mattole Beach decades before. It was the long and winding road home through Oregon and Washington before heading East and South.

Scott McNally was in no hurry. He would stop and get a room whenever he felt a little tired. The drive allowed him to become lost in the memory of Bonnie's Sunset.

After Doctor Green and Eli had finished all their distribution runs and stashing their cash, they returned to the cabin - and Bonnie - to share a farewell meal with the Compton boys. Eli would leave out again the next morning to bring them back to Compton. That would be the last act of closing out the season.

After the meal, the Compton boys returned to their tent, and Bonnie took a long bath while Doctor Green and Eli cleaned up from the meal. Doctor Green then changed into his pajamas in the hope of enjoying some recreational time with Bonnie.

When she emerged from her bath, Bonnie was wearing a pale pink, semi-sheer nightgown with embroidered flowers and butterflies that were meant to tamp down on some of the sheerness.

Doctor Green noticed her baby bump. The vision of her standing on the other side of the living room from him made him melt in his love for her. She was feeling it, too. Their eyes became lost in each other from twenty feet apart.

Suddenly, the main door to the cabin was thrown open as the two Compton boys barged in and charged at Doctor Green and Bonnie.

One of the boys ran over to Doctor Green and held his arms behind his back with one arm and wrapped his other arm around Doctor Green's neck. While he was doing that, the other boy was holding Bonnie from behind with one arm around her ribs and the other hand holding a boxcutter, blade extended, to her neck.

Oddly, neither Bonnie nor Doctor Green had shown any physical reaction to the aggressive entry, nor to the assault. They were still lost in each other's eyes...like they were communicating on a metaphysical plane. Their calmness further agitated the already jittery boys.

The assailant holding Bonnie at knife-point shouted nervously, "Where's 'The Rifleman?' Where's 'The Rifleman?'"

Doctor Green, remaining focused on Bonnie's eyes, responded in a flat tone. "He went outside to take in the sunset."

Then the boy behind Doctor Green shouted, "We want the money! That's all we want! Give us the money, and nobody gets hurt!"

Bonnie's eyes were so locked on Doctor Green that she wasn't even blinking. She spoke softly to Doctor Green. "Help them."

The boys couldn't figure out what was going on and started shouting louder, repeating their demands for the money. Bonnie's soft voice was barely audible through the boys' shouting. Again, "Help them." Doctor Green's attention was so finely focused into Bonnie's eyes that she didn't have to speak. He could hear her in his soul.

The boy behind Bonnie shouted at Doctor Green, "This is your last chance, mthrfkr!"

Bonnie kept repeating to Doctor Green in such a low voice, "Help them...Help them," that it kept increasing how jittery the boys were getting. The boy behind Bonnie was freaking out because of the calmness between the two soulmates, and he was getting beyond agitated that Doctor Green was not listening to him.

In his nervousness and his frustration and his anger, he suddenly punched the blade of his boxcutter into the side of Bonnie's neck. Immediately, blood started pumping out from the wound.

Doctor Green instantly stepped out of his restraints and started briskly walking toward Bonnie. The boy who had been holding him turned to run while shouting at his partner, "What the fck, mthrfkr! What the fck!" Bonnie had slumped to the floor when her assailant let go of her to flee with his partner.

Both boys ran out the back deck door while Doctor Green's assailant was shouting, "There went the money you dumb-ass mthrfkr!" as they ran down the deck stairs and away from the cabin toward the woods.

Before Doctor Green arrived at Bonnie's limp body on the floor, Eli, who had been listening, sprang out of the bathroom, looked at Bonnie on the floor, ran straight across the living room to the broom closet, pulled out his sniper rifle, and bee-lined it out onto the deck through the open door.

Doctor Green sat on his knees next to Bonnie and wrapped his hand around the back of her neck to put pressure on her spurt-pulsing wound. His medical training made him know that it would be of no use, but he kept his hand tight on the wound anyway.

He moved to a cross-legged sitting position on the floor so he could hold her head in his lap. Her body was already unresponsive, but her eyes were still locked onto his. Her lips were moving, mouthing, 'Help them...Help them.'

Doctor Green had heard Eli's footsteps stop at the deck rail. He knew the faint sounds of Eli taking a knee and setting his elbow on the rail to support the rifle. Doctor Green also knew what was next. He removed his hand from Bonnie's neck wound and used both his blood soaked hands to cover her ears tightly.

Then there came the sound of the bolt action loading a bullet into the chamber, followed almost immediately by the explosion of the bullet leaving the barrel.

Doctor Green took his hands off Bonnie's ears. Her eyes were still open but had no light in them. Her lips were no longer moving.

Doctor Green knew from Physiology Training that the brain processes sound even after it shuts down control of all other body functions. So Doctor Green placed his sticky blood soaked hands over her ears tightly one more time.

The sound of the second bolt action was quickly followed by the echoing report of the second bullet.

Doctor Green knew it was over. He removed his sticky hands from Bonnie's ears, pulling her beautifully shining sandy blonde bloodstained hair away from her sun-kissed, lightly freckled face as he went to cradling her head in the crook of his elbow.

Science hadn't yet discovered how long the brain processed hearing after death, so Doctor Green softly and tenderly sang Bonnie's favorite song, *You Can Close Your Eyes*, to her for about a half hour while gently rocking her head over his lap.

Eli had hiked into the woods to confirm his kills. He had then dragged each lifeless body back to the cabin and left them on the ground by the bottom of the deck stairs.

When Eli finally came in from his chore, he picked up a chair cushion and, with the cushion in hand, knelt down in the pool of Bonnie's blood. He lifted her head enough for Doctor Green to peel his hands off her face and hair and get out from under her.

Doctor Green took the cushion and laid it under Bonnie's head. They both gently rested her head onto the cushion on the floor.

Doctor Green went to their room and retrieved her favorite blanket. He laid it out on the floor about eight or nine feet from Bonnie. Then he and Eli each put a hand under her armpits and dragged her through the pool of her own blood and onto her blanket. They wrapped it over her from both sides.

Then Eli and Doctor Green began performing the last rites.

4.3 BREAKING UP IS HARD TO DO

It took all that night and the next day for Doctor Green and Eli to secure the three adult bodies in heavy-duty contractor bags and to seal the bags tightly to the bodies with duct tape...and to perform their other last rites. They only had necessary conversation during their unpleasant tasks, but one of those conversations was their agreement to not bother cleaning up the cabin...that they would burn it on their way out. They also agreed to bury the bodies where the years of money they had accumulated was vaulted.

When they came across a hand-held sledge hammer and a stone chisel that was among the tools that would go with Eli, Doctor Green suggested they keep those out to mark the large boulder that had kept their treasure safely pinned down against natural nature and human nature so well for a decade...or however many years it had been.

They both knew that they were leaving this land of Oz, never to return, and that the world of clocks and calendars was in each of their futures. Each of their Kansases.

They both had understood from the beginning that the criminal nature of their industry would follow them the rest of their lives, and so to protect each other in the event of one of them being discovered, they would never have any kind of contact ever again. As they prepared to go to 'the boulder,' they both dragged themselves through their final chores with that sad knowledge. Along with the other sad knowledge.

After a night of cat naps, they made a day of trips on the four-wheelers to where their nondescript trucks were parked.

They loaded the three bodybags into the bed of Doctor Green's pickup truck and covered them with bags of Doctor Green's clothing and what little other personal items he was taking with him. Eli handed Doctor Green his sniper rifle wrapped in a blanket. "I want to end up someplace where I won't need this. I filled your PJ ammo box with 165 grain .308's. You should be in good shape to wage a valiant war."

They were not new to the risks of traveling with prison-inviting contraband. They maintained their 'we've-done-the-best-we-can...whatever-will-be-will-be' attitude one more time.

After the last of the tools were loaded on the four-wheelers to make the final trip to Eli's truck, they emptied six 5-gallon gasoline containers of gasoline all inside and around the cabin. Then they each lit a match from opposite ends of the cabin and hurried back down on the four-wheelers to the trucks...before the smoke would draw the attention they knew it would.

All the building tools were tightly packed in the back of Elijah's pickup.

They followed each other for the two hour mountain-road drive to the Trail Head parking area at Mattole Beach. It was empty...as they had hoped it would be.

They made three walking trips down the tree line on the back side of the beach, one 200-foot trip for each bodybag, then carried each bag up the narrow rock seam where no trees grew, from which they followed the familiar foot trail that they had stomped over the years, to the huge boulder that stood alone on the low bluff overlooking the beach.

With each bodybag delivered to the boulder, they silently went through the familiar task of finding the steel beams and the railroad-track fulcrums and the hand shovels that were hidden around the woods.

With all their implements of engineering collected to the boulder, they went about the work of lifting the big rock and suspending it above their 'bank.'

They removed the heavy plastic that enveloped two oversized duffel bags and stacked the bags down the footpath a ways. They then had to dig out more earth from under the rock so all three bodybags would fit in the hole.

With the four bodies in place, and both men breathing heavily from their labor, they just stood over the open grave for a minute. Not a word was spoken. The church bells all were broken.

They then went back to the task of removing the steel beam supports holding the boulder up. In unison, they both made the final lift and removal of the beams. The boulder settled into its final resting place.

Before carrying their cash back to the trucks, they took turns chipping away an inscription in the face of the boulder looking out over the ocean. That took a couple of hours. They shared one pair of goggles that Eli had snatched when they brought the last of the three bodybags. They finished in time to watch the sun set over the placid plain of water.

When the sun was gone, Eli turned back to the rock and ran his fingers in the carving they had made. As Eli turned toward the footpath to leave, Doctor Green also ran his fingers through all the letters of their inscription.

The duffel bags weighed over 100 pounds each, all in $100 bills. Later, when Eli got to the town where he would make a go of it in the construction business, he calculated, by weight, that there was over five million dollars in each bag. He never would have an interest in counting it.

They put Doctor Green's half of the money in the bed of his pickup in place of where the bodies had been, but they had to re-pack Eli's truck in order to bury Eli's cash bag under all the tools. It was all to bolster the chances of an uneventful twelve-hour drive South for Eli.

There were no handshakes as they each got into their trucks. Departing handshakes were always understood to mean, 'until the next time I see you.'

There were also no words. They had had many years to say all they had to say. And they had.

They both started their trucks, they each put their hand on their shifters, they both looked over at each other, they both nodded, then they both put their trucks into gear and headed out in the opposite directions of their individual destinies.

4.4 HELEN MAYER

John Watkins arrived at his Memphis FBI office on Monday morning, straight from the airport, to sign his retirement papers. The adrenaline of the moment kept him from sleepwalking.

Some of the staff people had wanted to give him a party, but he declined, saying that his career of working with the greatest, most dedicated group of professionals in the world was his reward, and that he didn't want all of that to be summed up in a party. The memories would be his continuing celebration.

John got home around lunch time. His wife was still at work. He turned on the TV to find out what daytime TV was like. He surfed for about 10 minutes and decided he'd better get a hobby. Maybe make good on that paper about the last F4 downed in Vietnam.

He daydreamed remembrances of the 'Officer Down' case. He reviewed in his mind all the images from the years of mental work, and action plans, and carrying out those plans. The progress toward the goal as well as the setbacks. He was still daydreaming when Jackie came in from the garage and set her things on the kitchen island.

John hugged her for what she thought was going to be a quick 'hello' hug, but he wouldn't let go. She hoped he wasn't going to have a mental breakdown from nothing left to do.

She waited till he was done, and he, thinking he'd probably have to come up with an explanation, slowly let go. She tilted her head back to look at him in his face just to make sure he was OK. Then she started putting a small bag of grocery items in the fridge.

Her last move was to pull out a chilled bottle of white wine. Then she reached below the upper cabinet next to the fridge and slid two inverted wine glasses from the rack. She poured.

She lifted her glass to his and asked, "Well...how did the retirement go?"

He dinged his glass to her's and said, "I didn't give the Nazi salute...so...I guess it went pretty well."

Jackie thought he had lost his mind. Already. On the first day of retirement.

4.5 OH YEAH LIFE GOES ON

Grammi Nancy had not felt her whole self at Christine and Robert's wedding. A two year struggle through medications and treatment seemed sadistic. Mark and Charlene were at her side, along with pregnant Christine and Robert. Eli came into the private room with an old, battered, battery-operated boombox.

He set it on a mobile tray next to her bed and inserted an old, old cassette tape. He pressed where there used to be a 'Play' button and adjusted the volume to louder than normal.

Aretha Franklin belted out *You Make Me Feel Like A Natural Woman*, and Eli just waited, holding her hand and watching for a reaction from his wife of near fifty some odd years. Eli never had learned how to count time.

Less than a minute into their song, Eli got what he was looking for. Through the morphine, she smiled. She smiled all the way to the end of the song when Eli pressed where the 'Stop' button used to be. The room was silent once again. But Nancy was still smiling. And so was Eli.

She opened her eyes to see him bent over her, looking into her eyes. She could only keep her eyes open for about five seconds. Then her eyes closed. A few moments later, the machine to which she was attached made a steady tone sound. Charlene reached behind her father and pulled the plug to silence the machine. Grammi Nancy still had that smile on her face.

Eli spoke at the funeral. It was tough for him to get through recounting how they met and fell in love. How he never could have been a provider and a father and a grandfather without her. That all the nice things people have ever said about him were really about her in him.

He read from Nancy's favorite poet, Emily Dickinson:

> The Bustle in a House
> The Morning after Death
> Is solemnest of industries
> Enacted upon Earth –
> The Sweeping up the Heart
> And putting Love away

We shall not want to use again
Until Eternity –

He finished by saying that his "Nance had started her journey with soft and sensitive skin on the soles of her feet. But that with each act of kindness and goodwill that she showered on others, her soles became tougher and more resilient to the pain from the places where she chose to walk to perform her acts of giving of herself. And that by the end, she had developed diamonds on the soles of her feet. And those diamonds were testimony to the fact that there was no place she could not go to perform her acts that would bring joy and relief to others. The soles of her feet were a tribute to the end of her life well lived.

"Now those diamonds will protect and sustain the soles of her feet for the moment for which I patiently wait."

Eli bowed his head. "Lord, keep her feet ready so she can come running whenever someone special crosses over that River Jordan to see her again."

Robert Smith continued to make things better at *Washington Construction*. Two years after the wedding, his Profit & Loss responsibility for all renovation work was paying big dividends. His ability to keep all the operational gears greased and keep all his paperwork in order was the basis for the announcement that he would now get full responsibility for all new residential construction, also. The future was being laid for Robert to take over the commercial/industrial side of the business to coincide with his father-in-law's desire to retire sooner rather than later.

Christine had picked up Robert from work to accompany her to their 18-week prenatal care appointment. While they were in the waiting area, Robert was well aware that this was another example of his brave new world.

'My mother, and her mother before her, and another mother before her, ad infinitum, never saw the inside of a doctor's office. The closest they ever came to health care was accompanied by the blaring siren of an ambulance on a bumpy ride to an emergency room. If that.'

The nurse had been getting images on the screen of the ultrasound but didn't say anything. She waited for the Doctor to come in.

The Dr. asked, "Do you want to know the sex of the baby?"

Christine looked at Robert. "Of course we do!"

The Dr. got a still image on the screen and used his pen to point out the penis.

Christine looked back over at Robert. "It's so big! You should be proud!"

The Dr. laughed and said, "Yes. It's a boy."

On the way to drop Robert, who had the ultra-sound picture in hand, back off at work, Christine asked, "So, have you thought of any names for your son?"

Robert answered more quickly than he needed to. "Only one. Scott."

Christine noticed how quickly he answered. "Scott? Where in the world did *that* come from?"

Robert was lost in a memory. "Mother."

Christine looked at him with a squinting and wrinkled face to indicate he was being weird.

Robert snapped back into the present to ask Christine, "Have you thought of any names for *your* son?"

Christine got a little lost in herself as well. "I was expecting it to be a girl. I'll have to give boys' names some thought."

John Watkins had decided to work the Vietnam writing project in earnest. A lot of the work was via email, but he'd make a trip to get the authenticity of a human voice, 'the true timbre of humanity,' he would call it, from time to time.

His biggest highlight of the project was being invited to what would be the last quinquennial reunion at Ernie's place in Highlands Ranch. A group photo of all the generations of Ernie's Search & Rescue heroes would be the cover photo of his completed history of the event. There were 363 people in that picture. John had it made into a 4-foot x 3-foot poster and, with a little resistance from his Jackie, paid for and mailed a copy to the remaining heads of the eighteen families Ernie had hosted over the decades. John had been so diligent to get each of the participant's names so that he could have each person's name meticulously printed in tiny white letters across their chest in the poster.

John had made it a career discipline to never mention an FBI case to his wife or daughter, nor any of his work activities related to any of his cases. But in his retirement, he made one...and only one...exception.

John would re-construct the many pieces of a person's life from the pot farming story to his family without mentioning any names but one. Bonnie Lass. He saw her as a hero that never got to be a hero. He told his wife and daughter and son-in-law about her, chapter by chapter over time, and would often repeat events randomly about a girl who summoned her own strength to escape her circumstances. How she summoned her own strength to avoid the temptation of being taken care of by anybody but herself.

He would say things like, "She embodied the ideal of the American Dream...pull your*self* up. She was aggressive to find her own healing...diet, exercise, meditation. To build her own strength. To control her own choices. To control her own destiny. None of which could have come about but for the mercy to let her find her own way, that mercy being the wild card that Bonnie herself would have had to admit was out of her own control. Striving for self-determination, but accepting the refreshment of 'a gentle rain from heaven.' The girl that never got to finish her chance that she had created for herself." John would never mention her backstop. Her silent supporters.

There was always an air of sadness in John Watkins' details. He pined about her out loud more than once, "All the work and the focus to be the overcomer she would become...and that she would never get to become."

Jackie and MaryLou and Brandon would say, "It makes you want to go back in time and give her a chance to be all she could be. And it sounds like she could have been a lot."

John's family would often encourage him, "Tell us again about how she..." He couldn't reveal it, but whenever he told and retold the stories of Bonnie, in his mind, he always saw the last Boomers with her, backing her up without getting in the way. Giving her all the room she needed to become whole on her own terms.

4.6 KNOCK KNOCK KNOCKIN'

Scottie's body had become like his work boots. Worn and lived in.

As he tried to adjust to the ever increasing affects of age, the property got harder and harder to maintain. He knew that, like time and gravity, nature isn't all that overpowering. It was a weak force, weakened further by how slowly it encroached. But it was relentless. And *that* was the source of its ultimate dominance...like time and gravity.

His attitude kept him in the game. 'I've done the best I can...whatever will be will be.'

One morning, before what he knew was going to be an exhausting chore, he skipped breakfast under the influence of an unsurpassable urge to do a little soft-shoe.

He queued up Frank Sinatra's *New York, New York* on the computer. Then he soft-shoed around the tile floor in his stocking feet in front of the unlatched bookcase.

With his eyes closed, he swept back and forth with his air partner. At one point, he thought he felt her backside brush against his as they passed. He thought nothing of it until, during a point when their arms slid down each other's arms, he felt her hand take a hold of his hand. That made him open his eyes.

Nothing. No-one.

Then the soft-shoe ended.

The computer randomly played a song by Cintron next. *Oye Como Va*. Scottie loved the Cintron version because of the added verse in English.

The African rhythms interlaced with Latin melodies made Scottie shuffle and slide through his cha-cha steps and body moves while he stuffed his stocking feet into his work boots. After he performed the last rite of lacing his boots up, he shuffled and spun his way out the door to collect his tools for a morning of riverwalk maintenance.

When Scottie stepped outside his front door, he looked up and saw a woman standing twenty or so yards away from him. She had a baby on her left hip, plus a three-ish looking boy clutching her left leg, and a four- or five-year old girl standing on her right side, held close by the mother's free hand on the little girl's shoulder. They looked peaceful.

They were all four staring at him with placid smiles when the children began to look up at their mother, whispering what appeared to be questions, followed by broader smiles and head-nodding. Scottie wondered, 'Do these people know me?'

Scottie looked around for a car. But there was none. He looked up the driveway to see if there was a cloud of dust from a car leaving. But there was none.

He knew they could not have traipsed through the woods and up the hollow. 'Must have been dropped off a while ago.' He knew he would have heard from Miss Dolly, old and decrepit as she was now, if a Black family had moved into the neighborhood.

As he stared at the family, he wondered, 'Why didn't the driveway alarm go off?' Then he heard an anciently familiar sound. Scottie turned back to look at his house. 'That's not the driveway alarm.'

Scottie knew there was food in the fridge. The house was unlocked as always, and the no-longer-secret bookshelf to the basement was open. So, he walked to the shed to get his pruning tools. He didn't dwell on the oddity of the encounter.

When Scottie came out of the tool shed with his scythe for knocking down the tall weeds and grass on the riverwalk, he saw another woman in his driveway. She was walking with children in tow. Her and her children's features were Hispanic. There was a man about her age walking behind her. The group of them, like the first mother and family he saw, was looking at Scottie as they walked in his direction. They all started smiling at each other as though they recognized Scottie. Scottie heard that sound again. He looked up the hollow from whence the sound came. Then, once again, he looked around the yard area for a car, and then up the driveway.

When he looked up the driveway, he saw more people walking toward his house. Different sizes and combinations of family groups. He saw many different race characteristics as though they were coming from beyond his part of the country.

He looked from side to side into the woods, then again up the driveway. In the driveway, the coming crowd was even more dense. They crowded his driveway far beyond the first rise and dip. And the air seemed to be filled with that faint ringing sound.

'What is this about? Why are these people coming here?' But then a rational explanation came to him. 'The New York State Thruway has been closed.' That was the best he could make sense of it. Little did he know that this is where they had all been told to come.

With his scythe slung over his shoulder, he turned and descended the curvy and rugged tractor path to the river for his day's work.

The day was overcast. The chance of rain was high. But Scottie thought to himself that he would work until he couldn't. 'Never let the *threat* of rain stop a day's work.' He started at the downstream entrance to the riverwalk, off that corner of the bottom field.

It was after midday when he made it all the way to the section of riverwalk that the boys had named *The End of the Line*. He felt it was reasonable to feel some energy drop and thought he'd better get back to the house to eat something. That's when the first raindrops fell. Scottie thought that maybe he'd better sit on the flat of the bent ironwood tree to rest before making the big climb home.

He felt a draining as he sat, the rain drops accumulating on his already sweat-wet clothing, the scythe resting on his shoulder, held securely by the wrapping of his arm. He could feel his blood pressure was falling.

'No worries.' He started to flex muscles and breathe deeply. It had worked before to restore him. But he got distracted by the white caps of a rapid being formed by the increasing current. 'It must be raining more heavily upstream.'

He started to see little stars appear and disappear on the whitecaps...then all around. He knew he was about to pass out. He looked for a soft spot on the ground where he could lie down to make his transition to unconsciousness less bumpy.

As he looked for a spot, the ground came to him. He lay there for a bit with the blade of his scythe having come to rest between his shoulder blades and his neck. Then there were no more stars.

The rain came hard. And for a while.

The ground around him became muddy soft and held him for that while. But the rain turned into a thunderstorm flood, and the river started to rise even more.

Within a couple of hours, the river had risen over the banks. The raging river was near to fully covering Scottie when a rapid current separated him from his scythe and inched his body, jerk by uneven jerk, to where the bank had been before the flood. He finally got swept away from the bank shrubs, then into the open flow.

It was a fast ride to the dog's leg where he got caught in a logjam of trees accumulated from upstream because of the floodwater. Then the rain suddenly stopped. It was a little while longer before the flood started to recede.

As the logjam shifted from the falling water, Scottie was let go. He drifted with the current into the rapids below the dog's leg until the current washed him onto the sandy beach at the swimming hole. He felt the sand on his palm, so he dug his fingers in. That allowed him to use his free arm to keep turning his body until he was where he could use both arms to push himself away from the sand and the water. He pulled his knees up under himself and found his balance to stand up.

He dragged his feet through the receding water until he got to the edge of the riverwalk bank. There, he climbed off of the swimming hole beach and back onto the riverwalk.

Once he was stable on the riverwalk, he draggingly made the short walk to the uphill climb, back to where the entrance was to that corner of the bottom...where his workday had begun.

He stood under the canopy of the entrance just as the early evening sunlight found an opening below the horizon and reflected a glow off the undersides of the remaining disassembling clouds. He had never seen the gloaming on the bottom field more vibrant. He, once again, heard the distant clanging of giant tuned bronze echo off the surrounding terrain.

As his hearing and the sight of the magnificently lighted field mesmerized him, he noticed someone waving to him from the farthest corner. A younger woman, maybe a teenager, but probably not, was waving a hand while she made the long walk across the field toward him. He waved slowly back at her as he studied her approach.

While watching her, he heard a child shout, and he looked to see a little girl with familiar features bearing down on a soccer ball that she kicked with all her might. It went sailing into a group of small children, all chasing the ball to try and kick it amid giggles and shrieks of joyful play.

As Scottie began to feel the echoing sound of bronze penetrate his being, he looked to see that young couples were standing around the edge of the field, halfway in conversation with each other while halfway watching the children frolic in the neatly trimmed grass. They all looked so comfortable...like they knew that this place had been prepared just for them.

The young woman finally arrived in front of Scottie with the most calm and peaceful smile as Scottie had ever remembered seeing. He knew her. He tried to absorb the moment.

As the echoing sound of harmonic metal clanging seemed to be getting louder...'as though in celebration,' Scottie thought...Scottie noticed even more parents on blankets enjoying picnics while they watched the children. Every time the edge of the field became more packed with revelers, the echoing sound of bells got louder.

The din of the revelers drawn to the frolic became louder with every look. And the number of children chasing balls around the field became so large that, when they moved, it was like a flock of birds or a school of fish, so dense that they seemed like one large moving body.

The young woman who had arrived in front of Scottie stepped into him and gently engaged him in a full frontal hug. He thought he heard her say, 'Welcome,' though he never saw her lips move. She pressed the side of her face into his chest. The embrace felt like a permanent fixture of Scottie's being.

As Scottie kept drinking in the sight of the ever increasing crowd and the celebration clanging sounds coming up the hollows from the Methodist Church, an echo of his own thoughts wouldn't diminish. 'How did all these people know this place was here?'

While pondering that question, he looked down at the woman in his arms. 'Oh.' She tilted her head back until their mutual gaze reassured Scottie that they were melded as one.

At some point, they moved to a side embrace, Scottie's arm over her shoulder, her arm across his back, holding onto him at his waist.

From their corner of the bottom, they stood in silent wonder, surveying all the activity and playful energy that covered the field so densely that the finely cut grass could no longer be seen.

As their shared moment continued to well up into an ever increasing tranquil joy, Scottie noticed that the woman was nodding her head in silent affirmation. That's when he saw her lips move. That's when he heard her say it.

"Well done."

4.7 THE HEART IS A LONESOME HUNTER

Loquisha Davis had spent years listening to the wailing and moaning of Jamal's and Muhammed's mothers and grandmother and, after many years, and well after Muhammad's death, she caved into consoling Jamal's mother and grandma by sharing her secret...that she had seen the boys at the man's house seven or eight months after she dropped them off there. That he was the one who spirited Muhammad off to his new life and had, presumably, done the same for Jamal. But that where he sent them was never known to her until Muhammad turned up dead outside Denver. Grandma claimed she was about to die and wanted to meet and question the man who had taken and sent her boys from her.

Loquisha, once again, caved to the emotional pleas and agreed to make the trip to Scottie's property, knowing she was going to be crucified for it.

On the ride down, Loquisha told her passengers, "Don't be surprised to find out that Jamal has died, too. Everybody dies. We don't always know how. Sometimes they're just gone, and we never see them again. We never know."

Loquisha pulled down Scottie's driveway to see three local Sheriff's cars. One had Miss Dolly in the front passenger seat with all the windows down. Loquisha lowered her window as she neared the scene.

The new Sheriff approached Loquisha's car. "Yes, M'am?"

"We're here to see Scott McNally."

The Sheriff raised his eyebrows. "Are y'all friends of Mr. Scottie's?"

Miss Dolly was listening closely to the conversation. She frailly shouted, enough to be heard by the Sheriff and the visitors, "Scottie ain't never had no nggr friends. Get them the hell outta here before I call the Law."

The Sheriff bent a little closer to Loquisha and spoke in a little more hushed tone. "Sorry about her, M'am. What were you saying about knowing Mr. McNally?"

Loquisha told him, "He's just somebody that I used to know. My friends and I were out for a drive, and I thought I'd introduce them to him."

The Sheriff asked, "When's the last time you saw Mr. Scottie, M'am?"

"Oh, it's been years. Why? Is there something wrong?"

The Sheriff explained, "Mr. Scottie brings the daily mail to his neighbor over there, and she called me and said she hadn't seen him in a couple days. She added that it was not like him to not let her know when he wouldn't be home to bring her her mail."

Loquisha asked, "A few days? When I knew him, he had a car and a truck. Are they both still here?"

"Yes, M'am. They're both in the garage." He pointed to the closed garage door. After a moment he added, "Miss Dolly, over there, said he's been slowing down lately."

Loquisha got a bit worried. "Do you mean...mentally?...like he mighta wandered off and not know his way home?"

The Sheriff nodded his head while looking down at the ground. "That's what we're fearing, M'am."

"Oh, my." Loquisha had some sad pictures enter her mind. She didn't know if she was going to cry from worry. "Bless his heart. He hasn't called me in years. But if I hear anything..."

The Sheriff offered, "Thank you, M'am. And, again, I'm sorry about Miss Dolly's mouth."

As Loquisha drove away, they could hear Miss Dolly yelling at the Sheriff, "Don't you be apologizing fir my mouth, Sheriff. It's a good thing you run them nggrs off. I know people who'd make sure a nggr don't last a day in these here parts..."

Loquisha raised her window back up. Jamal's mother asked, "So, there's no way to know, now, what might a happened to my Jamal?"

Loquisha nodded lightly and silently through her own wondering.

As they got onto the Railroad Bed Road, Grandma mumbled clearly enough for all to hear, "In these parts, it ain't the *poe*-leece you got to fear. It's the neighbors."

Upon returning to his office, The Sheriff issued a Silver Alert for Scott McNally.

4.8 SUNRISE

The timer on the stove dinged. John Watkins announced through the doorway to the living room that the cake was done cooling. "Ten more minutes to showtime!"

He slid the first layer onto the cake dish and collected his homemade-from-scratch buttercream frosting. Once both layers were frosted, he stuck the oversized #1 candle in the top, lit it, and carried the cake into the living room singing, "Happy Birthday to you..."

Jackie, MaryLou, and Brandon were playing with their baby girl and joined in the singing. The baby had no idea what was going on.

Jackie asked her daughter, "MaryLou, I know the hospital's been keeping their thumb of pressure on you to come back to work. Have you and Brandon made a decision yet?"

MaryLou said, "They keep upping the offer. It's gotten to where Brandon and I feel if I'm going back to work, it has to be because I love the work, not because the money is irresistible. I've had our little precious for a year now. A good daycare, plus Brandon and me shifting our schedules around to have max face time with her...I told them to give me a start date."

Then she turned to her dad who was looking at Jackie. "What about you, Daddy? It's been forever since you finished your Vietnam writing. So...what's your next retirement project?"

John looked at his wife, Jackie, who was gently smiling and nodding.

John turned to his granddaughter's parents. "Your mother and I have left no stone unturned talking about this...because we wouldn't bring it up to you without having done our due diligence. Eh? Brandon? Pretty good lawyer talk?"

John moved to be arm in arm with Jackie and turned to both kids. "How would you feel about your mother and me doing full-time daycare for little Bonnie Lass? It would be our full-time job."

MaryLou looked at Brandon, both beaming about the surprise and the coincidence. Holding her husbands's hand, MaryLou said to both her parents, "We've already talked about it, too. We could have no greater joy but for our Bonnie's care to be your chosen work." She looked at her husband. "Brandon has a new saying that he's proud of."

John and Jackie were expectant, feeling all the positive energy in the room.

Brandon looked at his wife, and then back to his in-laws, so happy, and said, "Work is the physical manifestation of...

4.9 BLUE SKIES

Robert Smith entered the house that he was just getting used to calling 'home.' He'd been held up at his office by a phone call from a fellow City Councilperson.

Once inside his front door, he pressed the button to close the one-of-seven garage doors where he had parked his pickup truck. His kids came running to him with 'Daddy attention' desires.

Four-year-old Elijah made it to him first and jumped into his arms. Robert beamed, "Hey, Elijah! Nice to see you, too, buddy!"

Two-year-old Alison ran and grabbed onto her Daddy's leg. Robert lifted her up with his other arm, "Hey, Ali," and kissed her on the cheek. Then he kissed Elijah on the cheek as he set him down.

Christine called out from the kitchen with the baby in her arms. "Hey, Baby. I appreciate that you've worked all day to keep the lights on, but I'm in need of some break time." She was walking right up, passing the baby to him as she finished speaking. "Knock on my door when supper's ready."

Robert took the baby. "You know we're gonna make a great big mess, don't you?"

Christine acknowledged him with, "Deal. I'll do the clean-up," and started walking toward the sanctuary of their bedroom.

But then she suddenly stopped and turned back to him. "Oh, I almost forgot." She changed course back into the kitchen.

She came out with an envelope in her hand and said, "A letter came for you today from the FBI in Tennessee. I thought I shouldn't open it in case my fingerprints got on it." She laughed at her own humor.

Robert slowly set Ali down and moved baby Jamal to his other arm as he faded away inwardly.

"What's wrong, Daddy?" asked Elijah Scott, looking up at him from the floor.

Robert's black skin hid that all his blood had instantly drained, but it couldn't hide that all his facial muscles had collapsed.

Christine opened the envelope for him, reached inside, and pulled out the FBI letterhead. His mouth was unconsciously open as he thought, 'Oh, no, Babe,' and then he felt his spirit leave him.

He read the letter silently. Neither the kids nor Christine had ever seen this mood shift before.

"Dear Eli,

"A phone call from a former colleague interrupted the peace of my retirement yesterday. He was calling to inform me that a person of interest I had come to know toward the end of my career, our mutually known Scott McNally, was identified from a part of his bare skeleton.

"All that remained was his skull and a small attached piece of his vertebrae. It had been discovered in the bank brush, twenty-one miles downstream from his Little Buffalo River property, by a fisherman on the Big Buffalo River. It is assumed he died in the river at his home and was, over time, washed downstream by the rain storms.

"The recovered part of his skeletal remains showed no signs of head trauma, and he was identified by dental records locally.

"His death certificate lists the Date of Death as unknown. However, a footnote presumes it to be the day a neighbor reported him missing thirteen months earlier.

"Cause of Death was checked off as 'Undetermined.'

"I thought you might want to know that your former ParaJumper team member, your fellow combat Silver Star recipient, and your former farming partner, about whom you shared so many warm memories, has passed.

"Good luck with the great-grand-kids. And a final thank you for your generosity and friendship. You're a true American hero in every sense of the word.

"With the highest respect and the warmest regards to all whom you love...

"John Watkins"

Christine spoke when he got to the end of the letter. "Baby?...Are you OK? You're worrying me. Are you crying?"

Robert looked up and snapped back into the present. He handed her back the letter, wiped his eyes, and looked at and kissed baby Jamal, still in his arm, who was staring wide-eyed at the whole scene, himself.

Robert said softly to Christine, "This is a letter for Grampi. It's from the guy who was at our wedding...the guy that Grampi helped with his Vietnam story."

"Yes. I remember meeting him in Grampi's study with you one time." She turned the envelope over. "But it's addressed to you, Baby."

Robert took the envelope and looked at the handwritten address. His brain spun quickly through some flashbacks...of both Scottie and Grampi Eli having military experience, but Scottie never saying anything about the Air Force or Vietnam...of Scottie delivering Robert to Pacific Palisades, even stopping in front of *The Washington Construction Company* office.

Some meaning had started to come into focus...but as the pall over every part of every day of Robert's life since Nashville was starting to evaporate, the deeper meaning of Grampi Eli and Scottie knowing each other would have to wait. Shards of an unfamiliar sunshine were slowly accumulating for a breakthrough.

Robert, still speaking softly, rationalized to Christine, "Maybe Grampi's FBI friend wrote the letter before he knew of Grampi's death, and then addressed it after he found out. I don't know." Robert was still in ponder mode. "Do you remember Grampi ever saying anything about that guy being an FBI agent?"

Christine was trying to remember. "I don't think Grampi said anything about that the one time we met him before the wedding. And I didn't hear him say anything about it *at* the wedding."

Blood was returning to Robert's face. "In any event...it's a warm and thoughtful letter. We'll put it in our memory box of Grampi treasures."

Christine had a lingering concern about how Robert was feeling. "You OK, Baby? I thought I was losing you there for a minute."

Robert opened his arm and walked into Christine to hug and assure her. He knew the letter was meant to be addressed to him. He knew the letter was *for* him. "We miss Grampi, don't we, Babe?"

Christine nodded her head against his chest. She was snuggled up to baby Jamal, too.

Robert whispered in her ear, "Let's never forget that Grampi was the first person you wanted me to meet when you were interested in me. I've always felt that without his approval, we could have never gotten together."

Christine started tearing up at the memory of Grampi Eli.

Robert felt there was so much more he didn't know. Knowing Scottie, he presumed it was by design. He wondered about whether Grampi Eli had knowledge of all those things that had brought Robert to Eli's family.

But then there was also that new feeling that was entering Robert. A feeling of 'clean.'

He remained holding Christine closely with baby Jamal in his arm, and with Elijah and Ali holding tight to their Mommy's and Daddy's legs. The little ones were feeling something that was in the moment...but not understanding what it was.

Robert started rocking ever so slightly. He kissed Christine's ear ever so lightly. Over and over. Then he stopped and whispered, "Everything's gonna be alright."

Christine had never thought there was any other option.

4.10 ASHES TO ASHES

John and Jackie Watkins had loved the years of full-time daycare to little Bonnie Lass. But the pre-school years, and then the kindergarten year, were precursors to a coming day when her world would start to grow exponentially beyond John and Jackie and her parents.

One day during that kindergarten year, little Bonnie had been doing some exploring while John and Jackie were busy with chores.

John was sitting on the couch in the living room scrolling through a newsfeed on his phone. He looked up to see her walking out of his study with a relic in her hand and a question on her face.

John had been hyper-vigilant to store his old service weapon in a hard-to-find place. He stored the empty bullet clips in a separate hard-to-find place. And he stored a box of bullets in the small fireproof safe he kept in the back corner of a high closet shelf.

The pistol had a plastic-coated steel cord that snaked its way through the open chamber, then through the clip cavity, then through the trigger guard. It was held securely in place with a heavy lock. It was that pistol she had found in the back of a bottom desk drawer behind a stack of some file folders.

Little Bonnie's question made Jackie stop what she was doing in the kitchen and peer out to see what was going on.

Little Bonnie had raised the entangled piece of steel up to her eye level and, looking at John with the blankness of inquisitivity, asked, "What did you do in the war, Grandpa John?"

Jackie leaned against the kitchen wall, out of sight. She cherished these moments. These were the moments that had come to define their lives. And she knew they would soon disappear.

John let little Bonnie put the relic in his hand. He placed it on the couch cushion next to him and patted the empty space in front of Bonnie with his other hand.

Little Bonnie climbed up and maneuvered herself next to and up close to her grandfather. John put his arm over her shoulder and held her firmly to himself.

"I met a girl who was the most amazing Princess I had ever met in the entire world. She was a very active Princess. She studied books. She learned about good foods and how to make them delicious to eat. She learned lots of great ways to exercise her body. And she knew how to choose the right friends. She had the greatest friends in the world."

Little Bonnie was looking up her grandfather. She was intent on hearing every detail.

"What was her name, Grandpa John?"

"I could tell you, Sweetheart, but then you would know too much. You would know the great secret of where your name came from."

Bonnie thought he would just tell her, but John had paused to gauge her interest.

"Tell me, Grandpa John. What was her name?"

"Her name was Bonnie Lass, Sweetheart. And she was special beyond what 'special' had ever meant before...

Jackie Watkins was walking in the front door from seeing little Bonnie Lass onto the school bus for another day of Second Grade. John was cleaning up after the school-day breakfast. John thought he was hearing a ghost from the past when his phone sounded with the first four ominous sounding notes from Beethoven's Fifth Symphony. The last time he had heard those notes was when he found out about the identified remains of Scott McNally.

"Boss? Did you butt-dial me?"

John's former and almost forgotten boss was laughing. "No, John. I just had to call you to tell you that you have to be the worst FBI agent in the history of FBI agents."

"Oh, no, Boss. Not another pep talk."

"John. That Sheriff that had called me about the McNally remains? He called me again this week."

"Yeah, Boss? What'd he want?"

"He called to say the McNally property had finally been cleared through Probate for sale at public auction."

"Yeah, Boss. Why would I be interested in that? I spend my days gluing bird feathers onto wood carvings."

"He called to say that a young hippie-type couple bought the place. Yoga and vegetable gardens and music and dancing types. He knows about them because they had called him to come out to the house after they had moved in and were setting up shop."

"OK, Boss. This sounds like you're calling me with gossip...and it's still ringing in my ears that I'm that worst FBI agent in history."

"Well, John. This goes way beyond gossip. The reason the young-ins called the Sheriff was because they were going through McNally's computer and they came across a file that was titled *FIX*. They thought it had to do with how to do maintenance on some of the equipment around the property or house things. But when they read it, they found out it was a radical extremist manifesto. That's how the Sheriff described it."

John became half-interested to hear where this was heading.

"It turned out to be a history paper about Germany after World War II, and how America never cleaned house like that after the Civil War...and that America needed to outlaw White Supremacists and their symbols the same way Germany did to the Nazis. The document had a lot of historical detail in it."

Watkins thought to himself, 'So, you think it was extremist for the Germans to outlaw the Nazis?' But what he said was, "So, you're calling to tell me that McNally was a radical?" Watkins was having trouble getting his mind to rise to the level of having a full interest in this phone call from his former boss.

"No, John. I'm calling to tell you that McNally wrote a dedication in the front of his manifesto. The hippie kids called the Sheriff because they knew the two names McNally listed. The two names had become folklore heroes...legends...in certain circles across America."

"OK, Boss. The worst agent in the history of the FBI is all ears. What'd it say?"

"Let me read it to you, John. This is going to blow your mind...

"This prescriptive history lesson is dedicated to the memory of Muhammad Dogg Jefferson and Jamal Ali Jefferson. I feel personally responsible for both their deaths. I know I could have done more for both of them.

"In the two years that I mentored them, I did the best I could. Their deaths would have never been necessary if the prescriptions in this paper had been implemented after the Civil War in the United States of America."

Watkins was silent.

"John? You still there?"

"Yeah, Boss."

"Well, then, why don't I hear you jumping up down and turning furniture over in celebration?"

"How's that, Boss?"

"You were right, John! You were right all along! It *was* McNally! It was McNally the whole time! We don't know how he pulled off the details...but this is as close to a confession from the grave as anyone could hope for. We're treating it as a deathbed confession. And now we know that McNally did it because he was a radical extremist. That was the motive you could never put your finger on, John."

John Watkins was seeing something in McNally's dedication that his boss wasn't. He kept his mouth shut.

"Boss? I'm having a little trouble connecting the dots, here, to me being the worst FBI agent in the history of FBI agents. My memory is that there *was* a day when I listed a possible motive being McNally's desire to 'resolve racial inequities."

"John. Can't you see it? You're the worst agent ever because you *knew* McNally was the guy...*and you never caught him*!" John Watkins' Boss started laughing. "Can't you see it, John? We all thought you were crazy for chasing a hunch...but you were right! Your hunch was right! You're the man, John. You always *were* the man...and we almost *fired* you over it."

John was not as excited as his boss. "OK, Boss. Now I get it. What you really called for was to say I'm the *best* FBI agent in the history of FBI agents?"

"John, I'm not going to be that direct. I don't want you get the big head. But I *am* going to enter this manifesto...with it's all-telling dedication...as the closing document of the 'Nashville Officer Down' case. Both the kids are dead according to the guy who helped them. And we all know that dead men don't tell lies."

John felt his boss didn't understand the meaning of the phrase 'dead men don't tell lies.'

"But the *rest* of the story, John, *is* gossip. But I'm going to share it with you anyway.

"When the Sheriff went out to the house, the kids had engaged him for a long time and weren't shy about showing off the place to him. When they were explaining where the manifesto came from, he saw they had a brand new computer. The big-screen and expensive kind. Plus, they had a full-blown movie entertainment system in the living room. And all the furniture was new and expensive...lots of leather.

"Then they showed him around the outside. He said they had two brand new cars in the garage and, when they showed off their equipment sheds, all the tractors and mowers were brand new. And, to boot, the kids were wearing brand new clothing."

John had a picture-of-explanation forming in his mind, but he was patient for the end of the story. "So? They're rich kids. That doesn't sound implausible."

"Except, John, that the Sheriff told me he started asking around his fellow elected officials and County employees. The Probate Court Clerk said there was a problem with their funds to clear the sale of the property...that the Clerk had to wait for two checks to come in, one from each of the kids' parents."

John was back into agent mode. "I don't get your point, Boss. The most common thing in America is for wealthy parents to help out their kids."

"But, John, the checks were in two different amounts. That means that one of the parents couldn't afford their whole half. So there goes the 'wealthy parents' theory. Plus, if one of the parents had been wealthy, they wouldn't have required the other parents to contribute.

"Plus, the County Clerk said they registered the brand new cars in cash. Old cash. Plus, the bank teller said they were wearing rags when they set up their account, but now it was all high-end hippie glamor."

"So, you're telling me, Boss, that they're a rags-to-riches story?"

"C'mon, John. Have you been gone so long that you don't remember your theory about McNally having a secret stash of money?"

Watkins was way ahead of his boss.

"That's the explanation, John. The kids found his stash. And they're too young to know their lavish spending could invite some unwanted peering into their lives."

There was nothing in John's former boss' call that was a revelation. But John wanted to feign interest.

"Well, Boss, I guess I should feel proud. That's why you called, right? So I could feel proud?"

"John, when I heard all this new information, I felt like I want you back on my staff. If that were possible, I'd never doubt you again."

"Thanks, Boss." But John just wanted to get back to his bird feathers.

John Watkins didn't get anything done the rest of that day. By the time little Bonnie Lass got off the school bus and came running into his arms with a giant leap, John had already resolved that he'd never known anyone throughout his entire career at the FBI who could put a better bow on a case to get it closed than Scott McNally had done.

Some of John's thoughts went to Robert Smith. John knew from the bookshelf that Mark Twain was part of the boys' time with McNally. 'News of my death has been greatly exaggerated.'

At one point in his rambling thoughts, he had laughed out loud. 'I feel personally responsible for both their deaths.' It had taken the better part of the day for the smile to wear off of John Watkins' face.

'It was so brief. It was so simple. But that's all it took to get the case closed. That sly little bastard. I always knew there was more to him than what he showed.'

4.11 SOMEWHERE OVER THE RAINBOW

One day, Robert and Christine will have the pool house remodeled. An out-of-place, impossibly heavy, army-green metal box with a name in large capital letters on the lid will be found in the attic and be brought to Robert.

Nostalgia is the reliving of warm memories. Mystery is the pondering of things unknown.

Robert will bathe in both.

But that will be a long, long time from now.

Milton Keynes UK
Ingram Content Group UK Ltd.
UKHW031831300124
436988UK00013B/899